Anybody
Any Minute

Also by Julie Mars

The Secret Keepers

A Month of Sundays:
Searching for the Spirit and My Sister

Anybody
Any Minute

JULIE MARS

St. Martin's Press   ✖   New York

Dobbs Ferry Public Library
55 Main St.
Dobbs Ferry, NY 10522

This is a work of fiction. All of the characters, organizations, and events portrayed in this novel are either products of the author's imagination or are used fictitiously.

ANYBODY ANY MINUTE. Copyright © 2008 by Julie Mars. All rights reserved. Printed in the United States of America. For information, address St. Martin's Press, 175 Fifth Avenue, New York, N.Y. 10010.

www.stmartins.com

Library of Congress Cataloging-in-Publication Data

Mars, Julie, 1951–
    Anybody any minute / Julie Mars.—1st ed.
        p.   cm.
    ISBN-13: 978-0-312-37869-1
    ISBN-10: 0-312-37869-6
    1. Middle-aged women—Fiction.   2. Psychological fiction.   I. Title.
    PS3613.A7695A79 2008
    813'.6—dc22

                                                            2008010602

First Edition: June 2008

10   9   8   7   6   5   4   3   2   1

Dedicated to the memory of my sister Shirley,

who wanted it on the record that she did not approve of certain parts

acknowledgments

I am deeply grateful to Joan Schweighardt and Daniela Rapp. Thank you for making this happen. For your encouragement and help, I thank Julie Carter, Jennifer Egan, Michele Meyers, Chris Newbill, Julie Reichert, Laura Robbins, Julie Shigekuni, and Whitney Woodward. For inspiration, life support, and the past twenty-six years, I thank Robert Farris.

Anybody
Any Minute

one

"Y ou *what?* You *what?*" Tommy's voice, which he rarely raised, was so loud Ellen held the pay phone receiver a full arm's length from her ear.

"Calm down, Tommy," she said.

"You call me up and say you put a *house* on your Optima card and you're telling me to be calm? Damn it, Ellen, I—"

"It was a *cheap* house," she cut in. "You just wouldn't believe how cheap real estate is up here."

"Yeah, because nobody in their right mind lives there. You've flipped, Ellen. Is there a state hospital nearby? You go check in right now. No, stay where you are. I'm calling the state troopers to pick you up."

Ellen let silence resonate over the phone line for a few seconds and then said, "You finished?"

"What got into you?" Tommy demanded, but the heat was gone from his voice, and Ellen imagined that by the next afternoon he'd be milking this for all it was worth. She could just picture him, sitting in a booth at Michael's Pub with all his lawyer buddies from the public defender's office. "Guess what my wife pulled?" he would say as he jiggled the ice in his Early Times and ginger ale. "She goes away for a week to visit her sister in Montreal, right? And before she even gets there she puts a fucking *house* on her credit card." She could almost hear Bill Foster now. "Way to go, Ellen!" he would chant, raising his clenched fist in the air the same way he did twenty-five years ago when he was into black power; "Way to go, baby!" She smiled to herself. The idea that she was still capable, at forty-six years old, of doing something outrageous thrilled her, and she felt a warm rush of self-love.

"Oh, Tommy, you're gonna love it. It's a little run-down, you know? Nobody's lived there for years, but I always wanted an organic farm, and—"

"Hel-*lo*, Hel-*lo*," Tommy yelped. "Excuse me, Miss, but could you put my wife back on? Ellen Kenny?" Ellen stopped talking and thrummed her fingers on the metal shelf inside the phone booth. "Excuse me, Ellen," he continued, "but this is the first I'm hearing about your lifelong wish to be an organic farmer. I'm going into shock over here."

"Look, Tommy, it's obvious we can't talk about this now. I'll call you in a couple days . . . give you some time to get used to it."

"Don't hang up, Ellen." His voice was thick with warning.

"It's a done deed. Bye, Tommy."

"Don't hang up, Ellen." This time the singsong rhythm that particularly irritated her had been added.

"I'm gonna call you from Karen's. I love you. Bye."

She reached toward the phone. From the receiver, she heard "Ellen? Ellen! Ellen!" just before she pressed the disconnect button and everything went silent. Sighing, she backed out of the phone booth and glanced up and down Main Street, Lamone, New York. It might have been prosperous once, back in the 1890s when most of the buildings went up, but now many were half-burned, boarded up, empty. She noticed a flat, six-foot, wooden ice-cream cone halfway down the block and started toward it, hoping for a cup of coffee. She definitely needed one. It had been a crazy day so far.

Ellen peeked in the door of the ice-cream parlor but the row of video games beeping, whirring, and speaking out loud in robot voices put her off, and she backtracked to Newberry's, where a huge fluorescent orange GOING OUT OF BUSINESS SALE sign was taped across the front windows. She pulled the door open, spotted the lunch counter, and slid onto a Naugahyde stool as far away as possible from the only other customer in the place, a cigarette smoker eating ham and eggs.

"Just a coffee," she told the waitress.

"Regular?"

"Sweet'N Low and half and half," she answered. It soon appeared in front of her and she sipped it gratefully. Tommy called it her "caffeine fix with white death and fat calories." She smiled affectionately, thinking of her husband. They had been married seventeen years. Their marriage had crashed and nearly burned twice, but they had managed to stagger away from the wreckage—together—both times. A realist, Ellen viewed their relationship as average to above average for people married that long. Not great, if such a thing existed, but far, far above the murky marriage swamp that many couples sunk into. She liked Tommy and he liked her. They still enjoyed each other's company, and though sex had become something of a special event between them, they were both relatively good-humored about that particular loss and took it in their middle-aged stride.

But suddenly Ellen experienced a little stab of terror. What if her outrageous act, which she thought was actually rather charming, backfired and Tommy got fed up and divorced her? One thing she knew for certain: in marriage, anything could be the final straw. If it all collapsed, would she really, at her age, find happiness as an organic farmer? Was it even remotely possible for her to find serenity in a broken-down old farmhouse, a shack really, that sat on the steep slopes of a mountain town famous all over the North Country for its arctic winter temperatures and its overpopulation of black flies? She felt a bubble of hysteria rising inside her, ordered a refill of her coffee, and through sheer force of will, reestablished her tunnel vision. She could not allow such peripheral fears and doubts to distract her from her modest goal, which was simply to be herself. That didn't sound like much for a woman of her age and experience but it was, and she was determined to devote herself to it.

Using a plastic stirrer, she swirled her coffee with such intensity that a whirlpool formed in the middle. Ellen stared into it, mesmerized. It carried her away, back in time, to the end of the sixties when she was living in Somerville, Massachusetts, in a house populated by so many flower children that her share of the rent was only twenty dollars a month. She was a sociology student at Tufts, but her class load had diminished each term in direct proportion to the increase in her extracurricular activities, which included floating in an inner tube in Walden Pond while reading novels by Colette or Henry Miller, and waiting tables at a basement jazz club in downtown Boston.

One night after work, very late, she'd stood on Mass. Ave. to hitch a ride across the river into Cambridge. A beat-up '62 Plymouth Valiant stopped for her and she climbed in. It reeked of pot and beer.

"Where to?" the driver asked.

"North Cambridge. Porter Square," Ellen answered. Her house was a quick walk from there.

"Right on my way," he said, pulling out into the light traffic.

Ellen braced herself, stiff-armed, against the dashboard because, clearly, the driver, a long-haired hippie wearing a leather vest and no shirt, was totally stoned. But then, at that time, everyone was always shit-faced and somehow simultaneously immune from harm. He stared, obviously transfixed, into the lights of Central Square, negotiated the turns and tunnels of Harvard Square with extreme concentration, and whooped with glee over the fact that the Wee Bit O' Gloucester Bar on the first floor of the Quality Motor Inn had suddenly become the I Did It My Way Lounge. He insisted on driving her to her

door, but once they turned off Mass. Ave. into the warrenlike streets of
Somerville, the driver seemed to lose control of the situation. He veered to
the right and scraped a parked car.

"Shit," he said in a low voice as Ellen screamed. Peering intensely through
the windshield as if they were in the midst of a blinding snowstorm instead of
a clear summer night, he made a left, too wide, onto Lowell Street and broad-
sided a car on the other side of the block.

"Shit," he said again as he continued slowly up the hill. Ellen got out midway up the hill, giddy with relief to be safely home. She watched his car turn
left onto Highland Avenue and disappear.

For some reason, the memory of that driver's profile, staring straight ahead
and totally focused as all the havoc he created melted into nothingness behind
him, inspired her. It became a secret and private source of strength. And
somehow, she felt certain, buying this farmhouse was part of keeping her eyes
focused on her goal, just to be herself, no matter how much hollering Tommy
did or how terrified she suddenly felt at Newberry's lunch counter. This was
somehow meant to be.

That's what she had to believe.

two

ut how had it happened?

B Ellen reached into her purse for a pen and prepared to review her whole day. Bestowing order on chaos was her favorite pastime, and she gleefully yanked a paper napkin from an overfilled dispenser and jotted "Step One" onto it in block letters. She warmed her hands on the sides of her coffee cup as she thought.

Step One: She'd kissed Tommy goodbye at the breakfast table, walked to East Eleventh Street to retrieve the Honda (which they still shuffled back and forth across the street to conform to parking rules), and sped out of the city on her semiannual visit to her younger sister, Karen, who ran a café on Rue Saint-Paul in the old section of Montreal.

Step Two: Five hours and 250 miles into the trip, she'd impulsively pulled into a rest area to consult her road atlas. It was a straight shot into Montreal on the Northway, Route 87, but the mid-May day was spectacular with its blue sky and tree buds, and she suddenly wanted to slow down, to meander her way through the Adirondack mountain towns, to see fresh laundry hanging on outdoor lines and kids playing with Tonka trucks in the dirt. With her finger, she traced a route that would take her through Keene Valley, Lake Placid, Saranac Lake, Lamone, Trout River, then across the border into Quebec, Huntingdon, Ormstown, Mercier, Chateaugay, Montreal. She folded the map onto the passenger seat, and when Exit 30 appeared, she snapped on her blinker and left the highway.

Step Three: Feeling a general euphoria that she assumed was a severe attack of spring fever, she'd wound up and down the mountain roads, past rivers swollen with melted snow and woods so thick they barely allowed sunbeams to slant through them. Ellen tuned the radio to an oldies station and sang loudly along. She knew all the words to every song, including, to her dismay, "Alvin's Harmonica" by Alvin and the Chipmunks. But when the opening chords of Smokey Robinson's "I Second That Emotion" played, she cried, "Yes! Yes! My favorite!"

Rocking out to the beat in the driver's seat, she distinctly remembered the precision footwork of the Miracles, the way they strolled and twirled in perfect unison in their high-waisted pants and Cuban heels. And that was when she realized that she was desperate to stretch her own legs and pulled into a parking space not far from LaFleur's Country Real Estate on Main Street in Lamone. The office was located in an old brick building on the edge of a river that rushed through the center of town. Picturesque, Ellen thought, as she stared down at the rapids far below. Peaceful.

Step Four: Mildly curious, Ellen stopped to examine the Polaroids in the front window of LaFleur's. The prices—big, old houses with acreage for $30,000 or less—astonished her. She had lived through the eighties in New York, when tenement dumps sold for six figures, so these prices seemed to be from some era long buried and forgotten. At the right edge of the window, inside a red Magic Marker border and under a sign that said BARGAINS!! FIXER-UPPERS! HANDYMAN SPECIALS! Ellen noticed a blurry photo of a small farmhouse. Shaken, she stepped forward for a closer look. For the last decade, she'd had a chronically repeating dream in which she walked down a narrow, weed-filled country path into a clearing where this very farmhouse stood. It had probably been a charming cottage in its heyday, but in her dream and in the photo, it looked as if it were perilously close to just lying down once and for all among the green weeds. She never entered the house in her dream, never even stepped onto the rickety front porch.

"You've just got a thing for abandoned houses," Tommy said when she gave him her first dream report on the white farmhouse many years before.

"I do?" She was puzzled.

"Like every time we're on the Thruway and we pass the Suffern exit, you launch into that poem by Joyce Kilmer," he said. "'Whenever I walk to Suffern, along the Erie tracks.' That one."

"I do?" She said again. "Every time?" But she did love that poem, had loved it since the second grade when she voluntarily memorized it from her poetry textbook.

I go by a poor old farmhouse, she continued to recite in her mind, *with its shingles broken and black. . . . I suppose I've passed it a hundred times, but I always stop for a minute . . . and look at the house, the tragic house, the house with nobody in it.* All seven verses were burned into her long-term memory.

"See something you like? I'm Roger LaFleur." He had long legs, white hair, and an Amish-style beard. Ellen pointed in a stupor to the picture in the window.

"That one?" he said. "It's up in Eagle Beak. House plus fourteen acres for eleven thousand five. That's the most they'll take." He paused, and when Ellen smiled, he added, "Nice day. Want to take a quick ride up?" Ellen glanced at her watch. Three twenty. She was only sixty-five miles from Montreal. Why not take a look? She'd kill an hour and avoid the rush-hour traffic, too.

On the ten-mile drive up the mountain, Roger related the circumstances surrounding each FOR SALE sign. "That one? Kids grown and the house was too big. That one? Owner in a nursing home." Ellen nodded politely, but secretly she felt dizzy, as if she'd been lifted high into the air, and the upper part of her stomach, right below her ribs, was shaking.

Step Five: Roger turned into the driveway. Ellen saw the peeling paint and sheer curtains disintegrating behind wavy windowpanes, and a great giddiness overtook her. "Watch yourself on the steps," Roger advised as he flipped expertly through a ring of keys. But Ellen didn't worry about turning an ankle or crashing through a rotted wooden plank. She felt surefooted, as if she knew the place intimately.

"How long has it been for sale?" she asked as she followed Roger inside.

"Since Viola de Beer died," Roger said. "That'd be 1988."

Seven years, Ellen thought as she mentally subtracted 30 percent from the asking price. She made a cursory swing through the three tiny downstairs rooms and the two bedrooms upstairs under the eaves, not even spending ten minutes inside. "Comes with everything, right down to the dish towels and the silverware. All you need to bring with you is your fine-tooth comb," Roger said to her back as she exited and crossed the porch. Ellen was barely listening.

"Of course, it's a little run-down," he added halfheartedly as they climbed back into his car. Ellen was silent. Except for his voice, the whole world was deliciously silent here, at the top of the mountain. Roger backed out into the dirt road. "There's a dug well, and them kerosene pot burners keep it nice and toasty in the winter." He seemed to deflate. On the way back down the mountain, though, Ellen politely kept up her part of the conversation. And then, when Roger made the final turn into town, she asked him to stop at the Key Bank. He glanced quickly at her, his white eyebrows shooting up and down like the tops of two question marks, but he said nothing except, "No problem."

Step Six: Ellen marched in, digging both her Optima and MasterCard out of the side compartment of her purse. She had collected a tall stack of credit cards with huge cash advance potential. Tommy laughed as she checked yes to every "guaranteed approval" credit form that arrived in the mail, licked the return envelopes shut, and sent them flying right back out. He thought it was hilarious because she was so cheap. She never spent any money on herself, and she frequently spouted a baroque, ten-minute diatribe that Tommy had titled "How America Blew It Thanks to Credit Cards, by Ellen Kenny." Yet Ellen liked the concept of potential cash, and as she stood in line behind a farmer in knee-high rubber boots who stunk of cow manure, the idea of actually taking some made her feel like a high diver, bouncing at the end of the board. She stepped up to the window. "I'd like a cash advance," she said, pushing her Optima card, with its $10,000 limit, under the thick glass. "Eighty-five hundred, please." The cashier didn't even get an okay from the bank officer.

Step Seven: Tucking her wad of cash into her purse, she rejoined Roger in the car. He drove two blocks up Main Street and parked in the tiny lot next to his building. Feeling smug euphoria, Ellen watched him from the corner of her eye. Didn't he know something was up, she wondered. Couldn't he smell fresh cash, she wondered.

"So," he said as they approached the front window, "can I show you something else?"

"Let's go inside," she said, preceding him through the unlocked door to his dusty office. She dropped into a wooden swivel chair. "Eighty-five hundred dollars, cash. Take it or leave it."

"What?" Roger sputtered. "You're making an offer?"

"That's right."

"Well, hell, let me get on the phone." He flipped through a bulging Rolodex, chuckling deep in his throat. "Let's just hope Viola's no-goodnik son is home. He should be. Rodney never worked a day in his life so far. 'Course he might be passed out in a ditch somewhere or in the detox unit." He yanked a tattered card from the file and held it up like a trophy. "Here it is," he said.

Ellen rocked back in her chair. Suddenly, she felt lazy, as if she were already on her weather-beaten front porch listening to the buzz of the hummingbirds as they raided the lilac bushes. She felt so dreamy that her eyes closed and her chin dropped toward her chest, but when Roger slammed down the phone and said, "He went for it!" she jolted awake.

"Let me just dig out a purchase order," he said, pawing through his desk. Then, with no warning, he pulled a camera from the bottom drawer and snapped her picture. "I like to get these candid shots," he explained, tearing the Polaroid print off the edge of the camera, "so you'll always know how you looked when you bought the farm. Just kidding. That's a little real-estate humor."

As Roger did the paperwork, Ellen waited for her image to emerge. When it did, she let out a yelp of laughter. "Gee, Ellen," Roger said, peering over her shoulder and using her first name, which he had just copied from her driver's license, "you look like you just got hit over the head by a two-by-four."

He was right. She laid her wad of cash on the desk and then pushed it in a pile toward him. He smiled in a way that brought to Ellen's mind the famous words of P.T. Barnum: There's a sucker born every minute. She swallowed the large lump in her throat.

Which brought her up to Step Eight: telling Tommy. That had been relatively painless, though she was sure there'd be at least three steaming messages waiting for her when she finally arrived at Karen's.

She pushed away the last half of her third cup of coffee, lifted her purse from her lap, and surreptitiously took another peek at her photo, which Roger had stapled to her offer-to-purchase form, along with a receipt for the full purchase price. He had given her the name of a local lawyer, whom she called from Roger's office. The lawyer took her MasterCard number for the down payment on his fee. Because it was a cash sale, he said, she'd be closing in a month, at most.

"Fine, fine," she said and hung up.

"Well," she said in Roger's general direction. "Well."

"Well, well, welcome to the North Country," he answered, extending his hand. She shook it, feeling as if she'd just gotten a diploma she hadn't really earned.

three

Karen had asked her to stop at the duty-free shop and buy two cartons of Craven A cigarettes and a fifth of Jack Daniel's. Ellen left them on the front seat as she pulled into Canadian customs. "*Bonjour,* hello," said the agent, who looked to Ellen like a baby in a uniform. "Where do you live?"

"Eagle Beak," she answered without hesitation.

"What is the purpose of your visit to Canada?"

"I'm going to Montreal to see my sister."

"Okay. Go on."

Ellen stepped on the gas. "Eagle Beak?" she repeated to herself in confusion. "Why did I say that?" Yet it was natural, as if her two decades in New York had simply vanished. Nothing changed that quickly, she mused, but then she noticed the speed limit given in kilometers and the road signs all in French. She glanced in the rearview mirror. There was America, two hundred feet away, complete with a sign for hot dogs and an old election poster that said JIM JACKSON FOR SHERIFF nailed to a telephone pole. She shrugged her shoulders. Who knew how quickly everything could change? Or why or when or if it even made a difference?

The road to Montreal ran alongside a winding river, meandering through green farmland and little villages named for saints. Ellen was glad she'd exited off the beaten path and found the real world, though parts of it scared her. The bloody Jesus Christ, laid out in a Plexiglas sarcophagus in somebody's front yard. The angry billboards, covered with images of scalps and tomahawks, that protested the provincial police presence on the Kahnawake Indian Reserve. And as the old Honda labored up the entrance ramp to the Mercier Bridge, the St. Lawrence River below looked black with resentment at having been tamed for barge and freighter use.

Still, Ellen was exhilarated. She cruised into the Centre Ville lane and barreled into a tunnel that would spit her out a stone's throw from Karen's café.
Her sister was thirteen years younger, a natural beauty who tucked her baby's
bottle into the waistband of her black spandex miniskirt. Her son, Olivier, was
now eighteen months old. Ellen had a little Guess For Kids outfit, two educa-
tional games designed to strengthen hand-eye coordination, and a yellow stuffed
duck for him. For Karen, she had a bottle of orange bath oil beads in lavender
petals, a photo album from the Metropolitan Museum of Art, and a short pink
angora sweater that she bought on a whim after she and Tommy had howled
their way through the movie *Ed Wood*.

Ellen loved to see Karen behind the counter of her café, steaming milk for
cappuccinos and bantering with her customers in French. She loved her sister's strawberry blond hair, pulled upward into a classic but sexy twist, and she
loved Karen's business partner, Regine-Marie, who moonlighted as the drum-
mer in a blues band that was booked six months in advance. In fact, Ellen
adored everything about her visits to Montreal, including the fact that there
was usually on-the-street parking within half a block of the Café L'Alibi. She
hopped out of the car, walked to the café, stepped inside, and was temporarily
blinded by the darkness.

"Ellen!" Karen cried, running full tilt from behind the espresso counter.
"Ellen!" Ellen had learned to expect Karen's continental greeting—back and
forth two times, four little cheek kisses—and she managed to follow the right
choreography. When it was over, though, she grabbed her little sister in a bear
hug and squeezed. Karen felt so fragile, all delicate bones and wisps of her signature scent, a spray cologne called Rain that actually evoked the obvious
connection.

"You look great!" Karen said, stepping back. "It's so good to see you."

Ellen smiled. She knew she did look great as seen through her sister's eyes.
It was possibly the thing that gave her the warmest feeling about Karen—that
she seemed to have sailed in a private capsule through the decline-of-
everything in the eighties with no apparent damage to her values. Karen, and
in fact her whole lifestyle of late nights, love children, and loft living, always
sent Ellen reeling back to the sixties, to Somerville, to the era when being a
"beautiful person" started and ended with the inside, not the outside, of who
you were.

Because Ellen was quite sure, by the standards of the mid-nineties, that her
looks were not even in the ballpark of great. Gravity had lowered all her important body parts with the same precision that a tow truck lowers a broken-
down car to the ground in front of the garage. Nasolabial grooves, otherwise
known as "marionette lines" as she'd learned from a late-night infomercial on

plastic surgery, were etched into her face from the edge of her nose to the corners of her mouth. Her hair, once a deep coppery shade of auburn, had faded to some noncolor, and even fifty sit-ups a day could not keep her stomach bulges at bay.

"I went from baby fat to a beer belly to a forty-year-old belly," she had sobbed one night to Tommy as she stood in front of the full-length mirror in their bedroom wearing a flowered one-piece bathing suit. "My whole life is over and I never even got to wear a bikini."

"If I remember correctly," Tommy commented, a small smile tugging at his lips, "you've spent most of your life refusing to wear a bathing suit at all."

"That's *different*," she shrieked, "and let's just leave Truro out of this, okay? You're always trying to drag Truro in by the neck."

Tommy, sitting up against a cloud of pillows in bed, placed his book on the nightstand. "I'm not always dragging Truro in by the neck," he said. He had a delighted look on his face, as if he were pleased that this moment had recycled by again. Truro, an Atlantic beach on the eastern shore of Cape Cod, had taken on mythic symbolic proportions in their marriage. It could at any moment be taken out of mental storage to prove any point from how impossibly different to how exactly alike Tommy and Ellen were. It could be used like lighter fluid to ignite the flames that either one of them might use to warm the other, or, just as likely, to fry them. And it all grew from their first formal date, though neither the word *formal* nor *date* was much in use at that time.

It was July 31, 1970—Ellen's twenty-first birthday. She sat, alone and depressed, on a park bench in the Cambridge Common listening to the long line of conga drummers. Their pounding energy had always inspired Ellen before, pulsed through her like hot Caribbean blood, but that day the relentlessness of the beat and all the accompanying musical loops and swirls just added to the headache she'd climbed out of bed with at eleven o'clock. Finally, she left, moving mostly unconsciously toward the comfort of a chocolate ice-cream frappé at Brigham's in Harvard Square. She sat at the counter, perilously close to melting into big tears of self-pity.

"Hey," a voice said, "why so sad?"

She didn't even look up. "It's my birthday," she pouted into her ice cream. "My friends are having a party for me out on the Cape, but I slept through my ride. And I don't have money for the bus."

There was a short silence. "Hell, I got a car," the voice said. "Let's go."

She raised her eyes, and there was Tommy: the sexiest guy she'd ever seen in her life. "Wow," she breathed, and he threw his head back and laughed. Ellen didn't know where to look first: at his perfect white teeth, at his long, deep dimples, or at his dreamy black eyes, which seemed well worth taking a chance on.

This is a guy I could love, she thought as they sped down Route 3 in his VW Beetle. Irish, working class, son of a New York City fireman. First in his whole extended family to finish college, though it had taken him six years, including summers, while he worked full time as a sheetrocker. And then, the impossible had happened. Admission to Harvard Law School. A scholarship. ". . . and a beautiful summer day with a beautiful chick. My life is perfect. What can I say?" he said, turning toward her in his sexy dark glasses. Then that smile again. Ellen felt a big jolt in her chest. And when he impulsively reached over and took her hand, placing it beneath his on the solid muscle of his thigh, she felt indescribable bliss. This is it, she thought. Oh boy.

And then they got to Truro.

Tommy left the mid-Cape highway and followed Ellen's directions until she finally motioned him to park against a dune in Newcomb's Hollow. He had hurried around the car in time to get a full view of her rear end as she leaned into the VW's backseat to pull out her canvas beach bag. Then they climbed the dune together, hand in hand. For years afterward, whenever he would tell the tale, Tommy would admit that he planned to take her in his arms and kiss her, but he was temporarily stunned by the sight of the sea. When he finally turned around, she had just stepped out of her blue jeans and her red underpants and was pulling her T-shirt up over the most beautiful pair of breasts in the world.

"Hey, it's my birthday," she laughed. "Might as will get in my birthday suit." Tommy obviously thought he'd hit the jackpot. But then, as she stuffed her clothes in her bag, he caught some movement to the left. A man was running toward them, his penis, a sunburned pink sausage, flopping up and down in the breeze. "Ellen!" he called. "Hi!" Tommy spun around and suddenly, as if he'd just adjusted binoculars, it all came into focus.

"This is a *nude* beach," he sputtered.

"Yeah," Ellen answered, offhandedly, as her friend, the naked man, joined them. Ellen introduced him as "Fettuccine Alfredo" and he laughed and said, "Alfie."

"This is a *nude* beach," Tommy repeated, as if it were the first sentence he'd ever learned and he wanted to practice it.

"No shit, Sherlock," said Alfie. He turned to Ellen. "Did you bring the stash?"

"Would I forget?" She reached into her bag to produce a carved wooden box and handed it to him. He opened it. Inside was a loose lid of marijuana.

Alfie rummaged through it and found a joint. "Oh good, there's one rolled." He lit it and took off with the stash box under his arm. "Come on, we're waiting for you."

Ellen started after him. Tommy stepped forward and grabbed her arm.

"You had *pot* in my car?" His black eyes were angry now. "How could you be so stupid?"

"Lighten up, man," she said, pulling away.

"I'm a *law* student. You could've got me busted and wrecked my whole life. Did that cross your mind?"

Ellen was silent. "You're kidding, right?" she finally asked.

"No, I'm not kidding!" he yelled. "I worked my ass off for this, and, sorry if it's not cool enough for you, but I take it seriously. You don't understand that because you obviously don't have a serious bone in your body. Or much of a future, for that matter." His neck had turned a deep crimson.

Ellen was stung. True, it hadn't occurred to her to mention the pot. But why did he have to go all judgmental? For his information, she was secretly terrified about her future, which looked blank and parched from age twenty-one. And, if anything, she thought of herself as too serious, serious to the point of depression. She held her breath for a few seconds. "Tell you what: it's my birthday and I'm not gonna get upset. Thanks a lot for the ride. Good luck in law school." She turned away.

"Fuck you," he said.

"Asshole," she responded, walking off. The last thing Tommy saw was the long-stemmed red rose tattooed on her left cheek.

He never saw her again until they met by chance during rush hour on the No. 6 train in Manhattan eight years later. "Excuse me, Miss," Tommy had said over her shoulder as they hung from adjoining subway straps, "but don't you have a flower tattooed on your ass?"

She whirled around.

And there was Tommy.

That same smile.

This is a guy I could love, she thought.

When the train stopped at Eighth Street, they got off together.

four

Karen served Ellen a café au lait in a tall glass mug. A strawberry and a kiwi slice were speared on a long plastic stirrer that read, "*Vous avez toujours un Alibi*" on one side and "You always have an Alibi" on the other. Ellen sat at a small table in the corner, waiting for her sister to attend to the last details of her workday. Just being in the café, like the kiwi, was a treat for Ellen. Around her, men with loopy curls flirted outrageously with pouty women. People were smoking and reading Kafka.

"Okay, all finished. Let's go get Olivier," Karen said. "You won't believe how big he is." When they hit the street, Karen tucked her arm through Ellen's. Ellen squeezed it against her waist as they walked toward the car, unloaded the trunk, and proceeded around the corner and into the cobblestone alley where Karen, Olivier, and Olivier's Peruvian father, Cocho, lived. It was a building made of granite, built during an early round of construction in Montreal in the 1780s. From their windows on the fourth floor, the top, they could watch the river traffic a block away.

When Cocho, a musician, was traveling, as he was now, Olivier stayed during the day with a Vietnamese family on the ground floor. They ran a fruit and vegetable stand that the local loft dwellers, relatively few in number by big-city standards, relied on heavily for their last-minute, and often first-minute, food needs. Olivier and the two Ng children happily played hide-and-seek and roll-the-can in the storeroom amid huge burlap bags of rice and trays of wheat grass and bean sprouts in different stages of development.

Because the aisles were so narrow, Ellen, burdened with packages and a suitcase, waited on the sidewalk. She saw Karen stoop down and lift her little dark-skinned baby, covering his sweet face with kisses and placing him on her hip as if it were custom-made to fit him. Then Grandmother Ng said something in Vietnamese, to which Olivier responded with a few words. He squirmed to get down, and when Karen placed him on the floor, he ran on his fat bowlegs into the back room and emerged with a green plantain banana. Karen laughed as she hoisted him up again.

"Here's Auntie Ellen," Karen cooed. Ellen, unsure of what to expect, opened her hands toward him and he fell forward into them with a happy giggle. Ellen was overwhelmed with gratitude and buried her nose in the creases of his neck. The smell of a baby—she had always loved it. She loved babies, period. But she and Tommy had never been able to have one. It was her fault, as such faults go. She'd suffered enormous guilt and begged Tommy to adopt, but he'd resisted. Child-free, not childless, was a fine way to live, he'd said.

They climbed up the four flights and went in, dropping everything just inside the door. Olivier was off and running. "Don't worry about him; the whole place is kid-proof," Karen said as she flopped onto a huge old couch and kicked off her fashionably strappy sandals. "So talk to me, Ellen. What's happening?"

Ellen felt a flutter of excitement. It was always an incredible relief to talk to Karen. Her sister listened with full attention, as if each of her cells were vitally engaged and determined to absorb every word. At times, Ellen felt it was almost scary to be listened to so carefully. Yet she felt a sudden resistance to telling Karen about the house she'd bought just two hours ago. It was the same feeling she got when she was on the verge of blabbing a secret she'd sworn to keep forever.

"You've got a funny look on your face," said Karen. "The cat that swallowed the canary."

"I got fired," Ellen blurted out, and Karen laughed.

"Is that all? What happened?"

"What didn't happen?" Ellen responded, her arms jerking upward in a gesture of hopeless disgust.

"Give me the play-by-play. I haven't heard a getting-fired story from you since you told PBS to take their love and shove it."

Ellen felt little tugs all around her mouth. She loved these stories, too, particularly the climaxes, those moments that had all too frequently repeated themselves in her job life, when tensions and gripes had built to a feverish pitch, when everything was wrong, wrong, wrong, and then suddenly it all faded into white background noise, and she, like a half-cracked biblical prophet in a loincloth, would hear her own clear voice announcing the bare truth to anyone who would listen. It was actually very simple. After a certain point, she snapped. It was all so sudden, like a revolution, and, as in any revolution, heads fell. And one of them was always hers.

"Well, we were in this so-called creative staff meeting—" Ellen began.

"Oh, good," whooped Karen, "a staff meeting!"

"—and Reginald was doing his usual petty tyrant routine. Ranting and raving and terrorizing the college kids doing arts management internships. And for some reason, he got onto this . . . *thing* about the copy machine in his office. It was right out of Captain Queeg and the strawberries."

Ellen warmed up as she told the story. She had worked for Reginald Eubanks, an independent producer-director of highly acclaimed political documentaries, as chief researcher for four years. It sounded impressive and people would ooh and aah when they learned what she did, but privately Ellen mainly felt career cynicism. When she measured the stress of reporting to a powerful manic-depressive against her chump-change salary, she always came up short.

"So we were all sitting around this huge round table that Reginald imported from Burma or someplace and everybody's slumped down, sitting on their necks, and he's carrying on and on about how every time he needs a personal copy of anything, the copy machine is broken again because none of us morons can manage to push the right button. Then he demands that we all report at seven in the morning for an in-service, he called it, on mastering the copy machine. This is after a forty-five-minute tirade, mind you. And then he takes this long, dramatic pause, and in this very condescending voice, he says, 'And I'm not going to be here. Would you like to know why?'"

Karen had a look of great anticipation on her face. "And you said . . ."

"I said, 'Because you're a fucking asshole, Reginald.'"

And suddenly Ellen was howling, laughing so deeply that tears gushed down her face and Olivier reappeared to check out the commotion. "The crew took me out for champagne," she finished in between bouts of near hysteria. She knew, even as she roared, that this laughter was coming from some other place than the story she was telling, some hysterical part of her that could only be accessed at random. She loved it when it came—being delivered to that place inside her that was full of laughter, even if it was crazed and maniacal.

She shook her head.

Fired again.

Karen beamed affectionately from the couch.

"And on the way up here, I stopped and bought a house on a credit card advance," Ellen added, feeling spent and therefore somewhat sobered.

Karen's eyebrows arched. "Uh-oh. What's Tommy-the-Bear have to say about this?"

"I don't know. Maybe we should check your answering machine." Ellen giggled. Karen got up and went to the other end of the loft. She returned with two cold Labatts. "No messages," she said as she handed one to Ellen.

A bad sign, Ellen thought as she wiped a stray tear from her cheek with the back of her hand.

five

Ellen was at the point of collapse before she finally gave up and went to bed. Across the loft, Karen was deep in conversation with a couple who dropped in unannounced just after midnight. Ellen couldn't recall the last time anyone had just shown up at her and Tommy's door in New York. Maybe never. And she could count on one hand the number of times she'd been up so late in the last year. The cadence of the French, punctuated by short little laughs, soothed her, and she snuggled under the lightweight flannel blanket that Karen had drawn over her shoulders. The blanket smelled of incense, a pleasant mix of smoke and spice.

How did genes get distributed in any given family, she wondered lazily. Was it as random as she suspected? In her mind, Ellen watched a drunken farmer, out in the black dirt of a well-tilled field. Bathed in silver moonlight, he dipped into a burlap bag of seeds and flung them far and wide. In the morning, waking up hungover (a rare event in his hard life), he would slowly realize that the neat rows of vegetables he had planned were not to be. This year, the corn and peas would tangle up together and red tomatoes would grow out of the cucumber mounds. That was how haphazard it was, Ellen thought. Looks, brains, talent, proclivities: all seeds tossed at random into the Great Mother. No one could predict what would grow.

Karen, for example, was born calm. She was forward-looking, precise, and undistracted by the temptations in her path. She had received a prestigious, full scholarship to Bennington College, where she majored in romance languages and minored in music. Immediately, and without any agonizing, she'd joined the Peace Corps and spent three successive two-year assignments in a refugee camp in Honduras, where she worked in the fields by day; by night, she arranged and conducted the camp chorus, which she had also created. People who heard the refugees sing called it a miracle. And then she'd taken her three $5,000 paychecks, for two years service each, and opened the café with Regine-Marie, whom she'd met when Regine-Marie passed through Honduras on an extended winter vacation. And two years later, when Karen and Cocho discovered she was pregnant, Karen felt nothing but happiness.

Ellen, on the other hand, had been an agitated child, a baby who had to be taken for a long ride in the car every night before she would fall asleep. She had grown into an alienated, angry teenager, and in college, she had switched her major five times and taken nine years to graduate. Her life seemed to be composed of hurdles that got higher as she got older, and she felt so much moment-to-moment friction that it was no surprise to her when any one spark ignited and burned whatever she'd built up to the ground. Her career life, for example. Ellen had been working nonstop for thirty years, and what did she have to show for it? Just the latest "Get the fuck out." Reginald's final words were shrapnel, mental shrapnel, and it would take a long time for her to pick them out of her psyche, no matter how hard she laughed in front of others. And she did not absolve herself of guilt. What she had said to Reginald was outrageous. It was also true, but that didn't count.

"What makes you think anyone cares about the truth?" Tommy had once asked, years before, after a similar event.

Ellen was astonished. "I can't believe I'm hearing this."

"What?" Tommy asked, perplexed.

"This disrespect for the truth. You're a lawyer. You're supposed to be committed to it."

"Lawyering has nothing to do with truth," Tommy commented. "Besides, we're not in a courtroom, Ellen. We're talking about life here. And in case you haven't noticed, most people just try to get along, which eliminates the truth-telling."

This possibility was enormously depressing to Ellen. To her, the truth was the only thing worth hanging onto, the only possible reference point in life. Knowing the truth, she thought, kept a person sane; a vigilant quest for it automatically made a person worthwhile; those who avoided it were mentally and morally weak. More than that, she believed the truth had healing qualities, that a single blazing exposure to it could neutralize pain, insult, and sorrow. The truth, she thought, was freedom. She loved it with a deep, absorbing passion.

"And anyway," Tommy added, "who appointed you the burning bush of truth?"

Ellen tried to compose herself. "People need the truth, Tommy," she said in a voice not unlike a growl.

"Why?" There was gentleness in his voice.

She hesitated. "Because it orients people."

"So when it's lost or buried or even threatened," he mused, "you have to blurt it out. Just so people don't get confused."

"Right. Public service."

"You nut," he said, pulling her close. "Maybe you're right. But remember what always happens to the messenger." He lifted her wavy hair off the nape of her neck and kissed her there. "Don't let them kill you, Ellen," he whispered. "I can't live without you, honey."

Ellen woke up reaching for Tommy. He wasn't there. She opened her eyes and didn't recognize anything. But then she saw Olivier, in his yellow sleepers. She lifted the summer quilt into a tent and he climbed in. They started a spirited game of peekaboo, Ellen noticing that he screeched with happiness each time the darkness ended.

She understood that because, while she fully expected several new worlds to open before her at any moment, she could not help but feel the nearly unbearable pressure of thick darkness all around her: no job, Tommy's silence, her new credit card debt, and worst of all, the strange yet indisputable inner certainty that she was growing tired, too tired to fight the tide anymore. What if it carried her far, far away from everything that mattered?

"It's like I'm on an iceberg, floating out to sea," she confessed to Karen over a breakfast croissant, "and . . . well . . . it's warming up."

Karen studied her. "What's wrong, Ellen?"

Ellen had no ready answer. "Did you ever study Erikson's eight stages of human development?" she finally asked. "Because I think I got prematurely blasted into the final phase: integrity versus despair. You're not supposed to get there until you're in your seventies."

"Can that happen?" Karen asked.

"Look, if it can happen to anyone, it'll happen to me. And I say that with all good humor." Actually, Ellen believed that she, like most of the sixties hippies, aided by hallucinogenic drugs, had been propelled, while in their twenties, into the infamous midlife crisis that usually shot the legs out from under mature forty-five-year-old adults. Looking back, she often felt sorry for her fragile, youthful ego, relentlessly forced to confront problems of meaning that were out of its league. She had naturally expected coping with life to get easier, but now decades had passed, and a fog of doubt and confusion had set in. It had actually grown denser in the past five years. Ellen felt gypped that a person could lose her moorings just at the point when she expected smooth sailing.

In a way, though, it was funny, she thought. Life's unpredictability. Anything could happen. To anybody. Any minute.

"Did I ever tell you about the time I went home for Mom and Dad's fortieth wedding anniversary?" she suddenly asked.

"No," Karen answered. "Where was I?"

"You were in Honduras," Ellen supplied. She was better at keeping track of time than Karen was. "Forty years!" she said. "It's such a milestone! So Tommy and I drove up there the night before, planning to take them out to a nice dinner to celebrate. We got there late, and when we came up on the porch, we could see them both through the living-room window, conked out in their matching La-Z-Boys. Dad's head was dropped forward, like his neck had come unhooked, and Mom's was the other way, back against the chair, and her mouth was wide open."

They had looked so incredibly vulnerable, she'd thought at the time. Alone in a house, asleep in front of the boob tube. Her mother wore a knee-length quilted bathrobe and crocheted slippers with pom-poms on the toes. Her father was dressed as he always was: dark trousers, a plaid dress shirt, a cardigan sweater. Ellen had felt a rush of tenderness that made her reach for Tommy's hand and dig her fingers in.

"Anyway, they basically just said hello and went right up to bed. But the next day, the actual anniversary, Tommy slept late and when I came downstairs, they both acted like nothing special was going on. After a while, I cornered Mom in the kitchen, and she said Dad hadn't given her anything: no card, no flowers, not even a 'Happy Anniversary.' So I went looking for him and found him puttering in the garage. 'Dad,' I said, 'did you forget your anniversary?' Guess what he said." Ellen paused, leaning forward.

"I have no idea." Karen's voice was cautious.

"He said, 'As far as I'm concerned, I'm not married.'"

Karen's eyes widened. "Really?"

"Yep. So I said, 'If you're not married, then what have you been doing for forty years with Mom?' And he looks up from the lawn mower he was fixing, and, I remember this perfectly, he says, 'Wandering in the desert.' His eyes were so sad I just ran out of the garage."

Karen said nothing.

"So when I got back inside, Mom asked me what he said. I tried to come up with a lie, but I couldn't, so I told her: 'He said as far as he's concerned, he's not married.' I left out the forty years in the desert. And she dries off her hands—she was doing the dishes—and sort of collapses at the kitchen table and just holds onto the sugar bowl with both hands. And then she looks straight at me and says, 'There wasn't a day in this marriage that I didn't think of leaving.'"

Karen pushed back from the table as if she needed more room to absorb her

Dobbs Ferry Public Library
55 Main St.
Dobbs Ferry, NY 10522

sister's words. "God, a double whammy," she said. "Why haven't you ever told me this?"

"Oh . . . why know?" Ellen said. And then she repeated it. "Why know?"

"But it's so . . ."

"It was truly surreal," Ellen sighed. Both were silent for several seconds.

"So did you and Tommy take them out?"

"Well, you know how Mom liked to go to the Sizzler for the early bird special, so we went there, but nobody mentioned the anniversary. We ended up talking about seafood. What kind of fish everybody liked, who liked sea scallops and who liked bay scallops. Like that. I felt weird for weeks afterward."

Karen took a long, deep breath. "Did they hate each other?"

Ellen shrugged. "I don't think so. I think they were both just incredibly honest."

The two sisters stared into the froth in their coffee cups. "Do you ever miss them?" Karen finally asked.

"Not really." It made her melancholy. "Why? Do you?"

"Every day," Karen answered. "Every day."

Was that possible? Ellen wondered. Their parents had been dead for years. Joyce went first in 1990 of a massive cerebral hemorrhage, and Norman, seven months later for no reason at all except his heart stopped beating. Twice, Ellen and Karen had met in White River Junction, Vermont, to bury a parent. And after it was over, neither of them could get away fast enough. When the old house was sold and the bills paid, Joyce and Norman Hart, after seven and a half decades on Planet Earth, broke even with $3,800 to spare. By mutual consent, Karen and Ellen placed it in a joint checking account as a family emergency fund that could be used at will by either party, no questions asked. In fact, with the whopping 1.5 percent interest it was earning, it had mushroomed to just under $4,000.

All of which made Ellen's purchase of the house in Eagle Beak even more irrational. Eagle Beak was, if anything, even less of a town than White River Junction, which at least had a main street and two square blocks of active downtown life. Eagle Beak had nothing but a one-person post office and a tiny grocery store with a single gas pump. There wasn't a Thai restaurant or a movie theater that showed documentaries by the likes of Reginald Eubanks for seventy-five miles. Ellen had left White River Junction on the day she graduated from high school, fled to the excitement of Boston. But Boston had not been big enough to hold her, and she packed up and moved to New York City. And now, for no apparent reason, she'd turned her back on the Big Apple, which she still considered the center of the universe, and made a commitment to fourteen acres of picker bushes and beaver ponds and a dream image that she had never understood at all.

And, more confusing, she had to face the fact that she might've turned her back on Tommy, too. And why? For what? All marriages lost their excitement. All husbands and wives forgot about the miracle of the other and periodically felt the chilly fingers of alienation tightening around their necks.

Didn't they?

six

Ellen arrived at her new old house on June 9, a Friday, not quite four weeks after she'd so whimsically purchased it. The Honda was packed to the roof with essentials ranging from a ghetto blaster and a box of blues tapes to a carton of Middle Eastern and Asian food treats. On the long drive up from the city, her mood had vacillated between absolute terror accompanied by misgivings of every possible sort and a breezy kind of peace that prompted her to dig through her tapes to find Patsy Cline and sing along. When she was younger, she'd always secretly aspired to be a backup singer in a girl group. Now she secretly wanted to be the star, the Diana Ross or the Smokey Robinson. She wanted to be the center of attention, the major talent who sang her whole heart out for a crowd of thousands. In my next life, she thought, I'm putting my order in, God.

Ellen chuckled to herself as she sped north on the Thruway. She was always putting her orders in to God, and almost every one was for her next lifetime, as if she considered her current one a washout, a write-off. Still, she was steadfast in her expectation of two present-life rewards from God: the first one was to reach a state the ancient Greeks called *ipsissimus*. Roughly, the translation was "she who is most herself." Of course, Ellen supplied the feminine pronoun and probably her own interpretation of what it meant, but she knew that back in the days when the Greeks were building the Parthenon and sitting on the hillsides to watch Sophocles' latest play, *ipsissimus* was thought to be the highest level of human development. And since you didn't need any special, expensive equipment to pursue it and probably couldn't get instruction as to how, Ellen had named it her dearest long-term goal and asked God to place her on that path. Her second request was that, when it came time for her to die, she would spontaneously combust.

"Look at this picture!" she'd once said to Tommy, shoving the coffee-table-sized book into his lap. "I'm not making it up." After all, there was visual proof. An old man's foot, neatly tucked into his bedroom slipper, rested to the side of the toilet. His aluminum walker was tipped over and the walls were scorched. "See? He went into the bathroom and *boom!* He was gone. Nothing left but one foot. Spontaneous combustion." She reached over her husband's shoulder to turn the page. "See? There's another one. An old lady was sitting in her chair and then *boom!* Gone! Nothing there but a scorched spot and some ashes on the doilies."

"Ellen," Tommy said, "stop yelling '*boom*' in my ear."

Her eyes were as bright as lighthouse beams. "It only seems to happen to old people. It must be biochemical." She pushed the book onto the couch, climbed onto Tommy's lap, and put her arms around his neck. "Oh, Tommy," she said, "I hope it happens to me. What an exit."

"Maybe it hurts," Tommy said.

"Nah, it couldn't," Ellen answered. "God, just imagine how you must arrive in the next world if there is one."

"Not with a whimper but a bang," Tommy said.

"Uh-huh," Ellen said, just imagining.

How many times had she climbed onto Tommy's lap over the years, she wondered. It was such a silly thing for a grown woman to do, and yet she loved the stability of his thighs beneath her, like iron beams. Sometimes, resting on his legs like that, she thought of Tommy as the framework upon which her whole life was built, a thought that brought both comfort and anxiety.

But there'd been no lap-sitting when she told him about her plans to move to Eagle Beak for the summer. She'd been back from Montreal for ten days. Tommy had more or less dismissed her house purchase by the time she'd returned to New York. "What you do with your money is your business," he said on her first night back, "but I don't want any part of it. I'm not spending my vacations doing carpentry, so you're on your own with this, honey." It had been a relief to Ellen. "It'll give Karen and Cocho a place to go when they want to get out of the city," she said reasonably. "It's so close to Montreal." "Whatever," Tommy answered.

The following week, Ellen had halfheartedly made job calls, letting the relevant people know she was available for hire. But in her heart, she didn't want to work. She studied her bank accounts—savings and checking—and figured it out on paper. She thought she could keep up her end and skin by financially until October if she was careful. Flat on her back on the couch in the living room, her favorite thinking position, she let her mind drift anywhere it desired to go, and it always carried her to Eagle Beak, to the tiny white farmhouse she'd just bought. She saw herself in a big straw hat planting a garden, watering it, shucking peas on a porch swing.

Then she would get up, stand at her apartment window, and look down at the street, and she knew her heart just wasn't in the city right now. Really, she thought as she recalled an image of herself from several months before, crying as she came up from the L train platform on First Avenue and Fourteenth Street because it was so incredibly noisy down there, she hadn't been on speaking terms with New York in quite a while. She wanted to get out. She wasn't sure why, but those words kept repeating way at the back of her mind. *Get out.* She finally told Tommy that she wanted to move away for the summer. She had to get out, she said.

He was quiet afterward. He took off his tie and jacket and hung them carefully in his closet, as usual. Then he took off his shirt and put it in the bag to go to the Chinese laundry on the corner. He pulled on his gray sweatpants and sat on the edge of the futon. "Ellen," he said in a soft voice, "are you leaving me?"

Suddenly Ellen remembered her mother's words: there wasn't a day I didn't think of leaving. Could Tommy feel that way? Was that why this was his first question?

"Do you want me to leave?" she asked, terrified.

"I just want to know if this is it. If this is the beginning of the end."

Ellen felt paralyzed by panic.

"Do you want it to end, Tommy?"

"Goddamn it," he exploded, "stop acting like I'm the one who just announced I'm taking off. I'd like to know what the fuck is going on around here, okay? Stop turning everything around."

Ellen started to cry.

"Oh, great, here come the tears." Disgusted, Tommy yanked a sweatshirt out of the dresser. "I'm going out," he growled and he left, giving the apartment door a good slam behind him.

"What did I do?" Ellen asked the emptiness. She was both confused and angry. Confused, because she couldn't understand why Tommy would interpret her innocent little summer adventure as a veiled statement about their marriage. He knew that she was honest to the point of recklessness when it came to discussing their marital problems. Angry, because his reaction served to remind her how unwilling the world-at-large is to make a little room for anyone to be herself. It made her want to start packing that very minute. Maybe she should pack up everything she owned. Just get out.

Tommy came back two hours later. No surprise, he had been drinking. Ellen pretended to be asleep although it was only nine thirty. Tommy undressed and climbed into bed, pulling her toward him while she simulated sputtering to consciousness. "I don't want a divorce," he whispered in her ear.

"Who said anything about a divorce?" she asked. "This isn't about us, Tommy. It's about me."

"I'm sorry," he said. "I'll miss you." Ellen turned her face to avoid his breath, which smelled like sour beer. Over the years, in fights, she had even accused him of a failure to overcome his Irish heritage, and lately, she had flatly refused to buy him booze of any sort, though she felt hypocritical when she bought it for herself. Lying tense and motionless beside her husband, Ellen waited for his breath to deepen into a loud, wet snore. She loved Tommy. She did. But lately their timing was off. The cylinders weren't firing as they ought to. She wanted to feel excited by her husband, but, basically, he bugged her. He spent too much time at work. He took her for granted. He drank too much. He refused to talk about their relationship. "If it ain't broke, don't fix it," he'd said when she'd recently suggested a marital makeover, one that included scheduled sex dates, a course in communicating from a higher level of consciousness, and couples lessons in the art of sensual Thai massage. They needed a romantic tune-up.

So when Tommy came home early every night for the twelve days before she left, Ellen played along. Hand in hand like two kids in love, they strolled through the neighborhood or sat outside the dog run in Tompkins Square Park and watched the puppies tumble in the dirt. Ellen felt such tenderness toward Tommy it hurt. He was trying to do everything right, she knew. Trying to polish up their day-to-day life so it would shine when she thought about it from afar. She was touched that he would go to the trouble, but her intuition told her it wouldn't help. Anyone could distinguish a flurry of semidesperate activity from the daily grind. Not that she expected to put their marriage under a microscope while she was in the country. She didn't. But even as they intertwined their fingers across the tables of the Indian restaurants on East Sixth Street, she felt some nameless, hopeless dread, and she knew that what was, was.

Tommy stayed home on the morning she left. Ellen surprised him by pulling back the sheets and teasing his morning half hard-on awake with her tongue. "It's time for your annual blow job," she joked as she gently fondled her husband's balls.

"Annual?" Tommy murmured. "I think we missed a few years."

Ellen laughed even though she knew it was true. Why had that little love token fallen away, like a hubcap that spiraled to the side of the road and embedded itself in the dirt as the car sped off and disappeared?

Actually, Ellen had a thousand theories about sex. In her younger years, sex had been her whole world: her laboratory, her university, her church. She had blazed a trail of glory through the various landscapes of sexuality, and she didn't regret a single act. She'd always been willing to experiment: it was that simple. Once, she had even given a group of sexually inhibited women detailed instructions on the art of giving head. "First, you have to adore the penis," she had begun. Even now, after all these years, she still felt seized by inspiration as she went to work on Tommy. The stupid look on his face only egged her onward to a peak performance, and she felt proud when Tommy howled during his climax. When she rested her head on his belly, he wound his fingers into her hair, gently twisting and releasing it.

"Hey, Tommy, remember my Japanese phase?" she suddenly asked.

"Yeah. Was I ever glad when that blew over." His voice had a husky edge.

"You were?" Ellen perked up. She slid up the length of her husband's body and tucked herself under his arm. "You were? Why?"

"It was pretty fucking weird, Ellen," he said. He was drowsy, right on the edge of a short nap.

Ellen buried her face in his armpit and chuckled. How long ago was that? Ten years? Twelve? While on a research project, she'd stumbled across a book of Japanese erotica. She had found the paintings extremely charged, but it was something else entirely that captured her imagination. "After the sex act is completed," the text said, "it is customary for the female partner to announce, 'Words cannot express the depth of my gratitude.'" Ellen's first response was feminist outrage. But then she looked again at the illustrations. The women were obviously having fun. What if there's something to it, she wondered. What if the principle behind the bulky shape of the words could lead her to new erotic ground, to some understanding that would transcend gender?

She tried the line on Tommy.

"Huh?" he said.

"Words cannot express the depth of my gratitude," she repeated.

"Yeah, it was good, baby, but don't get carried away," Tommy said. By the third time she said it, he demanded an explanation.

"So how does it make you feel to hear it?" she had asked after showing him the book.

Tommy thought for a while. "It makes me think you're up to no good," he finally answered, ruffling her hair. But Ellen persisted, searching inside herself for the place from which she could truthfully make that announcement, and Tommy put up with it. Eventually, she gave up. And now, a decade later, she learned that Tommy had been thrilled to see it go. Her experiment in passivity—a flop.

Tommy was snoring now. She was used to this, had even invented her own name for it: PPDI, or postpartum deprivation of intimacy. She took a long, slow breath, inhaling the musky smell of his body. Then she climbed out of bed and finished packing. By the time he was up, she was ready to leave.

She turned into her own personal driveway seven and a half hours later and switched off the car with a sense that this had always been inevitable. No matter what she'd done, fate would have conspired to place her here at this time.

The house looked adorable. Several little patches of daffodils were in full bloom and the spindly lilac bushes by the door were topped with beautiful purple buds. Yellow and purple, Easter colors, nature's symbolic color code for resurrection, had come a month late to the North Country. They were long gone from the city. I get two springs this year, she thought, as she climbed from the car and stretched. Around her head, black flies swarmed. She tried to chase them off by madly swinging her arms, but they were oblivious. By the time she reached the door and got inside, she had squashed two in her ear and one had flown into her mouth and gotten stuck on her tongue. "Get out, get out!" she yelled at the cloud of insects that had followed her from the car. As she slammed the door, it hit her: those were the very words that had driven her from New York. She felt a thud in her stomach.

The house smelled old, musty, and closed up. She wanted to fling open the windows, but the bugs, the bugs. She sank into a wooden chair in the dining room. It creaked and swayed under her weight. Suddenly, Ellen felt friendless, exiled for no reason. She saw herself trapped for months in this clammy, airless crypt of a house while millions of black flies and mosquitoes pelted the windowpanes.

Well, she thought, pushing the image away, I'll just make a list of what I need. List-making always cheered her. She walked to the wall and flipped on the overhead light. Nothing. She had arranged in advance for the electricity to be restored, but it obviously hadn't happened. With a sigh, she pulled her notebook from her purse and opened to a fresh page. Candles, she wrote. Screens, bug spray, Windex. She looked around. The place was shabby, even mocking. Where could she begin? Her eyes did a quick visual scan of the perimeter of the dining room and the kitchen. They snagged at a velvet black splotch up near the ceiling. Ellen focused on it. She resisted admitting what she already knew: it was a bat. Hanging upside down from the kitchen molding like Bela Lugosi.

She put her head down on the table and wept.

seven

Torture.

It was torture unloading the car and dashing through the mosquitoes with her arms full of electronic devices that she could not plug in. No music tonight, she thought, as she deposited her tape player on the living-room floor; no coffee in the morning. And no deli on the corner either. Possessed, she ran outside for another armful. She wanted to clean out the car and make a quick trip into Lamone. "For supplies," she said out loud, feeling very much the pioneer. *Supplies* was a word she had probably never used, not even once, in all her years in the city, but here, staring at the wall of trees and the underbrush creeping toward the house, here it was appropriate.

The pile of her personal belongings grew to a mountain in the middle of the living room before she stopped for a drink. It was uplifting, cozy, and familiar to head into the old pantry fully equipped with jelly glasses. But when she turned on the faucet and nothing happened, her jaw clenched. She marched to the table and picked up her pen. Water, she wrote in big letters on her list. Calamine lotion, she added, scratching a huge red welt on her forearm. Alcohol.

She started a second column under the heading "To Do." Call electric company. Call phone company. Find a handyman to get the water going. She glanced at her watch. It was six thirty—too late to do business. And it was a long time until Monday. Then she remembered the little mom-and-pop store at the curve in the road near the post office, and she ran to the car and backed out of the driveway so fast her whole body snapped forward when she hit the brakes. She took off in a cloud of dust.

A black dog the size of a small bear was draped across the doorway to the Eagle Beak General Store. It showed no interest in moving, so Ellen took a giant step over its back while simultaneously jiggling the doorknob and shoving her way inside. She almost fell into the candy rack before she caught her balance. A man with a Smith Brothers beard and a T-shirt that read "Ask Me No Questions, I'll Tell You No Lies" glanced up from the magazine he had spread out on the counter.

"Big dog," Ellen commented, trying to be neighborly.

"Useless," the man said. "That's his name."

"Must be great for his self-esteem," quipped Ellen.

"Old Useless can take it. He made a career out of being shiftless." He returned his eyes to his fly-fishing catalog.

Ellen collected the essentials from the half-barren shelves. She was astonished by the items she carted to the counter: Wonder Bread, peanut butter and jelly swirl, a six-pack of Bud Ice, ranch-flavored corn chips. Was this how America ate, she wondered. She remembered the red and blue balloons on the Wonder Bread wrapper from her childhood, but she had not seen it stocked in any store she'd entered in well over a decade. She noticed a bin of batteries and grabbed two handfuls. She would have music after all.

"You staying over to the lake?" the bearded man asked as he worked the cash register.

"Lake? No," Ellen answered. "I just bought Viola de Beer's place."

The man's finger hovered above the register key. He looked at her with renewed interest. "So you're the one," he said.

Ellen laughed and said, "That doesn't sound good."

"Name's Baldy," the man said, extending his hand.

Ellen resisted the urge to check out his hairline, which was covered to the eyebrows by a baseball cap. "Ellen Kenny," she said. "Pleased to meet you."

"We'll see if you still feel that way in a few months," Baldy said. He rustled under the counter until he produced a wrinkled paper sack and packed the groceries, tucking in, for her reading pleasure, a copy of the *Free Trader*. WIDEST CIRCULATION IN THE NORTH COUNTRY boasted the headline. Ellen paid up, climbed over Useless, and left. I'll have dinner by candlelight, she thought cheerfully as she drove the two miles back home. Maybe drink all the beers and pee in the bushes.

But when night came, Ellen was afraid to step out the door. The overwhelming silence and darkness, which seemed filthy, evoked images of ax murderers and inbred mountain perverts who would force her to squeal like a pig as they raped her. She played tape after tape: Otis Redding, Elvis, Aretha Franklin, but the music seemed frail and tinny, as if it were too weak to conquer the quiet. And above her head, Ellen heard the constant pitter-patter of mouse feet as they charged back and forth upstairs. She had closed the kitchen door so the resident bat could not nest in her hair, but she was still uneasy about it as she guzzled her Budweisers, her least favorite beer, in the candlelight, taking a gulp each time she needed to numb a new tendril of anxiety.

What's wrong with me, she wondered as she sank lower into Viola de Beer's old pea-green armchair, her fingers tracing the patterns of the hand-crocheted antimacassars with their various cigarette burns. Why am I so shook up? And then, in a boozy inspiration, it came to her: pretraumatic stress syndrome. She laughed out loud. That had to be it: utter, complete anxiety inspired by the sure knowledge that the stress that would ultimately do her in was yet to come. But it was close.

Pretraumatic stress syndrome.

Suddenly Ellen felt happy. She loved to invent new psychological disorders. She rose from the chair, ready to climb the steep staircase to bed. But walking made her dizzy, so she resettled on the lumpy couch at the other end of the room and fell into a deep, drunken sleep.

When she opened her eyes, thousands of tiny dust particles were suspended in a sunbeam that angled over her head to warm the wide pine floorboards. So much crap in this world, she thought angrily, even up here in the middle of nowhere. But being a morning person, Ellen was determined to seize the day. Bounding off the couch despite a pronounced headache, she tore through her suitcase until she found a tight V-neck sweater. She positioned her head in the neck hole with the V under her chin and her hair completely covered, tied the arms atop her head, and then scooted quickly through the kitchen to the woodshed to collect the fishnet she'd seen hanging there. Next to it, she found a pair of leather work gloves. Then she dug her Rayban sunglasses out of her purse and put them on, ready, willing, and able to fight the bat that still listlessly hung from the kitchen molding.

Fearlessly, she headed for the kitchen, dragging a rickety wooden chair along behind her. When she climbed up onto it, it swayed beneath her but held her weight, and one quick poke dropped the unprotesting bat into her net. She leapt from the chair, charged through the dining room, and heaved the bat, net and all, out the screen door and into the driveway.

A good job done, she thought with pride as she stripped off her gloves, glasses, and protective hood. She cracked open a Diet Pepsi, made herself a peanut butter and jelly swirl sandwich on Wonder Bread, and sat at the dining-room table. After a few bites, and in the absence of *The New York Times* or even the *Post*, she opened the *Free Trader*.

With the interest of a cultural anthropologist doing fieldwork, Ellen read through the first several pages of announcements for roast beef or ham dinners at various churches. She noted that there were "anonymous" groups, from overeaters to debtors to women who love too much, meeting with regularity right in the county. And she was amazed at the number of piglets for sale, fields of standing hay begging to be cut, and trailers for rent.

Halfway through page eighteen, she came upon an ad that caused her to momentarily choke on her swirl sandwich. "For Sale," it read, "Entire beer can collection and set of motorcycle leathers, size 46. Call 483-7978." She pushed back from the table to speculate on the advertiser. Had he suddenly grown up? Renounced his beer swilling? Seen the error of flying his size forty-six motorcycle colors? Was he in the midst of a midlife crisis, she wondered. For that matter, was she? Was this a kindred spirit, reaching out through the *Free Trader* for someone to relieve him of his past? She glanced once at the plate shelf that ran the entire perimeter of her dining room. How much room would a beer can collection take up, she wondered. Exactly how large was a pair of size forty-six motorcycle chaps?

Circling the ad with her red felt-tip pen, she refolded the paper New York–subway-style, into eighths, and set it to one side. Then she stuffed last night's list into her purse and headed to downtown Lamone to take care of business.

eight

With the precision of a military strategist, Ellen conducted one east-west and one west-east reconnaissance sweep of Main Street, just to orient herself, before she pulled into the parking lot of the Super-Duper. She had thought she was getting an early start, and perhaps she was by city standards, but here in farm country where the people rose with the sun, she was at the tail end of the morning rush and had to slowly circle the outer limits of the parking lot in search of a space for the Honda. With glee, she left the car unlocked and the windows rolled down.

Ahh, country life, she thought, taking a great breath. So intent was she on inhaling the sweet, fresh morning air that she failed to notice that the entire atmosphere reeked. She gagged and quickly pulled the hem of her T-shirt up to cover her nose. Frantically, she glanced around for the source of the terrible smell and soon located it directly across the road: a tractor moved slowly across a wide expanse of black dirt, flinging soupy cow manure far and wide.

Ellen hustled into the store, gulping its recycled oxygen with relief. Then she lost herself in the wide aisles of the Super-Duper, maneuvering an oversized cart around dozens of women who were at least twice her size. In the city, she usually felt perilously close to being physically unacceptable. Here, she was on the cutting edge of fitness, a model of self-control, and she sailed past the Hostess Twinkies and the Chips Ahoy! with a little burst of self-righteous pride. She made her calls from the pay phone in front of the store, securing promises of light, phone, and cooking gas by noon on Monday.

Ellen wanted to call Tommy, but it seemed unfair to blast him out of his Saturday morning snooze at eighty thirty-five A.M. Left to his own devices, he usually rose at ten on the weekend, then spent a good fifteen minutes preparing himself a cappuccino or a latte in the restaurant-grade espresso machine he'd bought himself for his forty-ninth birthday. Ellen's eyes had widened at the price tag, but she chalked it up to a mini-midlife crisis and silently thanked God it wasn't an apple-green sports car or, even worse, a young babe for a girl-friend. Every Saturday, she would go to the Hot Bagel on Fourteenth Street while Tommy slept off his hard week's work and buy him his favorite: garlic and onion with a schmear of vegetable cream cheese, which he would consume with his hot drink.

What would he do without her to provide this little gustatory pleasure? She imagined him, barefoot, groggy-eyed, and groping for the white bagel bag she always deposited next to his personalized coffee mug. She decided to find a diner and linger over her own cup of coffee for half an hour, then call. It would still be a little early for Tommy, but she was dying to tell him about her triumph over the bat. She could almost hear him humming the theme to *Batman* in her honor.

But when she stopped forty-five minutes later at the phone booth in front of Newberry's and dialed their number in New York, nobody picked up. Even the answering machine was turned off. Ellen dialed again, more carefully, and let it ring eight times—an absurd number given the size of their apartment—but it was clear that Tommy simply wasn't home.

"Hmmph," she snorted as she replaced the receiver. An irrational ribbon of anger caused her hands to form fists at her sides. Where was he? She'd only been gone one day and already he'd altered his lifelong routine and pulled the rug out from under her. Of course, she realized her reaction was drastically out of proportion to the event itself. And as she drove parallel to the Salmon River, which rushed in the opposite direction from Eagle Beak, she grilled herself, as Tommy would say, about her motivation. "You should've been a short-order cook," Tommy had once commented. "You always got yourself or somebody else on the grill." But she had to know the truth.

And the truth was painfully obvious: she was way too dependent on Tommy. One time, he'd failed to answer the phone, and she was sure he'd pulled a fast one. Her blood had begun to boil and doubts about his fidelity had instantaneously popped up like spooks at the edge of her imagination.

Ellen was sorely disappointed in herself. And what was worse, this was an old theme, one she had grappled with, it seemed, forever. All the moments when she'd tried and failed to overcome her basic insecurity were familiar stepping-stones in her psyche. With a deep sigh, she chalked up her reaction to the morning's phone call to Tommy as the latest in a long line of failures. By the time she pulled into her overgrown driveway, she was thoroughly depressed. And climbing out of the car, she heard a mysterious sound—a weak *cheep-cheep*—and traced it to the bat, trapped in the string of the fishnet in the blazing sun. She was shocked to see how stunning it was up close, the velvety blackness of its body and wings, its sharp teeth, the tiny little heart visibly pounding against its chest as it struggled. Without thinking of her snood or gloves, she worked it free and placed it under the shade of a lilac bush. It no longer seemed willing to fly, and she saw with alarm that its wing was completely dislocated. *Cheep-cheep* it moaned as she climbed the crumbling cement steps to her door and returned with her leather gloves on.

"I'm so, so sorry," she whispered as she kneeled in the dirt, and, with horror, leaned forward to snap its little neck.

nine

Summoning the healing spirit of Mr. Clean, Ellen threw herself into a major scrubbing frenzy. For hours, she hovered above a chemical cloud of disinfectants and scouring products that came in spray bottles. Bit by bit, the grime on the windows retreated, the cobwebs vanished, and the generations of dead houseflies disappeared from the windowsills. Of course, it would have been easier with running water, but Ellen refused to whine about what couldn't be remedied at the moment.

Visible demonstrations of her own control always cheered Ellen. She liked clear, attainable goals that could be crossed off her mental checklist, one by one. She tore through the closets and dressers, sorting the contents into three piles: laundromat, dump, and Goodwill. By late afternoon, she noticed with satisfaction, her shabby little farmhouse shimmered with the pride of ownership.

But she couldn't stop. She loaded her car full of old blankets, sheets, and towels and headed back down the mountain to Lamone. She had seen two laundromats and, since she had nothing better to do with this particular Saturday night, she intended to do all six loads of wash, rinsing away any sign of the house's previous tenants, and read the latest gossip rags, too. Plus, there was probably a pay phone she could use.

But Tommy didn't answer. Ellen glanced at her watch. Almost six thirty. Maybe he went to an afternoon movie or an early dinner. Maybe he just stepped outside for some fresh air pollution. There was no reason to panic or allow herself to feel resentment or anger. She vigorously snapped the warm sheets as she folded them and layered them in a blue plastic bag. Tommy was in New York, the center of the universe, and there were at least a thousand things he could be doing.

And she was in Eagle Beak, sweeping up mouse turds.

"Why am I here?" she asked herself aloud as she sat in Viola de Beer's old armchair in the dim candlelight. "Why were *you* here, Viola?" she suddenly asked the empty house. She held her breath, half expecting an answer, but none came. Then she remembered: Viola had raised a son. She had probably wrestled her living out of the earth and devoted half her time to survival. That was what Ellen needed. Less time to think. Less time to boil in her own mental oil. Tomorrow, she decided, no matter what, she would put in her garden. She would start small, and do it all by hand, rise with the sun and work up a healthy sweat in the fields. Ellen Kenny, nature girl. A woman who ran with the wolves.

She climbed the steps to her bedroom under the eaves and snuggled beneath a fresh-smelling patchwork quilt that had miraculously survived both the wash and the spin cycle. Although it was after nine, it was not quite dark, and crickets and frogs, or so she assumed, were conducting a lively sing-along outside her window. She was not relaxed in this wilderness, but at least she wasn't plastered, like last night. And she knew she would feel more secure when a simple flick of a switch flooded the room with light and the toilet could be flushed on demand.

She could make it to Monday, she was certain. And she wouldn't even try Tommy again until she could dial in the comfort and privacy of her own kitchen. Two could play at his no-contact game. Even as she formed that thought, though, a tear worked its way out of the corner of her eye and down her cheek. "I miss you, Tommy," she whispered. "I really do." And then she caught a passing wave of sleep, and rode it safely through the night.

Ellen slept straight through dawn despite her determination to get up with the sun, though, because a flotilla of dark storm clouds effectively blocked any sign of sunlight. The air turned cold, like a late fall day in the city, and through a veil of sleep, Ellen heard an angry rumble not unlike the one the A train makes as it rounds an underground bend on its way into the West Fourth Street station. Am I late for work, she wondered lazily, grateful in her drowsy dream state that she had a comfortable seat on which to wait for the subway. But then a wet splash hit her in the face and her mind instantly delivered her to the worst possible scenario: some pervert had jacked off in her face. It had happened to her work friend, Carol, as she had been quietly absorbed in a book on a bench at Thirty-third Street, and neither Carol nor Ellen had ever gotten over it. It established an entirely new level of big-city terror—one that ranked right up there with getting raped or murdered or kidnapped by a phony taxi driver.

"No!" Ellen screamed, sitting bolt upright in her bed, frantically slapping at the offensive wet spot on her cheek. "No!" she yelled again, as if her revulsion could rewrite history. And suddenly it came into focus, her bedroom under the eaves with its faded vertical rows of lilac bouquets and ornate ribbons and bows in the same hue. Another cold splash hit her forehead. Ellen looked up. A whole circle of engorged drops hung at the edges of a brown water stain on the ceiling. And outside her windows, the rain was an opaque silver sheet.

Ellen jumped up with a mighty roar and shoved the iron bed and all its freshly laundered linen out of harm's way. She ran down the stairs for a container to catch the drips, realizing to her horror that there were leaks everywhere. By the time she had placed a pot, a pan, or a bowl under each minor cascade, the pantry shelves were bare and the house was a domestic obstacle course. The rain pounded on, a solid sheet from sky to earth that invited no intrusion.

Positioning Viola's armchair away from the leaks, Ellen conducted a prolonged assessment of the level of dampness in the house. No wonder it smelled moldy. Probably the edges of every floorboard were green with slime and the wallpaper was alive with broccoli-shaped microbes. She would definitely need to fix the roof. She would sue Viola's son Rodney for failure to disclose and force him to pay for it, too.

Slowly, the windows fogged over. How long could she sit in a chair and do nothing before she would lose her mind? How long could a cloudburst last? Eagle Beak wasn't in the tropics, after all. It was practically on the border of Canada, where the air was supposed to be crisp and dry.

Every half hour, Ellen dumped the containers that had filled in the interim. On one such tour, it occurred to her that she should save the water, collect it for recycling purposes. That's what a pioneer would do. She remembered the huge, heavy-duty garbage can crammed under the kitchen counter. She had filled it with empty cleaning bottles yesterday, but she quickly lifted the plastic liner bag out and dragged the can to the dining-room door. She would place it outside under the edge of the roof where the rain ran off in torrents.

Taking a deep breath, she opened the door and stepped out. It was chilly, and within a few seconds, Ellen was drenched to the skin. Amazingly, it felt good, and she suddenly realized how essentially dirty she felt. She typically took two long, luxurious baths each day—one to enter and one to exit. Abandoning the barrel, she ran inside for soap and shampoo, stripping her wet clothes off and tossing them into the tub.

Giggling like a child, she entered the spurt of cold, fresh rainwater pouring off the roof and soaped up. She even shaved her legs and underarms and shampooed her hair twice. The runoff, more intense than any showerhead, exhilarated her and she felt an irresistible urge to take a romp around the front yard.

Perhaps it was the heady return to cleanliness that distracted her, or the sound of the raindrops as they drove themselves into the soggy earth beneath her feet, but she didn't notice the low rumble of the truck approaching her driveway until she was quite sure it was about to make the turn between her two grand old maple trees. Panicked, Ellen sprinted for the dining-room door. She knew she was invisible in the downpour and the safety of the house was only thirty feet away. But when she leaped up the three steps, ready to blast into the cover of home, she found the door was locked. It had swung shut in the wind.

Through the sheets of rain, she could barely decipher the outline of a pickup truck at the end of the drive. The rain barrel, she thought. A fifty-five-gallon hiding place! If one was big enough to cram a Mafia guy into for a one-way trip into Biscayne Bay, it was big enough for her. She scrambled over the side and crouched low just as the truck door slammed and footsteps stormed past her, within five feet. Squatting down Asian-style with her chin on her knees, she noticed for the first time the water lapping against her private parts. It was quite deep already and filling fast. I hope I don't have to stay here too long, she thought with terror, long enough to drown. That would be the grand payoff of a life well-spent: drowned in a rain barrel on her first weekend in the boonies. She could see it all now—being unceremoniously dumped out, naked, rigor mortis already set in to keep her eternally in the cannonball position.

She heard a loud pounding on the door, then a man's voice. "Mrs. Kenny?" he yelled. "You in there?" It wasn't Baldy from the grocery store and it wasn't Roger LaFleur—her two male reference points in the entire North Country. "You in there?" he persisted. "It's Rodney de Beer."

Viola's no-goodnik son! Ellen crouched even lower and held her breath as the runoff poured into the barrel and the rain pelted her head like miniature BBs.

"I figured you might need the pot burner on," he yelled, "and I want to tell you about the roof!"

"Yeah, buddy, you've got some explaining to do," Ellen mumbled angrily under her breath. Or so she thought until she heard him say, "What? Who's that? Where are you?"

Ellen quickly considered her options: if she stayed quiet, he might initiate a search. She'd be a sitting duck, trapped as she was. Or, since she'd blown it anyway, she could simply announce herself. She was freezing and her teeth were chattering. Maybe he could get that kitchen pot burner to work and she could warm up.

"Where are you?" Rodney repeated, a little louder this time.

"I'm in the rain barrel," Ellen said.

"In the rain barrel?" He was obviously taken aback. "What're you doing in the rain barrel?"

"I'm locked out of the house."

"Well, come on out. I won't bite you. And we got a spare key hid right here anunder this shingle."

Anunder? Even in her ridiculous situation, Ellen noted with interest the new North Country preposition.

"I can't come out," she admitted. "I don't have any clothes on."

"You're nekked?"

"Yeah."

Rodney paused for the briefest second and then said, "To each his own."

"Yeah, well there's a poncho in the shed off the kitchen. Could you get it and throw it to me?"

"Okay."

She peeked over the edge of the barrel and could barely make out his shape against the door frame, but she heard it when he gave the swollen door a good shove and stepped inside. A moment later, he returned. "You want me to just toss it?"

"Please, and then turn around."

Rodney threw the olive-green poncho within a foot of the garbage can and Ellen crawled stiffly out and put it on. Summoning all her dignity, she headed for the open door. Thankfully, Rodney was bent over the pot burner in the kitchen with his back to her as she scooted around the corner and ran up the stairs, feeling for all the world like the distant cousin of the streaker who set the tone at the 1974 Academy Awards show.

ten

Dried and dressed in a warm sweatshirt and jeans, Ellen descended the stairs to formally meet Rodney de Beer. There was no way to pretend she hadn't been nude and hiding in a rain barrel just five minutes before, and she fully expected to be the laughingstock of Eagle Beak, and maybe Lamone, before nightfall. But she could handle it. It wasn't the first time she'd ever been embarrassed in her life.

But the shock of seeing Rodney in her kitchen neutralized all her anxiety. Unconsciously, she had expected the infamous no-goodnik son to be a rebel without a clue, a strapping stud in his twenties with a jailhouse mustache and a pack of unfiltered Camels rolled in his shirtsleeve. But Rodney looked to be pushing sixty-five. He was stoop-shouldered with a set of false choppers that proved, beyond a reasonable doubt, that in the world of dentures, one size definitely does not fit all. His eyes were almost buried in the folds of loose skin that hung like curtains from his eyebrow ridge and what remained of his steel-gray hair had been carefully parted low on one side, swept over the top of his head, and plastered flat with some hairdressing fluid. Ellen detected no twinkle in his eye that implied he'd taken a secret peek as she scampered by. All thoughts of the rain barrel episode ceased to exist as she moved toward him, her hand extended.

"Looks like you got a few leaks," Rodney said with no hint of irony.

Ellen dropped her hand. "That's the understatement of the year."

"See, the problem is the rain's coming from the northwest. It don't usually come this hard from the northwest."

Ellen, expectantly waiting for more, suddenly remembered an old boyfriend from the sixties, from Somerville. He was chronically late and his arrival time had become a hot potato between them. Ellen's foot would tap and her blood pressure would mount as she waited for an explanation, but he would inevitably shrug and say, "Baby, who knows if time is really accurate?" She had hated both the suspense and the hope of a genuine answer, and she felt that same way now. But what could Rodney possibly say? That the rain was not accurate? Who knows if it's raining at all? Cynicism rose like gorge in her throat.

"See, the roof don't leak unless the rain comes from the northwest," Rodney explained.

"Why is that?"

"The wind gets anunder the shingles during the winter and loosens 'em up. Once it warms up, say in a couple weeks, the tar will expand and them shingles'll be tight again. It's a goddamn shame we had to have this hard rain so early in the year."

Ellen weighed this information. It sounded somewhat logical, but then, if you thought about it for long enough, so did "Who knows if time is really accurate?" But she was determined that this geezer was not going to pull the wool over her eyes. This wasn't *Green Acres*, after all, and she was no Eva Gabor.

"You owe me money back, Rodney," she said. Her voice carried no charge, no hint of hostility. "You didn't disclose. And furthermore, I don't like the idea that you held out about the spare key. You could've strolled in here anytime you wanted."

"I was gonna tell you where it was," he said defensively. "You ain't been here but two days. Anyway, what would I want to come in here for?"

"That's not the point," Ellen said, realizing that she didn't really have a point. So what if he knew where the spare key was? He hardly looked like a rapist or a robber. He seemed totally flustered, with his pink pate shining through the gray strands of hair and his rubber galoshes forming two puddles on her kitchen linoleum. And he *had* come out in a near hurricane to start a fire for her. But she didn't think it wise to back away from the line she had just drawn in the dirt.

"We'll let the lawyers handle it," she said dismissively, and then added, "I'd offer you a cup of coffee but the stove's not working and neither is the electricity."

"You could heat up some water on the pot burner," Rodney offered tentatively.

Yes, Ellen thought, coffee, and she quickly filled a small pan with bottled mineral water and placed it on top of the heater while Rodney explained the intricacies of turning on the old heater. These included humping a five-gallon jug of kerosene up a ladder in the woodshed and dumping it into a gas tank that Rodney had hung on the wall. He said it came from his mother's last car—a '63 Oldsmobile.

Ellen wasn't really listening because it was simply too difficult to comprehend. In order to activate the seventy-five-year-old pot burner, she had to go somewhere to buy fuel, schlep it here and there, purchase long-stemmed matches, and scrub the creosote out of the chimney. Hadn't these people up here ever heard of thermostats? And now Rodney wanted to lead her on an orientation tour that included such things as priming the shallow well pump, flushing horse dung into the septic tank, and hustling the raccoons out of the crawl space over the front porch.

"Look, Rodney, could we do this another time? I'm on overload here and I can't absorb another thing."

He looked at her curiously. She probably seemed like a spoiled brat to him, a privileged New Yorker who could hire someone to manage the chores. And when it occurred to her that it was true, she felt shame and wanted to change the subject.

"Tell me about your mother," Ellen suddenly said, lining up the coffee, Cremora, and pure cane sugar next to two stained porcelain mugs on the counter.

"She was a bitch on wheels," Rodney said. "By the time she died she was shriveled up like a prune and didn't weigh no more than eighty-eight pounds, but there wasn't a man, woman, or child in Eagle Beak who wasn't scared to death of her." He sat down at the dining-room table, grunting as if it were a relief to be off his feet.

"Gee," Ellen lamely commented.

"She was mean as a snake her whole life," Rodney added. "Sick in the head."

Ellen looked around. From the crocheted doilies to the sheer curtains, from the dinner dishes trimmed in a rose pattern to the sewing box complete with thimbles and a strawberry-shaped pincushion, the house that Viola de Beer had vacated some eight years before looked delicate and gentle. It had that soft, feminine touch that usually went with homemade cookies and frequent little hugs.

"There wasn't one person besides me who would dare to step over the threshold, and that includes the nun from St. Helen's parish church."

Fortunately, the water had just begun to bubble and Ellen was able to distract herself by measuring out teaspoons of coffee and transporting all the paraphernalia to the table. "The first cup of joe I've made in my new house," she announced, placing a cup before Rodney. He raised it in a toast. "Good luck," he said, and they clinked their cups together high above the tabletop.

Irrationally, Ellen was seized with a strong desire to know exactly how Viola died. Perhaps she had spontaneously combusted right out of her pea-green armchair, eighty-eight pounds of human dynamite. Perhaps Ellen had been mystically drawn here for that reason, like a pilgrim to a far-off temple. "Was she ill for a long time before she died?" she tactfully asked.

"Who?"

"Your mother," Ellen answered, unnerved.

"No." Rodney did not seem prone to add more details and Ellen felt ghoulish probing.

"I guess I'm just curious about her," she said, ready to put the topic to rest for the moment. "You know, living in her place, using her cups, sleeping under the quilts she made. It just gets you wondering. That's all."

Rodney lowered his coffee to the table, his faded blue eyes boring into her brown ones. "When you look into the abyss," he said in a clear but quiet tone, "the abyss looks into you. Remember that."

Ellen nearly dropped her cup. Rodney de Beer was quoting Nietzsche! Or was it Goethe? She promised herself to look it up.

"God, Rodney," she said, "you're intense." They sat in silence for a few seconds before Ellen remembered her manners. "Would you like some more coffee?" she asked.

"No, I better be pushing off," he said. "This rain'll end by tonight sometime. They're calling for sun tomorrow."

"Well, you'll be hearing from my lawyer about the roof," Ellen said in a businesslike tone as she rose from the chair. She didn't want Rodney to think he was off the hook just because they'd shared a cup of Taster's Choice.

"Whatever," he responded, slipping into his yellow raincoat and matching hat.

"Thanks for turning on the heat," Ellen added, somewhat saddened to see her company go. Once Rodney disappeared into the downpour, Ellen amused herself by dumping out the containers that had filled with rainwater during his visit. Then she made herself a second cup of coffee and mulled over Viola's emerging profile as the wicked witch of the west. Or, more correctly, Rodney's subjective description of his mother as such. Not that Ellen doubted Rodney. He seemed like a no-frills kind of guy who probably lacked the imagination to invent a Mommie Dearest for himself. Plus, his story would be easy enough to check out, should she ever choose to do so—and she probably would because Ellen was a die-hard detective. She liked following up on leads. Like a pit bull, she could sink her teeth into any topic and not let go, no matter how inconsequential. It was what made her an exceptional researcher. But usually she turned her talents to more demanding tasks than documenting the life and times of the late Viola de Beer.

She stared out into the steady stream of rain, realizing with a start that she was already borderline desperate for stimulation. She hadn't counted on this.

Somehow her mental picture of life in the country centered on peace, tranquility, and beauty. What she'd found, thus far, was agitation, tension, and the gnawing proximity of panic. She felt seriously afraid that, stripped of her hectic New York City schedule and her demanding work life, she might simply fizzle into nothingness. And it had only taken her two days to realize it! Ellen figured that must be the world record for the decline and fall of a female ego at the end of the millennium.

By early Monday morning, she was officially out of her mind. The torrential rain was reduced to a listless drizzle but the mud formed a massive suction cup that relieved her of her Reebok when she placed her foot down on the site of her potential garden. Planting the corn was clearly out of the picture and she couldn't get in the Honda and gun it down the dirt road because the phone person was due sometime before five.

He arrived at four thirty. Ellen waited with bated breath for his diagnosis. She secretly suspected he'd need to return in the morning, that some small but important part of the phone system was missing from the shelves of his panel truck. But within fifteen minutes, she had a dial tone and she quickly pounded in Tommy's office number, not even waiting for the rates to drop in five short minutes. Edna, the secretary, said Tommy was not in the office. He had called in sick. Ellen didn't want Edna to know how out of touch she was with her own husband, so she hung up quickly. Then she called her home number on Tenth Street. The machine picked up.

"Tommy? You there?" Ellen asked. No response. "No? I just called to give you my new phone number." She repeated it into the phone. "I tried you at work," she added casually, "but Edna said you called in. Are you sick or what? Call me, okay? Love you."

She hung up, thoroughly deflated. She needed something to do, right now. Badly. Her fingers beat on the tabletop. She studied them, shocked at the aggressive rhythm of her pent-up energy. When she noticed the red stain beneath her hand, she thought she was bleeding and raised her fingers in shock. But then she recognized the Magic Marker circle she had made around the ad in the *Free Trader*.

The beer can collection! The size forty-six motorcycle leathers!

Without any hesitation, she dialed the number.

eleven

fter four rings, Ellen heard a male voice. "Yeah?" it said.
   "Hi," Ellen began with cheery enthusiasm, "I'm calling about your
ad in the *Free Trader*." He said nothing, forcing her to specify, "About
the beer can collection?"

"I got cone tops, flat tops, and pull tabs. Foreign and domestic," he said.

"Well, I'd like to see it." She could hear country-and-western music in the
background, some female whining about a broken heart. The man took a long,
deep breath as if he was inhaling on a cigarette.

"You know where Porkerville is at?" he asked.

"Porkerville?" she repeated, astonished that any self-respecting town would
permit itself such a name. "I'm afraid I don't."

"Where you coming from?"

"Eagle Beak."

"Porkerville's almost right next door. Just follow the main road past the
post office and take a left at the Y six miles out. I got a trailer on the left just
after the Porkerville sign. Got some truck tires piled up in front and painted
orange. You can't miss it." He took another drag on his cigarette. "You coming
over now?"

It seemed like a ridiculous thing to do, but she was committed. "If it's convenient."

"S'all right." He hung up.

In her heart, Ellen knew she would never buy a beer can collection. She
wasn't interested in beer cans, and collections of any sort made her uneasy.
Collectors were hoarders and misers who blocked the free-flowing circulation
of objects and got away scot-free, their basic greed somehow whitewashed. Society gave the nod to collectors, stood back in admiration of their dedication

and precision. Though beer cans were hardly Impressionist masterpieces or pre-Columbian treasures robbed from dead Mayans.

She spotted the Day-Glo tires and made a sharp right into a narrow driveway that sliced between two rows of tall pine trees. The Honda bumped over the ruts into a clearing where a decrepit Airstream trailer sat up on concrete blocks. Four bucket seats, obviously liberated from a muscle car, waited in a row to the left of the front steps and a satellite dish of epic proportions stood in a gravel circle before a shed that bulged with unidentifiable bits of machinery. The shed roof was covered with a royal blue tarp held down by yet more tires.

Ellen got out of the car. "Hello," she called. "Anybody here?"

A huge German shepherd ambled around the corner of the trailer. His head was supersized with the traditional mask across the eyes and ears that pointed skyward, but the dog's body had been shaved, a buzz cut that made him appear to be clad in a set of stained long underwear. Ellen laughed, a little bleat that she hoped would not hurt the dog's feelings. He showed no sign of aggression or even interest as he proceeded across the driveway and flopped down in the dirt next to Ellen's rear wheel.

"Hey there," she said as the dog closed his eyes and began to snore.

"No use talking to him now," a voice commented. "He's got the sleeping sickness. Narcolepsy."

Ellen turned toward the source. Emerging from the torn screen door was a man who appeared to be in his early forties. Had she been younger, she would have assumed he was older, but Ellen had become familiar with the post-forty appearance gamut and was no longer surprised to see a potbelly, sagging jowls, white whiskers, or a fashion felony. It all depended on how a person lived— and this guy had obviously lived hard.

"I didn't know dogs could get narcolepsy," she said with a slight nod toward the dog asleep in the dirt.

"Mutley's not a dog. He's a rocket scientist."

The man had descended the two steps from the trailer. He wore a black T-shirt with the sleeves torn off, the words "Party 'til You Puke" barely visible across the chest. His hair, thinning on the top, hung in light brown strings to his shoulders, and his ill-fitting blue jeans appeared to be fake denim.

Ellen extended her hand. "Ellen Kenny, from Eagle Beak," she said.

"Rayfield Geebo of Porkerville," he answered and they both laughed. It was the first moment of pure merriment that Ellen had experienced in the North Country and she instantly felt five pounds lighter. Then, suddenly, she was swept into one of her laughing fits, carried away on a current of uncontrollable giggles that quickly became guffaws. Rayfield Geebo kept a loose grip on her hand, as if he intuited that she needed an anchor of some sort.

"I'm sorry," she sputtered through the tears that were beginning to veil her eyes. Rayfield said nothing, but he observed her closely and without self-consciousness. He seemed neither intimidated nor insulted by her outburst. When her fit subsided, he released her fingers and she brushed away the last of the tears. "Whew," she said, "I guess I needed that."

Rayfield hesitated. "You don't look like a beer can collector," he commented.

"You don't look like a guy who'd sell off his beer can collection either."

"Touché," he said with a shrug and then added, "Well, if you want to see it, it's in the back." He started around the trailer and Ellen followed. He led her to an aluminum outbuilding, a miniature Quonset hut. It struck Ellen that Rayfield Geebo's entire world seemed to be constructed of lightweight tin: his house, his beer can museum, the cans themselves. If she got to know him better, if she came to care about him as a person, she'd casually mention all the research relating Alzheimer's disease to aluminum, just as a point of interest.

The door to the shed was padlocked and Rayfield lifted a ring of keys hanging from a spiraled plastic cord attached to his belt loop. He fitted one into the lock, and they entered the Quonset hut with reverence. Shelves stood floor to ceiling with just enough room in between for comfortable browsing. Rayfield had rigged up a spotlight on an orange extension cord from the trailer and when he snapped it on, arcs of light reflected off the various beer cans.

Ellen had no idea of the protocol. Should she step forward to examine each label? Gasp in shock? Run her fingers over the rims of the cans as if they were fine antiques made of mellowed wood? Then it occurred to her: she could ask questions.

"Exactly how many cans do you have?"

"Over thirteen hundred," said Rayfield Geebo.

"Hmmm," Ellen responded, leaning forward as if to study the specimens. "How long have you been collecting?"

"Since I started drinking. When I was twelve."

"Hmmm," Ellen said. "I see you've got an Olde Frothingslosh here." She had no idea if the can she selected was rare or common. It was a blind stab, a bluff.

"Got a couple," Rayfield said. He had moved to the doorway and was leaning against the casing, watching as Ellen moved along the shelves.

"How much are you asking for the whole collection?"

"I'd like to get what it's worth."

"And how much is that, in your opinion?"

"How much is it in yours?"

To her, it was worth the number of cans multiplied by the five-cent deposit on each and that was it, but she dared not admit this to Rayfield Geebo of Porkerville, whose beer can collection rated its own outbuilding.

"Well," she said, stalling, "I'll have to study what you've got here."

"I got an Iron City and a Hamms keg can," Rayfield said.

"Hmmm," Ellen answered.

"I got a Schaeffer olive-drab government-issue World War Two."

"Hmmm," she said again.

"I got the first Bud Gold."

"You do?" Ellen answered. She had painted herself into a corner, and there was no way out. Rayfield was even symbolically standing in the only exit. He was a big man, she realized; at least six-two in his sock feet. He was a beer drinker and a motorcycle rider. How had she allowed herself to be trapped with him in a Quonset hut in the middle of nowhere?

"You don't know shit from Shinola about collecting beer cans, do you?" Rayfield said in a conversational tone.

"No, I don't," she admitted in a small voice.

"What'd you come here for, really?"

For Ellen it was a fork in the road. "I wanted to broaden my horizons, learn about something brand-new," she could say, improvising on the spot. Or she could tell the truth. She turned to face him. "Because your ad in the *Free Trader* made me curious. I wanted to see the guy who wanted to sell off a beer can collection and a set of motorcycle leathers." She knew she was taking a risk, but she had, in general, a good record with bikers. Once, back in Somerville, she'd pulled into a neighborhood gas station run by the Grave Cheaters. The temperature gauge in her '67 Chevy Malibu convertible was in the red zone and she'd opened the hood and leaned in to see if there was an obvious leak in the radiator. She wore a pair of shocking pink corduroy jeans and two oversized bandanna-style handkerchiefs tied together, hippie-style, to form a halter top. A biker known as Rat was helping her.

Suddenly she heard the roar of an engine and an even louder voice. "Hey!" it said, and Ellen stood up and turned around to see the big kahuna of bikers perched on a Harley with gleaming tail pipes. "Can I eat you?" the biker said, and Rat let out a whoop of laughter.

"You're an asshole," said Ellen. And in the end, the big, bad biker had turned into her friend. He traded her defunct Malibu for a Dodge Dart that had run faithfully for a decade. They often laughed about that initial meeting. "What? Didn't nobody ever say that to you before?" he had asked.

She looked Rayfield Geebo straight in the eyes. "And," she added, "I thought I was gonna lose my mind unless I went somewhere or did something. I've only been up here for three days, and I'm already half nuts. Nothing's going right. The mosquitoes are eating me alive. I don't have any water in my house. The roof leaks. My husband isn't answering the phone and—" She stopped, afraid she might begin to cry.

Rayfield Geebo didn't respond for a few seconds. Then he said, "You want a beer?"

"Yes, please," said Ellen.

Meekly, she followed him out of the Quonset hut. It had been a long time since a gentleman offered to buy her a drink, though, for all she knew, Rayfield Geebo would charge her for it. Even if he did, Ellen still felt oddly touched by his kindness and his benevolent presence, despite the biker trappings and the prepubescent drinking history.

"Park yourself here and I'll bring out a couple cold ones." He indicated the bucket seats propped against the side of the trailer. Ellen sat down. Because of the position of the seat, her knees were at eye level and blocked her view of the small clearing that passed for a yard. She would have liked to study it in detail, but she would've had to open her legs wide to see, and she simply could not do that. The importance of primly clamping the knees shut to keep the boys from getting any ideas had been firmly embedded in her psyche by her Catholic school upbringing.

Rayfield returned with two cans of Milwaukee's Best, which retailed for under two dollars a six-pack. He handed one to Ellen and dropped down next to her, not even leaving one bucket seat between them.

"Yeah, life's a bitch," he said as he cracked open his beer.

"And then you die," Ellen replied.

"Have a nice day," Rayfield said, and they both tipped their beers high and guzzled. Rayfield lit a cigarette and used the ashtray built into the armrest of his bucket seat. As Ellen expected, he blew a large smoke ring. Just before it floated out of range, he put his finger through it. "Can't let it die a virgin," he said. After that, neither spoke for several seconds, though the silence was lazy and surprisingly comfortable.

"So where's your husband at?" Rayfield finally asked.

"He's in New York," Ellen answered. "At least, I think he's in New York. He hasn't answered the phone since I got here. Then I called his job and they said he hadn't come in. So who knows? Maybe he flew the coop. Maybe he moved in with an aerobics instructor with breast implants. I don't know."

"Maybe he joined the French Foreign Legion," Rayfield contributed. "Maybe he went gay and found himself a boyfriend named Bubba."

"Anything is possible," Ellen said, taking a swig of beer. "That's one thing I really, really know."

"That's one thing I found out recently," Rayfield said, and then added in an undertone, "Boy, did I."

Ellen's ears perked up. "What happened?"

Rayfield sent out another smoke ring and watched it evaporate as it rose to the top of the pine trees.

He looked at her sideways. "You ever hear of Peyronie's disease?"

"No, what is it? Some kind of cancer?"

"It's something only men get. It turns your dick into a donut."

"What?" she said stupidly.

"It turns your dick into a donut," he repeated.

For the first time, Ellen entertained the possibility that Rayfield was insane. He thought his dog was a rocket scientist; he thought his dick was a donut. There was probably some technical term for this illness.

"You get these lumps in it, see? And they start to grow, and when they get big enough, the doctor told me, he said, 'They change the direction of your erection.' Starts to go in a curve and keeps curving 'til it's a full circle."

He revealed this deadpan, with no visible sign of embarrassment, as if he were teaching a Biology 101 class at a community college. Ellen was shocked by the path of Peyronie's destruction, if any of this was actually real, but even more bowled over that any male could or would speak of his precious penis with such detachment. He blew another smoke ring, deflowered it, and continued.

"There ain't no cure for it."

Ellen struggled to come up with something to say and then settled on, "Does it affect your urination?"

"Oh, I can piss like a racehorse," he said. "Probably all the beer I drink. But I'm forty-three years old. Prostate trouble's probably coming down the pike right now."

"Well, my husband's almost fifty," Ellen offered reassuringly, "and he can still urinate." Tommy had told her that most of the guys in his age range had started to make jokes about waiting at urinals for the party to begin.

"Anyway, sex is out of the picture," Rayfield said matter-of-factly, "and my wife left me 'cause I couldn't perform no more. Shit, I was more shook up to hear her use the word 'perform' than I was about not doing it. But hey, shit happens. Want another beer?"

"Yeah," Ellen said, and Rayfield pushed himself out of the bucket seat and went inside the trailer.

How the hell did I get here, Ellen wondered. Catapulted onto the evolutionary path of Rayfield Geebo's pride and joy, the Geebo family jewels. The Geebos of Porkerville, that is. But she couldn't allow herself to laugh. Rayfield reemerged from the Airstream with a beer in each hand. He settled in beside her once again, both of them staring straight ahead as if they were expecting a movie to start at any moment.

"This must be hard on you," she said.

"Oh, very funny," he responded.

Ellen was nonplussed. She hadn't intended to pun. "I didn't mean—" she began, but Rayfield cut her off.

"Believe me, it'd be a lot worse if I gave a shit," he said.

So where did they go from here? If you started off a casual conversation with the deepest intimacies, what did you do next? Talk about the weather? Ellen remembered when her friend Kathleen had confided that she'd met the man of her dreams, but the prognosis for romance was poor. "If you let him tie you up on the first date," she'd sighed, "what do you do for an encore? Blow him in a meat locker?" There were no easy answers to those questions. The love of Kathleen's life never called her back, and she instituted a mandatory getting-to-know-you policy, which went completely against her grain.

"Did you know Viola de Beer?" Ellen asked conversationally. "I just bought her house."

"I hope you know a good exorcist," Rayfield said.

Images of Viola's aged head spinning three-hundred-sixty degrees while green slime ejected from her mouth flashed on the screens inside Ellen's eyelids. "You think she was possessed?" she asked.

"No doubt."

Ellen felt irrational panic but forced herself to calm down. "Rodney did say his mother was a bitch on wheels," she said.

"You know Rodney?"

"I met him once."

"You ever see his sculptures?"

"He's a sculptor?" Ellen asked, incredulous.

"Best chain saw man in the North Country."

"Really?" Ellen didn't even know sculpting with a chain saw was possible. "I'd like to see his work sometime," she added politely.

"Just go over to his house," Rayfield said. "You want directions?"

"No, I really can't. Actually, I have a lot to do. I better be heading off. Thanks for the beers." She pushed herself to the edge of the seat, to the position of a deep knee bend, and gave herself a heave-ho.

"I guess you ain't making me an offer on the cans."

"Let me think about it," Ellen said. "I'll be in touch." She walked to her car, hustled Mutley away, and backed down the long driveway. "Sorry about your donut-condition," she called out the window. She was quite tipsy from the two beers in short succession, but she felt more relaxed than she had before she'd met Rayfield Geebo of Porkerville.

twelve

It was sunset as Ellen negotiated the curves along the narrow highway to her new home. A ribbon of magenta clouds stretched across the sky above the mountains, and the top quarter of the sun, a flaming disk, was quickly sinking out of sight. The beauty took Ellen's breath away and she pulled to the side of the road and got out of the car to watch.

Stepping from her car, with all the humid, green silence around her and the intense colors overhead, Ellen felt deeply reverent. Quite tipsy, she raised her arms, wide open, and threw her head back so that her breasts rose up before her like two mountains. She felt suspended in time, tuned only to the steady pounding of her heart within her.

But she snapped out of it when she suddenly heard the squeal of the tires of a gleaming, new pickup truck coming to a stop beside her. She lowered her arms as the driver rolled down his window. The entire landscape, reflected in the glare, seemed to disappear into a dark void as he cranked. Ellen waited in suspense, and finally saw that it was Baldy. "Been in any good rain barrels lately?" he called, and then howled with laughter at his own joke.

What could Ellen say? She did not want to defend herself. It hurt her that Rodney de Beer had told on her, but there was not a thing she could do about it. "You New Yorkers! You're all nuts," Baldy said, and then he waved, rolled up the window, and drove off. Well, Ellen thought as she stepped toward the car, that was unnecessary—and even cruel. At least you expected it in New York where the natives were famous for the variety of ways they said "Fuck you!" to each other. Here in God's country, you hoped for more.

She climbed back into the Honda with a heavy heart and drove home well below the posted speed limit. Naturally, the house was dark when she pulled into the driveway. The electrician had been delayed until tomorrow, and another long night stretched out in front of her. The Rayfield Geebo diversion had not lasted long. In fact, the bit of light it had shed on her dark loneliness was fading fast.

And then, as she inserted her key in the lock, a miracle happened. The telephone rang. Frantically, Ellen turned the key and pushed the door open. She ran to the phone and grabbed it.

"Hello," she panted.

"Ellen?"

"Tommy?"

"You sound out of breath."

Ellen sat down, curling the phone cord around her finger and smiling like a fool. "I was just coming in, that's all. How are you?" She hesitated. "Where are you?"

"Fine. Home. So how's it going?"

Ellen did not want to cry. She didn't want to tell him that a few minutes ago, the one and only local merchant had poked fun at her on a public highway. She didn't want to demand an explanation of his whereabouts when she'd called or why he hadn't shown up at work. Ever since she'd surrendered to her Eagle Beak impulse, she'd felt guilty, as if she was on thin ice with Tommy, and she didn't want to crack it and disappear into the cold, dark water.

"It's great," she said, trying to put a little oomph behind it. "How's it going with you?"

"Excellent," he said. A brief silence followed.

"I tried to call you. Several times," Ellen said in her best conversational tone. "Nobody home."

"Yeah. I took off for the whole weekend. I think your 'Freedom for All' campaign is affecting me." Ellen noticed that his voice was buoyant, loaded with barely contained excitement. A fear began to tug at the inside edges of her lungs, making it difficult for her to breathe.

"So where'd you go?" she asked.

"Bermuda!" Tommy said.

"Bermuda!" Ellen repeated. Tommy had gone to *Bermuda*.

"Yeah. I was coming home from work on Friday and I saw one of those travel posters on the subway. You know, the pristine beach, the deep blue sea . . ."

Yeah, Ellen supplied in her mind, the postadolescent goddess in a thong bikini with total absence of cellulite in her ass and thighs.

". . . anyway, I figured, Why not? The minute I got in the door, I called the travel agency and I was in a cab headed for Kennedy within ninety minutes."

Even given her pretraumatic stress syndrome, there was no good reason to ask her husband if he had gone to Bermuda alone. She resisted the urge to probe, knowing it was totally out of line. After all, hadn't she bought a house on a similar whim? Hadn't she packed up and left New York? Hadn't she spent the afternoon discussing a gentleman's penis?

"So how was it?" she asked.

"Fantastic! You're not gonna believe this, Ellen, but I actually went surfing. Of course, I was the oldest guy out there and I never made it to shore, not even once, but hell, I did it. I always wanted to give it a try."

"You did?" She had no idea that Tommy secretly desired to hang ten.

"Well, it wasn't a driving need, but yeah, I always wanted to surf."

"Good for you, then," Ellen said, and she meant it. "What else did you do?"

"The usual. Sunbathed, swam, ate in four-star restaurants, drank tropical drinks with fruit stuck on the rim."

"Sounds great." Tommy had probably been applying sunscreen when she'd been hiding in the rain barrel. He'd probably been perusing a glossy, eight-page menu while she was making instant coffee on the kitchen pot burner.

"I even stayed an extra day. Called in sick at work. Why not?"

"Yeah, why not?" Ellen echoed.

"I feel like a million bucks."

Ellen, who felt like ten cents, could only sigh.

"How about you?" Tommy asked. "How're you making out as Nanook of the North?"

"Okay," she said cautiously.

"That doesn't exactly sound enthusiastic."

"Well, there are a few problems with the house."

"Like what?"

Why recite the litany, Ellen thought. For what? "It's not worth getting into," she said, feeling a surge of self-containment. Instead, she told him about being locked outside in her birthday suit. She mentioned that some of the locals believed the house had cooties left over from the late Viola de Beer. One had even recommended an exorcism. Tommy roared. To Ellen, it was a very beautiful sound.

But she didn't mention Rayfield Geebo, the beer can collection, or the presence of such a thing as Peyronie's disease on Planet Earth. She would save that whole story for a lull in some future conversation.

"Anyway, I just got back and I'm starving." Tommy wanted to hang up.

"Where're you gonna go?" Ellen asked, holding on.

"Maybe the Thai place."

"Tommy?"

"Yeah?"

"You think you might ever come up here for a weekend?"

"Sure," he said, "how about the Fourth of July."

That was weeks away.

"Sounds good. Well, bon appétit!" Ellen gently hung up the phone.

Tommy had gone to Bermuda while she rotted in Eagle Beak. It made her want to give up. But give up what? Her chance to find out who she was, minus the marriage and career frills? Her opportunity to be of the earth, a bona fide nature girl? Whatever happened to *ipsissimus*? Was she a man or a mouse? Wearily, Ellen climbed the stairs to her bedroom under the eaves. Eight o'clock was a perfectly respectable time to go to sleep.

In the morning, the sun shone with a brilliance that called out for Rayban sunglasses. Ellen trotted to the Honda for a quick dash to the Feed & Seed store. It was time to plant the garden—late, actually, but for this year, late would have to do. She whirled through the aisles like a benign typhoon, sweeping packages of seeds and skinny tomato plants, a watering can, and a straw sombrero into her cart. Garden hose and organic fertilizer! Tools for digging, spading, and hoeing the corn! Arugula, endive, portobello mushroom seeds! Ellen wanted to grow her own gourmet treats. She wanted to live the healthy life, eat directly from the dirt. It was a shock to see the cash register tally up more than two hundred dollars. She pulled several twenties out of her wallet, refusing to worry. The world was full of opportunity! Maybe she'd launch her own line of produce. She was sure she could get top dollar for arugula in the city.

Dousing herself with bug repellent, she collected her garden tools and headed off to the fields in search of a flat spot, and before long, she came to the perfect site. Unfortunately, the grass had already grown a good eight inches, which could complicate her initial tilling of the soil. But she expected hard work, and she was not afraid. Dropping all her equipment on the ground, she selected her shovel and placed its pointy tip into the earth. A great giddiness overtook her, as if she, like a great ship, had just been hit over the head with a bottle of expensive champagne. "Here I go," she announced to the universe. She placed her foot on the shoulders of the blade and threw her weight on it. The point pushed down an inch and stopped. Must be a rock, Ellen thought, moving slightly to the left. She tried again. Still no go.

Maybe I need to pull this grass up first, she mused, slipping her hands into her work gloves. If she had to become a human lawn mower, so be it. She dropped to her hands and knees and began to tug at the clumps of ragweed. They resisted, but Ellen pressed on, inch by inch. She hadn't even cleared a square yard and already her knees felt bruised and the small of her back ached. When she tried to stand, she felt like the first Neanderthal to get the bright idea of straightening up to become a biped. Why bother? It was so much easier to crawl.

Ellen wiped her brow and shooed away the cloud of mosquitoes that hovered just outside the halo of spray-on insecticide. She tried the shovel again in a different spot, and actually managed to turn over a spadeful of earth. Fat slugs that reminded her of blue-veined Viennese sausages squirmed in the moist dirt. Ellen, responsible for their obvious disorientation, tried not to look too closely.

By the time the sun was high in the sky, she had cleared an area approximately the size of a nine-by-twelve rug. The palms of her hands were beginning to blister inside her work gloves and she had developed a raging thirst. With a sense of accomplishment, she dropped her shovel to the ground and headed toward the house. The old swing on the front porch beckoned her. She deserved a rest.

The packets of seeds on the dining-room table waited in readiness, and Ellen could just imagine the relief each would feel as it was placed in the dirt, a part of it all, the cycle of growth. The only thing she'd watched grow in the city had been the number of homeless people gathered in the park under her window. She sighed as she settled into the porch swing. She was weary, and her eyes wanted to close. Bring on the darkness, she thought as a huge yawn from deep within worked toward her throat, causing her mouth to open wide to let it escape. But the stuff of this particular yawn seemed bigger than any previous one in her whole, entire life, and she stretched her mouth even wider, as if an invisible wave of negative energy were passing through her. An image of Edvard Munch's *The Scream* popped into her mind, and as a private joke she placed her two hands at the sides of her face and imagined herself on a bridge in a drab European capital. And then the moment passed and she lowered her hands to her sides. But when she tried to close her mouth, nothing happened. In fact, her mouth seemed to be stuck in the wide-open position, as if a sociopath had wedged a stick into the gears.

Ellen sat bolt upright. She fingered the hinge of her jaw. It didn't hurt and she felt nothing obviously out of alignment, but, nevertheless, her jaw had jumped its track. "Relax! For chrissakes! Relax!" she commanded herself, and, using all her powers of will, she sent relaxation like a smart bomb to her mandible. But it didn't help. Lockjaw! she thought. The terror of her life from ages five through twelve. She must have accidentally stepped on a rusty nail! And now she was doomed to spend her remaining years with her tonsils visible to the world. And Edvard Munch thought he had something to scream about.

To make matters worse, Ellen heard the sound of a motor and stood up to see the electrician turning into her driveway in his reconstituted bread truck. She could see him, apparently standing up to drive, through the windshield of a big moving box that had a series of lightning bolts painted above the hand-lettered name: BOYEA AND BOYEA ELECTRIC. The repairman hopped from the truck and headed toward the dining-room door. Ellen went to meet him, pausing briefly to glance at herself in the wavy old mirror.

If it was strange for the electrician to be greeted by a middle-aged woman with her mouth wide open, he did not let on. "I'm Fred Boyea, the electrician," he said when she appeared at the screen door. "Took me long enough to get here, right?"

"Ahh canh hawk," Ellen said, pointing vigorously to her mouth. "Ny nouh inh htuck oh-hen." Aside from being in the dental chair, she had never attempted to conduct a conversation with her mouth stretched to its maximum capacity. M's were simply impossible; so were s's and p's.

"What?" said Fred Boyea.

"Ny nouh inh htuck oh-hen," Ellen tried again. "I hah who go who a hah-hital."

"Your mouth is stuck open?" Fred said. "How'd that happen?"

Ellen waved his question away. "Where inh huh hah-hital?" she asked.

"The hospital?" Fred repeated.

Ellen nodded. "I'll drive you down there," Fred said. "You're my last call today."

Ellen grabbed her purse and pulled the front door shut behind her. She covered her mouth with both hands against the mosquitoes and black flies and she ran toward the truck. The passenger seat was so high her feet didn't even touch the floor.

Fred fired up the engine and they backed out of the driveway. "I never heard of anybody getting their mouth stuck open," he said as he maneuvered down the road. "Did you?" He glanced at her across the expanse of the truck, which was bigger than Ellen's bathroom in the city. She shook her head.

"Well, there's a first time for everything, I guess," he said stoically. When she stopped to think about it, though, it was no major shock to her that she was bouncing along in a reconditioned bread truck with her mouth frozen into the "on" position. She had had more than her share of freaky body events. When she was born, the umbilical cord was wrapped around her neck, cutting off her oxygen supply and turning her skin, according to her mother, violet blue, and she'd spent her first two weeks in an incubator trying to warm up. Her left eye wandered off on its own when she was exhausted. Her feet were flat and her ankles caved in. Two years ago, while placing a personal expense receipt on Reginald Eubanks's office spindle, she somehow miscalculated and rammed her hand down on the spike. It went straight through and the poor secretary had to pull it off. And once, when she was twenty-four and had spent a month traveling in Costa Rica, a mosquito had stung her, depositing eggs from the tropical botfly into her thigh. A month later, she had given birth to a one-inch larva that had, unknown to her, grown inside her very flesh and finally pushed its way out through her skin. A gaping maw was nothing in comparison to that event, which very nearly drove her over the brink and took five years to place on the back burner of her mind.

On and on they drove, down the mountain, along the river, and into Lamone. Fred dropped her at the emergency-room door, declining to come in but promising to wait in the parking lot until he heard from her.

"What seems to be the trouble?" asked a nurse wearing a baby-blue pantsuit uniform.

"Ny nouh inh htuck oh-hen," Ellen said, pointing at her jaw.

"Oh, dear," said the nurse as she passed a clipboard across the counter. "If you'll just complete the paperwork, the doctor will be right with you."

Ellen was at the age where she was particularly sensitive about appearing to have a double chin, and the position of her jaw was not flattering. Plus, her lips were dry and it was hard to swallow. Fortunately, there were only two other patients, and the doctor was available within fifteen minutes. A serious Indian man wearing a white turban, he probed and poked for several moments before he announced that if the muscle relaxers he was about to administer by injection didn't work, he was probably going to have to break her jaw to free it. She would be wired shut for six weeks.

This can't be happening, Ellen thought. There was only so much a person could bear. The doctor gave her a shot and left the examining room. She stared at the mint-green walls in a stupor. She imagined him returning with a rubber mallet, the swift blow to her jaw, and the misery of forty-four consecutive days in metal braces. Tears of self-pity splashed down her cheeks into her open mouth. A broken jaw. She would definitely have to leave Eagle Beak to recuperate in New York, abandon her silly organic farm fantasy once and for all.

She felt a slight bit groggy and began to massage her jaw. Beginning at the ridge of her cheekbones, she pressed her thumbs against her teeth, along the underside of the bone that seemed to run from her upper jaw to her lower ear. She had never studied anatomy, nor acupressure, and had no reference points. The jaw bone connected to the . . . what bone? she asked herself, trying to feel the intimate internal arrangement of the cartilage through her skin.

In the midst of her technical self-examination, she felt a little click followed by a noticeable lessening of tension. Tentatively, she attempted to close her mouth, just a fraction. It actually moved. Slowly, Ellen closed her mouth. Her jaw ached, but a wild gleefulness telegraphed itself to every cell in her body. When the doctor stepped back into the room, she ran to him and threw her arms around him as if he were a long lost brother.

"It unhooked!" she exclaimed. "Right in the nick of time, huh?" She could read the relief in his eyes, which made sense. No reputable doctor looked forward to bashing a terrified patient in the face with a hammer. Ellen floated out to the reception area. She felt like Miss America on her triumphant stroll down the runway. She could almost hear Bert Parks crooning in the background. But she didn't dare smile.

"Mrs. Kenny?" the baby-blue nurse called. "Fred told me to tell you he decided to run some errands. He figured you'd be tied up for a while. Said he'd be back by three." Ellen glanced at the clock on the wall. Ten to two. She stepped through the emergency room doors into the sunlight with a glowing sense of well-being. She had an hour to kill. Without a plan, she began to stroll the tree-lined street. Along both sides stood old Victorian houses with rocking chairs on the porches and hanging baskets of flowers. She felt appreciative of the perfection of it all, as if being able to close her mouth had simultaneously permitted her to open her eyes.

On the corner was the town library, a beautiful stone building with multi-paned windows. Magnetized, Ellen ascended the marble steps and opened the stately wooden doors. As a researcher, she spent countless hours in libraries of all descriptions. She loved the wooden drawers of the old card files, the well-stocked magazine racks, and the Dewey decimal system. Even the dust motes thrilled her. On automatic pilot, she moved toward the computer terminals that provided Internet access.

"Peyronie's disease," she typed in.

The computer quickly found a match and Ellen began to speed-read. She felt inhibited by the lack of a notebook, a ballpoint pen, and her glasses. But as she scrolled through the collected wisdom on Peyronie's disease, the twentieth-century scourge that would one day turn Rayfield Geebo's dick into a donut, she felt a surge of personal power. Ellen Kenny was born to research.

Before she left the library to meet Fred for the ride home, she had a firm grip on the fundamentals of Peyronie's disease and was relatively certain that Viola de Beer, despite her shameful reputation, had never been arrested, committed to an insane asylum in the state of New York, nor taken part in any form of political insurrection.

thirteen

L et there be light," Fred Boyea announced dramatically as he flipped the switch in the dining room, and suddenly the ancient fixture above Viola's table came to life. "Let there be water," he continued, moving toward the kitchen sink and turning on the faucet. A spitting sound, a few spasms on the part of the spigot, and a stream of water the color of well-steeped tea issued forth.

"Hurray!" Ellen cheered.

"The water should clear up once you use it for a while. If it don't, I'll have to come up with a mud-sucker."

"A mud-sucker?" Ellen repeated as she paid Fred in cash. He promised to check back two days later. "And thanks for taking me to the hospital," she called as he headed down the steps.

"Gave me an excuse to sit in Huck's bar in the middle of the afternoon. I ain't done that in six months."

Ellen laughed. Life's little pleasures.

Speaking of which, she had light! Water! Phone! Heat! It was as if she'd been in a time warp and had finally found her way to the present. She surveyed her modest empire with a feeling of love. Then she remembered the roof and wrote a quick note to herself to contact her lawyer the first thing in the morning. Rodney de Beer would have to pay for the repairs. Once that was done, she'd be in business.

This called for a celebration. She could dash to the store, but she was somewhat afraid to see Baldy. She wasn't in the mood to be the butt of more bad jokes. Then she remembered a tavern she'd passed on her way to Rayfield Geebo's. Tucked under the tamaracks, it sported a peeling painted sign featuring

Yogi Bear's sidekick. BOO-BOO'S BAR—WE PUT THE BOO BACK IN BOONIES, it read.

A woman alone, a redneck bar in the wilderness: it could be a recipe for disaster. But one of the landmarks of her middle age was her new invisibility. It was a double-edged sword for sure. Secretly, she sometimes missed the hoots and howls of the construction workers and the steaming once-overs from strangers on the street—the very things that had made her go ballistic in her prime. But she was nothing more than a bump on a log now, and the chances of getting into any real trouble were next to nil. She pulled a brush through her hair, tied it up into a sloppy ponytail, and started out in search of a glass of fine wine.

There were two pickup trucks and an old Ford Escort in the parking lot of Boo-Boo's. She put on her bar-entering persona like a coat, and stepped into a small, dim room that had no less than a dozen stuffed deer heads on the walls, not to mention stuffed deer feet, bent at the ankle and pointed upward, which functioned as coat hooks. And behind the bar were two raccoons, a small red fox, and a great horned owl. The sight of all the wildlife demoted to decorative purposes almost caused Ellen to do a U-ey, but at the last second she decided to stay for a drink. Just one.

The bartender, a senior citizen with her hair dyed a flaming red, ambled over. Ellen suspected that wine in Boo-Boo's came in a box with a built-in spigot, so she went for a vodka tonic, which cost her a whopping dollar-ten. But the atmosphere was hardly celebratory. The bartender watched *Wheel of Fortune* on a six-inch TV, and the only other customer in the joint was an overweight man with blond hair and a pink face who seemed to be meditating on the principles of ice cube suspension. After ten minutes of silence, broken only by the guesses of the contestants on the game show, he cleared his throat and said, "Put me on a hamburger, will you, Alice?"

Ellen could just picture him flayed over a huge beef patty as a giant bun was lowered. Only his feet and hands would stick out beyond the lettuce leaves. Alice climbed off her stool and deposited a frozen hamburger into a skillet. She carried it to a stove, which was located behind a partition. Soon the odor of frying meat filled the air. Ellen finished her drink and self-consciously placed a thirty-five-cent tip on the bar. She left. So much for triumphant celebration.

When she pulled to the edge of the gravel parking lot, she made a right toward Porkerville. It wasn't attraction toward Rayfield Geebo that sent her tooling along in his direction. She had rigorously examined herself on that particular score. Attraction implied a desire, admitted or not, for sex. Sex with

Rayfield sent chills down her spine. Everything about him, from his "party 'til you puke" mentality to his cigarette smoking was a complete turnoff. Besides, he couldn't have sex if he (or she) wanted to, so what would be the point of an attraction? It would be sexual suicide.

No, it was not romantic chemistry that drew her to Rayfield. He simply embodied, literally, a compelling project to work on. Perhaps she could help him, and Ellen, who had the heart of a humanitarian, reaped great satisfaction from the performance of good deeds. To fight for the underdog, to participate in the revolution, to refuse to take no for an answer—these were her strengths. And Rayfield Geebo was certainly an underdog. A man unable to face the music with an erect penis was the *capo de tutti capi* of losers. The lowest guy on the totem pole. A societal bottom feeder.

And essentially, Ellen liked Rayfield.

She spotted the orange tires and put on her blinker. Down the driveway she drove, into the heart of the Geebo compound. Mutley, asleep at the bottom of the steps, didn't even wake up until Ellen slammed the car door. Then he raised his head in relative disinterest and just as quickly dropped it back into the dirt.

"Rayfield?" called Ellen. "Are you here?"

She heard a minor commotion in the trailer and then a form appeared in the doorway. Rayfield stepped through, wearing a pair of forest-green sweatpants cut off at mid-knee and nothing else. Ellen was somewhat shocked to see his hairy chest and beer belly, which looked not unlike a very progressed pregnancy. His legs, from the knees down, were as white as a fish's underbelly and totally devoid of muscle definition.

"It's me, Ellen Kenny," she said. "We met a few days ago."

"For chrissake, Ellen, I know who you are," said Rayfield. "I still have a couple of my marbles left."

He came down the wooden stairs, stepping over Mutley with the grace of a ballet dancer.

"Listen, I don't think I told you this, but my job, what I do in New York, is I'm a professional researcher," she said. She seemed to be stuttering. "In fact, it's kind of a passion of mine. And after we talked, I got kind of interested and I went to the library to check out Peyronie's disease."

Rayfield's face was totally deadpan. He said, "Yeah?"

"Just out of curiosity, you know? But I have a few leads and I'd like to help you out if I can. Free of charge."

Rayfield shifted his weight from one foot to the other.

"Maybe there's something that can be done," Ellen added.

"Jeez, Ellen," he said, "it's nice of you and all, but you shouldn't get your hopes up. I mean, even if something worked out, you're not really my type. I'm into fatter women."

At first, Ellen could make no sense of what he said. When it finally registered, a strange mix of outrage and hilarity possessed her. "You think I'd do this to get *laid?*" she blurted out. "By *you?* You must be crazy!"

Rayfield was perplexed. "Why else would you bother?"

"Oh, forget it," Ellen said. "Look, Rayfield, I don't want to get in your pants, okay? Trust me. Do you want my help or not?"

"Sure, if you're giving it away."

"All right," she said, feeling somewhat slighted. What had she expected? That Rayfield would kiss her ass? "I'll be in touch," she said as she climbed back into the car and made a three-point turn in the driveway. She saw Rayfield vanish into his trailer without so much as one backward glance.

The absurdity of the whole exchange hit her about two miles later, and she began to giggle. He likes fatter women, she reminded herself. I don't have a snowball's chance in hell with Rayfield Geebo. Actually, it was a rare experience to be rejected as too boney. It made her feel good that, at least on Rayfield Geebo's planet, she had come up short in the weight department. And her hips measured in at forty inches! Rejection had never felt so wonderful.

Back at home, Ellen indulged in the luxury of electric light and reviewed her eventful day. She had broken ground on her organic garden, turned the earth by hand as the pioneers had done. She'd unhinged her own jaw, achieved electricity, and water, even if it was brown, was coursing through the veins of her house. She'd launched a new medical research project and begun to dig into the past life of Viola de Beer. She'd taken herself out on the town and dropped in on a new friend. And soon, she would climb into her iron bathtub for her first official bath, even if it did resemble sitting in a cup of coffee. It had been a big day.

Of course, it was all relative. A big day in New York might include fifty phone calls, a power lunch, six cab rides, and an evening at an avant-garde interpretation of *Hamlet* in which Hamlet was played by a woman and the famous "To be or not to be" speech had been tossed out. A big day in Mexico had been a new bun in the bakery, a tourist to buy her a beer, and a swim in the moonlight in a tidal pool. In Somerville, it had been a morning joint and a fuck, an afternoon drink and a fuck, and a late set of Miles Davis live at Paul's Mall followed by dinner in Chinatown at three in the morning, preferably with one of the musicians in the band, and a fuck. You simply adjusted the definition of a big day according to what was available and didn't look back. At least, not if you wanted to stay sane.

"But who knows if sanity is really accurate?" she suddenly inquired aloud.

Or how her big day in Eagle Beak ultimately stacked up against any other day. Who was doing the measuring anyway? And what, exactly, was there to measure? Ellen, lost in thought, had begun to examine her hand in the circle of light cast by Viola's brass floor lamp. A few small blisters had appeared on the palm of each hand, the result of her morning's labor. Dirt was packed in under her fingernails, which were ragged already, and her wedding ring seemed like a belt that was cinched too tight around her ring finger. A few brown spots had begun to expand on the back of her hand.

The phone rang, an intrusive echo in the silence. Ellen ran to prevent it from sending out yet another shock wave.

"Hello?"

"Ellen? Bill." Bill Foster was Tommy's colleague in the public defender's office, had been for close to two decades.

"Bill? What a nice surprise!"

"So how are you? What're you doing up there in Hell's Half Acre?"

"Just sitting here watching my skin age," Ellen answered.

"Sounds like a party." Bill laughed.

"Oh, yeah," she replied, wishing she could come up with the witty rejoinder they both expected. "So anyway, to what do I owe the pleasure of this call?"

"I'm gonna be in Lamone tomorrow afternoon," Bill said. "I have to depose a witness, a guy who's incarcerated at Franklin Correctional. I just happened to mention it to Tom, and he told me that Lamone is next door to where you're at. Let's have dinner and get plastered."

"God, it'll be great to see you."

"You want me to bring you anything from New York?"

The only thing that came to mind was cheese-filled tortellinis from the Italian grocery down the block from her apartment on Tenth Street, but she couldn't expect Bill, on such short notice, to invest in a cooler and go to the trouble of filling it with ice to keep the homemade tortellinis in tip-top shape for the three-hundred-fifty-mile drive.

"Not that I can think of."

"Okay, so I'll call you when I know what I'm doing and we'll pick a place. It'll be late afternoon, early evening."

"I'm thrilled."

They hung up. Ellen reviewed the layout of Lamone in her mind. Had she passed any restaurants that weren't greasy spoons? Was there a place with white tablecloths and waiters who could list the specials from memory? She wanted to find a restaurant where they could spend hours without either guilt or self-consciousness about hogging up a table for two during the dinner rush.

She couldn't wait to relate the woes of her first several days in Eagle Beak. Bill Foster, a great listener with a talent for playing the straight man in her impromptu comedy routines, deeply appreciated a good belly laugh. Ellen knew she could frame the Eagle Beak adventure in a way that would put him on the floor.

She and Tommy and Bill and his first wife, a Korean beauty named Soyeon who'd ultimately left him for another woman, had spent at least two weekends a month together for years, forming a foursome that worked in every possible permutation. In fact, they still got together once a year for dinner at Windows on the World in the World Trade Center. Bill's second wife, Marta, a modern dancer, had kept Bill on a much tighter leash, and for the six years of that marriage, their friendship was conducted on a catch-as-catch-can basis. In Bill's last half-decade of bachelorhood, they had fallen into a comfortable, easy-going relationship that felt more like family than friends. His surprise visit was a bonus she had not even thought to hope for. She took her bath and went to sleep happy, full of anticipation of the new day waiting to dawn just beyond the silhouette of Eagle Beak Mountain.

By the middle of the next afternoon, Ellen had doubled the size of her garden and planted half her crops in neat rows. Her tomato plants, each with its own stake and protective wire cage, stood proudly in the sun, and two cucumber mounds rose like miniature Adirondack peaks. Ellen had deposited stones, pushed up by the frost over many years, along the edge of the garden, the beginning of a hand-built wall right out of a Robert Frost poem. With her watering can and her straw hat, she felt like a decal on a country canister.

She placed a call to her real-estate lawyer, whom she'd never met, and informed him of Rodney's failure to disclose the condition of the roof and spoke to the part-time employee at the Chamber of Commerce regarding a decent restaurant. When Bill called at five o'clock, she had a plan prepared and ready. Two hours later, she drove into the parking lot of the Super 8 motel. She wore a linen dress in a fashionable shade called eggplant and sandals that managed to look stylish without sacrificing the Podiatrist's Association seal of approval. Bill answered his door and immediately pulled her into a giant bear hug.

"Here she is," he said, "the queen of the jungle." He released her before she had time to luxuriate in the moment of human contact. "You look tan."

"I do?" Ellen asked. "It must be residue from the water in my well."

"Well, whatever it is, you're looking *fine*. I guess the great outdoors agrees with you. You hungry?"

"I could eat."

"Let's go. You drive." He lifted a light jacket off the back of a chair, unintentionally allowing Ellen a moment to admire what her mother would have called his physique. Bill prided himself in keeping in shape. He worked out twice a week at Gleason's Gym and jogged five miles along the East River every working day. He and Marta had looked like a pair of gods on the beach, while Ellen and Tommy resorted to oversize T-shirts for camouflage. For some reason, that brief memory made her sad, dampened the edges of her mood. Even if Rayfield Geebo thought she was too skinny, one look at Bill Foster reminded her that self-preservation in the forties was hard work, and she had become a fitness lollygagger.

"I haven't seen a black face on the street since Albany," Bill commented as they progressed down Main Street.

"Bet the jail was full of brothers," Ellen said.

"You got that right."

It hadn't occurred to Ellen that the town showed about as much ethnic diversity as a Westchester country club in the 1950s, and she felt a little stab of shame. White guilt. It made her even more cognizant of the surreptitious glances of the other diners in the restaurant, a renovated barn in which wagon wheels and leather horse collars were prominently featured.

"So what do you think of Tommy's trip to Bermuda?" Ellen asked just after their second round of drinks had arrived. She knew she was fishing where fishing was strictly off-limits.

"You should've seen him when he got back to the office on Tuesday. He looked five years younger."

"I think it's important to surrender to your impulses from time to time," Ellen said evenly, even though what she really wanted was to scream, "Does he seem happier without me? Do you think he'll blossom on his own and file for divorce before September?"

"Speaking of impulses, are you glad you bought the Ponderosa? Man, I howled when Tom told us you put it on your credit card."

"I knew you would," Ellen said. A small silence followed. It was, paradoxically, a direct communication, and Bill was great at reading subtext.

"That bad, huh?"

"It's . . . complex," said Ellen.

"What isn't?"

Ellen could see her face reflected in the windowpane. She looked miserable. Bill reached across the table to touch her hand, which was holding on to her vodka martini for dear life. "Are we having a midlife crisis, dear?" he asked in an old lady's voice.

"Do women get them?"

"I'm sure they do." He had removed his hand from hers, and she missed it.

"Is that when the rug gets pulled out from under you and you suddenly find yourself flat on your ass in front of a bunch of stiffs? And all the stiffs are parts of yourself that expected more from you?"

"That's one way to describe it." He was not laughing. The level of seriousness in his brown eyes made her uneasy, and she felt herself switch tracks.

"Hey! Don't let me get maudlin here!" she said. And she launched into an animated rendition of her life in Eagle Beak. She hit all the high points, including her first trip to Rayfield Geebo's pad in Porkerville.

"What size does Tom wear? You oughta buy him the leathers," Bill said. "I think we're about to witness the rise of one of his long-repressed subpersonalities."

Again, Ellen felt the cool fingers of fear press into her neck. All conversational roads led to the same place: Tommy would find himself in greener pastures without her, and she would lose him. And suddenly—afterward she would blame it on the three martinis she'd consumed before she had even ordered her fried mozzarella sticks—she found herself blurting out her (but not Rayfield's) closely guarded secrets.

If there were an organizing theme, it would have been the loss of her younger self—the self whose breasts passed the pencil test, the self that had (and sometimes used) the power to control men, the self that had hitchhiked across the entire country twice with no fear, or went out for a cup of coffee at seven on a Tuesday and didn't get home until Friday. Her young self had flatlined, and she was adrift.

"It's all gone," she lamented through teary eyes. "I spend half my time looking in the mirror, wondering how my head got stuck on my mother's body, and the other half trying to hold my stomach in in public. It's like I fell off a cliff into middle age. I'm just not attractive anymore. And I've lost my charm."

"All that charm? Lost? You don't know what you're talking about, Ellen. You're still a babe. You're just an older babe."

"Don't try to cheer me up," she said. "Let me put it this way: if I put up a bird feeder, I wouldn't get one stinking bird." Even she could see the humor in it, and Bill laughed outright.

"Look Ellen," Bill said, "were we or were we not finalists in the Olympic fuckathon of 1978?"

Ellen looked up, startled. "Yes," she said in a tiny voice.

"Knowing that, would I lie to you?"

She didn't answer.

"Hell no, I wouldn't. And I'm telling you, you still got it. So derail this depression, girl. You're gonna be over the hill soon enough. Don't rush it."

Suddenly, Ellen felt better. She excused herself and went to the ladies' room to freshen up. She cupped her hands under the faucet, filled them with cold water, and splashed it on her face. Her eyes, red and swollen, called out for cool cucumber slices, and her skin looked blotchy under the fluorescent lights. She stared at her reflection in the mirror.

"Pass the baton, Ellen," she said. "Just give it up."

But she didn't want to. She wanted to hold on, or perhaps reverse time and start again, minus the sense of dread that had so often kept her from enjoying every precious moment of her youth. She figured, conservatively speaking, that she had had far less than a quarter of the fun that was available to her in her life. And the sad thing was, according to the reports of her women friends, she had had a lot more than most.

As she patted her face dry with a scratchy paper towel, she allowed herself to remember the day and night she'd spent with Bill Foster seventeen years ago. She had been highly shocked at the dinner table when he'd brought it up. They had not spoken of it, not once, in all the intervening years, and she had all but deleted the file from her mental hard drive.

It was less than a month after she'd run into Tommy on the No. 6 train. They had immediately gone for a drink, laughed off the birthday incident in Truro, and luxuriated in their intense mutual attraction. Tommy, in his dark suit and tie, seemed exotic in his upward mobility, while she supplied the dash of funk. They became inseparable, peeling off each other like Velcro in the mornings and meeting again in the late afternoon, the minute Tommy finished at the courthouse. Ellen would wait in City Hall Park; Tommy would finally arrive. Suddenly, the city would seem thrilling.

On one such day, she met Bill Foster.

Young, gifted, and black, she thought as they all strolled together toward Chinatown for an early dinner. The expression was out-of-date even then but it fit, and Ellen began to mentally sort through her Rolodex for single woman friends who deserved a guy who was sexy, articulate, and gainfully employed. Plus, he had an actual music library, which consisted of the best jazz, rhythm and blues, samba, calypso, and modern classical selections of the past forty years.

Ellen had just scraped together enough money to buy herself a stereo—her first since an unruly boyfriend had hurled her last one off the roof of her house in Somerville in a fit of jealous rage. But just working part time and barely capable of making her rent, she couldn't imagine building a decent record and tape collection. That is, until Bill offered her free access to his records and his state-of-the-art stereo setup. They made arrangements for her to spend her afternoons at his loft under the Manhattan Bridge on the East River in Brooklyn. In three days, she had dubbed forty-three tapes.

On the fourth day, she was so lost in his musical paradise that she failed to clear out before Bill arrived home from work. He strolled in just as the first strains of "Girl from Ipanema" filled every corner of the room. Ellen, stretched out on the couch, watched him samba in from the door, swinging so sweet and swaying so gently that when he passed, she, like the boys on the beach of Ipanema, couldn't help but go, "Aaaahhhh." Bill pulled her from the couch onto the dance floor. With a confident tug on her fingers, he reeled her in, and they ended up cheek-to-cheek. Soon the giggles started. And the record changed, and the first bottle of Bordeaux was opened, and the hip action in the dancing became more and more suggestive.

And then, long after they both wanted to, they kissed.

People use words like *hunger* or *greed* or *lust* to describe sexual appetite, but none of those words described Ellen and Bill. They simply fell into each other's bodies in a feeding frenzy that stood outside all known boundaries and every previous definition.

"I gotta have it," he whispered.

"I know, I know," she said.

They made love on every horizontal surface in his loft and standing up in the kitchen, too. In between, they danced. Bill called for take-out Chinese food and ran to the storefront restaurant ten blocks away to collect it and bring it back home. They fell asleep, raw and glistening with sweat, their hair soaking and muscles aching. And when the alarm went off ninety minutes later, because Ellen was already in love with Tommy and Bill was his closest friend, they promised each other to forget what happened, never to mention it under any circumstances, never to let it happen again, never even to think of it, never.

And they hadn't.

Until tonight.

Now the taboo had been broken, and Ellen's one and only lie (by omission) to Tommy was free-floating in the universe. Would it find its way through the bars on the bedroom window on Tenth Street? Would she find it harder to look Tommy in the eye when she finally saw him on Independence Day?

With a sigh, she returned to the table.

"I was about to call in the SWAT team," Bill said. With a piece of garlic bread, he was wiping up the last of the tomato sauce on his plate.

Ellen smiled. "Just putting myself back together."

When she dropped him off, she asked him point-blank not to tell Tommy that her fantasy life in Eagle Beak was, so far, a bust. Bill agreed. Now they had two secrets. Ellen felt deeply disturbed by this all the way back up the mountain.

fourteen

Ellen woke up with a pounding headache. Too many martinis and too much emotion. She climbed out of bed and carefully groped her way to the bathroom, where she took three aspirins and splashed some cool brown water on her face. She had a strong craving for salt-and-vinegar potato chips.

Quickly, she got dressed, decided to let bygones be bygones, and drove to Baldy's. Useless was sprawled across the door, as always, and Ellen hung on to the jamb to steady herself as she stepped over him. Baldy sat in his easy chair behind the counter. The leg rest was up and a mug of coffee steamed on the arm. There was nobody else in the store.

"Aspirin?" he asked.

"Actually, I'd like some potato chips." She was standing in front of the rack even as she said it.

"It's the salt," Baldy said. "Best thing in the world for a hangover."

"You seem to be an expert," Ellen testily replied.

"I can spot a hangover a mile away," he said. He hadn't even climbed out of his chair to ring up the sale, so she tore open the bag and stuffed several chips in her mouth.

"I just overindulged a little last night," Ellen said defensively.

"None of my business," answered Baldy as he finally shifted his chair forward and got out to make change. Ellen, her jumbo-sized bag of chips under her arm, munched her way to the car. When she pulled into her driveway, she discovered Rodney de Beer in the process of unloading a long wooden ladder from the back of his truck. "Rodney, what're you doing?" Ellen called, clutching her bag of potato chips like a star quarterback with a football.

"I got a call from Ray Dufus. He told me you were filing a complaint against me about the roof. So here I am to fix it."

"*You're* gonna fix it?" Ellen asked. "Isn't that sort of a big job for a"—she was going to say "a man your age" but she didn't want to insult him—"for one guy?" she finished.

"Beats paying somebody else to do it." He wrestled the ladder to its end and balanced it.

"Well, do you know what you're doing?"

"I put the last roof on, didn't I?"

"That would be the one that leaks," she said. "Right?"

"It only leaks when—"

"I know. When the rain's from the northwest."

"Ray just said I had to fix it. He didn't say I couldn't do it myself."

Ellen felt too miserable to argue. It didn't matter anyway. Let Rodney give it a try if he wanted. "Potato chip?" she asked as she passed by him on her way to the door.

"No, thanks. I'm a popcorn man."

Ellen made a pot of coffee as Rodney, wearing overalls over a short-sleeved shirt, carted his rickety ladder to the corner of the house and disappeared. A few minutes later, he was back with buckets of black tar and a tool belt the likes of which she'd only previously seen on the Village People. He seemed too old and frail to support it, but he attached it to multicolored suspenders, buckled it around his hips, and leaned into the truck cab for a baseball hat that had "I Drink Milk" written across the front in cursive.

Within minutes, he began a persistent hammering on the roof. With her hangover, it was worse than Chinese water torture. *Blam! Blam! Blam!* Plus, the awful stench of tar soon filled the air. Before she even finished her first cup of coffee, Ellen knew she couldn't take it, so she freshened up and collected her car keys, planning to spend the morning in the library researching Peyronie's disease. Then, once the sun relented a bit, she'd put in the last of her garden seeds.

As she walked up the driveway, she turned to inspect the situation on the roof. Her heart sank when she saw Rodney balancing himself on the steep pitch with nothing more to hold him than a two-by-four he'd nailed down.

"How you doing up there?" she called, suddenly sorry that she had made such a fuss about the roof.

" 'Bout as good as can be expected," he called back. "Where you off to? You gonna go meet that colored fella again?"

Ellen was speechless. "We use the term African-American now, Rodney," she finally said. "What do you people do up here? Send gossip out in Morse code to each other?" She was actually yelling. "And furthermore, I don't appreciate your shooting your mouth off to Baldy about the rain barrel episode!" She wanted to stop to compose herself, but she simply couldn't. "Why'd you do that, Rodney? For what?"

"Well, gee, Ellen," he called, "it was funny." He had turned to sit on the peak of the roof. "It made a good story. Didn't you tell it to anybody? Your husband, or that colored fella? Or is that your husband?"

He was right, of course. It was a funny story and she had already told it twice herself. Plus, she knew that Tommy would call upon her in the future to repeat it—at dinner and cocktail parties when the subject of country houses came up, and she would glory in it. And as for Rodney's use of the word *colored*, well, nothing else had changed in Eagle Beak in fifty years. Why should she expect the vocabulary of Rodney de Beer to be politically correct? Why get mad at a skunk for stinking?

"The African-American man I had dinner with last night is a close family friend from the city, up here on business," she said haughtily.

"Didn't look like much business got done after the martinis started up."

"How do you know this?" she demanded.

"I was sitting right there in the bar. I waved to you, but you sailed right on past me."

"I didn't see you," Ellen said.

"Well, I saw you."

He spread gooey tar on a shingle and nailed it down. It looked like hard labor. And the sun was already blistering. Ellen turned to leave. "The house is open if you want to take a break," she called.

"Thank you."

The cool, quiet air inside the library was like salve on a bad rash. Calmly, she sat down at the computer terminal and initiated a search on Peyronie's. Her fingers flew over the keyboard and photos and technical illustrations of penises, which did have a certain visual affinity to donuts depending on the degree of circularity, appeared on the screen. Ellen read the captions beneath each one, taking care to position herself in the stony-faced librarian's line of sight. She didn't want to be booted out of the library on a morals charge.

Like many diseases, Peyronie's was a mystery. And while certain urologists were trying to solve it, progress was minimal. Some correlated it with high levels of stress. Ellen couldn't imagine Rayfield as stressed-out, but who knew? He had mentioned that his wife had left him, and he didn't appear to have a job. Maybe his life was in shambles.

Acupuncture would probably help, Ellen suddenly thought. She drove the computer like an Italian sports car, hitting PRINT again and again, even at fifteen cents a page. The nearest alternative medical practitioners were across the border in Canada, in a town named Cornwall, which didn't appear to be so very far from Lamone. An exploratory expedition was in order. She clicked into exchange rates for foreign currency and was gratified to learn that the American dollar spread 32 percent farther just a few miles away. She would make an appointment for herself as well as Rayfield. Ellen appreciated a good acupuncture tune-up, and she made it a point to get her body overhauled in such a way at least twice a year.

She glanced at the big clock in the reading room, wondering if, perhaps, they could get an appointment today. It was just after eleven. There was no phone in the library, so Ellen stepped out into the muggy heat and started down Main Street. This was the second time she'd strolled this way, and she already found comfort in the familiarity.

Rayfield answered on the second ring. He agreed to a trip to Cornwall, provided the treatment didn't exceed twenty-five dollars, and she promised to check it out and let him know within a few minutes. A quick credit card call to Cornwall confirmed that Dr. Yi, who was Korean and spoke very little English, had time to see two new patients at two thirty. The cost, which amazed Ellen, who was used to New York City where charges for alternative medicine rivaled those of board-certified brain surgeons, was within Rayfield's budget. She quickly redialed and asked him to meet her in front of the library in a half hour.

"Where's it at?" he asked.

"You don't know where the *library* is?"

"Nope."

"Jesus H. Christ, Rayfield," she cried, "it's a big stone building on Elm, right off Main Street. You can't miss it. Come in and I'll show you some stuff about Peyronie's you should know."

"Nah. I'll wait for you out front."

They hung up. She wondered if he would show up in his "Party 'til You Puke" T-shirt and his green sweatpants cut off to homeboy length. Maybe he'd come in his biker outfit, she thought with a giggle, one last hurrah before the right buyer came along. However he looked, whatever he wore, it had nothing to do with her, she reminded herself. The last thing she needed was to get personally invested in Rayfield Geebo's appearance. Besides, she wasn't going to win any fashion awards herself. She sported a pair of turquoise canvas deck shoes with red-and-white-striped trim, black pedal pushers with obvious grass stains on the knees, and a T-shirt of Tommy's that had a map of Italy, "The Land of Pizza," on the front. Little pizzas marked the various cities: a thick-crusted slice for Sicily, a calzone for Florence, and so on. She considered running home to change, but when she looked around she realized she didn't look any worse than any other middle-aged woman on Main Street. What good was being in Rome, after all, if you couldn't let yourself do as the Romans do?

She sat down on an ornate iron bench under an elm in front of the library to wait for Rayfield. With her eyes closed, she counted back through the days since she left New York. It would only be a week tomorrow, and yet she felt as if her cells no longer held the memories that could connect her to her former self. Time, she mused: maybe it wasn't really accurate after all. Rayfield soon showed up in a noisy pickup truck. He parked in the shade and sauntered toward Ellen looking very dapper in a clean white T-shirt, his fake blue jeans, and flip-flops.

"Let's take your car. My muffler's got a hole in it."

"So I heard. Sure. You know the way to Cornwall?"

"I can get us there."

They walked to the Honda and Rayfield crammed himself in, like a clown in a miniature circus car. His knees were up under his chin, and his head almost touched the roof. He quickly lowered the window and let his meaty arm rest there. He directed her out to Route 37, and soon they were speeding through the countryside. Lush green fields lined both sides of the road.

"They don't really know what causes Peyronie's disease," Ellen said, by way of opening the conversation, "but it could be related to stress." She left a pregnant pause that Rayfield didn't fill. "Have you been under a lot of stress lately?" she persisted.

"If I had any less stress, I'd be asleep," he answered and Ellen chuckled. Stress was the occupational hazard of living in New York City, and she couldn't imagine a single person who felt free of it.

"But didn't your marriage just break up? That's got to be stressful."

"It don't feel stressful."

"Really? I'd fall apart if my marriage cracked up."

"If you're so worried about it, why'd you leave your husband and come up here all by yourself?" He was holding a cigarette in his hand, but had made no move to light it, which Ellen appreciated. She hoped she wouldn't have to tell Rayfield Geebo that she didn't allow smoking in the Honda.

"I don't have any idea," Ellen answered and she meant it.

"Most likely you won't know what you're doing here 'til you leave. Then you'll see it in the rearview mirror."

"Exactly!" Ellen said.

They drove for many miles in silence. "I'd like to stop for smokes on the rez if you don't mind," Rayfield finally said.

"The rez?"

"The Indian rez."

Ellen hadn't known they would pass through one. She perked up, always a sucker for a cross-cultural experience. But when they arrived, it looked just the same as the rest of the North Country, except for the high-stakes bingo games and the cheap gas. Ellen filled the Honda while Rayfield went inside and returned with three cartons of cigarettes. They climbed back in the car and took off.

"It's not like I don't miss her," Rayfield suddenly announced. "Old Double-Wide and me had our share of good times."

"Double-Wide?" She knew a double-wide was a type of trailer popular in the area.

"That's what I called her."

"She must've loved that."

"Usually I'd call her Wide Load," he added in a nostalgic tone. "I didn't mean nothing bad by it. She was a big girl, but I liked her size. She knew it, too."

"How big was she?"

"I guess she ran about two fifty, two seventy-five."

"Jeez," said Ellen. "That is big."

"I felt like a little pat of butter on a big hot biscuit." His tone was even more wistful and for a second Ellen wondered if Rayfield was going to cry. "Anyway, we were on the rocks for a long time before she left. Guess I got used to it." He gestured to the bridge across the St. Lawrence. "Cost you two bucks to get into Canada."

Ellen dug in her purse as she steered onto the bridge. Stopping at a rather grand tollbooth, she thrust her two crumpled dollars at the uniformed attendant.

"What's this?" he demanded.

"It's two bucks."

"Madame, this is the Canadian customs office."

Ellen shot a dagger look at Rayfield, who had a big, stupid grin on his face. "I'm sorry, Officer," she said, at once removing her sunglasses. "I thought it was the tollbooth."

"Can you step out of the car, please?"

Ellen undid her seat belt, envisioning herself bent over the hood, spread-eagled, like on the TV cop shows.

"What about *him*," she said, pointing at Rayfield through the open window. If she was going down, she was bringing Rayfield with her. "Look, Officer, this is my first time over the bridge. I thought this was the tollbooth. I didn't mean any disrespect." She looked contritely down at the pavement.

"Do you have anything to declare?"

"No, nothing."

He bent down to stare in the car window. "I see you have some cigarettes."

"Those aren't mine. They're *his!* I don't even smoke. I don't even like people who smoke." Ellen felt a red rage building against Rayfield Geebo, who sat wedged into the front seat with an innocent look on his face.

"Are these your cigarettes, sir?" asked the customs agent.

"Nope," Rayfield said without looking at Ellen.

"Rayfield! You liar!" Ellen screamed. She all but threw herself into the car window and grabbed the cartons of cigarettes. "Here!" she said, shoving them into the agent's hands. "Take them."

The agent studied her. "Madame, I'd like you to step inside for a Breathalyzer test."

The four martinis she'd consumed the previous night flashed into her mind like a psychedelic slide show from the sixties. Was there enough residue to skew a Breathalyzer test? She knew that even the poppy seeds on a bagel could cause a positive on a urine test for drugs. Nervously, she followed the agent inside, while Rayfield, who had climbed from the car with a merry look on his face, leaned against the hood and lit a cigarette.

"Officer," she said politely, "this is all a misunderstanding. I'm not drunk. My passenger told me there was a two-dollar toll, and I just made a wrong assumption. We were just going to Cornwall to see a doctor, and he bought the cigarettes on the Indian reservation. He intended to take them home to Porkerville, not sell them in Canada."

The young agent remained tight-lipped as if he resented the very sound of her voice. Meekly, she submitted to the Breathalyzer test and passed with flying colors. The agent escorted her back to the Honda and even returned the cigarettes. "Next time get your cigarettes on the way back home," he said.

"Oh, yes, Officer," Ellen said as she started the car and pulled away. She wanted to throw Rayfield out of the car, but she dared not create any disturbance on the bridge. The tollbooth suddenly appeared one hundred feet beyond the customs house. How could she have missed it? She paid the two dollars and continued on. The air stunk, as if factory waste was pouring into it from a million chimneys.

"Remind me never to do any crimes with you," Rayfield commented. "Some partner you'd make." Ellen turned toward him, her jaw hanging loose in shock. "They're *his* cigarettes!" Rayfield mimicked in an exaggerated tone. "Officer, they're *his* cigarettes!"

"Yeah, well you didn't tell the truth," she sputtered.

"I had to teach you a lesson," Rayfield said, "about being a partner."

She slowed down so she could momentarily take her eyes off the bridge. She didn't want to drive into the river. "I am not your goddamn partner, you nitwit," she said, and then she saw him crack into a big smile and before she knew what was happening, she was howling with laughter and so was Rayfield.

"I thought I was gonna get strip-searched," she said through her convulsions.

"Spread 'em, lady," hollered Rayfield, and they roared even louder.

"Shit, I didn't mean for you to give the two bucks to the customs guy, but, shit, it was so funny. Did you see his face?"

"Did you see mine?" They howled on until the fit passed.

"Shit," Rayfield said. And it crossed Ellen's mind that Rodney de Beer would probably enjoy this story. She would tell him when she got home, by way of making up.

According to the digital clock on the dashboard, they were almost an hour early for their appointment. For reasons unknown to her, she felt responsible for the day's entertainment, as if, by the sheer fact of her gender, she was an automatic, lifetime member of the Gracious Hostess Club.

"Want to stop for a cup of coffee?" she asked.

"Sure. We got time to kill."

It was a phrase Ellen hated, but she let it go and pulled to the curb in front of the Canadian equivalent of a Greek diner in New York. Without consulting Rayfield, she asked for the No Smoking section only to discover they didn't have one.

"You lose," said Rayfield as they settled into a booth and ordered two cups of coffee. Rayfield smugly lit up, but she noticed that he pulled the ashtray to his edge of the table and exhaled the smoke out of the corner of his mouth. The crazy laughter they had shared in the car had surprised them both and moved their budding friendship forward several paces.

"Rayfield," she asked impulsively, "what do you think of me?"

"I don't think about you. No offense."

"I just wondered," she said, embarrassed.

After a brief pause, he said, "I guess you seem lonely and desperate." The words stung, but she'd asked for it. Across the table, Rayfield straightened up from his usual slouch. He looked to Ellen like the most sincere pumpkin in the pumpkin patch, and it touched her.

"What do you think of me?" he asked.

Ellen reminded herself to be careful. "You seem like a character in a movie." She would never tell him it was *Deliverance*. But she could see that wasn't enough of an answer. "You have a very good sense of humor, but you seem like somebody who might give up too easy. That's just an impression. I like you, Rayfield." She quickly added, "In a friendly way, I mean."

He considered this as he patted up a coffee ring with his paper napkin. "Are you one of them women who likes to take in stray dogs?" he asked.

She was confused. "Are you talking about real dogs?" she asked. "Because I've never had a dog."

"I'm just telling you in a nice way that I ain't a stray dog. No matter what you think. No offense."

Should she be offended? It seemed to Ellen that he, if anybody, should be offended. It was becoming very convoluted.

"Lonely and desperate, huh?" she joked. "I ought to put that on my grave-stone, just under 'Astrological sign: Leo.'"

"You a Leo?" he said, raising his eyebrows.

"Yeah. How about you?"

"Scorpio."

"Fire and water," Ellen commented. "A steam bath." Rayfield nodded as if he understood exactly what she meant.

"By the way," she said, abruptly changing the subject, "did you see a specialist about your problem? A urologist?"

"Sure I did. That's how I know what I got."

"How many times have you been back to see him?"

"I only went the one time."

"Rayfield, why didn't you go back? You should establish a relationship with your health-care practitioner," she lectured.

"Look, I ain't gonna have no relationship with a doctor whose first name is Bippin. I mean, I ain't prejudiced or nothing, but come on. I couldn't understand a word he said. For the first fifteen minutes he was talking to me, I thought he was saying 'peanuts' instead of penis. I couldn't figure out for the life of me what kind of problem I could be having with peanuts. Hell, I never eat peanuts."

Ellen laughed. Wait 'til he gets a load of Dr. Jin Gyoo Yi. "The guy you're gonna see today is from Korea, by the way," she said.

Rayfield threw his eyes to the ceiling and shook his head.

"Hey, they've got a five-thousand-year head start in medicine. Let's go." She drained the last of her coffee. They paid at the front register, and a few minutes later, they parked at a meter down the block from Dr. Yi's storefront office.

"Bombs away," said Rayfield as he struggled out of the car.

The reception room of Dr. Yi's office was sparkling clean and furnished in the minimalist style. Full-color charts of the human body with all three hundred and sixty-four acupressure points labeled hung on the wall, and a large cabinet with a glass front contained plastic bags of twigs, roots, and berries. A middle-aged Asian woman, presumably Mrs. Yi, greeted them in broken English and handed Rayfield a clipboard and a pen. On it was a miniature version of the charts on the wall—a front and back view of a human body, male, with the energy meridians indicated in blue and red.

"Make mark where is problem," said Mrs. Yi, and both Ellen and Rayfield giggled as he made a bold circle around the hanging phallus. He handed the clipboard back to Mrs. Yi, who did not react. She led Rayfield into a small examining room and closed the door. Ellen felt she should go in too, as interpreter, but she hadn't been invited. A few minutes passed and Mrs. Yi emerged from the room. Through the crack, Ellen could see Rayfield seated on an examining table with a metal rod, attached by wire to a machine that looked like a Geiger counter, in each hand. Dr. Yi watched the dials and listened to the beeps as he moved yet another rod into different positions in Rayfield Geebo's left ear.

"Your husband?" Mrs. Yi asked as she closed the door.

"No," Ellen said quickly. "Just a neighbor." She hadn't even used the word *friend*.

"Very fat. Not good." Mrs. Yi was pointing to her own stomach.

"Oh, yes. Well, it's called a beer belly."

Mrs. Yi nodded, handing Ellen a clipboard with the female figure on it. Ellen accepted it before she realized she didn't have any specific aches and pains. "Do you know the word *depressed?*" she whispered.

Mrs. Yi nodded, her lips pursed.

"I'm depressed," Ellen said. "What should I circle for that?" The head? The heart? Was there an equivalent of the human spirit on the acupuncture chart for women? Mrs. Yi escorted Ellen into the room adjoining Rayfield's. She could smell moxa burning from next door. A little burst of hope lit up Ellen's psyche. Maybe Dr. Yi could help Rayfield. Maybe Rayfield's penis would slowly unwind and he could get back together with Wide Load and live happily ever after. She smiled to herself at the thought as she lay down on the table and closed her eyes. Mrs. Yi was already inserting thin needles into her forehead, hands, and feet.

She had told Mrs. Yi that she was depressed. This was a word Ellen had never before used to describe herself, at least not out loud

Rayfield and Dr. Yi seemed to be in a prolonged conversation on the other side of the wall. She couldn't hear their words, though she tried. Finally, she let herself relax, imagining the chi arriving like the cavalry at every cellular outpost in her body. When Dr. Yi entered the room, she was in a near-dream state. He spent several minutes checking her five pulses and then stared at her tongue as if he'd entered a trance.

"Your husband . . . very powerful," said Dr. Yi.

"He's not my husband," Ellen said emphatically. "My husband is a lawyer in New York City." She wanted to nip any identification between her and Ray-field in the bud. Yet Dr. Yi, an expert, had called him powerful. Was she miss-ing something? And what about *me*, she wanted to scream. I'm right here! I just announced I was depressed! Fuck Rayfield Geebo! Dr. Yi removed the nee-dles from her body and motioned her to turn over onto her stomach. Lifting her T-shirt, he began to press in along her spine. "Your heart afraid," he said as he worked. "You need open your heart."

For once, Ellen had nothing to say. But suddenly tears began to pour out of her eyes, as if his words had unlocked her private floodgates. She felt raw, vul-nerable, and ill-equipped for whatever was in store for her, bad or good.

"I make special tea for you," Dr. Yi said, ignoring the puddle of tears that was spreading across his examining table. "You need be strong to open heart."

Ellen's throat cramped shut. And still Dr. Yi's thumbs, or perhaps knuckles, drilled into her and the tears fell unabated.

By the time she crawled off the table, she felt like a war veteran: drained, weak, and beaten in spirit. She felt pale and shaky as she took her first step to-ward the waiting room, where Rayfield sat in a straight-backed chair. Dr. Yi stood in front of his glass cabinet, placing twigs, berries, and roots into Ziploc freezer bags. He had four bags full before he stopped, and they were all for Ellen. Guess it takes a lot more medicine to open a heart, she thought with re-sentment, than it does to untangle a donut dick.

In the car on the way back, Ellen was subdued while Rayfield was ani-mated. "I felt like a goddamn human pincushion!" he ranted. "First he stuck me with needles and then he burned some kind of powder on them and I had to say 'Hot' when it got too much. I never heard of this stuff." He kept right on babbling while Ellen placed her thoughts elsewhere. She wondered why and when she had closed her heart. Could she have been born that way? A side ef-fect of spending her critical bonding period in an incubator? Or had it just thickened over time, like a callus that grew tougher with each little disap-pointment? Was it even true at all? Who was Dr. Yi to tell her her heart was not open? She had been married for seventeen years, after all. You didn't do *that* with a dysfunctional heart.

But that, of course, was simply not true. Ellen suspected that at least half, if not more, of the long-married couples had shut down and gone out of the love business. For the last five years, in her weaker moments, she agonized that she and Tommy were nothing more than a comfortable habit with each other.

"Do you have to go back?" Rayfield asked.

"Huh?"

"Did he tell you to come back?"

"Yeah, in two weeks."

"He wants me to come back every other day for five times."

"You gonna do it?"

"I don't know." Rayfield hesitated for a few seconds. "He told me no alcohol or coffee or smokes for the next ten days."

"You think you can manage that?" Ellen asked, her voice heavy with doubt.

"If I wanted to, I guess."

"Dr. Yi said you were very powerful," she said.

"He did? What'd he mean? Strong?"

"I really don't know," she said. "Had he ever heard of Peyronie's disease before?"

"Hard to tell. His English ain't that good, y'know. I had to use hand signals." Rayfield pointed at his crotch and then used his fingers to pantomime a penis in its transformation from flaccid to erect. Then he turned his hand over and proceeded to roll it up.

"He got the picture?"

"I guess so. I don't know, though. A hundred twenty-five bucks." He shook his head.

"That's not much money," she said. Even as the words left her lips, she felt the deep shame of the privileged class. Worse, she was tempted to push on, deliver a lecture about self-destructiveness, but at the last moment, she skipped it. They were already crossing the bridge back into the States. Ellen averted her face as they sped past Canadian customs, determined not to catch the eye of the agent who'd mistaken her for a drunken smuggler. On the U.S. side, they were just waved through.

"What're all those sticks he gave you for?" asked Rayfield.

"To make a tea."

"What kind of tea?"

How should she answer? "A tea to make me stronger," she finally said. Rayfield did not press for details, and Ellen didn't supply any. When they arrived in Lamone, she dropped him off at his truck, said a cursory goodbye, and continued on up the mountain to Eagle Beak.

When she pulled into her driveway at five, Rodney's truck was gone, though his ladder still rested against the side of the house and his roofing paraphernalia was scattered across the yard. She filled her watering cans at the outside spigot and lugged them to her garden. The tomato plants were already drooping, and the turned earth looked parched. It took six trips and more than an hour before Ellen felt her arugula and cucumber seeds had had a sufficient drink on a hot day. Then she went inside to make her tea.

She stood at the stove, absentmindedly observing the water bubble up between the sticks and twigs. Unidentifiable berries, indigo in color, danced on the top, occasionally diving or getting sucked under. An unfamiliar smell rose up. It brought with it images of deep forest and damp moss.

Dr. Yi had said her heart was closed.

Was this tea the key that would unlock it? Should it be unlocked?

Carefully, she poured the liquid through Viola's tea strainer. Then she sat on the front porch swing, sipping her cure, which tasted like dirty lake water, and watching the shadows grow and the light change, and she went to bed early and dreamed that she had tossed her wedding ring into a stylish European briefcase that was resting open on the kitchen table on Tenth Street. When she went to retrieve it, for Ellen had in real life never even removed her wedding ring from her finger, it suddenly changed into her high school graduation ring, which she'd worn for three months before she lost it while skinny-dipping with three football players. The dream was mildly disturbing. She woke up wondering if a seventeen-year marriage, even if it ended that very day, could be called a "brief case" by anyone at all in the modern Western world.

fifteen

Rodney arrived at eight the next morning, ready for another day on the roof. He brought with him a box of chocolate-covered donuts, which he arranged in a pyramid on one of his mother's flowered plates from the pantry. Ellen made coffee as Rodney set two places in the dining room and spread a copy of the new *Free Trader* at each one. She was secretly amused. She had played this scene with Tommy a million times, except they read *The New York Times*, and she made comments about culture, politics, and trends, not church socials, garage sales, and plans for the Firemen's Field Day.

Rodney was a fastidious eater. He used a fork to break apart his donut and patted his lips with the edge of his paper towel after every fourth bite. He wore reading glasses obviously purchased off a drugstore rack. Occasionally he'd "hmmph" about something, but he, like Tommy, never read anything out loud.

"Rodney, I hear you're a sculptor," Ellen butted in.

Rodney raised his eyes to peer over the top of his glasses. "That's right."

"How long have you been at it?"

"Oh, about thirty years, I'd say."

He didn't seem prone to chat, but Ellen persisted. "How'd you get started?"

Rodney put down his paper and removed his glasses. "It was building up in me for a long time," he began, and for a brief second, Ellen imagined the artistic impulse burgeoning in Rodney de Beer, gathering fire until it burst forth in a blaze of creative glory. "But one day I thought I was really gonna do it. Take a chain saw to my own mother. I ran out into the woods where an old tree was—it was struck by lightning a long time before that—and I just started to hack away at it. I didn't even know what I was doing, but when I was done, I had one of them gargoyles, like they have over there in Paris, staring me right in the face."

Ellen, spellbound, forgot all about her chocolate donut. Her mind raced in two directions at once: first, she had always felt that the absence of gargoyles was the single greatest loss of modern architecture. And here, right in the middle of nowhere, Rodney de Beer, a simple country boy, was attempting to reinstate them on the back forty. Second, of course, was the idea that this same Rodney, this mild-mannered, fussy donut eater, had come close to carving his own mother into slices of bologna with a chain saw.

"Jeez, Rodney," Ellen said, "remind me to stay on your good side."

"Anyway, I just couldn't stop. Every day I was at it out in the woods. It got a lot easier when I bought myself a saw with a fourteen-inch blade. Jeezum! I started out with the thirty-incher. That was heavy."

"Are they still out there? The statues?" Ellen asked, staring out through the window. She was imagining taking a stroll through her very own woods, a monument to Rodney's personal demons.

"A couple are. But the ones I got serious about, I cut down and took over to my place to work on."

"Have you ever sold any?"

"Why, yes. That's how I make my living."

"Really!" Ellen was impressed. How many artists could live off their work in the nineties? And Roger LaFleur had said Rodney had never worked a day in his life. "I'd like to see them sometime."

"Sure."

"Where do you live, anyway?"

"'Bout four miles from here. Still in Eagle Beak."

She wanted to ask him about Viola. What could drive a man to want to take a chain saw to his mother? But, unlike her usual self, she hesitated to barge in. Maybe she should handle the volatile Rodney de Beer with kid gloves. Anyway, he was already back into the *Free Trader,* and Ellen followed suit. She read for a few moments. "Listen to this!" she said. "Giveaway: German shepherd dog. Can catch Frisbee." She whooped with laughter until she read the next few words: "Call Rayfield" and a phone number.

Rayfield Geebo was trying to get rid of Mutley, the narcoleptic canine!

"Do you know Rayfield Geebo?" she asked Rodney.

"Everybody knows Rayfield."

"Why would he suddenly decide to give his dog away?"

Rodney looked pensive. "Maybe he's losing his mind," he said.

"Maybe he's losing his *mind?*" Ellen repeated. "This is the first explanation that pops into your head?" She took a bite out of her donut. "Why? Has he lost his mind before?"

"Not that I know of." Rodney returned to the paper. He was only on page three. At this rate, Ellen thought, he'd never make it out of her dining room and onto the roof. And since further conversation about the state of Rayfield's sanity was obviously not forthcoming, Ellen decided to set a good example of the work ethic. "Guess I'll go out and do some watering and weeding," she said as she sprayed bug repellent on her sombrero. Rodney didn't even look up. She purposely slammed the screen door behind her, hoping it would break Rodney's train of thought and motivate him to get a move on.

"I can't believe Rayfield would just dump Mutley," she muttered to herself as she lugged her watering can back and forth to the pea patch. What makes a man turn his affection on and off like a kitchen faucet? What happened to commitment, the famous bond between himself and his supposed best friend?

To be fair, she reminded herself that she had never even reached square one when it came to pets. She hadn't had one since her black and white cat, Lulu, was run over by a UPS truck when Ellen was in the seventh grade. Ellen had been devastated. The prettiest girl in the class, Antoinette, had patted her on the back and said she knew just how Ellen felt, which had set off yet another round of uncontrollable weeping. She had felt an ache so painful in her chest that she sat all through prayers, religion, and history classes with her hand placed over her heart, as if she were pledging allegiance to the flag. Every few minutes, she checked it to see if it was bloody.

Was that the moment her heart closed? Was it all because of Lulu? Suddenly, Ellen felt tears in her eyes. Lulu, mother of six kittens, champion cat-napper, beloved lap-sitter. Lulu had never asked for anything and gave all. Ellen would never forget opening the back door of her house to go to school and seeing little Lulu flattened on the pavement, like a miniature bear rug. Her mother, in a supreme display of courage, had peeled Lulu off the street and laid her to rest under the apple tree in the front yard. Ellen had missed a half day of school and had to take a note from her mother to Sister Alphonsus. She had never had another pet, never wanted one. Down came the tears, onto the green beans and the pepper plants. Why would Rayfield turn his back on Mutley? She didn't know who to feel sorrier for—Rayfield or his dog.

Five minutes after she finished watering and weeding, she was in her car, speeding toward Porkerville. Experiencing compassion and cold-blooded rage in equal proportions, she felt like a strange combination of a social worker and a hired hitman, a role for an actor of the caliber of Robert De Niro. And she felt like Bruce Willis.

Rayfield was sitting out in front on the second bucket seat from the end. Ellen noticed that he had neither a beer nor a cup of coffee in his hand. She stepped from the car to confront him.

"Rayfield, why are you giving Mutley away?" she demanded.

"I'm sick of him," he answered. "Good morning, Ellen. Nice to see you, too."

"What do you mean you're sick of him?" She was towering above him now, arms akimbo.

"I mean sick of him. There's something wrong with that friggin' dog."

"Well, there's something wrong with you too, Mister. Do you think Mutley would give *you* away?"

"I don't know and I don't give a shit. What's it to you, anyway?"

Ellen abruptly chose a different tack because, obviously, the direct approach did not work with Rayfield Geebo. Her college preparation in social work would come in handy here. She dropped into the next bucket seat. "Why don't you tell me why you feel this way about Mutley?" she cooed.

"Oh, for chrissake, Ellen, don't give me any of that share shit." His voice was mild, but she could tell he meant it. "What's with you anyway? You get outa the car and I get nuked. The next minute, you're sitting next to me playing nurse. Some nurse you are. Florence the Ripper."

Ellen snorted. "That's good, Rayfield. Florence the Ripper." But then, in spite of herself, she realized it *was* good. "That's good," she said again, but this time she added an appreciative laugh. Florence the Ripper indeed.

"Shit, Rayfield, here I am again," she said.

"So I see."

"Why are you giving Mutley away?" For the first time, she actually wanted to know.

Rayfield hesitated. "He's Wide Load's dog. It makes me feel bad looking at him."

Ellen considered this. "Well, what if nobody wants him?"

"I'll take him down to the pound. They don't kill 'em there, y'know. They keep 'em."

"Look, Rayfield, maybe you're just in a phase. I mean, won't you miss the company?"

"What company? He's always asleep. He bugs me."

"What the hell, I'll take him," she said impulsively. "Not permanently," she quickly added. "Just for a couple weeks, until you decide if it's really what you want to do. Maybe you could call Wide Load and work something out with her. Where is she anyway? What's her name, anyway?"

"Debbie," he said in a wistful tone. "She's living over in Skerrie."

Ellen could easily imagine how the name Debbie had affectionately mutated into Double-Wide and then continued on in its evolution to Wide Load. She herself had called Tommy every variation of his name from Tomko to Thomassio, from Tomelog to Tombosis. But she vowed to refer to Rayfield's ex as Debbie in the future. No woman should be called Wide Load by a total stranger.

Meanwhile, Rayfield had gone off around the edge of the trailer in search of Mutley. Soon they returned. Mutley's hair had progressed from a buzz to a short crew cut.

"Rub him down with Skin-So-Soft to keep the skeeters off him. I'll give you some," said Rayfield. He cared! She could just picture Rayfield lovingly slathering Mutley with Skin-So-Soft as they launched each new day together.

"Come on, Mutley," said Ellen. "You're gonna stay with me for a little while. Just *two weeks*," she said, loud and clear with a pointed glance at Rayfield. She opened the car door for Mutley to climb in, but instead the dog slumped into the dirt next to the car and closed his eyes.

"Aw, come on, Mutley, be a sport," Rayfield chided. Finally, he stooped down, gathered the sleeping dog in his arms, and tossed him into the backseat of the Honda.

"How much does he weigh?" asked Ellen.

"Better'n a hundred."

Ellen was astonished. She doubted she could heft Mutley around like Rayfield did. Rayfield went inside to get Mutley's dishes, food, and insect repellent. He also collected a grimy sleeping bag from under the front steps and, holding it by the corner, carried it to the car. "That does it," he said. "Be sure to keep him on a low-fat diet."

"You're kidding, right?"

"Oh, what the hell. Give him what you want." Rayfield slammed the door in the dog's face. "Good luck, Mutley." There was nothing for Ellen to do but get in the car and turn the key.

"Remember, Rayfield, two weeks. Just a cooling-off period," she called out the window.

"Okay." He stood, fat and unshaven, wearing his homeboy cutoffs and a T-shirt that read, "Join the ARMY! Travel the World! See Exotic Places! Meet New People . . . and Kill Them." But his right hand had clasped onto his left wrist. Ellen remembered seeing a documentary on John Wayne in which he had said that, to him, that was the position that telegraphed the essence of male vulnerability. The Duke had used it for the last scene of *The Searchers*. Suddenly, Rayfield looked like a little boy, lonely and afraid in the big, bad world. A little boy watching his best friend move out of the neighborhood.

"Don't feel bad, Rayfield!" she yelled out the window. "I'll take good care of Mutley!"

She passed the LEAVING PORKERVILLE sign and continued on to Eagle Beak. Somehow, she had acquired a hundred-pound dog with a crew cut. She vaguely remembered reading, perhaps on the page-a-day dog calendar in Reginald Eu-banks's office, that shaved dogs were prone to suffer sunburn. Perhaps she should get some sunscreen for him.

She pulled up in front of the store. Useless, the canine welcome mat, raised his head and looked in Ellen's direction as she ascended the steps. She bent down to scratch his ears, something she had never done before.

"Hey, Baldy," she said. Baldy was stacking Ritz crackers on the shelves in the rear of the store.

"Hey, Ellen. How goes it?"

"Okay, I guess. I seem to have gotten myself a dog."

"Shit, if I'd've known you wanted a dog, I would've gave you Useless."

What was this? Was every dog owner in Eagle Beak willing to turn Fido over to the first stranger that came down the pike? "How long've you had him?"

"Eight years."

"And you'd really give him away?"

Baldy stopped stacking. "Yeah, but only to a good home."

Ellen leaned back against the counter. "I don't get it, Baldy. How could you give your own dog away after all that time?"

"Shit, I don't know. Maybe 'cause it'd be less pressure."

Ellen glanced at Useless, listening to their conversation with sad eyes. How much pressure could he add to Baldy's life? Wasn't meaningful coexis-tence possible? A tapestry of mutuality, as Dr. Martin Luther King, Jr., had said, in which beloved others were experienced as support rather than pres-sure? She'd only had a dog for five minutes and already she was turning it into an issue of eternal, unconditional love. Zero to sixty in less than a second, Tommy often said. Often wrong, never in doubt, Tommy often said. Lighten up, Tommy often said. But no matter how she tried, she couldn't turn off her mind. It produced a running commentary that would put Woody Allen's to shame. Privately, she viewed it as an illness—hopefully not fatal.

"Got any Milk-Bone dog biscuits?"

Baldy directed her to a shelf and she opened a big box right in front of him and gave one to Useless before she even stepped up to the register to pay up. She grabbed sunscreen from a display of products that included lip moisturizer and clip-on sunglasses.

"Where'd you get the dog?" Baldy asked.

"It's Rayfield Geebo's dog, Mutley."

"You mean Debbie's dog." It was a statement of fact.

"I guess so. Anyway, it's not permanent. I'm just taking care of him 'til Debbie and Rayfield decide what to do." She put a ten-dollar bill on the counter. "So you know Debbie, huh?"

"Sure. She makes fork bracelets. I sell them during the summer when the rich folks are at their camps. She didn't show up this year, being that she left Rayfield and all."

Ellen hadn't seen a fork bracelet since the sixties, and she felt a sharp stab of nostalgia. Fork bracelets, tie-dye, and Indian print bedspreads. It had been beautiful.

"Is there a big market for fork bracelets?"

"She'd sell a couple. I just wanted to help her out." Baldy looked off. "You know, now that you got me thinking about it, I believe I have one or two left over from last year." Together they went to the shelves on the far wall where Baldy kept such incidentals as envelopes, candles, and a few assorted, out-of-date toys for kids, such as Silly Putty and packages of jacks. A cardboard box lined with tinfoil sat at the back of the shelf, and in it were displayed two of Debbie's bracelets. Their tines were twisted backward into curlicues and the handles were bent into an oval. Impulsively, Ellen put one on. It wasn't Harry Winston, but she liked it. "How much?" she asked.

"She asks five bucks."

"Sold."

She felt all the gleefulness of a little girl playing dress up as she carried her dog paraphernalia down the steps and into the car. I should've bought some silver polish, she thought as she drove back home, where Rodney was on the roof with his tar bucket. There was a slight wind but Ellen knew his tool belt would anchor him unless a tornado kicked up. She opened the car door. "Come on, Mutley," she said cheerfully. "This is your new home. Come on!" The dog opened his eyes but made no move to get up. "Come on!" Ellen said with even more enthusiasm. "Let's go!"

Still, he didn't move. She went around the car, opened the other door, and pushed him out from behind. He landed on all fours and stood there. Quickly, Ellen opened the tube of sunscreen and rubbed it into his back and shoulders. "Good boy," she said. "Want a biscuit?" She reached into the box on the front seat and offered one to him. He accepted it, but held it in his mouth as if he were too exhausted to start chewing. After a few minutes, he headed for a shady spot and collapsed under the maple tree.

That's that, Ellen thought as she filled his water dish and placed it in the dirt next to her front steps. She had expected her whole life to change now that she had taken on the responsibility of Mutley, as if some very specific difference in each passing moment would suddenly emerge. But that obviously was not to be. One more expectation laid to rest. With a sigh, she went inside. The breakfast remnants were still on the table, so she cleaned them up, tucking the two remaining donuts back into the Freihofer's box.

She wanted to talk to Tommy. It was just after twelve. Perhaps she could catch him at his office, though she knew it wasn't likely. The phone rang three times before she gave up. On the fourth ring, Edna would pick up and Ellen didn't want to talk to her. She noticed that her mood was doing a fast nosedive and decided to sit on the front porch to witness its descent.

What caused these erratic emotional changes? Over the years, Ellen had attributed them to many things: too much sugar, not enough protein, too much alcohol, not enough pleasure, too much stress, too little sunshine, too much idealism. And at forty-six, she had become somewhat acclimated to her rapid ride up and down the mood scale. She saw her moods as psychic waves— tempests or high tides on the astral plane. She often felt that if her inner weather were externalized, she would be declared a disaster zone, entitled to massive federal emergency aid. There was not a thing she could do about it except wait for it to pass.

Ellen listened to the *blam, blam, blam,* of Rodney's hammer overhead and watched Mutley dream on, oblivious to the black flies that darted around his head in a bug frenzy. Country life was harder than she'd thought. Insects swarmed, weeds grew, and days stretched on and on, from early morning until late night. No wonder farmers worked themselves to exhaustion. What else was there to do? Play a game of solitaire?

"I have no identity," she suddenly announced. It had become clear to her right there on the porch swing. When her old reliable markers—city husband, city life, and city job—were removed, she floated like a disembodied spirit. What's more, she felt compelled to haunt her own past. She didn't look ahead anymore. She looked back, to the sixties. Were the answers there? She doubted it. Answers were implemented on a daily basis in the present moment. And whether you had them or not, you had to keep on keeping on.

Rodney appeared as if by magic on the other side of the screen. "That Rayfield's dog?"

"Yeah."

"Sucker," said Rodney.

"Yeah," Ellen answered, defeated.

Rodney stood still for a moment. "What's wrong? You look like you just lost your last nickel."

Ellen sighed. "I'm having a personal crisis. I know I'm supposed to be doing something important, but I don't know what it is."

"I'll bet it ain't laying around the porch feeling sorry for yourself."

"No, it ain't." She could feel his eyes on her in a gentle way. Ellen had often been told that her eyes were like laser beams that actually hurt as they sliced into people's privacy. Rodney's were like a warm mineral bath.

"I gotta go home after another bucket of tar. Why don't you come along? Take your mind off'n your troubles."

Ellen got up. "I'll be right out." She made a pit stop in the bathroom where she redid her ponytail and splashed a little brackish water on her face. Rodney was waiting in the truck. He didn't back out of the driveway until she was safely buckled in.

"How come you didn't move in here when your mother passed on?" Ellen listlessly asked, just to make conversation.

"Too many bad memories. But you know what? Since you got here, the place seems kinda cheerful."

"Really? I haven't felt very cheerful."

"Well, by comparison to before, it's cheerful," Rodney said confidently. "Believe you me."

Ellen felt a little lift in her spirit. "So what'd you do? Buy your own place?"

"Well, I didn't have no father or nothing when I was a kid, and I struck up a friendship with an old mountain guy, kind of like a hermit. Name was Leland. He was good to me, kind of a fill-in father. I ended up moving in with him when I was not much more'n thirteen."

"How old was he?" Ellen's child abuse radar alarm was beeping.

"Old. Pushing seventy."

"How come your mother let you go?"

"I don't think she cared. And once I was out, she just sort of forgot about me. I didn't forget about her, though. Leland wouldn't let me. I saw her every weekend. Did the work around the place for her, you know."

"And then when Leland died, you stayed over there?"

"Yep. He left everything he had to me."

"How long did you live there with him?"

"About twelve years. When I was eighteen, he got sick with liver disease. I was hoping to join the Ice Capades, but I stayed on to take care of him instead. He died six years later. That was forty years ago, but I never left. Never even went to the Ice Capades again."

Ellen was silent as they sped past the post office and the general store. "It's a sad story, Rodney," she said.

"Don't I know it."

She stole a glance at him and saw that his eyes were dry. No sign of self-pity there. They bumped along a narrow dirt road up a steep incline. The milkweed and brambles reached the truck windows, and Ellen pulled her arm inside to avoid getting scratched. Then, suddenly, the road took a sharp right into an open area.

"Oh, my God! Oh, my God!" Ellen yelled. "Stop the truck!"

"What? What?" He slammed on the brakes and they both pitched forward.

"I have to look at this." She yanked open the car door and hopped out. From this high point, the whole North Country was laid out below like a world in miniature. Lakes shimmered in the intense sunlight, and barns and farmhouses dotted the countryside. Wildflowers, deep shades of burnt orange and lavender, provided the color that many people only saw on calendars from the National Geographic Society.

But it wasn't the landscape that took Ellen's breath away.

It was the sculpture. Or at least, the sheer volume of it. Because before Ellen could focus on the particulars of a single piece, she was overwhelmed by the simple phenomenon of production. Hundreds of pieces, thousands of pieces, acres of pieces, as far as the eye could see. Bears and bald eagles, Indian chiefs and bunny rabbits. It was as if a forest of trees had suddenly shapeshifted. Obviously, Rodney had not spent an idle moment in decades. It would be impossible, Ellen thought, to produce this much work unless under the influence of absolute obsession.

Or the desire to murder your mother, she reminded herself.

She stepped off the dirt road into the realm of Rodney de Beer's imagination. Like Alice in Wonderland, she fell into a deep trance. Her footsteps seemed directed by a force not her own, and her fingers reached toward the first piece, anxious to experience its contours firsthand.

"Them eagles are big sellers," said Rodney, effectively breaking the spell. "I can hardly turn 'em out fast enough. All these ones are sold already. I'm just drying 'em out a little more."

Ellen slowly twirled around. Eagles were flying, resting, stretching their wings. Some had small animals in their claws. Some sat peacefully atop tree trunks. "You do these with a *chain saw?*" Ellen asked, amazed.

"Yeah, but on most of them I use some other tools, too. I branched out after I got some experience." On and on, through the sculpture woods, Ellen wandered. She had many questions, but Rodney had lagged behind to open a package of gum. Through the sea of statues, Ellen saw Rodney's house and barn in the distance. A well-tended garden bursting with roses and tulips and cosmos circled each building and ran along the path between them. "It's paradise," she said, though Rodney was too far behind her to hear. She had left the Americana wing and entered a section rife with Christian lore. Life-size Jesuses hung on crucifixes, crosses with crowns of thorns at the crosspiece, and bleeding hearts abounded. Gaunt monks with shaved heads clutched rosaries, and angels, hundreds of angels, from cherubim to seraphim, smiled down on her.

Ellen was suddenly overcome with a deep desire to lie down in the grass and take a nap. Perhaps it was the stillness and the peace. Maybe it was just a case of extreme sensory overload. She stretched out at the base of a praying virgin and closed her eyes. All she heard was the distant chirp of the birds and the buzz of the honeybees. She drifted away, back into her childhood, when she'd been obsessed with little plastic figures, less than two inches tall. She called them "the little people" and had boxes and boxes full in every shape and size. Confederate soldiers and flappers, farmers and ballerinas. Each stood on its own little base, and all were meant to be viewed face-on because, being pressed out of molds by the thousands, they were flat with hardened plastic oozing out of their seams. Ellen had set up whole villages, created baroque stories for each one, and she didn't spare the tragedy. Bullfighters were gored and presidents were blown out of *Air Force One*. All the figures were pale pink. Two thousand could fit in a shoe box.

"Ellen! Wake up!"

Ellen opened her eyes. Rodney was kneeling over her.

"Hey, Rodney," she said sweetly. She felt like she'd been asleep for hours.

"What'd you do? Catch the sleeping sickness from Rayfield's mutt?" He was still kneeling over her, like a medic over an accident victim. She lay in quiet repose in the grass, the very image of serenity.

"It's your work, Rodney."

"It put you to sleep?"

"It knocked me out."

Rodney sat back on his heels. Ellen watched feelings flash across his sagging face. "Well, I'll be goddamned," he said.

sixteen

Ellen spent the whole afternoon at Rodney's. He left, went back to the roof, but she could not make herself get in the truck with him and leave. Happily, she wandered from sculpture to sculpture, standing in front, circling around, speculating on when he had done it. And why.

She recalled a visit to another, more official, outdoor art gallery. It was the end of the sixties, and she was driving from Boston to New York with a classical piano player named Jeff. They'd dropped some mescaline while on the Thruway, heading south. Both were flying high when they noticed a sign for the Storm King Art Center. Ellen turned on her blinker and exited at Newburgh. Though it was only a few miles, the drive to the art gallery seemed interminable. Finally, at the end of a winding road, they passed though a gate. All around them, massive metal sculptures sat atop grassy knolls.

Jeff and Ellen moved toward the first one, which appeared to be an airplane wing polished to a silver glow. The glint blinded Ellen and she lowered her eyes until they haphazardly focused on the wood chips that surrounded the base of the sculpture. She bent down to pick one up. The color tones from red to black and the woody layers of grain fascinated her, and she passed it to Jeff. "Look at this!"

He turned it over and over in his hand. "God, it's beautiful."

They threw themselves onto their stomachs and proceeded to study each individual wood chip, handing them back and forth with considerable reverence. They stayed there until the sun and the airplane wing had joined forces to cast an unexpected shadow over them, and simultaneously, a security officer came along and threw them out. "Fucking hippies," he said as he hustled them to Ellen's Dodge Dart. Just more than an hour later, they had arrived safely in New York with wood chips stuck to the front of their sweaters and several precious ones hidden in their pockets. Ellen had later placed them on the dashboard, where they remained for many years.

She missed the sixties. But Rodney's place was an oasis in the nineties. She allowed herself to doze off several times, waking each time with a sense of profound contentment. Eventually, she meandered on to Rodney's house. It was a big place, rustic. Old barn boards, gray with age; a spacious front porch with three old rockers and barrels of flowers; a screen door that had *Welcome* written across it in wooden scrollwork.

She tried the doorknob, and it turned.

She stepped inside. The room was perhaps twelve-hundred square feet, all wood, with thick beams running across the ceiling. An old, ornate woodstove, right out of *Country Living,* stood in the center. Everything was completely neat. The place would go for eight thousand a month in New York—and that was without the antique furnishings that decorators reverently described as "distressed." Ellen noticed a major floor-to-ceiling bookcase, maybe fifteen feet long, and several portraits, probably in oil, that were impossible to see at this distance. Was there one of Leland? Viola? Blue Boy?

Though she wanted to poke through drawers, look in closets, and search for scrapbooks, she quickly backed out through the screen door. RESEARCHERS WILL DO IT WITH ANYBODY: she suddenly remembered that old bumper sticker, popular with the library set for a brief moment in the seventies. It was true. But Rodney was not a research subject. In fact, until a few hours ago, she'd viewed him as a pain in the ass, a lollygagging geezer with an attitude.

She plunked herself down in the first rocking chair to revise her attitude toward Rodney. He was not the deadbeat, the no-goodnik, that she'd assumed he was. In fact, he was a live wire. Creative energy snapped through him, and he left a wide trail of work in his wake. She could even make an educated guess at his evolution from primitive to elegant. She could just imagine Rodney churning out bald eagles like a day job, then sanding the African-looking masks with twelve-hundred grade paper in his spare time.

And she had him tarring her roof on the off chance that the rain would come from the northwest again! She was so ashamed. She knew it wasn't wrong to stick up for herself. It had taken her years to develop that particular habit and she was proud if it. But she had gone after him with the vengeance of a pushy New Yorker, and now, sitting on his porch, gently rocking, it seemed silly. It was exhausting being yanked from one point of view to the next. She'd be glad when Rodney finished with the roof, and she could forget she'd ever threatened him with a lawsuit.

She heard the sound of his truck coming through the pine trees and stood up.

"Hop in. I'll run you home," Rodney called.

Ellen buckled in as he did a three-point turn and headed back down the driveway. "Damn hot up there on the roof today. I was sweating like a pig. But I got the one side all but done."

Ellen was absolutely astonished that he showed no interest or even mild curiosity about her reaction to his artwork. She had known many artists, good and bad, and therefore accepted that to allow two words on any other subject to escape your lips after you'd viewed the latest masterpiece was tantamount to treason.

"Rodney, I want to talk to you about your work."

"For God's sake, Ellen, I'm going as fast as I can. I'm not as young as I used to be, you know."

"I'm not talking about the roof," she said, exasperated.

"Well, what *are* you talking about?"

"Your sculptures!" she almost screamed. "Your sculptures!"

"What're you so mad for? Stop yelling at me. I had enough of that in my life."

Ellen took a deep breath. "I'm sorry, Rodney. But it's . . . it's unnerving. You've got all this work here and you don't even know what I'm talking about when I bring it up. Sheesh. I'm sorry I yelled at you. I don't even know why I yelled." She held her breath for a few seconds while Rodney pouted.

"Probably for the same reason you took on Rayfield's dog," he finally said.

"And what might that be?"

"Because you don't know what you're doing anymore."

Ellen stared out the window for a full minute. "Let's start this whole conversation over. Rodney, I'm truly amazed by all the work you've done. Where'd you get your inspiration?"

"From books," he said, a little chill in his voice. Ellen waited. "Leland had a lot of books," he finally added. "He was a college graduate, you know. And he traveled the whole wide world with the merchant marines before he got fed up. He studied all the time."

"Was he an artist?"

"He appreciated beauty," Rodney said, very quietly. "And he believed that trying to make something beautiful, no matter what it was, was a high calling."

"Did he like your sculptures?"

"He never saw 'em. He died just before I got started."

"What a shame." She meant it.

"Did you go in the barn?"

"No. Why?"

"I got my best stuff in there. Next time, take a peek if you want."

"You mean I can come over again, even after I yelled at you and made you mad?" She noticed a familiar tone in her voice: the sound of making up.

"Lots of folks come up to look around. If you want to be one of them, it's fine with me."

She placed her hand on his arm. "Thank you, Rodney."

"Don't mention it."

Then she remembered that Rayfield had once offered to give her directions to Rodney's yardful of sculptures. Was Rayfield one of Rodney's regulars? It was hard to picture.

"It was a great day," she said. "Just great." She had forgotten all about the gloom that had set in as she sat on the porch swing watching Mutley sleep. He was still snoozing in the same place when Rodney dropped her off.

"I'll see you in the morning," said Rodney as he shifted into reverse. "That's if it don't rain." He smiled. She waved goodbye and went inside.

She called Tommy at home, and he answered on the third ring.

"Hi, Tommy."

"Ellen! I just tried to call you."

"You did?" She was surprised and pleased.

"Yeah. How you doing?"

"Good," she said. "Everything is under control."

Tommy laughed. "Your supreme goal in life," he said.

"How about you?"

"I bought a NordicTrack," he said. "It's right in the middle of the living room. It's huge. Every night, I turn on the tube and ski over the Alps."

Right in the middle of the living room? That probably threw a monkey wrench into her decor, but she didn't comment. After all, she wasn't there to see it. "What brought this on?"

"I figured it's now or never. It's time to lose the love handles once and for all."

"You should come up here if you want to feel skinny. Half the people are tubs."

"Yeah, well, half the people in New York are anorexic, so it all evens out in the end. Anyway, who's counting?"

"Yeah, who's counting." It occurred to Ellen that she had not stepped on a scale in a week. At home, it was the first thing she did, right after her morning pee and before her first glass of water.

"By the time you get home, I'll be Charles fucking Atlas."

"Legs like tree trunks!" Ellen contributed, remembering the ads in all the magazines of her youth. "Don't let anybody kick sand in your face at the beach! Don't be an eighty-seven-pound weakling!"

"Ski the Matterhorn in the comfort of your own living room while watching reruns of *F Troop*." Tommy laughed. "So what have you been up to?"

It was time to tell him about Rodney de Beer, but she stopped herself. She would take him to Rodney's over the Fourth of July weekend. "I got a dog," she said.

"A what?"

"A dog. His name is Mutley and he's narcoleptic."

"What?"

"Dog. Mutley. Narcoleptic."

"Christ, Ellen, what're we gonna do with a dog? We live in a five-floor walk-up, remember?" He stopped talking to wait out the wail of a police siren on the street. When it faded, he added, "Ellen, I feel compelled to say this, for the record. I do not want a dog."

"I know that, Tommy. And you don't have one. I do."

"Let me clarify, then. I don't want a dog in our shared New York apartment."

"And I don't want a NordicTrack in the living room." She could almost see Tommy stiffening. "Look, Tommy, I didn't mean that," she said quickly.

"Yes, you did."

"Well, I did, but I don't. I take it back, okay? I'm glad you got yourself a ski track. Put it anywhere you want. I'm not even there. What difference does it make where you put it?"

"I still don't want a dog." His voice was tight.

"And you shall not have one. Mutley's only here for two weeks."

"Good."

There seemed to be nothing left to do but hang up and start over another day. With a sigh, Ellen studied the calendar on the kitchen wall, a free gift from Baldy's store. Eighteen more days until Tommy came. They would speak several times before that. And Mutley would be long gone. Speaking of whom, it was time to feed him. Ellen carried the dog food outside. Mutley was still snoozing under the tree. When she walked to him and sat in the grass, he slowly opened his eyes. Ellen placed his head in her lap and began a slow, systematic head massage. She scratched his ears and stretched the skin hanging below his jaw. His dewlap, she thought, astonished that she had absorbed so much dog trivia from Reginald's page-a-day dog calendar. Mutley shifted to another position to offer her easier access to his shoulders. From deep within, a low groan emerged.

"Sing those blues, Mutley," she said. And he did. The more she rubbed, the longer his moans became. The whole canine history, from domestication to routine castration, was there in Mutley's voice. It was more animation than she'd ever seen in this dog. "Sing it for me," she whispered as she gazed into Mutley's deep brown eyes, which looked almost purple in the evening light. She made a tentative attempt to imitate his sounds, which only egged him on. Soon they were improvising together, a soulful duet. At its end, Mutley heaved himself to his feet and staggered, as if drunk, to his food bowl.

Rayfield's *Free Trader* ad had said "Can catch Frisbee." For the first time, Ellen tried to imagine it. Mutley, galloping full-out, his muscles rippling under the surface of his shimmering coat. Rayfield lied, she thought. This dog would no more chase a Frisbee than he would fly around the living room. She made a mental note to stop at Kmart and get the best Frisbee money could buy. If Mutley showed no interest, she would deliver a lecture on the ethics of advertising to Rayfield Geebo.

Lost in her reverie, she failed to notice the mosquitoes that swarmed around her head. When the first one struck, she slapped herself hard on the forehead and charged back into the house. From inside the porch, she called Mutley. She would not leave him outside to be eaten alive in the yard. She fluffed up his sleeping bag to make a comfortable bed and promised to let him out to relieve himself before she went to bed. Mutley climbed the porch steps, collapsed onto his pallet, and began to snore.

seventeen

At first light, Ellen climbed out of bed, determined to get her watering done before the sun rose too high. She let Mutley off the porch and filled her watering can. To her surprise, Mutley accompanied her across the yard, down the narrow path through the brush, and into her garden. He's bonding, she thought with an interesting mixture of panic and pride.

Mutley sat at the edge of the garden as she moved down the rows, sprinkling the spindly tomato plants and tiny green shoots that were already peeking through the dirt in several places. Soon she would feast on food she had grown for herself, by herself, in a patch of land she had cleared with her own two hands. It was a miracle on the same caliber as the loaves and fishes. Something from nothing.

Back and forth she went with her water buckets. Each time, the dog tagged along. Ellen patted him on the head, and, before her third trip, she covered him with Skin-So-Soft and gave him a dog biscuit she had previously tucked into her pocket. This launched her into a long meditation on caring: if you took care *of* something, would you end up caring *about* it?

She went into the house to look up the word *care* in her Merriam-Webster's pocket dictionary. The first seven definitions were all wrapped up in images of fear, anxiety, and responsibility, but number eight seemed appropriate: to feel a liking, fondness, or inclination. Ellen stared out the window into the woods. She loved the dictionary but was baffled by it. How did words acquire meaning? How did anything? She was so absorbed in her musing that she didn't even hear Rodney's truck pull into her driveway.

"What're you doing?" he asked from the other side of the screen door.

"God, you scared me. Come in. I was just looking up a word."

Rodney went directly to the kitchen where he started the coffee. "What word?"

"Care. To care."

"Don't you know what that means?"

"I thought I did but now I'm finding out it's mostly about worry, fear, and anxiety. Look." She pushed the dictionary toward him, and Rodney put on his reading glasses and bent over it.

"Well, I'll be goddamned," he said.

Ellen got up and arranged yesterday's donuts. "Guess why I looked it up?" She felt she had a secret ripe for telling.

"Why?"

"Because I was trying to figure out if I cared about Mutley. Yesterday I sat under the tree and"—suddenly she felt the first vibrations on an incoming laughing fit—"and I gave him a massage and sang him a lullaby and . . ." But she was laughing too hard to get the words out. Rodney stood uncertainly for a few seconds and then joined in. In the midst of it, the phone rang and Rodney, standing right next to it, simply reached over and answered it.

"Hello? Yes, hold on." He giggled, and then he passed the receiver to Ellen.

"Who was that?" Tommy demanded.

"That was Rodney."

"What's he doing there?"

"We're having an orgy. Pass me that dildo, will you, Rodney?" Rodney's eyebrows shot up and he covered his mouth with his hand.

"Very funny," said Tommy. "And here I thought you were lonely."

"I told you, he's fixing the roof."

"Right."

Ellen was momentarily speechless. Was it just a guy thing? Some sort of biological territoriality, like pissing at every corner of the yard? Or could Tommy actually be jealous?

"Call Karen," he snapped. "She's hysterical. Something about Cocho."

And he hung up. Ellen didn't even remove the phone from her ear. Tommy had not hung up on her in seventeen years. How dare he? But then, the meaning of his words registered, and her outrage vanished. Something about Cocho? Karen was not the type to get hysterical. Quickly, she dialed Karen's number and got a busy signal. She tried again. Busy. She hit redial three times to no avail and felt a terrible tightening in her stomach.

"I'm going to Montreal," she said to Rodney. "Something's wrong at my sister's. If she should call, tell her I'll be there by eight thirty." She grabbed her purse, ran out, squeezed the Honda past Rodney's truck, and disappeared from

Eagle Beak in a cloud of dust. Her heart pounded and grisly images of murdered bodies were coughed up from her unconscious.

High anxiety. Worry. Fear.

She cared. She cared about Cocho in relation to Karen and Olivier, but she
also loved him for himself. He was a sixties kind of guy, a free spirit who didn't
even acknowledge that the corporate world existed.

Down the mountain she sped, along the very roads she'd traveled on the
day she'd impulsively purchased her house less than five weeks before. In that
short time, everything in her life seemed changed. But she knew she'd simply
done a geographical, in the parlance of the twelve-step programs. Changed
her location instead of her attitude.

If something serious had happened to Cocho, the change in Karen's life
would be catastrophic. Ellen tried to shake her fears away and concentrate on
the road, but she couldn't. Anything could happen to anybody, any minute,
she knew, even as she desperately hoped that Cocho had been passed over by
the fickle finger of fate. Onward she drove, her fingers gripping hard onto the
steering wheel. At eight twenty, she was standing on the street under Karen's
window, hollering her name. Karen appeared in the fourth-floor window and
tossed down the keys to the street door in a red wool sock. Ellen, a veteran of
a five-floor walk-up for more than a dozen years, tore up the three flights, two
steps at a time. Karen stood in the doorway. Her eyes were swollen into two
slits, and her whole face was mottled in shades of pink and maroon.

"What happened?" Ellen asked as she flew to her sister and gathered her in
her arms. Karen crumpled against her.

"There was a car accident."

"Cocho? Is he . . . ?" Ellen could not say it.

"He's in a coma." Karen's face was buried in Ellen's shoulder. "They don't
know."

Ellen led her sister back inside and closed the door. Olivier looked up from
the pile of oversized blocks he was stacking into a pyramid. He smiled when he
saw Ellen, then reached for a wooden spoon and knocked down the top blocks.

"Where is he? You have to go right now," she said.

"He's home in Peru. It happened in the mountains on his way back to
Lima from his family's village. They . . . it took them six hours to get him to a
hospital. . . . They didn't know who to call." Karen wiped her nose on her
arm. "His best friend was killed."

"You have to go to him." It seemed the most important thing. It was what
she would do if something happened to Tommy, even if he were in Timbuktu.

"I can't take Olivier," Karen said. "And I can't leave him here."

"Olivier will stay with me. It doesn't matter how long." Ellen's voice was solid and decisive. "Now, go take a hot bath and let me call the airlines."

"Really?" Karen was in a daze. She walked down the hall, bumping into the wall on her way. Ellen had never seen her so disoriented. During their parents' funerals, Karen was stoic and strong.

"Want to come stay with Auntie Ellen?" she asked, stooping down to kiss her nephew's head. He offered her his wooden spoon. The gesture, so trusting, made Ellen's eyes sting, but she willed the tears away and settled into the chair next to the phone.

When Karen emerged from the bath, Ellen had made a plane reservation for two o'clock. She had used her own credit card to pay for the ticket. For years, all the plastic cash had remained dormant in the darkest reaches of her shoulder bag. Now she had ten thousand bucks racked up. But she couldn't think about it.

Karen had collected herself a bit. "I need to get to the bank and stop by the café and go to Regine-Marie's," she said as she tied her sneakers.

"We'll all go," Ellen said. Karen and Olivier had never been separated overnight before, and Ellen knew her sister was full of misgivings of every sort. But she couldn't take her son with her. He didn't have a passport. He would need shots. She didn't know where she would stay, or how long she would be gone. There was a cholera epidemic in Peru. A hospital, hotbed of germs, was the last place for a baby. Karen repeated all these facts out loud, over and over again. "Just go to Cocho and don't worry about Olivier," Ellen responded each time.

In a blur, they traipsed through the city, packed Karen's old knapsack, and drove to the airport. Olivier waved bye-bye to his mother as she disappeared down the tunnel to the plane. Ellen watched with him at the window until the jumbo jet backed away from the gate and lumbered toward a far-off runway.

"Well, it's me and you, kid," Ellen said as they walked hand in hand down the corridor toward the exit. She was already exhausted and hoped that Olivier took an afternoon nap because she desperately needed one. But it was not to be. Regine-Marie arrived to help Ellen schlep Olivier's port-a-crib down the stairs and into the car. They loaded the car seat, a bag of assorted toys, a jumbo-sized box of disposable diapers, and a stuffed bear half the size of Mutley. Ellen had Olivier's birth certificate and a notarized letter from Karen giving her permission to take him out of Canada.

"Why don't you just stay here?" Regine-Marie asked. "You would have a great time in Montreal, and Olivier could be at home."

"I've got a dog and a garden to take care of," Ellen answered, amazed that it was true. Suddenly, she was living the American dream: house and a car, baby and dog. All the things she'd sidestepped for forty-six long years were now crashing down on her like flying debris in a tornado. It made her dizzy.

She locked up Karen's loft, stopped to let Olivier say goodbye to the Ng family in the market, and soon melted into the white tile tunnel to the Mercier Bridge and home. It was the first time she'd driven in a car alone with a baby since legislation in the seventies had made car seats mandatory. It seemed strange to have Olivier buckled in behind her, all alone in the back, leaving her to check over her shoulder as she kept up a constant stream of baby babble from the front.

She barely knew her sister's great love, had spent perhaps a grand total of ten days with him over several visits. Even then, he'd seemed more spirit than flesh. Even the music he produced had the gentle touch of wind instruments made from reeds and wooden pipes. "He seems like he could just lift off at any moment. Just start floating," she had said to Karen on her first visit. Karen had laughed, delighted. "Not to say he isn't sexy. *Gawd*," Ellen added, pretending she had touched something very hot and had to blow on her fingers. "But he's so ethereal. Or elusive. Just not what you think of as down-to-earth."

Maybe the earth, with all its gravity and wild spinning through space, was not strong enough to hold on to the spirit of Cocho. Maybe it was going to fly home soon, leaving a body behind to turn slowly to dust. He was at the portal, for sure. If all the words of the near death experience section of the pop psychology section of the bookstore were accurate, he could be walking down the tunnel toward the light right now as the faces of the dead smiled and beckoned him onward.

"Don't go, Cocho," Ellen said. "You hear me? Come back. Stay and raise your son." She glanced over her shoulder again. Olivier was asleep, slumped to one side of his car seat, his lower lip hanging open. "Come back, Cocho," she whispered again.

eighteen

Ellen had a feeling of immense relief as she gunned the Honda's motor along the straightaway before the sharp incline up to Eagle Beak Mountain. She felt like a little iron filing, irresistibly drawn forward by a big magnet at the top of the world. And as she sped along, she had the sensation that the tall pine trees on either side of the road subtly acknowledged her return, like concerned parents listening for the sound of the front door late in the night. When the car finally reached the end of the long ascent, when she could release the accelerator pedal as the road flattened out into a high plateau under the shadow of the mountain peak, Ellen felt filled with deep peace, even though this hamlet, with its weather-beaten shacks, its proliferation of trailers, and the total absence of activity, was hardly her idea of paradise.

Mutley was asleep under the tree when she turned into the driveway, though she could barely see him in the high grass of her front yard. Amazingly, she hadn't given a single thought to cutting it. It had seemed like a magic carpet, rippling in the wind. But Olivier would barely be able to plow through it. She couldn't remember seeing a lawn mower anywhere. One more thing to deal with, she thought as she cut the motor.

Olivier woke up screaming, and Ellen hurried around the car. When she opened the door, he was thrashing around, stiff-legged, in his car seat, his little face a deep purple and his fists flailing to beat the band. "It's okay, honey," she said as she fought with the buckle and lifted him out of the car. "It's okay." But Olivier obviously did not agree. He kicked harder, and Ellen finally put him down in the tall grass, which seemed to surprise him somewhat.

"Let's go see the doggie," she said with enthusiasm. "Where's the doggie?" It did not help that Olivier spoke no English. Of course, he didn't really speak any language at all, but his babyish word collection included French, Spanish, and Vietnamese. Ellen had actually helped Karen formulate a language plan for her infant son, which included such concepts as Karen only speaking French and Cocho only speaking Spanish, just to keep the linguistic threads separate in Olivier's impressionable little mind. It had sounded good at the time.

"Where's the doggie? Let's go find the doggie," Ellen repeated with cheery animation. Olivier continued to scream, even as she picked him up and carried him through the grass toward the maple tree. Mutley hadn't moved but his eyes were open. Suddenly, years' worth of front-page stories from the *New York Post* flashed before her eyes: GERMAN SHEPHERD KILLS TODDLER, INFANT MAULED BY STARVING SHEPHERD, K-9 GOES CRAZY. Even a dog fact from Reginald's calendar arrived unsummoned into her mind: "Babies emit a scent that confuses dogs. This sometimes results in aggressive acts. Always monitor your toddler around strange dogs." And there she was, delivering Olivier to the tiger pit. But Mutley remained his usual mellow self when Ellen deposited her nephew on the ground.

"Hi, Mutley," Ellen cooed, and Olivier, distracted, abruptly ceased screaming and commenced to pound Mutley's head and ruffle his whole-body crew cut. "Mutley's a nice dog. Nice Mutley. Be nice, Mutley," she added, though it hardly seemed necessary. "Are you hungry, Mutley? Let's go, Olivier. Let's go feed Mutley." The dog heaved himself to his feet and all three slowly plodded through the tall grass to the house. Olivier tugged free of Ellen's grasp and waddled a few steps ahead. His chubby legs, deeply creased in three places from the knee to the hip, were sturdy but somewhat unreliable on the rough terrain, and he fell into a heap that left a grass stain on the back of his little sunsuit. Mutley paused and turned to give Ellen a look that seemed judgmental.

There was a note from Rodney on the dining-room table. "Dear Ellen," it said in beautiful cursive script, "I hope everything is okay with your sister— and you. You seemed beside yourself this morning. Well, good luck to you both. I will not be around for a few days as I have to travel to Albany to deliver a carving. Rodney."

Ellen felt a little thud of disappointment. It was as if Rodney, with his down-home coffee-and-donuts approach to life, had already become a fixture around the place, no different than the porch swing or the jelly jars in the pantry. He belonged there, banging his way across the roof, his tool belt circling his narrow hips.

Plus, she needed somebody to mow the grass, and she'd secretly hoped to palm this task off on Rodney. Now that she was thrust back on her own devices, though, she would need to get creative. But all that could wait until the morning. She had a baby to take care of, a car to unpack, a garden to water, a dog to feed, and a pot of open-the-heart tea to brew.

This is how the pioneer women must have felt, she thought. But she knew from her research on a Reginald Eubanks documentary about water rights in the Old West that one pioneer mom had died for every ten childbirths, so chances were the mom wouldn't be around, even if the baby was. And, of course, many of the pioneer babies died, too. Compared to that, carting her watering can along the path to the garden and pouring prepackaged kibble into the dog's bowl did not seem too difficult, especially since she knew it was all temporary. Mutley would go on to wherever Rayfield and Debbie decided. Karen and, hopefully, Cocho, would return from Peru to collect their son. The house would be closed up, and she would head back to New York where such old-fashioned survival issues had completely faded from the mass memory. Needless to say, others had arisen, the kind that sent petite women to martial arts classes or caused them to carry mace in their coat pockets. The kind that transformed the simple act of breathing into the equivalent of smoking a pack of unfiltered cigarettes every day. The kind that eventually carved every face into the "New York pinch," as she and Tommy called it.

"And just think! We're at the top of the food chain," she remarked to Olivier, noticing how compelled she was to fill the air with words, even if he didn't understand them. He sat on the crumbling bottom step as Mutley chomped through his daily meal and Ellen scurried back and forth to the car. She needed to talk to Tommy, and as soon as the port-a-crib was safely stashed in the dining room, she dialed the number in New York. "Hello?" Tommy said just after the second ring. He sounded breathless.

"Skiing over the Alps?" Ellen asked in a friendly tone.

"Nope. Just got in the door."

"Tommy," she began, not sure of what to say first. "Cocho's seriously hurt. He may not make it."

His voice softened. "What happened?"

"He was in a car accident. He's in a coma."

"Jesus."

"Didn't Karen tell you?"

"There was just a hysterical message. I didn't talk to her. She didn't seem to know you were up there. Didn't you call her?"

Ellen closed her eyes and clenched her teeth. Had she really not called Karen in over a week to say that she was more or less in the neighborhood? It seemed impossible. But she knew she withdrew from others when she felt overwhelmed.

"I guess not." She heard despair in her own voice. "Anyway, she took off for Peru this afternoon. I have Olivier."

"Are you in Montreal?"

"No. I'm home. Here."

"Is he okay?"

"So far." He was banging wooden blocks against the floor, reveling in the racket, and Ellen ignored it. "Tommy," she finally said, "all this stuff with Cocho . . . I just want . . ." Suddenly she was crying. "I just want you to know how much I appreciate your friendship over all these years."

"Ellen, I . . . I'm sorry I hung up on you this morning."

"Forget about it," she said.

"I got so mad thinking you had a guy there before eight in the morning, I even called 1-800-DIVORCE."

Ellen laughed. She had dialed that number herself at least six times over the years. "But then you suddenly remembered you're a lawyer," she said, feeling her tears evaporating like a puddle on a sunny day.

"No, not really. It's just that, after I cooled off, I realized that if there was a guy with you, I could accept it." He seemed to choose his words with extreme caution. "Because I trust you to do what you have to do, and . . ." Now his voice actually cracked. "It was never my intention to put you on a leash. That's not why I married you."

The tears started up again. "God, Tommy," she said.

"I just want you to know that I support you in what you need to do, whatever it is."

"But it wasn't anything, Tommy. It was just Rodney, over here to fix the roof."

"That's not the point."

"I know. And I appreciate what you've said." Was there really that much room in their relationship? Whatever the truth was, his words touched her deeply and she wanted to say I love you, I'll always love you, but her throat muscles had constricted, cutting off the flow of words.

"God, I hope Cocho makes it," Tommy said.

"Me, too."

"You just never know what's coming around the bend."

"You got that right."

There seemed to be nothing left to say, and it suddenly hit Ellen that Olivier hadn't eaten since noontime. She should cook him something nutritious, or at least give him a banana. "Well, I guess we've covered the waterfront," she said, a signal that she was ready to disconnect.

"Yeah."

"So I'll call you soon."

"Or I'll call you."

They hung up. Ellen felt warm all over, as if her blood temperature had just risen five degrees Fahrenheit. Such were the backflips of marriage. At eight A.M. the phone was slammed down in your ear; a few hours later, true love coursed through your arteries like a hot river. And best of all, Tommy probably meant what he said. He neither wanted nor needed to control her. That was Ellen's party line, too, but in her heart she never felt up to the ideal. While Tommy simply accepted the big ifs in life, Ellen was afraid of them. Not that it ever kept her from plunging in headfirst.

"How about some mashed potatoes with some sautéed vegetables on the side?" she said to Olivier as she began to rattle the pots and pans. "Let's have ourselves a sit-down dinner. Ice cream for dessert." Olivier listened to her with a curious look on his face. Ellen found the tops of two pots in the pantry and gave them to him to bang, like cymbals. She turned on an Otis Redding tape for motivation, and soon Olivier was perched on her knees and they were sharing a plate piled high with food as Mutley snored away on his sleeping bag on the front porch.

Olivier cried himself to sleep. "Mama! Mama!" he had screamed several times as Ellen gave him a bath in the kitchen sink and snapped him into a pair of pj's modeled on the blue-and-red Superman costume. She bounced him on her knee and paced with him until he finally gave up. Ellen, exhausted, collapsed on the bed after she lowered her nephew into his port-a-crib, which was set up just an arm's length away. She could hear his sweet, shallow breathing in the last seconds before she fell into a deeply satisfying dreamworld.

nineteen

I n the morning she called Rayfield.

"Is this a social call or are you trying to palm Mutley off on me?" he asked.

"Actually, I need a lawn mower, and I was wondering if you could lend me one. And bring it over. And mow the lawn," she said.

"I suppose you want me to front you five bucks, too."

"Only if you're flush."

Rayfield was so silent that Ellen was about to back down and laugh off her request for help. Then Olivier started to screech in the background. He wanted to go outside and couldn't manage to push the door open. The frustration was unmanageable.

"You got a kid over there?" Rayfield asked.

"My sister's son."

"Sounds like a screaming mimi."

"He's a great kid," Ellen said quickly. "I'd like to let him play in the yard, but the grass is up to his waist. So I have to mow it."

"Damn it, all right. I'll bring my old one over." Ellen gave him directions and hung up. She hadn't seen Rayfield in two days, hadn't even asked if he was going back to Dr. Yi. Her basic manners were slipping, she thought, if she could call up a man and ask him to mow her lawn without even covering the preliminaries. Twenty minutes later, he pulled into the driveway in his noisy pickup truck. Ellen stepped outside to greet him, Olivier on her hip. "Good morning," she called.

"If you say so," he replied.

"How are you?"

"Don't ask."

"Been back to see Dr. Yi?"

Rayfield yanked the tailgate down on his pickup and rolled an ancient power mower down two two-by-fours. "What's it to you?" he asked.

"Oh, touchy, touchy," said Ellen. Actually, it hurt her feelings a little.

Rayfield bumped the mower to the ground. "This ain't grass; it's hay," he said as he looked around, obviously miffed.

"Come on in and have a cup of coffee," said Ellen.

"I'm not drinking coffee. Or beer either. Or smoking."

"I wasn't planning to offer you a beer at nine in the morning. It's not the cocktail hour," she said.

Rayfield snorted. "The cocktail hour, my ass," he muttered under his breath. Ellen ignored his little display and asked, "Any medical progress?"

"Christ, Ellen, nothing happens overnight."

That's what you think, Ellen thought. The whole world could change in a split second, and it often did. She intentionally blocked a mental image of Cocho in a hospital bed, tubes wired into ten locations.

Meanwhile, Olivier squirmed to get down and Ellen set him on his feet on the overgrown weeds in the sidewalk. He immediately took off at a run, directly to Rayfield, and grabbed onto his legs at the knees.

"Hey, little fella," Rayfield said, stooping down until his beer belly flattened out along the tops of his thighs. "You are a fella, ain't you?"

"His name is Olivier. Like Sir Laurence."

"You like that truck, Ollie?" Olivier was banging his fist on the fender.

"He doesn't speak English," Ellen commented.

"He don't? Where's he from? Cuba?"

Ellen laughed. "Why Cuba?"

"Look at his hair, for chrissakes. Put a set of fatigues on him and give him a cigar and you got Fidel." Rayfield hoisted Olivier up in a movement that made Ellen stop and wonder if he had children of his own. "Got any milk?" he asked.

"Sure, come on in."

"Looks a hell of a lot cleaner than it did when Viola lived here," he said as he stepped past her. "Rodney must've hosed it down."

Ellen perked up. "You used to visit here?"

"Not exactly." There was an odd tone in his voice. But just then he stepped into the kitchen. "Wow! Where'd you get that?" he asked with sudden animation.

"What?"

"That washing machine."

It was an old electric wringer that had been crammed into the corner of the pantry and buried under several boxes of empty mason jars. She had tried to haul it out, but had only made it as far as the kitchen before she gave up.

"Man, my mother had one like this. I loved that machine when I was a kid. I used to feed the socks through the wringer for her," Rayfield said nostalgically as he inspected it.

Ellen had no idea what to say. This was definitely virgin conversational territory for her. And Rayfield had a faraway look in his eyes. Suddenly he turned to her. "Hey! You got any dirty laundry? Let's do a wash."

"I don't even know if it works," she said, resisting.

"Only one way to find out."

The image of her clothes sloshing around in brackish water did not please her, but she refused to be a party pooper. She went upstairs to sort through her pile of laundry, quickly removing her underpants and placing them in a separate pile.

When she returned to the kitchen, she saw that Olivier was perched on the kitchen counter while Rayfield hooked up the hose to the faucet and stretched the frayed cord toward the one and only electrical plug. Ellen dumped her load of dirty work clothes into the barrel of the washer with a sense of dread. She truly disliked this stick-in-the-mud part of her personality, the part that sometimes held back for no reason and wanted to drag everyone else off the front line of fun, too. Not that doing a load of wash in the kitchen was her idea of a big time. She squirted in some dish soap.

"We're ready to rock and roll," he said. "Go ahead, throw the switch."

Ellen stepped forward and pressed the button, and a slow trickle of brown water began to run into the clothes barrel. "She's working!" said Rayfield. "See that, Ollie?" He swept Olivier off the counter and poised his little feet on the edge of the washing machine. "That's water. Wa-wa." And then to Ellen, "It sure looks like shit though. Why don't you filter it?"

"It's clearing up, little by little," Ellen replied, defensively. "The guy said it'd take a week."

"Suit yourself." He turned his eyes back to the washing machine.

It was not in Ellen's nature to stand back and watch. She was too restless. Staring into the washer as it slowly filled did not have any immediate fascination, but Rayfield seemed to be transfixed in the same way that Reginald Eubanks was when he watched the rough cut of his newest documentary film. Ellen covertly studied Rayfield's face. It had become serene, as if the concentration necessary to observe the flow of water into the washer had lifted him out of his bad mood and transported him somewhere lovely.

The washer emitted a crack as loud as a shotgun, and simultaneously, the water flow ceased. The machine began to gyrate as water sloshed back and forth, creating waves that crashed against the side of the barrel. Soon, the weight of the water actually caused the whole machine to move.

"Stand back!" yelled Rayfield with delight. "This baby's gonna dance!" Olivier hooted with glee as Rayfield swept him onto his arm. "I remember this," he said. "My mother's used to shimmy like a table dancer. Bah, bup, bup, bup, bah, bup, *bah!*" Rayfield chanted, throwing his hips into it. It took less than three seconds for Ellen to join in. It was like having Cozy Cole in the kitchen, so intense was the banging. How often did anyone get to dance to a washing machine? She allowed herself a shoulder shimmy and segued into the Pony. Before long, Rayfield grabbed her hand and they launched into a mean jitterbug. And when the cycle shifted from agitate to spin, they broke apart to whirl like dervishes, with Olivier whooping with laughter and Rayfield hollering, "Oh, boy!" at unpredictable intervals.

Ellen sat down on the floor when she got dizzy, but the machine abruptly switched into rinse, and Rayfield pulled her to her feet again. The gentle whirring inspired a slow waltz and she moved without resistance into his arms. She could smell body odor and stale cigarette smoke in his clothes as he guided her around the kitchen like a tubby Fred Astaire.

"You've been practicing," she said.

"One of my many talents," Rayfield responded, lowering her into a deep dip. She could see both Rayfield's moon face and Olivier's toothy smile above her as he held her backwards over the linoleum floor. Then suddenly she was swept up and together they sailed toward the corner of the kitchen, doing an abrupt right angle turn before they would have crashed into the built-in ironing board. When the rinse cycle switched off, she felt disappointed to be set free. And then it all ended. The wet clothes were plastered to the sides of the barrel, and the washer had returned to its sleep state.

"Time to put those babies through the wringer," Rayfield said. One by one, he fed her work shorts and T-shirts through the ancient black rollers, and they fell like pancakes into Ellen's plastic laundry basket. "You got a clothesline?" Rayfield asked.

"I'll go outside and look," she said, still giddy from their impromptu dance routine. "Let's go, Olivier." She offered him her hand but he sat down on the floor. "*Où est Mama?*" he asked. Ellen had rarely heard him speak a full sentence.

"She's coming soon, honey," she said as she dropped down and took him onto her lap. "She's coming soon." Tears filled Olivier's deep brown eyes and began to drip down his cheeks and off his chin. "Oh, Olivier, don't worry, don't be sad," she said.

"Where is his mother anyway?" Rayfield asked.

"She's in Peru."

"Peru over by Plattsburgh?"

Ellen looked up, amazed at the limits of Rayfield's universe. "No, Peru as in South America. Her boyfriend was in a bad car accident."

"His father?" Rayfield motioned toward Olivier.

"Yes."

"Poor little fella. When's she coming back?"

"I have no idea."

"Then you shouldn't tell him she's coming soon."

"For chrissakes, Rayfield, he doesn't even speak English." Olivier's shoulders were shaking and his face was pressed deeply into Ellen's breast. She stroked his curls and rocked.

"You ought to tell the kid the truth," Rayfield persisted.

Ellen, afraid that her voice would scare her nephew, did not respond.

"Ollie!" Rayfield suddenly said in a loud, cheerful tone, "let's go mow the lawn. Come on, kiddo." Rayfield plucked him from Ellen's arms and headed toward the door. "Come on, *mon petit chou-chou*. Let's go. *Allons-y*." Olivier used his hands to push off Ellen's chest and ran to grab onto Rayfield's finger. "Let's go mow the lawn, buddy," Rayfield said as they disappeared through the screen door.

Chou-chou? Allons-y? Where did Rayfield get that, Ellen wondered as she crossed to the door and watched them make their way to the ancient lawn mower waiting in the tall grass. Mutley, in a grand display of interest, had risen to his feet under the maple tree. His tail was wagging in spasmodic jerks and finally he took one step in Rayfield's direction.

"Mutley, my man," said Rayfield as Mutley licked his fingers and made one long slurp across Olivier's face for good measure. "How's life treating you?" Rayfield put Mutley in a half nelson and flipped him to the ground. On his back, Mutley raised his paws high in the air and Rayfield and Olivier patted his stomach. Then Rayfield climbed onto the mower and placed Olivier on his lap. Together, they turned the key in the ignition and, with a mighty roar, the mower came to life. Mutley raised his head, made a thoughtful assessment, and promptly collapsed and returned to dreamland. Rayfield placed Olivier's hands on the steering wheel and off they putted, out of her immediate sight, leaving a swath of cut grass in their wake.

Ellen made herself a cup of instant coffee. So this was family life. The man on the mower doing chores, the dog, the baby boy, the house in the country, the vegetables growing in the garden, the car in the driveway, water boiling in the background for sound effects. She sat down at the table, as she had seen her mother do a million times. "Coffee break," her mother would say, as if she owed the world an explanation.

Could I have done it, she wondered. Raised a family, lived a normal life instead of a patched-together one in which she ascended and descended a minimum of twenty flights of stairs per day? Would she have an open heart, and therefore no use for strange Asian concoctions, if she had channeled love into the home fries she made from scratch in the morning? She watched Rayfield, oversized on the rusty lawn mower, his rear end hanging over both sides of the seat, and tried to imagine it. Of course, it wouldn't be Rayfield on the lawn mower.

But it hadn't happened with Tommy either, she thought sadly.

twenty

After Rayfield finished the lawn and left, the air was filled with the scent of freshly mowed grass. It bothered Ellen. Grass blood. She felt dark gloom upon her as she pulled weeds from her garden, throwing them into a pile of plant corpses, their lives cut short because they happened to be incarnated as crummy milkweed instead of classy tomatoes or cucumbers. She stood up among the rows of her garden and surveyed the lush green carpet of her lawn. At its edges, the brush and trees rose like a wall, ready to close in on her the second she turned her back. And the black flies and mosquitoes were swarming over her head, held back only by the repulsive layer of deadly chemicals she had smeared over every inch of exposed skin. She wiped her sweaty forehead with the back of her arm. There was nothing to do but ride out these waves of helpless misery. But just as she buckled her mental seat belt, the phone rang inside. Ellen scooped up Olivier and made a dash for the house, grabbing the receiver off the hook just after the fourth ring.

"Collect call for anyone from Karen," said a female voice. "Do you accept the charges?"

"Yes," Ellen cried, "yes." After a series of loud clicks, the line cleared and Karen's voice echoed as it beamed off a satellite circling the earth somewhere between Eagle Beak and Lima, Peru. "Hello?" she said.

"Karen, how are you? How's Cocho?" Ellen nervously bounced Olivier on her hip. His frizzy black hair reminded her of a hairdo she'd coveted whenever she saw it on the old *Soul Train* of her youth: the Afro puff.

"Mama?" Olivier asked sweetly.

"They're doing everything they can," Karen said. "His vital signs are weak."

"Oh, Karen, I'm so sorry. Are you okay? Are you okay?"

"I don't know. I spent the night with him, just holding his hand, telling him I need him and Olivier needs him." Her voice faded.

"Olivier is fine," Ellen quickly said. "He mowed the grass for me."

Karen laughed. "Very precocious child. Is he nearby?"

"Right on my hip."

"Let me say hello."

Ellen moved the phone to Olivier's ear. "*C'est Mama,*" she said. Olivier listened to Karen's voice with extreme attention. He held his hand in exactly the same position on the phone, as if moving it would break the precious connection to his missing mother. His little voice produced the word *oui* several times. Then, suddenly, he launched into what seemed to be at least two connected sentences in which the word *chien* figured. Olivier was discussing Mutley! Ellen had no idea Mutley loomed so large in her nephew's personal universe. We never understand the experience of others, she thought with sorrow.

Olivier shifted his eyes toward Ellen, which she took to mean that Karen was asking for her. He knows my name, she realized with a wide burst of love. "Can I talk to Mama now?" Gently, she took the phone. Olivier reached for it, resting his little brown hand on the receiver as Ellen placed it on her shoulder, wedged there with her jaw. The gesture brought tears to her eyes.

"He sounds good. He says you have a dog." Olivier began to thrash and scream. "Mama! Mama!" he cried. Ellen let him slide off her lap onto the floor. She covered the receiver so her sister could not hear him.

"We're fine, but really, how are you?"

"Can you manage Olivier for a while?"

"I love him," Ellen said, glancing nervously toward the living room into which Olivier had disappeared. "He's my main soul kid."

"Okay then, I'm going to stay until . . . until I know."

Ellen asked the name of the hospital and rang off. She ran after Olivier and found him sitting in the corner, his legs a wide V before him. "Mama," he sobbed. Ellen lifted him to her lap, kissing him again and again. "Let's have lunch, honey," she said, just to have something to say. Her heart ached as she spread the peanut butter and jelly swirl. It was piling up on her: the smell of the grass, Cocho's vital signs, the little brown hand resting on the back of the phone, poor homeless Mutley, Rodney's crazy mother, the green weeds creeping in at the edges.

And Tommy. Where was Tommy anyway? Why was she so far away from him?

Ellen felt a surge of anger as she answered her own question. Tommy was working. Tommy was always working. At first, when he'd elected to stay in the public defender's office, she'd been proud of him. Proud that he stuck to his lower-class values even after Harvard. But over the years, that pride had mutated into suspicion and then cynicism. When she asked him why he never tried to make it to the next rung of the ladder, he gave the same old answer—"I like my job. Somebody's gotta stick up for the poor people"—but she began to doubt him. Eventually, she accused him of being lazy, afraid, and unmotivated. "Look who's talking," Tommy said. "Look, Ellen, I know who I am. This is who I am. If you don't like it, do what you gotta do, but stop fucking busting my balls."

After several years, Ellen gave up. At holiday office parties, the young kids, just-graduated lawyers, would corner her and tell her Tommy was a local hero and a legend, and she would nod and try to ignore the fact that within five years they'd all be making more than Tommy. The whole issue was a sore point for both of them. And to top it all off, Ellen hated herself for being the wifely equivalent of a stage mother. But she couldn't help herself. His loser status in the world of lawyers bothered her.

She glanced up at the calendar. Twelve more days until the Fourth of July weekend. Maybe Tommy wouldn't even come. Ellen knew how it was in New York. If you left, the city closed over the top of your memory. People soon forgot you. New Yorkers rarely glanced backward, careening as they were, en masse, around the dangerous curves of the present, busy as they were yelling "What are you looking at!" at each other and trudging up six flights of stairs with fresh, handmade Italian tortellinis. Tommy probably had a case to prepare. He'd probably spend the long weekend with some drug lord from Washington Heights.

"Let's go out to lunch," she said to Olivier. "Let's doll up." She threw the swirl sandwich in the trash and carried the baby up the steep stairs to change clothes. Then they took off down the mountain, passing shrines to the Blessed Mother on the right and left. Every second house had an old bathtub shoved halfway into the dirt in the yard, the interior painted blue to raise associations with some distant grotto. Inside, a plaster of Paris Virgin Mary stood upon a globe or a crescent moon. Typically, her arms were ever-so-slightly raised, palms open to the world in a gesture that Ellen viewed as vaguely reminiscent of Al Jolson as he belted out the final bars of "Mammy."

"Holy Mary, mother of God, pray for us now and at the hour of our death, amen," she suddenly said. She had repeated that prayer more than a million times between the ages of seven and ten. According to the nuns, each repetition took thirty days off her afterlife sentence in Purgatory, and Ellen wanted to stockpile as much spiritual cash as possible. In fact, as a child, she had desperately wanted to be a saint, ghoulishly preserved like Mother Cabrini in a glass cabinet in a cathedral in New York City. The idea of Purgatory or, God forbid,

Hell, sucked her breath away. To burn forever was simply out of the question, and to live forever barred from the luxury of Heaven for not planning ahead was almost as bad. Ellen had repeated the "Holy Mother" with such speed that none of the words were clear except for the grand finale, the amen, which sounded in her rendition a bit like "Olé!" She counted the amens, refusing sleep until she had knocked fifty years off her future life in Purgatory.

Ellen didn't really mean to drive to Montreal, but it felt anticlimactic to dress up and then land in an orange booth in McDonald's, dipping cold french fries into a coagulated pool of ketchup. So she had driven across the border, unaware of the bucolic bliss on either side of the highway. Visions of cappuccino with kiwi fruit garnish lured her on. Maybe she would have a Camembert sandwich with avocado slices on whole wheat pita bread while Olivier moved from lap to lap in the Café L'Alibi.

Her muscles tightened as she checked the rearview mirror before changing lanes. Cars and trucks roared by on both sides and sunlight glinted off the basilica of St. Joseph's Oratory far in the distance. The radio, tuned to a French station, blasted some unfamiliar torch song in which an accordion was prominently featured. It made her want to cut her bangs and get her hair straightened. She wanted to wear Capri pants and high heels and large hoop earrings. I love the city, she thought with a dizzy burst of internal enthusiasm. To hell with country life and all it stands for.

Someone pulled out of a parking space directly in front of the café and Ellen glided in. Olivier, sound asleep in the backseat, stirred, and Ellen saw joy flood his face as he recognized the stone buildings and concrete sidewalks of his hometown. Regine-Marie was leaning on the counter reading a magazine when Ellen stepped inside. She glanced up and then bounded over to grab Olivier and smother him with kisses. Before Ellen could even sit down, a tall waitress with blond hair to her waist and deep burgundy lipstick had scooped out some ice cream for Olivier, a high chair appeared, and he was surrounded by a bevy of leggy women who wore short shorts to work.

Regine-Marie led Ellen to a corner table and sat down with her. "So how's motherhood?" she asked.

"So far, so good," Ellen said. Actually, the constant vigilance wore her out. She knew that, unless Olivier was safe in his crib, she had to keep her eyes peeled in his direction, and when he screamed, she felt totally helpless.

"He's a glorious baby," Regine-Marie said, watching Olivier with deep affection. "Good-natured."

"He's amazing, really," Ellen added, and she meant it.

"Any word from Karen?" Regine-Marie's gray eyes had grown fearful.

Ellen didn't want to say the words but she forced them out. "Not good."

Regine-Marie moved the salt shaker an inch to the left. "Hope and pray," she said without looking up.

"Hope and pray," Ellen repeated. Holy Mary, mother of God, pray for Cocho now and delay the hour of his death for many decades, amen, she said silently.

"Hungry?" Regine-Marie asked.

"Starved. I just meant to drive down to Lamone for lunch and I ended up here."

"Destiny at work."

"I guess."

"And looking very smart in your green dress, too."

Ellen smiled. "It covers a multitude of sins." She was thinking of her lumpy hips and flabby thighs.

"There are no sins," Regine-Marie said. "They don't exist in Montreal."

"Must be why I came."

"It's why everybody comes. Let me make you a sandwich." Regine-Marie pushed away from the table and disappeared into the kitchen. Ellen settled into her chair, admiring the funky elegance of the place. She was in the flow here, in this café. Part of the pulse. No sins, she thought. Could that possibly be true? Her mind drifted until it bumped into a line of poetry—John Ciardi's: "Let them all into heaven; I abolish hell!" he had written. A good philosophy of which Ellen wholeheartedly approved.

Regine-Marie arrived with a stinky cheese sandwich held together with wooden toothpicks from which festive curlicues of crinkly scarlet paper swirled. "*Merci,*" Ellen said as Regine-Marie sat down across from her. She wore a skimpy black blouse with spaghetti straps that revealed a fading upper-arm tattoo of a heart pierced with three sharp swords. Olivier was happily finger painting on the tray of his high chair with chocolate ice cream.

"Have you had any trouble covering Karen's shifts?" Ellen asked.

"Why? Are you looking for a café job?" Regine-Marie responded.

Ellen laughed. "Nope. I have my hands full at the moment."

"Really? You seem like quite the lady of leisure."

"I do?" Ellen was astonished. "How so?"

"Here you are, the very next day, back in Montreal."

"Was I just here yesterday?" Ellen asked, stunned to think that she had packed up the Honda and left this city less than twenty-four hours ago. It seemed so much longer. She had no clue why she was back so soon. And then she heard herself blurt out, "I'm scared."

Regine-Marie leaned forward. "For Cocho?"

"For Cocho. For Karen. For Olivier. For me, for you, for everybody. And for the planet. And that's just off the top of my head." Ellen tried to pass it off lightly, but it wasn't working. Regine-Marie's face was inches from her own. Ellen could see where she had amplified her lip line with the skillful use of a maroon pencil.

"Me, too," she said.

Suddenly, Ellen was sickened by the smell of the cheese, and she pushed her plate away. Her hands were white on the tabletop, as if they had temporarily merged into the Italian marble slab. Regine-Marie reached over. Her touch was warm, and Ellen could feel the hard calluses along her fingers. Maybe banging the drums kept a person in touch with the pulse of human life, she thought, the rhythms that go unnoticed, ignored, or avoided. Like death. Ellen had a powerful urge to get back in the car, twist on the ignition, and speed away. She stood up. "I need a cigarette," she said, though she didn't smoke, had never smoked, and would never smoke.

"Go take a walk around the block," Regine-Marie said.

When Ellen left the dim café, it was like stepping into an oven. She started to move, too quickly, through the heat, and rivulets of sweat ran between her breasts. Soon, she found herself standing in front of Karen's building, and she quickly let herself in and climbed the stairs. Inside the loft, dust motes tumbled in shafts of sunlight and then settled on the windowsills and tabletops. Ellen stood still, waiting for direction. The dark red bricks of the far wall looked orderly and solid, and the wooden floor, sanded and waxed, had a warm luster, as if a fire were burning somewhere deep within it. Out the window, she could see the cargo boats on the St. Lawrence and the cranes situated along the riverbank.

She went to the fridge and poured herself a glass of lemonade. On the kitchen table was a framed photo, propped up against a flower vase. In it, Karen, Olivier, and Cocho smiled from a park bench in Mt. Royal Park with the whole city spread out below them. Ellen studied the way Cocho's arm circled Karen's shoulders, the way she leaned into him and gazed fearlessly into his eyes. Olivier, standing to one side of Cocho, held a turquoise ball. He wore a baseball cap, backwards, atop his curls. Ellen lifted the picture and, like Karen, she stared into Cocho's dark eyes. They were hooded and foreign.

How had it happened, she wondered, that she did not truly know Karen's beloved? It was wrong, all wrong, unforgivable, and true. She carried the picture to the bedroom and lay down on Karen and Cocho's bed. Tears fell upon the pillowcase that smelled like rain, soaking it.

twenty-one

Ellen woke up, shocked that she had fallen asleep. A glance at the bedside clock indicated that she'd been out for just over an hour. Cucumber slices, she thought. She had read in a checkout rag that those were Elizabeth Taylor's first words as she greeted each new day. Of course, there was no maid here to cut up the cucumber and place it on her puffy eyelids, so Ellen forced herself to get up and examine the vegetable bin herself. She found a large, fresh cuke and set to work.

Ellen studied her face in the mirror before she applied the cucumber slices. Her eyes peered out from two ovals of pink skin that looked not unlike half-inflated inner tubes designed for the world's tiniest bicycle. Beneath the puffy part were green circles, the origin of which was an anatomical mystery. With a sigh, she flopped onto her back and covered her eyes with half-inch cucumber disks. Since no one was around to eat it anyway, she had sliced the entire thing and soon her whole face was buried under a layer of cool green vegetable matter. When she concentrated, she could almost feel the tension stored in the bags under her eyes being drawn slowly upward into the meat of the cuke. No wonder a lifelong babe like Elizabeth Taylor made this a habit.

Musing about Liz conjured up images of Tinsel Town and Malibu Beach, where women with ballistic tits played volleyball with surfer hunks on a daily basis. At forty-six, Ellen had finally accepted that she was not destined to be a Hollywood starlet, though periodically she still felt gypped. Secretly, she thought that Hollywood needed her, and it crossed her mind to pack up her cucumbers and go.

But then reality reared its ugly head, and Ellen knew it was time to harvest the cucumber slices, filled with psychic toxic waste, and return to the Café L'Alibi for Olivier. Unlike her, the poor kid hadn't even had a nap today. She could only hope that the sugar rush from all that ice cream would see him through until she could establish the maternal routine. She tucked Karen's family photo into her bag before she left.

It was unbearably muggy on the street, and the hair that straggled from her ponytail stuck to her neck in the sweat. She caught her reflection in a shop window and was suddenly seized with the notion that it was ridiculous for a woman of her age to have such long hair. In her youth, she'd had a name for women like the one she had become: old girls. At twenty, she had sworn she'd go gracefully and not embarrass herself in her golden years by clinging to pubescence.

Ellen darted into the first beauty salon she passed. It had posters of women for whom hair was art and a polished copper cappuccino machine. Fortunately, the stylist to whom she was assigned spoke English fluently. "I just don't want to end up looking like Brunhilda, the Olympic shot putter," she cracked, "or an old maid." The stylist, Monique, a woman with three nose rings and magenta streaks in her own black locks, laughed. "Trust me," she said as she lathered Ellen's head with shampoo that smelled like cloves. "I don't want to look like a flapper, either," Ellen added as Monique dug her fingers into her scalp.

The first cut was a twelve-inch swath from the crown of Ellen's head. As it fell to the floor, Ellen, for no apparent reason, thought of all the abuse she had endured from Reginald Eubanks as that hair grew. That was the hair of a researcher who slaved for an egotistical tyrant with a personality disorder. Like her list of work-related complaints, her ponytail had grown, weighing her down though she hadn't known it. Seeing it on the floor made her giddy. Goodbye, Reginald, she said in her mind. Good riddance, asshole.

She watched in fascination as Monique sculpted her new identity. When she stood up twenty minutes later, her head a mass of short waves that tumbled hither and thither, she felt positively lawless. At the last minute, she had her eyebrows reshaped, too, into two bold slashes that looked flung onto her forehead by a free spirit, perhaps a cosmetology Jackson Pollock or Anton Malevich.

She hurried to the Café L'Alibi, where Regine-Marie and all the other waitresses, gathered in a tight circle around her and raved at her spontaneous makeover. In her green dress and her new eyebrows, Ellen felt invincible. Harness it! she told herself as she bundled Olivier into the backseat of the car. Steer this chariot of temporary self-esteem into the fast lane! Eat my dust! she happily thought as she chomped into her Camembert sandwich, which Regine-Marie had thoughtfully refrigerated.

When she made the final turn into her driveway, it was almost dark and the buzz of the mosquitoes drowned out the chirping of the crickets. Ellen quickly rolled up the car windows and hung over the seat to free Olivier from his infant seat rather than do it from outside, thereby exposing both of them to multiple mosquito bites. Olivier's eyes drooped and he seemed to have no spine as she hefted him toward her, pushed the door open, and dashed to the house. Poor kid is pooped, she thought. And no wonder. He was living on peanut butter and jelly swirl and ice cream and flying back and forth across the border as frequently as the Mohawk smugglers from the Akwasasne reservation. Ellen vowed to be a better substitute mother as she tucked her nephew into his port-a-crib, neglecting to change his diaper even though he needed it. She dropped to her knees beside the crib to watch him breathe. What a phenomenon it was, this inhaling and exhaling the breath of life. We are all joined together in it, she thought. She got up and navigated the steep stairs, digging Karen's family photo out of her bag, then returned upstairs to place it on the nightstand, facing Olivier.

"Breathe on, Cocho," she said quietly as she continued to study the rise and fall of Olivier's tiny chest beneath the patchwork crib quilt she had found in one of Viola's old trunks. "Breathe on. I'll help you." She sat on the edge of the bed, breathing deeply, and imagined she was helping to fill Cocho's lungs with precious air. She lost track of time, and still she breathed for him, on through the night. In her dreams, she saw the white farmhouse among the weeds, and she studied it carefully. It was Viola's house, her house, but why was it in such disrepair? Why did it appear so forgotten when in fact it was full of life? The lawn was cut now, and the beefsteak tomatoes were growing in the garden. Why hadn't her dream image updated itself in her unconscious—a nod of acknowledgment from the other world. It was disturbing, as if the house were caught in a cycle of inevitable decay.

Therefore, she was relieved to be awakened by the sounds of Rodney's hammer on the roof above her head. Olivier was sitting up in his bed staring at the mysterious banging from above. The smell of fresh coffee had just begun to work its way through the cracks in the floorboards. Obviously, Rodney had used the hidden family key to let himself in. Why fight it? She might as well give in to Rodney de Beer and the customs of country life. If someone had entered her apartment on Tenth Street without permission, she would fully expect to be killed. Bloody murther. And with her luck, Tommy would end up defending the perp.

"Let's get cracking, Olivier. Another day is upon us," she said as she scooped him out of his bed and changed his diaper. When she descended the stairs, fresh donuts were already on the table, a powdered pile. She poured a cup of coffee, wondering for a split second if Rodney could be talked into climbing the stairs with a plate of cucumber slices, too.

She and Tommy had turned being waited on into an art form. Each would wake up but pretend to be asleep in the hope that the other would get up and make the coffee. Though they had never spoken of it, each knew what the other was up to. Every morning was a contest to see who could hold out longer. Luxuriating between the sheets as Tommy ground the coffee beans in the kitchen always filled Ellen with naughty glee. It was everything she could do not to gloat when he returned to bed with two steaming mugs.

She glanced up at the calendar from Baldy's store. Soon, Tommy would arrive for the long weekend. She vowed to wait on him hand and foot—bring his morning coffee, give him the side of the bed with fewer springs poking through, make him stuffed green peppers, and buy him the best bottle of full-bodied red wine in Lamone. Ellen wondered if Tommy missed her yet. Over the years, she had come to accept that she and her husband were different in every possible way. He liked oldies as background noise and she craved silence. He liked dim rooms and she preferred the glaring brightness of two-hundred-watt megabulbs. He thrived in clutter while she required surface order, even if the chaos was just stuffed into a convenient drawer.

Dunking her powdered donut into her coffee, Ellen found herself composing a mental list of the various ways in which she and Tommy had defined marriage during their years together. "It's like taking a perfect stranger and turning him into family," she had snarled once, "which is fine if you like being part of a family, which I don't." Another time she had equated marriage to slogging in the same rice paddy. Just before their tenth anniversary, she had looked up from the book she was reading in bed and said, "Gee, Tom! Just think—in a few days we will have spent an entire decade together," to which he replied, "Do me a favor, honey. When I fall asleep, smother me with a pillow," and they both laughed. At a particularly stressful moment, Tommy had even said that he believed that the wedding ceremony created an invisible third entity that put a gun to your head if you made a move to leave.

Frustration, Ellen realized, was the prime motivation for attempting to define marriage. When the chips were down, it felt like quicksand, mercilessly sucking you down. The rest of the time, it was more like a handmade cradle that rocked you gently to sleep. But even that sweet image irritated Ellen, and she made a conscious choice to get the hell off the subject.

"Let's water the garden," she said in Olivier's general direction as she tapped Skin-So-Soft into her palm and generously applied it to his skin. Powdered sugar covered the lower half of his face like a white beard. With his unruly hair, he looked like a composite drawing of Jimi Hendrix as he aged from babyhood to old age—if he had made it to old age, which he didn't. By simply thinking of a dead person, Ellen felt she had betrayed Cocho and she whispered, "Breathe on, Cocho," in an attempt to neutralize the moment.

"Hey, Rodney," she called, shielding her eyes against the sun. "How you doing up there?" He braced himself against the two-by-four he had nailed up for support and turned toward her.

" 'Morning, Ellen! Looks like you got yourself a new hairdo."

Ellen's fingers fluttered to her head.

"It makes you look ten years younger," Rodney yelled.

"Ten years? Ten *years?*" she repeated. "Thanks. And thanks for the coffee and donuts," she hollered. She was happy to see Rodney, though it was odd to launch into a morning conversation in which both parties were bellowing at the top of their lungs.

"Who's your little friend?" Rodney yelled.

"My nephew, Olivier. He's gonna be staying with me for a while." Suddenly she felt afraid that Rodney would call Olivier a colored kid. She didn't want to face that.

"Hello, little fella!" Rodney called. "Is your sister up in Montreal okay?" Ellen remembered that the last time she'd seen him, she had charged out of the house to be at Karen's side. Two days ago.

"Not really," Ellen answered. "I'll tell you about it later. We have to water and weed."

"Okay," Rodney said, and he raised his hammer high above his head in a worker's salute. Soon the bashing of his hammer filled the air. The sky behind him was bright blue, a particular shade Ellen had never seen before, and she paused for a few seconds to admire it. Mutley rose from under his tree, causing Ellen to emit a little bleat of shame. She had forgotten and left him outside all night, among the mosquitoes. "Mutley! I'm sorry! I forgot about you," she said as she ruffled his crew cut and rubbed him down with skin lotion. Olivier pounded his side and tried to pronounce his name.

Back and forth to the faucet they all traipsed. Ellen monitored Olivier's every movement, terrified that he might put a rock in his mouth and choke on it, as she dutifully pulled weeds and saturated each row of vegetables. Then she set about expanding the perimeter. She wanted a big garden, a huge garden, even if it meant she had to lug water back and forth all day. Even if it was too late to plant. She would get an early start next year.

Next year? Was she actually entertaining the concept of next year in Eagle Beak? She had unconsciously assumed her nature girl phase would blow over like all the rest of her careers. True, she couldn't be fired from this one, which put it in a whole new category. And it *was* satisfying to see the grass trimmed and the emerging plants. As she dug on, she piled rocks on the wall, and Olivier helped. Ellen could only hope he wouldn't get a hernia or that someone driving by wouldn't report her to the child labor police.

At ten thirty, everyone converged in the dining room. Ellen heated up her special open-the-heart tea and made a pot of fresh coffee for Rodney. Fastidious Rodney took Olivier to the kitchen to scrub the hardened sugar off his face with a tattersall handkerchief.

"I never thought to ask: do you have any kids, Rodney?"

"Hell, no."

"Any particular reason why not?"

Rodney stood up and seemed to seriously contemplate an answer for too long. "Not that it's any of my business," Ellen added. "Just ignore me. I shouldn't be such a Nosey Buttinski."

"I'm just thinking of how to put it," he said. "I guess I was afraid they'd be sick in the head."

"They wouldn't have been nuts, Rodney. You're too nice."

"You really don't know me," he said. "I have my problems."

"Tell me a story about Viola." Ellen didn't really know why she wanted to hear one. On principle, she disapproved of probing painful spots in another's past for her own personal entertainment, though in practice she did it all the time.

"What kind of a story?"

She didn't want to appear ghoulish. "Just the first one that pops into your head."

Rodney looked around the house, as if a visual cue might trigger the appropriate memory. "Well," he began, "she sometimes called me pumpkin. This was when I was just a boy. It always seemed kind of strange because even though it passed for an affectionate name, it never sounded like one when she said it, if you get my meaning. Then, oh . . . it must've been years later, one day I asked her what it was like to give birth and she said, 'It's like shitting a pumpkin.'" Rodney stopped to sip his coffee. He peered at Ellen over the top of his cup.

"Boy, that'll take the romance out of it," Ellen said.

"It gave me a sick feeling, I can tell you. One day, I figured out that every time she called me pumpkin, she was really calling me shit."

"Jeez," Ellen said, "that's awful." She wanted to reach out and touch him, to lay a healing hand on him, but it seemed inconsistent. You can't rip a person open and then stitch him shut and spend too much time patting yourself on the back for your sewing technique.

"I got over it," he said.

"How?"

"Leland helped me."

"What'd he do?"

"He told me my mother was too sick to know what she was saying. And he made me believe it."

"That worked, huh?"

"It worked for me."

It was the healing power of love, Ellen thought, and she rushed to the kitchen to plant a kiss on top of Olivier's furry head and turn up the flame under her open-the-heart tea. Olivier had pulled out all the pots and pans from under the sink again and was clanging them to beat the band. Ellen sat down on the floor with him.

"I just don't know how she could've been so totally awful and still crochet all these doilies and make all those beautiful patchwork quilts."

"It was her one talent." He pushed back from the table, carried his cup to the sink, and rinsed it.

"How much longer do you think the roof will take?" Ellen asked.

"Maybe three more good days after today if I'm lucky," Rodney answered as he pushed through the screen door. He headed around the corner of the house and reappeared on the ladder outside the window a few seconds later. Ellen watched as his body rose, rung by rung, out of sight. It would be good to have the hammering end, but sad to lose Rodney's company. There was something special about him and his no-frills approach to life. He could tell a heart-wrenching story and hardly miss a beat. Besides, she felt ashamed of bullying him into fixing the roof in the first place. When she weighed the occasional northwest rain against the image of that old man, an artist, spreading his bucket of roofing tar in the hot sun, it simply didn't balance out.

"Let's go for a ride," she said to her nephew. Anything to get out of the racket and away from the smell of tar. She had noticed a sign for a public beach on nearby Peak Pond. It was the perfect time to investigate, even if it meant squirming into her dreaded bathing suit and appearing in it in full public view.

twenty-two

The dirt road to the Peak Pond was filled with deep potholes, and Ellen drove it like an automotive obstacle course. Tall, spindly spruce trees lined each side with only the occasional driveway to interrupt them. On the right, an abandoned Cub Scout camp appeared. "I guess the local Cubs have gone down in flames," she commented to Olivier.

At last, the road dead-ended at the lake. A few cars had pulled to the side and parked, and Ellen noticed with a sinking feeling that Rayfield's truck was among them. It had never occurred to her that she would have to undress before an actual personal acquaintance. She freed Olivier from his car seat and gathered the beach blanket, towels, and pans and serving spoons she had brought in lieu of a bucket and shovel. Olivier held on to the fingers of her free hand and waddled as if hypnotized toward the dark water, in which a few people splashed. It was a spectacular setting if you averted your eyes from the side of the mountain, which had been clear-cut. It looked as if it had been shaved with a giant double-edged razor. Only stubble remained.

The so-called beach, dotted by a few towels and blankets, was only a bit wider than the road that led to it. On one particularly large blanket, Ellen saw two mounds of human flesh. The closer one was obviously Rayfield. Even in the glare of the sun, she recognized his cutoff sweatpants and the unmistakable contours of his beer belly. His head was turned away from Ellen, and he was deep in conversation with a rotund woman lying on her side, her head propped up on an arm that the word *meaty* did not even begin to describe.

Wide Load! Ellen thought. This was a bonus she never expected. She didn't mean to stare, but, as involved as they were in each other, they were clearly oblivious to her. Ellen couldn't help but notice the inches of cleavage that erupted from the top of Debbie's beach costume, which had as much in common with a sixties minidress as it did with a bathing suit. Rayfield could easily bury his whole face in the fold between Debbie's massive breasts. Because of her position on her side, Debbie's stomach seemed to have poured off her skeleton into a large lump in front of her, and her thighs evoked images of sumo wrestlers. Yet there was a beauty to her, a massiveness that made it clear why ancient peoples had favored tubby fertility goddesses.

Ellen spread her blanket out of earshot and, with only a semiagonizing burst of self-consciousness, slipped out of her loose sundress. She was amazed that a tan line had begun to form above her knees, where her work shorts ended, and at her shoulders. Obviously, her hours in the garden were giving her the healthy glow that paradoxically accompanies burnt flesh. Olivier seemed unsure of what to do next, and Ellen realized that this was probably his maiden voyage to a swimming hole. "Let's get in the water," she said as she helped him out of his T-shirt.

The tiny waves lapping at the edge of the lake were surprisingly warm, providing Ellen with a sensual rush as they covered and uncovered her toes. Olivier immediately squatted down and giggled. A second later, he flopped onto his belly in the sand and came up looking like one of the Mud People of the Amazon River basin. Ellen ran back to the blanket to get the saucepan and demonstrated the art of filling it up with mud and dumping it out in a perfect mold. Delighted, Olivier got busy, his spatula flying. With the sun beating down on them and the ring of gentle mountains, Ellen felt safe and protected. It was all so timeless out here in nature. She could be a cavewoman on a break from skinning a saber-toothed tiger.

"Hey," Rayfield grunted, fitting right into her prehistoric fantasy. Ellen looked up. From her position on the ground, she could see the underside of his hairy belly. She didn't even want to guess what he could see.

"Rayfield! How are you?"

"How would you be if your wife just told you she was getting married again?"

Ellen glanced quickly back to Rayfield's spot on the beach. "That's Debbie?" she asked, playing for time.

"Yep."

"Jeez, Rayfield, I don't know what to say."

He dropped into the sand beside her. "Hey, Ollie," he said flatly, adding a handful of dirt to Olivier's makeshift bucket. Ellen had never seen Rayfield so listless. A fly landed on his nose and he didn't shoo it away.

"Did you know she was seeing someone?"

"I had a feeling," Rayfield said with a sigh.

Ellen surmised that Debbie had probably met the new guy while she was still living with Rayfield—perhaps after Peyronie's disease had thrown the monkey wrench into their sex life. Rayfield had said she left four months ago. That seemed too short a time to find a boyfriend and progress all the way to matrimony. Rayfield and Debbie weren't even divorced yet as far as Ellen knew.

"Do you want her back?" Ellen asked.

"What's the use? You can't make somebody love you if they don't."

Ellen felt the cork blow out of her patience. "Why don't you fight for her?" she snapped. "Strategize! Seduce her! Show her no new guy could ever replace Rayfield Geebo."

Rayfield stared at her. "Wide Load needs a lot of sex and I can't give it to her," he said.

"For Pete's sake, Rayfield, there are lots of ways to please a woman. Get creative." She felt very wise. After a second, she reiterated, "You've got to fight for her if you love her." Rayfield, his eyes flashing with hope, glanced toward the blanket where Debbie was munching out of an oversized bag of ranch-flavored Doritos. Her chestnut brown hair was crimped in a Cleopatra style and sat on her head like a helmet. With all the extra weight, her chin seemed to proceed at a forty-five-degree angle all the way to her solar plexus. Ellen noticed that she wore fork bracelets on each wrist and had a large tattoo of Yosemite Sam accompanied by the words "Back off!" just above her ankle. Debbie stared at Ellen with undisguised curiosity. Ellen raised her fingers to form a little wave, but before she could direct it across the open space, Debbie abruptly turned away.

"I don't know," Rayfield said. "We had our shot and it just didn't work out."

"How long were you married anyway?"

"Oh, about fifteen years."

Fifteen years! Almost as long as hers and Tommy's. It sent a cold chill up Ellen's backbone. "I thought it was less than that," she mumbled. Would Tommy fight for her if she started to drift away? Would she be able to lure him back if he suddenly announced that he had met someone else and was preparing to take the flying leap into fresh love? Suddenly, her advice to Rayfield sounded hollow.

"You wanna meet her?"

Ellen got to her feet. "Sure." She left Olivier with his toys and started across the tiny beach a half step behind Rayfield. His stringy hair brushed his shoulders and his sweatpants had dipped dangerously close to the crack in his ass—something Ellen truly did not want to see, then or ever.

"Debbie, this is Ellen, the nut I told you about."

Ellen threw a playful punch at Rayfield's upper arm. "Hey!" she said, "Show a little respect." She shifted her eyes to Debbie. "Hi. It's nice to finally meet you."

"Hi," Debbie replied in a voice as breathy as Marilyn Monroe's or Melanie Griffith's. "You're the one who bought Viola's place, right?"

"Right."

"So how do you like it?"

Keeping Olivier in the center of her field of vision, Ellen dropped down to sit primly on the edge of the blanket. "I bought it on the spur of the moment without really knowing why," Ellen began. She had not told a living soul except Tommy about her dream of the house. Most people didn't accept that kind of hooey, though Ellen firmly believed in it. Once, in New York, on her way to an important meeting and running late, she had been overwhelmed with a desire for a Tootsie Roll. She darted into the nearest candy store and stood before the candy display, but there was not a Tootsie Roll in sight. She herself hadn't had one nor even thought about them for years. Maybe Tootsie Rolls had gone the way of Brown Cow all-day suckers and those little colored candy dots that came on a long strip of white paper, she thought as she'd dashed for the No. 6 train and wedged herself into a seat next to a blond woman with a slim briefcase on her lap upon which rested some official document. Ellen surreptitiously stole a glance at it. It was an annual report, and as the woman turned the page, there were the figures for the Tootsie Roll Corporation. Ellen yelped, and the woman gave her a cold stare and shifted her shoulder into Ellen's line of sight.

Precog was real, she knew. And so were ESP, prophetic dreams, déjà vu, and bending spoons through mind power, like Uri Geller did. But like all mysteries, they revealed themselves only to those with proven faith. These thoughts piled one on top of one other like a mental layer cake that Ellen was tempted to serve to Debbie. After all, Debbie already thought she was a nut. She probably knew all about the rain barrel episode and getting her mouth stuck open, too. Plus, it was nice to hear a female voice for a change. Girl talk, like going braless in public, had evaporated when she crashed through the barrier into middle age.

Rayfield conveniently chose this moment to speak up. "Mind if I take Ollie in the water?"

"Go ahead. Just be careful."

"Cripes, Ellen, what do you think I'm gonna do? Toss him into the deep end?"

"She's just nervous, Rayfield. Don't give her any crap about it," Debbie said. Rayfield shook his head and oafed off.

"Avoiding responsibility's been my lifetime goal," Ellen confided. "Then I show up here and before I even know what's happened, I've got a house to fix up, a garden that needs water"—she turned her head to keep a sharp eye on Rayfield—"an eighteen-month-old, a dog . . ." It was the perfect moment to find out Debbie's intentions regarding Mutley, but before she could form the words, Debbie said, "A guy," in a tone loaded with subtext.

"Huh?" Ellen said.

Debbie jerked her chins in Rayfield's direction. "Rayfield," she said.

"What do you mean 'guy'?" Ellen said stupidly. "You mean *Rayfield?*"

"What's wrong with Rayfield?"

"I'm married, for God's sake," Ellen blustered. "I'm not looking for a *guy*. Why? Did Rayfield say something?" Ellen would crown him if he had.

"No, but you two are pretty chummy."

Maybe Debbie was jealous. Ellen was torn between nipping this mutant fantasy in the bud and egging it on in the hope that she might somehow facilitate a reunion between Rayfield and his beloved Wide Load.

"It's just friendly," she said mysteriously. Let Debbie interpret that as she wanted.

"You seem pretty friggin' anxious to help him clear up his . . . condition," Debbie persisted.

"Look, I'm a professional researcher. Once I sink my teeth into something, I can't let go." Giddy panic began to boil up inside her. "How's he doing with that anyway? Any progress?" Ellen hoped there was. Debbie didn't say a word. She just regarded Ellen suspiciously.

"Look, we're starting off on the wrong foot here," Ellen said. "Let's change the subject." She paused for a brief second. "So what are your plans for Mutley?"

"What's it to you?"

"Well, I *am* an interested party," Ellen said, taken aback.

"Why?"

"Well . . . because Rayfield gave him to me."

"Rayfield gave you Mutley?" It was clearly news to Debbie. Her neck turned bright red as if it were filling up with fresh blood. "Rayfield!" she bellowed. "Get over here!"

Ellen was shocked at Debbie's tone. She sounded like one of those despicable Mommie Dearests who yank their children along by their upper arms, nearly dislocating their little shoulders in the process. She and Tommy never spoke to each other in such a way. It wasn't right.

Rayfield, however, seemed to take it in stride. He ignored her completely.

"Why don't you leave him alone?" Ellen said evenly. She would've added

"Pick on somebody your own size," but Rayfield was more or less in the same ballpark. She hadn't the slightest clue why she was sticking up for Rayfield Geebo. Perhaps to atone for all the times she'd seen those angry mothers abusing their kids on the streets of New York and been too afraid to step in. Or perhaps it was because she had never, before Debbie, felt free to conduct a conversation that broke all the rules of civilization. "You walked out on Mutley. It's not your business what Rayfield does with him anymore."

"Aw, shut up," Debbie said.

Ellen was completely nonplused. This was becoming surreal. She was heading toward fisticuffs with a woman she'd only known two minutes. Worse, she actually wanted to get into it, win, slay this current dragon. A moment from the sixties, from Somerville, erupted in her mind like a volcano. She had met a guy at a party and he'd taken an instant dislike to her, perceiving her every word as a direct confrontation. Unsure of how to handle it, Ellen had stubbed out the joint she was smoking in the potato salad this man had just heaped on his plate. It was her way of drawing a line in the sand, but instead of escalating the tension, it short-circuited it. Both had stared at the marijuana roach smoldering atop the mountain of potatoes for two uncomprehending seconds and then burst into healing laughter, the kind that had them both doubled over and slapping each other on the back. She still got Christmas cards from him every year.

Debbie was glaring at her with her chins extended. It was a clear message, like the tattoo above her ankle, that she was warning Ellen to back off.

"Don't even think of telling me what to do," Ellen hissed in a monotone, steady-eyed. It was an adaptation of the New York City street sign that she most loved: DON'T EVEN THINK OF PARKING HERE. Ellen felt like David with Debbie as her personal Goliath. It took courage to load her verbal slingshot instead of turning and running away. With the two fork bracelets and her crimped hair, Debbie looked like a wrathful ancient goddess, one that could order locusts or boils for periods of up to seven years.

The two women stared at each other under the hot sun of the North Country. In the midst of it, Rayfield, carrying a sopping wet Olivier in the crook of his arm, ambled up. "You rang?" he said to Debbie in a perfect imitation of Maynard G. Krebs, the hero of Ellen's youth.

"She says you gave her Mutley."

"Yeah? So?"

Point for Rayfield, Ellen thought.

"So Mutley's my fucking dog."

"Hey, you're lucky I took him. Rayfield was going to dump him off at the dog pound," Ellen said, shamelessly whipping it up. It was her golden opportunity to get even with Rayfield for his cigarette caper at the bridge to Canada.

"I did what I did," Rayfield said, essentially ignoring Ellen.

"Yeah, what're you gonna do about it?" Ellen piped up.

Debbie's voice hardened. "You go get Mutley. You bring him back home."

"No," Rayfield said. "You go get him and take him home to your new boyfriend."

"Nobody's taking Mutley," Ellen said for no reason. She pushed herself to her feet and extended her hands for Olivier to fall into. She knew she should escape before the prevailing winds blew her even farther off course. Why was she fighting for Mutley? She didn't want him. She lived in fear that she'd get stuck with him. It was insane.

"I'll leave you two kids to work it out," she said as she strolled away. She could feel the flab on her rear end jiggle a little as she made her exit. The logical thing was to pack up and go home, but she'd barely arrived and she had no wish to subject herself to a long day of Rodney's roof-banging. Besides, she was sick of giving in to the impulse to escape. If she'd exerted a little more self-control in that area, she would not have landed in Eagle Beak in the first place, let alone be calling out a female heavyweight. Still, it felt perverse to drop anchor where she knew she probably wasn't wanted. But hey, she thought, as she deposited Olivier back at the water's edge and helped him refill his sand bucket, it's a public beach. Behind her, Rayfield and Debbie spoke to each other in low tones. No words were discernible and Ellen didn't dare peek over her shoulder.

Long-married couples, she knew, turned their communication patterns into deep ruts. For years, probably, Debbie had been barking out orders to Rayfield, and Rayfield had treated each one like so much water off a duck's back. Whatever level of tension this created was obviously bearable to both. Or more correctly, it had been for fifteen years, at which time Debbie had strolled out the door, permanently. But did that eliminate the rut, or would they both stumble back into it each time they were together?

And what about the rut she was in with Tommy? On the surface, they were doing just fine. But just below it, it didn't feel so good. Ellen wasn't even certain she could define it, though she did take a moment to list a few complaints off the top of her head. She hated Tommy's drinking, but she put up with it. He was a workaholic who spent too much time at the office. He was infuriatingly steady. He never tried anything new. He was frequently emotionally distant. He was always tired and his sex drive was at an all-time low. She had to face facts: she'd probably put on blinders long ago and, with no peripheral vision, had failed to notice how high the walls of the rut were around her. Now that she had airlifted herself out, she didn't want to fall back in. One way to avoid doing the same old thing was to do everything differently. Like staying here at Peak Pond Beach, taking the heat of Debbie's Mutley-based wrath. She watched her shadow on the sand in front of her. Her new short curls formed an irregular halo around her head. "I abolish hell," she whispered as she splashed her nephew with warm water. "Let them all into heaven."

twenty-three

That night, Ellen had a dream about Viola de Beer. She was certain it was Viola, though she had never seen a picture of her nor heard a detailed description. In the dream, an old woman with deeply etched frown lines stood in an overgrown field in the midst of a thunder and lightning storm. Though rain pelted the earth, she remained dry. Her steel-gray hair was pinned up into a small bun, and she wore a simple dress with long sleeves. Because her arms were wrapped around herself, she appeared to be in a dark brown straightjacket.

Suddenly, Viola started to run. Her legs were powerful, almost manly, under her drab dress, and her bare feet grew bloody as she pounded over pointy rocks and through bramble bushes. Each time lightning struck, Viola's form was momentarily outlined in neon colors in the gloom. Ahead, Ellen saw a dark hole, a cave entrance not unlike the one leading to an abandoned iron mine in the rock face of Eagle Beak Mountain. It looked forbidding, cool, and dangerous, like a tomb, and Viola seemed hell-bent to get there. Before Ellen's eyes, Viola reached the entrance. She glanced wildly back over her shoulder, a look that nearly stopped Ellen's heart. Then she stooped low and entered. Darkness closed around her form and thunder crashed. Then the whole dream went soundless and opaque, and Ellen woke up, afraid. She lay in bed, comforted by Olivier's rhythmic breathing. "Viola?" she whispered fearfully as she pulled the patchwork quilt over her shoulders and turned onto her side. "Viola?" she repeated before she drifted back into sleep.

She woke early and this time, when Rodney appeared, she had his coffee and her tea brewed and yesterday's leftover donuts in place. She stood in the dining room like a black widow spider waiting for him to climb out of the truck and come to the door.

"You're up bright and early," he called.

"It happens every blue moon," Ellen replied, determined to contain herself until Rodney got settled at the table. The second his behind hit the chair she said, "I had a dream last night. I think your mother was in it."

"If it wasn't a nightmare, it wasn't my mother," Rodney said as he cut his donut into the bite-sized chunks he preferred.

"It was disturbing, but I wouldn't call it a real nightmare," Ellen said. "The woman I saw was tiny. She had a tight gray bun and skin that looked wrinkled and weather-beaten. Did your mother look like that?"

"What old lady don't?" asked Rodney. Obviously, he had never seen the well-preserved senior females of Park Avenue and Rodeo Drive, the septuage-narians who maintained the dewy skin of youth via collagen injections and biannual face-lifts, who wore their hair like Tina Turner and attended water aerobics classes five days a week.

"Was your mother tiny?"

"She weighed no more than ninety pounds soaking wet."

Ellen sipped her tea. "Did she wear her hair in a bun?"

"When she bothered to comb it."

Ellen dropped into her chair. "Rodney, isn't this sort of amazing? I dreamed up your mother without ever seeing her—without even seeing a picture of her."

"Well, I dream from time to time about Robert De Niro, and I don't think nothing of it."

"That's different. Everybody knows what he looks like."

Rodney was collecting the donut crumbs by pressing them individually onto the tines of his fork.

"Will you show me the sculptures you did up in the woods? The first ones—the ones you did to keep from killing her?" She distinctly remembered Rodney describing them as gargoyles.

"What? Now?"

"There's no time like the present," she said cheerfully. She always reverted to optimistic clichés when she wanted something from an older person.

"I ain't been up there in years." His voice was as full of doubt and misgiv-ing as hers was bursting with enthusiasm. "It's probably all overgrowed. And after thirty years, there probably ain't nothing left of them."

"Come on, Rodney. Think of it as a field trip. A roots tour."

"That's the last thing I need."

Ellen was not prepared for such resistance. "Humor me, will ya, Rodney?" she begged.

"Oh, okay, but let's go later after I get something done on the roof."

"Deal!"

Rodney finished his coffee and left, and Ellen and Olivier puttered in the garden with Mutley asleep in the nearby shade. Ellen could barely look at him. It would be just like Debby to leave him here for spite, she thought, just to get even with her for her imaginary affair with Rayfield. On the other hand, it had been years since anyone had even remotely suspected her of being the other woman.

Just the thought of threatening other women made her want to talk to Tommy. There was a slight chance he'd be in his office, so she dialed his number.

"Thomas Kenny," he said on the second ring. Ellen's heart expanded and was happy.

"Tommy," she said, "I just needed to hear your voice."

"Ellen?"

Who else would it be, she thought.

"How are you, honey?" he asked.

"Good. You?"

"Busy. I have to be in court in twenty minutes."

"Then you don't have time to talk," she said reasonably, though she had to summon all her self-sacrifice to form the words.

"Any word on Cocho?"

"None."

"That's tough."

"Yeah." There was a brief silence. "Let's talk tonight, Tom. I know you need to get off the phone."

"I'm gonna be out late tonight. I'll call you in the morning."

"Okay. Talk to you tomorrow."

"Are you all right, Ellen?"

"Fine." It was a lie.

"Because I have to go."

"Go in peace," she laughed, desperately wanting to end it all on a lighter note, even if it had to be manufactured out of nothing. They hung up. Tommy had inadvertently torn a hole in the curtain Ellen had pulled across her worries about Cocho. "Breathe on, Cocho," she said, her magic spell. Impulsively, she dialed the hospital in Lima, but the call did not go through.

Karen, not available. Tommy, not available. Even Rodney was not available, and she didn't feel like searching out Rayfield. Who was left? She had a Filofax full of names, but she felt (and was) disconnected from each one. She had pulled the plug on her life, voluntarily gone into the isolation tank long before she up and moved to Eagle Beak. Now she was three hundred and fifty miles away from her life, whatever condition it was in. And for what? For what? To dream about Viola de Beer, a known maniac? To resurrect her Catholic bedtime prayers on behalf of poor, comatose Cocho? To pick fights with strangers on a public beach? To heckle her new best friend into revisiting a personal but painful fork in his life path, the place he'd first transformed his rage into art?

Maybe I should go on Prozac, like everybody else in New York, she thought. If you cleared away all your distractions and the only feeling that surfaced was despair, it might be time to hop on the better-living-through-chemistry bandwagon. She'd loved drugs in the sixties when they represented rebelliousness. Now that they had made it into the mainstream, though, she resisted them. She'd rather rely on the fourfold breath endorsed by the Dalai Lama, though she had no idea what it was or how to perform it. Maybe she would make a trip to the library later to find out. In the meantime, she would have to fortify herself with her open-the-heart tea and try to view each difficult moment with ever-increasing detachment.

When Rodney finally descended from the roof, the sweat pouring down his red face in salty torrents, Ellen was reluctant to ask any more of him. He had done enough for one day. But over the hours, the idea of searching out his original chain saw sculptures had obviously taken hold of his psyche, and now he actually wanted to go. Ellen covered herself and Olivier with mosquito repellent and handed the bottle to Rodney. Then they all traipsed across the dirt road toward the woods, toward the rock face of Eagle Beak Mountain looming above. Even Mutley came along.

Aside from the lawn and the garden, Ellen's fourteen acres were basically a tangle of brush and berry bushes, rocks and trees, weeds and ancient barbed wire fences, collapsed and half-buried in the dirt. There was no path to follow, so Ellen hiked Olivier up onto her shoulders to keep him from getting scratched by the various thorns. He weighed a ton. Actually, Ellen's back had seriously ached ever since she took over care of her nephew. Rodney walked ahead, apparently following some inner compass. Determined not to lose sight of him, even for a second, Ellen stayed within six feet. She thought about her dream, how her imaginary Viola had charged through this same field toward the gaping mouth of the cave above and disappeared into its darkness with only one short, but chilling, glance back toward civilization.

"Is your mother buried on this property?"

"There are laws against that," Rodney said. He had his arms extended for balance, and the particular bramble patch he was stepping through created the impression that he was modeling a wide hoopskirt.

"So where is she?"

"She wanted to be cremated and throwed into the ocean. Why, I don't know. She never even saw the ocean in her whole lifetime except in pictures. Jeez, it's really growed up in here." He held back the brush so she could pass through.

"So did you do what she asked?"

Rodney hesitated. "In a way." He seemed disinclined to say more, and Ellen, pushing her way through the undergrowth, couldn't summon the concentration to pry. A few moments later, Rodney announced, "I think we're coming to it."

The old tree trunk stood in a small clearing. Ellen put Olivier down on the moss that grew like a living carpet on a huge, flat rock. Predictably, Mutley rolled over on his side and went to sleep. The top half of the tree had cracked off, obviously by lightning, and lay rotting on the ground. The vertical trunk, standing perhaps eight feet high, on which Rodney had launched his chain saw career, had survived many brutal winters in the North Country, and it had long splits in it and several areas where the bark had fallen off in long, curved chunks. The original gargoyle was more of a suggestion now, a monster that time had pounded on in determination to transform it, like everything else, into harmless dust.

"This sure brings back memories," Rodney said. "My mother was going at me and going at me, and before I knew what was what, I had the chain saw in my hands and I knew I wanted to have at it. So I just took off, running to beat the band. I ran all the way up here."

Ellen made a three-hundred-and-sixty-degree turn. She couldn't see anything but wilderness in any direction. "We're pretty far from the house."

"It was easier to get here then. It was mostly fields."

Ellen studied the sculpture before her. It definitely evoked images of the satanic beasts that mocked all of Paris from the steeple of the Notre Dame cathedral. Was it a picture of Rodney's individual rage? Or was it a form that simply demanded periodic expression in all the corners of the world? Did this image, and others like it, signify the irrational impulses of the human being? Could it contain them? More important, did they always crumble and disappear over time? This one certainly had.

Rodney sat down on a convenient rock and wiped off his forehead with his handkerchief. "Took me two solid hours to do this one," he said. "I was in a frenzy. Half the time, I was working above my head. That's hard on the arm muscles, believe you me. And I don't think I would've stopped, but I ran out of gas."

"Had you cooled off by then?"

"It got my mind off my mother. See, I never did nothing like that before. I had no idea I had it in me. So afterward, my focus kind of changed. I started thinking about what I could do instead of what I couldn't."

Ellen pondered this for several seconds.

"Did you ever show it to her?"

"Hell no. She had a way of taking things away from you."

Ellen removed a clump of moss from Olivier's mouth, and he started to scream. She moved him into her lap, but he wrestled away and she let him go. He waddled to a nearby rock and sat on it. "So what did you do with your mother's ashes?" she finally asked.

"Oh . . . I tossed them in the Boston Harbor." He sounded as if his mind was on something else.

Ellen laughed, a little bleat. "Well, that's the sea, too," she said.

"I went on one of them historical tours to 'Old Ironsides.' When nobody was looking, I just chucked her overboard, urn and all."

Viola of the Open Sea and the Oil Slicks! Viola of the Toxic Harbor Waters! Patron Saint of Ultimate Liberation, her ashes mingling with the remnants of the Boston Tea Party. Amen to her and all she stood for, and good riddance. Ellen climbed atop a mini-boulder and scanned the landscape, attempting to get her bearings. From this high perch, she could see the dark opening of the Eagle Beak iron mine. "In my dream, Viola ran into that cave up there," she said, pointing. "Did it have any special meaning to her?"

"Not that I know of."

Ellen felt the familiar thud of disappointment. She had hoped to find the bridge between real life and the dreamworld. She was a detective who knew there were clues everywhere but for some reason couldn't recognize them.

"I wouldn't get it into my head to go poking around in that cave," Rodney said. "It's an old iron mine, full of shafts. You'd either fall into one or get lost and never find your way out."

"Don't worry. Caves are not my thing." When Viola had entered it in the dream, it seemed acceptable that she would never come out again. Ellen scrambled down off the rock and sat down with Olivier, who had stretched out full length next to Mutley on the moss and seemed to be on the verge of a spontaneous nature nap. Ellen stroked his curls and watched as his eyelids lowered like old-fashioned shades over his eyes.

She turned her attention to the chain saw sculpture. The pointy ears of the beast were worn to stubs and its snout had broken off in some long ago wind, but Ellen could almost hear the roar of the chain saw as Rodney held it above his head and carved into the tree trunk. Now he was an old man who lived alone among the creatures of his imagination. They filled his hillside fields and his barn. They sat in front and backyards across several states. He gave them life and they gave it back.

Ellen felt a burning in her chest, as hot as the sun that had baked her golden brown in Mexico. She thought suddenly that she could actually discern the contours of her inner organs—her liver and gall bladder, diaphragm and bronchial tubes, lungs and pancreas. Her heart. It was a sacred moment.

"I love you, Rodney," she announced, shocking herself.

"Huh?"

"I love you," Ellen calmly repeated. What the hell was in Dr. Yi's tea anyway? Love Potion No. 9?

"That's what I thought you said."

"Don't get nervous." Ellen giggled. "I'm talking about person love, not the kind that causes all the trouble." She felt serene. Olivier was snoring lightly in harmony with Mutley and there were white butterflies riding the gentle air currents. "Thank you for bringing me here," she said.

"Why?" Rodney suddenly asked, and for a moment Ellen could not recall what he was referring to. Instead, she remembered a time a dozen years ago when, under hypnosis, she had been prompted by her hypnotherapist to explain why she loved her husband. "Because he just goes along, and then every once in a while he looks over his shoulder and says, 'See how I'm going along here, Ellen?'" she had answered. It had seemed so absurd that the therapist chuckled, almost breaking the trance. Ellen remembered it vividly, not only the words but the feeling that inspired them.

"Because you just keep going along," she said to Rodney. "Because no matter what, you keep on keeping on."

"That's what everybody does," Rodney said.

Then let them all into heaven, Ellen thought, but she said, "You got style, Rodney."

"And you got bats in the belfry, Ellen," he said. He smiled, as if he chose to tease her as a way to deflect her compliment and goodwill.

"I said something nice to you. Don't push it back at me," she snapped.

Rodney looked both startled and sad. He moved away from her, about an inch.

Now she felt repentant. "Wait! I take that back! I'm sorry, Rodney."

Rodney pushed himself to his feet. "Ready to shove off?"

"Okay." She picked up Olivier, slung him over her shoulder like a bag of imported coffee beans, and off they trudged through the briars toward home. With each step, Ellen regretted the verbal snipe she'd made at Rodney. She couldn't take it back, and she couldn't let it go. If she stewed in it too long, though, she'd end up throwing herself naked into a convenient briar patch, like St. Francis of Assisi did for pleasure. There were endless mortification possibilities for the truly penitent, though nothing she could do could erase the fact that she'd used her words to stroke Rodney de Beer with one hand and then slapped him silly with the other. She thought of Sister Monica, the terror of her second-grade life, who would stand, enraged, in front of the classroom, dandruff clearly visible in her eyebrows, and holler, "Get up here!" to some sinner who had not learned the correct catechism answers and then, after the poor kid humbly and fearfully slunk to the teacher's desk, she'd bellow, "Go far away from me!" It had happened to Ellen so many times that she never knew if she was coming or going. She even developed a way of doing a dramatic about-face at precisely the right moment that set the other children's mouths atwitch in their efforts to control their laughter. Now she was playing Sister Monica, and the worst part was that she didn't know why.

When they got to the driveway, Rodney made a beeline for his truck. "Whew, that was a workout," he said as he paused to extract the pickers and burdocks out of his socks. "I ain't been back in them fields for a month of Sundays."

"Thanks for taking me," Ellen said.

"Don't mention it."

"Rodney?"

"Yeah?" His hand was resting on the door handle now.

"I'm sorry I was so testy."

"You're making a mountain out of a molehill."

"I still wish I could take it back."

"Forget it. I'll see you in the morning. Bye, little fella," he said. Olivier waved bye-bye until the truck was long gone.

The second she entered the house, Ellen phoned Dr. Yi. It was a bit early for her follow-up visit, but she wanted to grill him about the open-the-heart tea she was drinking to the tune of six cups a day. If she was professing love to Rodney in the shadow of a gargoyle, then it must be working. On the other hand, she had deliberately instigated a fracas with Wide Load. Perhaps one or the other of these recent events was a backlash. She simply had to know.

Mrs. Yi answered on the third ring and gave her an appointment for the following day. As she hung up, it occurred to Ellen that perhaps she and Rayfield could book back-to-back appointments and drive over together. Then he could watch Olivier in the waiting room while she consulted with the doctor.

She dialed his number.

"Yo," he answered.

"Hey, Rayfield, it's Ellen."

"Oh, great."

"Your enthusiasm is touching."

"Yeah, well, I know you want something. What is it?"

"Hey, I'm truly offended. This is a social call."

"My fat ass," he said. "Give. What do you want?"

Ellen was tempted to belt out that old hit tune, "I Just Called to Say I Love You," but she didn't. "I just wondered if you worked out the Mutley issue with Debbie."

"What's to work out?"

"Jeez, Rayfield, Mutley's whole future for one thing."

Rayfield hesitated just long enough for Ellen to get nervous. "I see the New York City skyline in Mutley's future."

"Rayfield, don't you dare," Ellen growled.

"Serve you right," Rayfield said and he laughed, evilly.

Ellen decided not to take it up at the moment. "Are you still going to see Dr. Yi? Because I'm going over tomorrow and I thought we could drive together if you are."

"What time you going?"

"I set up an appointment at one before I thought of calling you. Want me to call them back and see if they can fit you in before or after?"

"I'll handle it. If you don't hear otherwise, I'll be pulling into your driveway at noon tomorrow." He hung up. Ellen sat down in the living room, unconsciously smoothing out the wrinkles on Viola's handmade antimacassars. She felt a deep need to sort out her thoughts, but they were all stuck together in a lump, as if her mind was filled with paste. It was impossible to unglue any particular thought, feeling, or idea, so she just sat there and listened to Olivier's babyish babble as he scratched his toy truck back and forth over the floorboards.

twenty-four

Ellen felt like a teenager the next morning, waiting for the phone to ring. Tommy had promised to call, so she focused on that instead of her curiosity about where he had been so late last night. She enjoyed the flutter of anticipation as she fingered her new waves back from her face and studied her reflection in the cloudy mirror above the bathroom sink. Ellen actually liked the crow's-feet, or, as she preferred to call them, laugh lines, that were beginning to stretch horizontally from her eyes. They reminded her of that exaggerated kohl eyeliner that Cleopatra favored, and she liked to think that each fraction of an inch represented a time she had laughed until her sides ached. The loosening of her jawline gave her much less pleasure. Her shoulders still looked okay, but her breasts were already settling against her rib cage. When she adjusted her bra straps to hike them up, the straps simply readjusted themselves down by the end of the day. She was seriously considering sewing them into place with something strong, like dental floss or fishing line.

Ellen Kenny was about to turn forty-seven, barreling through the decade so fast she rarely admitted to herself how difficult it was to watch life as she had come to know it carried off by the inexorable tide of time. Her good looks, her sex appeal, her ambition—gone! All gone! Her energy was watered-down and soon her vaginal fluids would dry up. Her menstrual cycle was AWOL, the rusty-colored blood arriving ahead of schedule some months and not at all in others.

The woman staring back at her from the mirror was not Ellen. Ellen was an old soul in a young body, not the reverse. Hair and skin, jowls and breasts, knees and buttocks—they were all slipping downward, returning to the earth according to Mother Nature's cruel plan. "Even my ears are lower," Ellen announced to her image as she studied the little vertical stretch lines that had formed at the point where her ears connected to the side of her face. It was totally depressing. She tried to stretch the skin back, upward into her hairline as, she had read in a checkout rag, Sophia Loren did, but her face just slid back downward, and Ellen began to cry.

Then the phone rang. Ellen didn't want to talk to anybody, not even Tommy. She threw herself on her lumpy bed and counted the rings. Each one was an assault. They stabbed the silence and left residual trauma in the form of echoes. One barely ended before the next began. There were seven before the house returned to silence, and then they started up again. Seven more, and then sacred stillness. She had barricaded off the top of the stairs so Olivier would not tumble down, and then set him free. She could hear him in the next room.

The image of Viola disappearing into the mouth of the dark cave appeared before her eyes. Viola's last look over her shoulder was permanently etched into Ellen's subconscious and taking on a life of its own, showing up in her thoughts, uninvited. She studied its strange mixture of terror and peace, dread and excitement—the look on the face of the moth as it dives toward the flame. Viola's glance had raised Ellen's blood pressure when she saw it in her dream, but now she felt drawn into it, like Richard Dreyfuss toward the spaceship at the end of *Close Encounters of the Third Kind* or Kevin Costner toward the meadow as he cleared the way for baseball in *Field of Dreams*. But Dreyfuss got to go off in a flying saucer and Costner got to solve a mystery from his past and watch a home game, too. What was in it for Ellen?

Cogitating this required a suspension of disbelief, not one of Ellen's more developed talents. She was a doubter, not a believer. She was a researcher and a realist. She knew from her reading that women's lives were traditionally split into three parts: virgin, mother, and crone. In theory, the first was full of potential; the second, maternal satisfaction. But part three was a big blank, unless you bought the notion that acquired wisdom made up for the loss of everything else. But what if your virginity was tossed off with abandon to a boy you never saw again nor wanted to? What if you skipped phase two entirely? What if Viola de Beer was coughed up from your personal unconscious as the quintessential crone? Just because she had made it to the finish line and been thrown over the railing of "Old Ironsides" into Boston Harbor, it didn't make her a perfect master, after all. Viola had, by all accounts, been a crummy person.

Was it crummy to let the phone ring fourteen times, thereby disappointing and possibly even worrying one's husband? She imagined Tommy standing in the kitchen on Tenth Street, slowly replacing the phone receiver on its hook. He would be puzzled, maybe even feel personally rejected. But Ellen didn't care. She had her hands full at the moment, just accepting her sagging face. Tommy would have to get along without her while she licked her wounds in private.

Olivier stepped into the room, dragging his favorite blanket behind him like the train of a bridal gown. It took only a few seconds for the entire room to fill with a vile smell. "Oh, good, fresh shit," Ellen said. She held her breath as she scraped Olivier's tiny buttocks. He was a beautiful baby, a beautiful boy, and she loved him more with each passing day, but being a substitute mother was exhausting. Her private psychic space was now crowded, and she missed her freedom. She had to watch Olivier every second. It required complete personal sacrifice. And it lasted so very long for mothers. No wonder modern women were saying no in record numbers. To her surprise, Ellen found herself feeling grateful that the full experience of motherhood had passed her by. For some people, caring cost too much. Perhaps, Ellen thought as she powdered Olivier's bottom, she was one of them. It didn't make her a bad person. Or did it?

"Let's go downstairs," she said, lifting Olivier to her hip. "I need my tea and you need cereal." She negotiated the stairs and arrived safely in the living room just as Rodney turned into the driveway. "There's Uncle Rodney," she said, and Olivier squirmed to get down.

"Hey, Rodney," Ellen called as he came in.

"'Morning, Ellen. Coffee ready?"

"I'm putting it on right now."

Rodney took his traditional place at the table and opened the paper sack that contained the day's supply of donuts.

"Anything new?" Ellen asked. His eyes were seriously bloodshot and Ellen was certain she could smell booze on him.

"Not a damn thing I know of," Rodney said and then added, "Well, one thing. After you told me about your dream and all, I remembered I had a couple pictures of my mother. So I went looking for them." He pulled a white envelope out of the bib pocket of his overalls and shoved it across the table.

Her psychic radar was beeping furiously. It wasn't hard to put the picture together: she had pressed Rodney about Viola, coerced him into a trip into no-man's-land. There, in the shadow of his gargoyle, she had played with his mind by declaring her love and then, instantly, turning on him. He had gone home and searched for pictures of his departed mother. Obviously, he had started drinking. Even at that moment, he pulled a silver flask from the pocket of his overalls and placed it next to his coffee cup. Ellen ignored that and didn't reach for the envelope either. "Jeez, I'm afraid to look," she said.

"You're the one who had to go and have the dream," he said. There was mean-spiritedness in his voice. "You asked for it."

"That I did," Ellen said calmly, but now she wanted to keep the truth at bay. With Rodney breathing down her neck, though, she couldn't wimp out.

"Quit stalling," Rodney said.

Ellen reached for the envelope and lifted the flap and pulled out three photos. Two were black-and-white with scalloped edges, a style of print so old that she only vaguely recalled it from her childhood. The third was glossy and in color. She put all three in a row in front of her on the table.

"Them black-and-white ones are from the forties," Rodney said. "I took them myself."

Ellen leaned forward to study the first one. "Was this taken here?" she asked in amazement, for there were only rolling hills, covered with grass, and a few scattered trees. The two maples at the mouth of the driveway were already fully grown and Viola stood leaning against one. She wore a cardigan sweater, a straight skirt, and socks with her lace-up shoes.

"Right out front."

"It looks so . . . so cared for. I almost didn't recognize it."

"A lot happens in fifty years," Rodney said as he stepped into the kitchen to pour his coffee. When he set the cup on the table, he opened his flask and dumped a healthy shot of whiskey into it.

"You're not going up on the roof today, are you?" Ellen asked.

"That's what I'm here for," Rodney said.

"But you're drinking. I don't want you to fall." She felt a little explosion of panic in her chest.

"Don't worry about it," Rodney said.

Not knowing what else to do, Ellen helplessly focused on the figure of Viola de Beer. She was probably in her early thirties in the picture, which was not only faded but also slightly out of focus. Viola's face was actually a double image and therefore not defined. She looked squint-eyed and scrawny, her chin was sharp enough to open a can of beans, and her body was slightly bent, as if her skin was stretched too tight over her skeleton.

The second picture had obviously been taken the same day. This time, Viola sat on the concrete steps leading to the front porch. Her knees were clamped together and bent to the side. Again, the image was not clear, though Viola's long, dark hair was visible, clipped back from both sides with barrettes. It was absolutely straight—the kind of hair that wouldn't make it into the fashion world until the British Invasion of the early sixties. "What color was your mother's hair?"

"Shit brown," Rodney answered.

"She looks pretty," Ellen said, not really meaning it but feeling compelled to say something, as if the right words might smooth out the tension that Rodney had brought into her dining room.

"Is she the one you saw in your dream?" Rodney demanded.

"I really can't tell. The woman I saw was so much older." Ellen shifted her attention to the third photo and then went pale. "Jesus, Rodney! I think it *is* her!" She lifted the picture up and stared into it from a few inches away. Viola's hair had turned slate-gray and her skin looked overbaked. She sat at this very same table, a cup—perhaps the same cup Ellen was using—in front of her. She was reading a newspaper, obviously a candid shot.

It's true, Ellen thought, that all old people become more or less generic, like babies. And her dream image was part Wonder Woman cartoon and part horror flick, but the woman who had raced through the fields toward the dark entrance to the Eagle Beak cave closely resembled Viola de Beer. Both had hardness to them and a look about the eyes that warned of extreme inner wildness.

"Are you sure?" Rodney asked.

"It's hard to say absolutely, but . . ." Ellen noticed that her mouth had gone dry. "This really freaks me out," she said, dropping the picture. She felt consumed with the idea that she had violated Viola's space, and now Viola was violating hers. It made her feel sick to her stomach. Her Catholic school heritage had created a deep fear of being possessed—and once she saw *The Exorcist* in 1972 and thought, in a panic, That could happen to me, she was a goner. "What if I start channeling her?" she said.

"For chrissakes, that don't happen," Rodney said, adding another shot from his flask to his coffee.

Ellen grabbed the flask out of his hand, ran to the sink, and poured the rest of the booze down the drain. "Stop drinking. It's not even eight in the morning." Rodney didn't move. He just watched her, beady-eyed. Then the phone rang and Ellen yanked the receiver off the hook. "Tommy?" she said, too loud, into the receiver, "is that you?"

"Ellen, what is it? Is there bad news from Karen?"

"No." The reminder of Cocho's predicament made her problems seem insignificant and stupid. "I'm just afraid I'm getting possessed by the evil spirit of the woman who owned this house," she said.

Tommy was silent for a few seconds. "Am I supposed to take this seriously?"

"I don't know." She was hyperconscious of Rodney, who sat like an owl in his usual spot, making Ellen feel vaguely belligerent. "Let's talk about this later when you have time," she said to Tommy.

"I have time now."

"But I don't," she lied.

"Well, then . . ." He said no more, waiting. Ellen had read that the average American could only tolerate four seconds of silence before he or she blurted out something about the weather. She wanted to get off the line before that happened.

"Let me call you back later, okay?"

"Okay," Tommy said, and he disconnected.

What was wrong with her? Every human interaction blew up in her face, and she was always the one lighting the fuse.

Rodney stood up. "I got to get to work," he said. He put on his cap and exited, slamming the screen door. Ellen collapsed into her chair, took a few breaths, and turned to Olivier. "Ready to water?" she asked, desperate to do something productive. Each day, she approached her little vegetable patch with a mixture of pride and fear. The plants seemed so fragile and so much could happen to them. But upward they grew, in tiny fits. She spoke to them as she stood over each one with her plastic watering can. "Hello, beautiful," she halfheartedly said, but, as she pulled out the weeds, including the roots, she kept wishing that she had not cut Tommy off. But it was too late. Too late.

She knocked off in time to take a luxurious bath with Olivier in preparation for her visit to Dr. Yi. Rayfield had not called, so she expected him at noon. By twenty of, she had put on a casual white dress that buttoned all the way down the front. She wore ballet-type slippers, and, with her new city haircut and her tan, she thought she looked like a new person. Tommy would not even recognize her when she picked him up at Dorval Airport in Montreal in a few weeks.

Rodney was having lunch when she stepped into the kitchen. "Well, don't you look nice. You going to a party?" Obviously, he had gotten over his bad mood. Probably the sun had baked the residual booze out of him.

"Nope. Just for acupuncture. I'm riding over there with Rayfield Geebo."

"Is he picking you up here?" Ellen heard an edge in his voice.

"Yeah, in a few minutes."

"Oh." Rodney concentrated on the ham sandwich he had brought from home. He chewed with extra care, his eyes averted from Ellen's.

"Is there something wrong, Rodney?" She felt a starburst of impatience. Rodney was getting as moody as she was. "You seem tense."

"Not at all," he said, obviously lying. He took a big bite out of his sandwich.

"Tell me," she said.

Rodney shook his head and pointed to his mouth. When he could finally speak, all he said was, "You taking Olivier with you today?"

"Of course I am."

"Then you must be going in your car, since you have the car seat."

"That's right."

"Well, don't let Rayfield block me into the driveway. I may finish up before you get back."

Ellen sat down. "Is there something wrong between you and Rayfield? Because I had no idea or I wouldn't have asked him to come over while you're here."

"Just drop it, Ellen."

At that moment, a racket erupted from outside. Rayfield parked on the road, cut his engine, and was soon strolling down the driveway toward the house. Ellen felt a tingle in her chest. Were Rayfield and Rodney headed for a showdown?

"Come on, Olivier. We're going in the car," she said to her nephew, who was prone on the floor studying a dust bunny. "Let's go!"

Rayfield arrived at the door. "Knock, knock," he said as he opened it and stepped inside. Rodney had not changed his position. "Hey, Ellen, hey, Ollie, hey, Rodney. I thought that was your truck out there."

"Hello, Rayfield," Rodney said.

"You ready?" Rayfield asked Ellen.

"Yep."

"Then let's hit the road."

That's it? Ellen thought with disappointment. No hair pulling? No colorful North Country dissing session? She wanted to get the issue, whatever it was, out in the open and help resolve it through her mediation skills, but that was clearly not going to happen. She had a whole afternoon to grill Rayfield, though. He was probably much easier to crack than Rodney, who had, for all practical purposes, been raised by wolves.

Rayfield did an about-face and started back down the crumbling concrete steps. Ellen scooped Olivier off the floor, picked up her purse, and said, "Be careful up there on the roof, Rodney."

"I'll be fine."

"Okay. See you later."

It sounded normal, even seamless on the surface, and there was nothing to do but smile and walk away. Ellen could hardly contain her curiosity. Obviously, there was bad blood here, but what could it possibly be? Rodney surely couldn't have made a play for Wide Load, and even if he had, Rayfield did not seem like the kind of man to carry a grudge for long.

She waited until they had reached the bottom of the Eagle Beak hill before she blurted out, "So what's going on between you and Rodney? And don't give me any of that foot-shuffling, ham-sandwich-eating crap that ends in, 'Aw shucks, Ellen, nothing's going on.'" Even she was shocked at the vehemence with which she had posed her question. Perhaps she had learned an unconscious lesson in direct communication from her new role model, Wide Load.

"It's a long story," Rayfield said.

"So tell me."

"I'm not in the mood."

They drove along in silence for several minutes. The quaint serenity of the countryside, complete with spotted cows and happy farmers, no longer seemed foreign, and Ellen no longer felt like a tourist in it. She knew it took twenty-one days to break a physical habit and many more than that to break a mental one. Obviously, her cells had realigned and now carried the expectation of peace and quiet instead of crowds, pavement, and noise.

"I miss the city," she announced suddenly, right in the middle of her bucolic reverie.

"Yeah? Why?"

"It throbs. I'm used to throbbing."

Rayfield turned toward her, and in her peripheral vision, she saw the outline of his head against the cloudless sky outside his window. "You're still throbbing, believe me," he said. Ellen caught her breath and focused on the highway, desperate to deny the wave of sexiness that had definitely just broken over both their shoulders.

"Okay, I'll tell you about Rodney," Rayfield said. "It was when Viola died," he started. But now Ellen didn't want to hear it. It was the door to greater intimacy, and she was afraid it might lead to a maze she could get confused in.

"You don't have to tell me this, Rayfield."

"Yes, I do." He took a cigarette out of the pack in his T-shirt pocket and held it in his hand.

"See, everybody hated Viola, and I did, too. But one day, and I'll never know why, I was driving past her house and I got the urge to stop in. It was almost like I went into a trance or something. It was like the force was drawing me down her driveway." Now he put his cigarette into his mouth. It dangled from the far corner as if it were stuck there with Velcro. "Anyway, I pulled in, and I saw the door to the house was open." He paused to audibly swallow.

"I called out her name. But nobody answered. This was in October, and it was already chilly, so the door open was, you know, a tip-off." He took the cigarette out of his mouth and rolled it between his fingers. "I went in."

Ellen gripped the steering wheel and took a curve in the road at high speed.

"You wouldn't believe how the place looked. There was crap everywhere—like half-eaten food and dishes that had crusted over and newspapers piled up and clothes thrown around. And it stunk to high heaven."

"Don't tell me! She was dead on the kitchen floor and the mice were eating her eyeballs," Ellen said.

"Worse than that," Rayfield said. "I went from room to room, looking for her and calling out her name, but she wasn't anywheres downstairs."

"This is a horror movie," Ellen whispered.

"I went up the stairs." His voice had grown softer, as if it came from farther away than his mouth. "I found her in her bed. She was ninety-nine percent dead, just skin and bones, and there was this awful stink in the room. She was out of her head, moaning and groaning. At first, she didn't see me there. 'Viola?' I said, 'You still with us?' and she looked over and—"

"And what?" Ellen shrieked.

"Well, she said, 'Rodney?' and she reached out toward me—well, really, toward Rodney—and I went over to her and took her hand because that's what you do at a time like that. I said, 'I'll go get Rodney right now, Viola,' but she wouldn't let go of me. She had her fingers just dug in. And she thought I *was* Rodney, y'know, so I just let her hold on to me. She kinda pulled me down close, down onto the bed, and her breath smelled terrible, like her insides were rotten."

Ellen reached over and put her hand, like a rudder, on Rayfield's shoulder.

"I could tell she wanted me to come in close to her, like she didn't have it in her to talk too loud." Back into his mouth went the cigarette. "I sat down on the bed and leaned over. Remember, she thought I was Rodney."

"What did she say?" Ellen asked, spellbound.

Rayfield did not speak, and the tension in the car thickened. "What did she say?" Ellen repeated.

"She said, 'I'm sorry.'"

"That's it?" Ellen had expected vindictive words of vitriol or a nontransferable curse. "That's nowhere near as bad as rats," she added dismissively.

"It didn't happen to you. Believe me, it was awful. She was like a talking corpse. But I knew it was real important, so I just said, 'It's okay,' and I ran out of there and tore over to Rodney's to get him. He was working in his shop and I just tore in there and pushed him into the truck and tore back. By the time we got there, she was gone. Rodney never has forgave me for leaving her alone at the end."

"But you went to get him."

"It ain't logical."

"Did you tell him what she said? Her last words?"

"Yeah, well, I was choked up and so was he, but I told him and he got even more choked up. He said he wouldn't't've left her at the end and if she thought I was him, then she left this world with a wrong impression of him. He was mad as hell. Told me I should've stayed because that's what he would've done. He accused me of not being man enough to see Viola through to the end. He's hated me ever since. That's when he started going on them binges, too. And that's the whole story."

Ellen felt as if she were in a box with an airtight top on it. "It doesn't seem fair," she finally said. Rayfield was staring out the window, chewing his lower lip.

"He may be right. Maybe running off after him was just an excuse. But at the time, all I could think of was I had to go get him."

"I think you have to go by what was real at the time. What good does looking back on it do?"

Ellen was shocked to hear this from her own mouth—she who constantly drifted in the past; she who spent as much time reflecting as living; she who so frequently obsessed on those previous forks in the road, wondering where she'd made her wrong turns and why.

"I ain't beating myself up about it," Rayfield said, "but sometimes when I play it back, sticking with her instead of running after Rodney, and I see his point. Probably nobody should die alone."

"If you ask me, the real mystery is why you even stopped there in the first place."

"That'll never get solved," Rayfield said. He looked out the window for several seconds. "Want a stick of gum?" He pulled a value pack of spearmint from his pants pocket.

"Sure," Ellen said.

He worked a piece halfway out of the pack and extended it to Ellen. She unwrapped it one-handed, popped it into her mouth, and chewed vigorously.

"You know something else? Besides Wide Load, you're the one and only person I've ever told that story to."

"Really?"

"Yep."

"Well, no wonder you've never gotten over it. I read somewhere that you have to tell a story sixty-seven times before it loses its psychological charge. Two down, sixty-five to go," she added glibly.

"I don't want it to lose its charge," Rayfield said seriously. "It's one of the most important things that ever happened to me. What am I gonna do? Just blab it 'til it goes away?"

"That's what I would do," Ellen chirped with a confusing mix of pride and shame.

"Yeah? Well, what would you have left after you got rid of it?"

"I don't know. Peace?"

"Bullshit. You ain't peaceful."

Suddenly, Ellen felt accused of something. "Yeah? Well, what do you get from keeping it?"

Rayfield was pensive. "Well, I get to face the question of who I am, I guess."

Ellen started to hear a ringing in her ears. It was the high-pitched tone she associated with her nervous system rather than the low-pitched one she assumed was her blood pressure. "You can ask that question anytime," she said.

"No," Rayfield said with conviction. "That question got to be hooked to something concrete or it don't mean anything."

"A lot of philosophers would not agree with you."

"Fuck them. This is me we're talking about."

Ellen controlled her impulse to argue.

"Rodney's got a point," Rayfield repeated.

"Yeah, but what good does it do him to stay pissed off for . . . what? Seven years?"

"Maybe he needs all that and more to face who he is."

Ellen inhaled, slowly and consciously—a technique she had developed over time to take in a serious moment and preserve it for future reference. "I wonder why you told *me* this story. Really, you hardly know me."

"I don't know."

"Well, I won't tell anybody else."

"Fat chance."

Ellen felt future guilt descend on her like the leather straps of a whip. She could just imagine herself blurting it out as conversational filler at a cocktail party in New York, if the circumstances seemed appropriate at the time. She'd done such things before. Her spirits plummeted, like an elevator with snapped cables.

twenty-five

All through Rayfield's acupuncture appointment, Ellen sat in Dr. Yi's waiting room, fielding Olivier and thinking about what happened so many years ago between Rodney and Rayfield. It was a story that, if sorted out correctly, would take her to some heightened understanding about the existential predicament of the human being, she suspected. To Ellen, it had the weight of the questions Socrates posed to Plato, the emotion of a lesson in Christian forgiveness, and the simplicity of everyday life. It had drama and mystery, pity and fear, rising stakes, a shattering climax, and a heart-wrenching denouement. It amazed her that it was happening in Eagle Beak, in real life, and not in the pages of a South American novel or onstage at the Public Theater in New York.

There was a moral lesson, too, Ellen was certain, but like Rodney and Rayfield, she dared not make too quick an assumption about exactly what it was. Her job was to resist her natural temptation to place experiences in neat categories and then forget them, like urns containing human ashes that were bricked into the walls in mausoleums, never to be disturbed again.

When Rayfield emerged from the treatment room, Ellen felt a flood of respect for him. Rayfield Geebo, torchbearer of mysticism and truth. And all the time, she'd been treating him like a circus freak. Once, while working for Reginald Eubanks, Ellen had met a contortionist who could throw his legs over his shoulders and walk backwards with his head dangling just above the floor. He could put a nail up his nostril, compress his inner organs into such a small area that he appeared to be less than four inches thick when viewed from the side, and swallow a Japanese sword. Ellen had lavished more respect on this man, who traveled the county fair circuit and often slept in the backseat of his Ford Cobra, than she had ever given to Rayfield. Seeing him emerge

from Dr. Yi's workroom and knowing he was fighting for a functional penis
brought tears to her eyes.

"Your turn," he said. "Drop your cocks and grab your socks," he added like
an army drill sergeant. Ellen sighed. It was a challenge to maintain an attitude
of deep respect when faced with the actual and not the idealized version of
Rayfield Geebo of Porkerville.

"I'm gonna walk Ollie around the block," Rayfield said, and Ellen nodded.
As she went through the portal to the inner sanctum, they went out the door
into the streets of Cornwall. Ellen kicked off her shoes and climbed onto the
table, where she stretched out with abandonment. Dr. Yi used a penlight to examine her tongue and sat with his fingers pressed into her wrists for a full
minute. She loved this part—the assessment. Take good care of me, she thought
as she gave in to him.

"You drink tea?" he asked.

"Oh, yes, six times every day."

"You feel change?"

"I think so." Actually, she knew she did, but she was cheap about commitment.

"Heart stronger," he said.

"I do feel more open," she admitted. He inserted a thin needle into the side
of her neck. If she turned her head, her larynx would be speared like an hors
d'oeuvre. Ellen closed her eyes. When she rolled off the table an hour later,
she was pleasantly foggy, but the mist lifted the instant she stepped into the
waiting room and discovered Rayfield and Olivier were still gone.

Where could he be, she wondered. Surely, a trip around the block couldn't
take all day. She stepped out into the muggy sunlight and scanned the street in
both directions. No sign of them. And they weren't in the car, either. It sat pa-
tiently at the curb, its tires in a rain puddle, as if it had found the perfect place
to soak its feet.

Across the street, a park bench was positioned under a shade tree. Ellen
dug her sunglasses out of her bag and moved toward it. She extracted a
Kleenex and attempted to wipe off some of the accumulated dust before she
sat down on it in her pretty white dress. She looked up and down the street.
No Rayfield. The worst possibility presented itself: Rayfield was behind some
Dumpster molesting her nephew. She shook her head to eliminate the image,
but her mind would not retreat: what did she actually know about Rayfield?
How could she possibly predict what he might be capable of? Modern parents,
at least those in New York City, never allowed their children out of their sight
until they entered high school—and then they were given beepers and cell
phones. A whole generation was being raised that had never experienced

youthful independence and freedom. Instead, they had appointments and scheduled playdates from the time they were in preschool, and twenty-four-hours notice was expected in case of cancellation.

The sun made her lazy and she found herself making a detailed accounting of the thoughts that were passing through her consciousness as she sat on the park bench. Rayfield was a demon, a hero, a demon. She was a shape-shifter, and Tommy was eternal, like the great rock of Acoma in New Mexico, where people had lived for more than a thousand years without changing a thing, if you didn't count the road that some Hollywood movie studio had constructed to the top of the butte to facilitate the making of a B movie. Spontaneity was a trait that was disappearing from the gene pool as modern-day survival of the fittest selected for youth with appointment books instead of independence and freedom. And where was Rayfield? Even if he were a child molester, he would hardly indulge his sick need when she was guaranteed to find out.

She stretched her legs out in front of her, did a slow neck roll, and raised her face to the sun. She imagined all her worry oozing like sweat out of the pores of her skull, sliding along the waves of her new haircut, and slipping away into absolute nothingness.

Within a few breaths, the city sounds seemed to melt into a dull hum, as if honeybees were doing bee business in some nearby rosebush. Ellen felt like a soft blanket had been tucked in around her body, and she actually heard her heart beating in the lub-dub lub-dub pattern her high school biology teacher had been fond of imitating. In her dreamy state, Ellen recalled a moment, perhaps ten years ago, when she had sat bolt upright in bed, out of a sound sleep, and announced in a voice that hardly sounded like hers the words, "Anything that is created from the universal substance is not designed to have needs."

"Huh?" said Tommy, as he sputtered awake.

Ellen repeated the words, slowly and distinctly, looking straight into Tommy's eyes in the dim light of their bedroom. She had never felt so calm in her life. Then she flopped back down and returned without delay to sleep. Out of amusement, Tommy had written down her sentence on his bedside notepad. When he produced it in the morning over breakfast, Ellen, who had only the vaguest recollection of speaking in the night, was fascinated.

"What does it mean?" she asked Tommy.

"Beats me," he answered.

"It means something," she said, staring at Tommy's notepad. "Anything that is created from the universal substance is not designed to have needs. Hmmm." All day long, as she sat in the library collecting statistics on women's employment patterns for a mainstream article she was ghostwriting, she thought about it. Each time she repeated it in her mind, she noted a small but

perceptible lifting of her spirits. By the time she got on the No. 6 train, heading downtown, she was almost giddy with the possibility that there was no real
need in the universe. Lack was an illusion created because so few humans
could transcend their own desires and appreciate the bigger cosmic picture.
For two weeks afterward, whenever she felt that tension or desire tugged her
behavior into a familiar rut, she repeated her mantra and she felt free. When it
wore off, Ellen was bereft. She had one big need after all, she ultimately
admitted—to believe. But before this new belief had been able to reconstruct
her whole personality, it had faded. The words she spewed out in the night lost
their meaning, or at least their power over her. Maybe Rayfield was right. Talking out loud drained the significance out of important events. It left them neutralized and lifeless. It was a terrible waste, Ellen thought. Lessons were so very
hard to learn. They always came too late, after the irreparable damage had
been done.

The bench beneath her shook slightly as the weight of Rayfield collapsed
upon it. Olivier landed in her lap, and her arms encircled him in an instinctual
way before she even opened her eyes. It felt liberating not to jump all over
Rayfield, not to nuke him, for disappearing with Olivier.

"I been teaching this kid some English," Rayfield said instead of hello. "Ollie, what's that?" Rayfield pointed at a pickup parked a few feet away. Olivier
did a reasonable job of pronouncing the word *truck*. "What's that?" Rayfield
asked, pointing up. "Bud," Olivier replied. "Birrrrd," Rayfield corrected. "Bud,"
Olivier repeated.

Ellen smiled. "You know something I read when I was doing research? Babies are born with the ability to pronounce every single sound in every single
language. As they grow, they limit the sounds they produce to the ones they
hear in their own environment, the ones that are reinforced in their own language. It's such a loss, really. I mean, Olivier could speak everything—Arabic,
Chinese, Russian—without an accent if he were exposed to them now."

"Like I said, somebody oughta teach this kid some English," Rayfield said.
"Ollie, Who'm I? Who'm I, Ollie?" Olivier pounded Ellen's chest with both
his hands. "C'mon, who'm I?" Rayfield repeated. Ellen burst into tears when
Olivier said, "Dada."

"That's not what I taught him," Rayfield defended himself. "C'mon Ollie,
say Rayfield." Olivier giggled as he tried to hoist himself up onto the bench.
His head of wild black curls, so like Cocho's, had highlights of blue and purple
in the sunbeam that slashed through the leaves of the elm trees that lined the
block. Ellen held on to him and pressed him against her as tears collected
along her jawbone and dripped off, like spring thaw.

"What're you crying for?" Rayfield asked.

"I'm afraid for Cocho," Ellen blubbered. "Olivier's father. He's so young, so young. And he has so much to live for, and . . ." She could not go on for a moment, and then she sighed, "It's just not fair."

"Not one thing in life is fair," Rayfield said as if he'd given this serious thought and meant it. "Come 'ere," he said and he put his arm around her shoulder and pulled her to him. His bulk had a calming effect. He was a big pillow for her to rest her weary head upon, and when his huge arm encircled her and pressed her close, she closed her eyes and let the tears saturate Rayfield's T-shirt, turning it from a faded red to a shade fashionably referred to as Bordeaux.

Breathe on, Cocho, she silently begged, but with each passing day, her prayer sounded flimsier and less likely to be answered. The idea of Karen, down in Peru, waiting by Cocho's bedside and perhaps repeating the same words that Ellen was, filled her with a black hopelessness, and she wept on while Rayfield rested his hairy chin on the top of her curls and held her close. Olivier had squirmed off her lap and was now standing on the bench. Rayfield hooked the fingers of his free hand into the back of Olivier's little overalls. Just like the family photo of Karen, Cocho, and Olivier, Ellen thought, and she cried harder.

After ten minutes of turbulence, Ellen dried the last of her tears with the edge of her hem and stood up. "Jeez," she said, "I feel like I just aged fifteen years."

"Take a nap," Rayfield said. "I'll drive."

At first, Ellen wanted to resist. To surrender her keys to Rayfield seemed dangerously symbolic. Jungians, she knew, called cars in dreams "personal vehicles." If someone else was driving yours, it was time to ask why. Of course, Jungians believed that all the persons in the dream symbolized an aspect of the dreamer herself. What part of her did Rayfield represent? Her aimless inner male, handicapped by a penis that could not stand up and be counted? Or perhaps the part of her that was tired of coping with the high-stakes world of New York City, the part that wanted to throw itself into a bucket seat, crack a beer, and blow smoke rings?

She glanced at Rayfield, who was busy buckling Olivier into his car seat. He could just as easily symbolize the aspect of herself that met life's troubles with a who-gives-a-shit attitude instead of turning them into a tragedy in which she played the tormented heroine. So why not let him drive, she suddenly thought. Maybe with Rayfield at the wheel, she would go someplace different.

She settled into the passenger seat and rested her head back as Rayfield adjusted the rearview mirror and moved the driver's seat back as far as possible to accommodate his beer belly. Her mind drifted to the few minutes on the park bench when she had snuggled against him and poured out her pain. Anyone passing by would have assumed that Rayfield was her life partner. If Tommy had seen them, he would have jumped to conclusions immediately. She would have too, if the situation were reversed and she'd observed Tommy with his arm around Wide Load.

But if Tommy was comforting anybody at all, it was much more likely to be a skinny graduate of Harvard Law School, a starry-eyed idealist doing her one-year stint in the public defenders office. Ellen imagined this brainy babe would have no conflict about getting her hair styled by Attila and investing in the stock market while her clients rotted in jail. Why even think about it, she asked herself? Why agonize? But her mind would not let it go. She'd always fretted that, if they broke up for any reason, Tommy would find a trophy wife while she would wind up with a deadbeat like Rayfield Geebo—and that was if she got anyone at all. In the world of second marriages, Tommy would fall up and she would fall down.

Rayfield made the turn onto the bridge. So far, he had not said a word. He drove with his left elbow out the window and the fingers of his right hand lightly in the six o'clock position on the steering wheel. Ellen closed her eyes, happy to be free of all responsibility for a few precious moments.

That's what's wrong with Tommy, she suddenly announced to herself: he's too predictable. Ellen knew every move he would make, probably before he did. Or every move he *wouldn't* make, she snorted to herself. Tommy had once told her that waiting to see what would happen was fun. "Sounds like passivity to me," Ellen answered. "Doing nothing is doing something," Tommy replied. "Sure, Tom," Ellen responded. Inwardly, she stewed after that conversation. She wanted a husband who took risks, especially at work. She wanted him to climb the ladder of success, but he wouldn't do it for love or money.

Besides, Ellen thought as she raked her eternal soul twin over her inner coals, he drinks too much. Even a guy like Rayfield could give up his beloved beer, cigarettes, and coffee, not to mention his voluntary decision to part with those symbols of his former life, his motorcycle leathers and his beer can collection.

"By the way," Ellen asked dreamily, "did you ever get a buyer for your beer cans?"

"Not yet."

"How about the leather outfit?"

"It's not an *outfit*, Ellen. It's a statement."

This was amusing. "Really? What statement might that be?"

"What do you think?"

"Jeez, I don't know. Born to lose? Live free or die? Wild and crazy guy?"

"Something like that," Rayfield said mildly. The breeze coming in the car window cooled her to the perfect temperature, and once she got her mind off Tommy, she felt as content and lazy as the cows chewing their cud by the side of the road. Rayfield seemed disinclined to talk, which suited her mood, too. Thinking and talking were work. Today, she wanted to watch where her mind went without reporting it aloud to anyone, not that anyone was interested.

What was the mind anyway, she wondered. When Reginald had done a documentary on Vietnamese boat people, Ellen had been fascinated by their habit of touching their chests in the vicinity of the heart each time they said the word *mind*. Americans, of course, would tap their temples, as if the mind lived within the gray matter of the brain. Why did the mind and the heart seem to be at odds with each other in the Western world, she mused.

This was not the first time she had visited this question. Two decades before, while she rode the train toward Wall Street, she had looked up from the novel on her lap and noticed that the whole subway car was full of men in suits and ties. There were only a few people standing, and the men seated tended to lean forward over their knees, their ties dangling. Suddenly, Ellen saw the ties for what they were: nooses cinched around the neck to symbolically cut off communication between the head and the heart. Onward she theorized, and soon she realized that all ties pointed to the penis. Obviously, they were stand-ins for the phallus. That's why guys in bow ties are considered geeks, she thought.

"Isn't it sick that women who go corporate often start wearing ties?" she asked Rayfield. He didn't even bother to answer. Instead, he turned on the radio and found an oldies station. Ellen detested oldies unless she turned them on herself. She listened with festering resentment as the Monkees belted out their signature hit. "We're the young generation, and we've got something to say," they sang, and Rayfield hummed along.

"I think it's ludicrous," Ellen butted in, finally opening her eyes, "that the Monkees actually thought they had something to say." She felt smug, as if she'd aimed a harpoon and it had penetrated deeply into its target.

"Yeah, well you wanna hear something even stupider than that?" Rayfield replied. "That Caspar Weinberger thought he had something to say."

Ellen yelped. "Good one, Rayfield!" she said. Laughing switched her mental track, and when the next tune started, she sang along happily. It was a Frank and Nancy Sinatra duet, and Rayfield joined in right on cue. When the refrain came, they both belted out, "And then I go and spoil it all by saying something stupid like I love you," hamming it up like a Las Vegas lounge act. Still, to Ellen, those three little words were beginning to have a familiar ring.

twenty-six

W hen Rodney nailed the final shingle into place and descended the
ladder for the last time, Ellen experienced a strange conglomera-
tion of delight and depression. For days, the hammering from
above had driven her to the brink of insanity. Each *blam, blam, blam* created
an eruption of her nerves. It was like having mental hiccups that wrecked the
overall continuity.

On the other hand, she thoroughly appreciated Rodney himself. When
she'd professed love, she realized afterward, she actually meant it. Seeing him
put on his reading glasses to scan the *Free Trader,* or observing him while he
cut his donut or poured himself another cup of coffee or even grumped his way
through a crabby booze-induced morning, tickled her from the inside out, and
their daily get-together anchored her and made her feel safe. For many years,
Ellen had lived under the illusion that intimacy was formed on the high peaks
and low valleys of the emotional landscape. She had thought that knowing
important secrets or being there at the moment when hope transformed into
despair or vice versa, or sticking together through nervous breakdowns, or coping with dramatic events—that was the raw material of intimacy. But now she
saw that being with someone when nothing happened, when routine set in
and boredom lurked on the periphery, that was intimacy, too. And it could
happen with an unlikely partner, not just a soul mate.

Ellen did not tell Rodney that Rayfield had spilled the beans about Viola's
last moment. She would have liked to facilitate a reconciliation between them
but that was less important than her evolution as a person, which required, she
had decided, keeping her big mouth shut more often. Sometimes it felt a bit
dishonest. She would find herself watching Rodney and wondering how and
why he kept his irrational grudge against Rayfield alive, what fed it, seven

years after Viola's remains had settled, like pirate treasure, on the floor of the sea. What did Rodney get out of it? Or perhaps the better question was, what did he avoid?

"Well, that's that," Rodney said as he washed his hands and accepted a giant Pepperidge Farm chocolate chip cookie. "She shouldn't leak no more, no matter where the rain comes from."

"Thank you very much, Rodney. It was a lot of work for you."

"It had to be done."

"I wonder if I really would've sued you."

Rodney studied her. "You would have," he said.

Ellen was offended. "What does that mean?" she asked. Rodney didn't answer instantly, so she added, "No, I really want to know."

"You're pushy, Ellen."

"Me? Pushy? I'm a pushover."

Rodney's slit eyes expanded. "You? A pushover?"

"That's right." She felt compelled to expand. "You know what Pablo Picasso said? He said there are only two types of women in the world—goddesses and doormats. I'm naturally a doormat. I had to develop aggression as a survival tactic."

"If you ask me, Pablo left out a couple categories."

"Like what? Like ball buster?" Her voice sounded as if someone had turned up the volume.

"Jeezum, Ellen, what're you getting so worked up about?"

"Hell if I know." She took a huge bite out of her cookie. "Maybe I'm just worried that, now that the roof is done, I'll never see you again. Did you ever think of that?"

Rodney looked truly mystified. "What do you want?" he finally asked.

"I want it to stay like it is. I want you to come over here and eat donuts with me and Olivier in the morning." She would have preferred a tone of petulance or poutiness, which was no doubt what a goddess would do. But as a reformed doormat, she just sounded bossy.

"I could do that," Rodney said.

"You could? But what about your work? Your sculpting," she added for clarity. She assumed that the roof job had kept him from creating his art, and that he would be anxious to return to it.

"I generally do my carving in the afternoons. In the mornings, I loaf."

"So coming over here wouldn't throw a monkey wrench in?"

"In what?"

"Your life. Your routine," she said impatiently.

"Hell, no."

"Yahoo!" It was a victory. She had secured herself adult human interaction once a day.

"Besides, all New Yorkers are pushy. We're known for it," she added. "We're proud of it."

"To each his own," Rodney replied.

"To each his *or her* own," Ellen corrected

"Whatever," he said. Within five minutes, he was gone. Ellen got onto the floor with Olivier and helped him stack up his wooden blocks. He enjoyed knocking them down, she noticed. Maybe the desire to see if things would crash was built into the bones and cells of the human beast.

That night, late, the phone rang. On a burst of adrenaline, Ellen levitated from the bed and dashed down the kamikaze stairs. She was becoming adept at negotiating them, but even so she didn't make it to the phone until the sixth ring.

"Hello," she yelled into the receiver, as if she could keep the caller on the line by pure volume.

"Ellen?"

"Karen?" Karen's voice was thin through the static. "How's Cocho? Has something happened? Are you okay? Any news?"

"It doesn't look good. He's very weak."

"He hasn't regained consciousness?"

"No. Nothing. He just lies there. I get up fifty times a day to check if he's still breathing."

"You must be completely worn-out."

"I am."

Ellen listened to the crackle on the line.

"I keep thinking about the day he left Montreal," Karen finally said. "His plane took off in the middle of the afternoon. He came by the café to get me to go to the airport. When we got to the car, he said he didn't feel like driving, so I drove. He took out one of his zampoñas and started to play very softly. It was the saddest music I ever heard. The whole way to the airport, I felt like my heart was breaking. I wanted to ask him to stop playing but . . . I never did. Now I keep wondering if that's going to turn out to be our last conversation. Just sad music."

"Oh, Karen, don't let your imagination run away with you," Ellen pleaded.

"I'm not imagining anything. This is real."

It was Ellen who was doing the imagining, and she knew it. She was imagining a happy ending. "Did you . . . on the drive to the airport . . . did you know what he was saying in the music?"

"Not really. It was haunting. It stayed with me. I hummed it for days afterward." She stopped talking. Several seconds later, she added, "It was a new song he was just writing. He told me the name of it was 'Love Game.'"

"Karen, you have to keep hoping."

"I know."

"I'm praying for him."

"You are? I didn't know you prayed."

"I've taken it up."

Karen laughed, a welcome sound. "How's my little boy?"

"He misses you, but he's fine. He's great."

"I miss him desperately. I had two males in my life, and now . . ."

"They're both still here, Karen."

"I know, but . . ."

There was another long silence and then Karen said she had to go. After they hung up, Ellen heated her tea and sat in the dark on the front porch swing to drink it slowly. Without knowing why, she mulled over Karen's words about her personal males—her lover and son. They completed Karen in some crucially important way. Females and males, males and females; it was all such a mystery.

Of course, Ellen's main male was noticeably absent. And her two stand-ins were, singly and together, the strangest male complements she could dream up. Was there any way to figure out how it worked? And what about the little budding male spirit Olivier, who had been placed in her keeping? Would he take root in her psyche and her life and blossom in a new way for her each passing spring? Would she know him differently because she had bonded with him over a summer in Eagle Beak, the summer his mother had to rush to his father's bedside in Lima, Peru? She would never have had this time with Olivier, never been able to be there for Karen in her hour of need, if she were in her normal life in New York City. Had she been working, Reginald would have forbidden her to leave for Montreal for an indefinite stay.

She pulled one of Viola's quilts up over her shoulders and stretched out full length on the porch swing. All over the modern industrialized world, connections were snapping like dried twigs. Extended families, community involvement, shared ceremonies—all out the thermopane window. The individualism of the West had accelerated independence at great cost, and there was no room left for a family disaster. When one struck, like a raging storm at sea, each individual was set adrift alone, clinging to his or her own piece of wreckage.

When her parents had died, one by one, both Ellen and Karen had been there, at their bedsides, but both had arrived within the previous twelve hours, summoned by a hospital employee, a nurse whose job description included making personal calls to the potentially bereaved in the middle of the night.

In the decade before their deaths, Ellen had seen her parents perhaps a total of eight days a year, usually over weekends, one per season. And even then, there was little to say. Ellen had sat with them in front of the TV set as if the living-room chairs came equipped with restraints preset to release when the tube was turned off. It drove her nuts, listening to boring sitcoms at top volume and belting out small talk during the commercials.

In Asia, Ellen knew, respect for the elderly was based not on the past but on the future. The aged were standing at the portal of the greatest mystery in human life—death. They deserved respect because at any minute, they could be called upon to step, alone, across that border, never to be heard from again. As her parents had grown old, Ellen had wanted to grill them about their insights and fears. She wanted to know how a person who was wrapping it up experienced both what had happened and what was about to. But when she'd screwed up her courage once and asked her father how he felt about death, he had said, "It's a good cure for living," and changed the channel. She had gotten much more out of her same-age friend Harold, who, fatally ill with AIDS, had described himself as being in the departure lounge of a cosmic airport. His view from there, he said, was expansive. It seemed to Ellen, as she watched him approach death's door, that he was prematurely transformed into an angel. Just being with him was inspiring. And healing.

Maybe Rodney was mad at Rayfield because it was Rayfield who had heard the two most important words Viola de Beer uttered in her whole life. Maybe his you-should've-stuck-with-her chant was just a cover-up for extreme jealousy. Ellen herself would not have missed Harold's last words to her for anything. "I'll get in the computer and mess everything up," he had said, knowing that she had a fear that year of being audited by the IRS.

Viola's final words were, in a way, right up there with W. C. Fields's "I'd rather be in Philadelphia" or Gary Gilmore's "Let's do it." They made a concise commentary and a strong personal statement. Of course, Rodney would have wanted to hear them. He'd probably needed to hear her say "I'm sorry" every moment of his life, before her death as well as after.

Would Karen always remember Cocho's last words, in the form of his sad rendition of "Love Game" played without explanation in the car on the way to Dorval Airport? Karen's heart had ached during that ride. Would she wish she told Cocho that, whispered it into his ear just before he walked down the ramp and into the plane? Would she always regret that she had simply felt it, lived with it, and made no comment.

"Breathe on, Cocho," Ellen whispered. "Please. I beg you." A great peace came over her in the dark of the front porch and she fell into a soothing, dreamless sleep.

twenty-seven

In preparation for Tommy's Fourth of July visit, Ellen mowed the lawn, scrubbed the entire house, and purchased fresh flowers from a local farm stand. She arranged them in Viola's jelly jars and placed them in every room. She weeded the garden, which was thriving, and even took the Honda to the U-Wash and gave it its first-ever shampoo and vacuum combination.

Tommy's flight came into Montreal at six ten Friday evening, but she and Olivier were already at the airport at five, sitting in the international arrivals terminal even as Tommy buckled into his seat belt at LaGuardia Airport in New York. Ellen bounced Olivier on her knee for a whole hour before the announcement of Tommy's plane. Then, heaving her nephew to her hip, she stood at the observation window and watched Tommy clear customs. He had come straight from work and still wore his tie, though it was lowered to half-mast and the top button of his shirt was undone. He carried a gym bag and a briefcase. When he broke into a big smile at the customs agent, Ellen felt astonished that, despite the pronounced New York pinch, he was still so attractive. Dimples cut into his face to make room for his wide smile and even from a distance his eyes looked charmingly devilish. Her heart filled with joy as she competed for space near the double door he would come through any moment.

"Where's Uncle Tommy?" she said to Olivier. "Let's find Uncle Tommy." Olivier looked around as if he knew who Uncle Tommy was, though of course he didn't. And then the swinging door opened and Tommy was with her at last. Ellen ran to him and fell into his open arms.

"You changed your hair," he said. "You look great. Let me get the full view." Ellen stepped back and did a slow spin. Her tan was darker now and her waves gave her the free and jaunty look she associated with women with predictable menstrual cycles.

"Wow," Tommy said as he pulled her to him and kissed her once, quickly, on the lips. "It's good to see you, honey," he said. "And Olivier, my man! Come to your Uncle Tom." Tommy put his hands out and Olivier dove forward. As they moved toward the parking lot, Ellen imagined they were just starting out, just a few years into marriage, and Olivier was their son. If they had had a child right away, he or she would be sixteen by now, a high school student. Time had certainly marched on for them.

"What a week," Tommy said. "I'm totally beat. How far do we have to drive?"

"It's only about an hour and twenty minutes, door to door."

"Why don't we stay in Montreal tonight? At Karen's. I love this town."

Ellen felt an irrational burst of rage. He didn't really give a shit about her organic farm. "We could do that," she said, supremely careful to keep her voice light and easy.

"Good. Let's get a great dinner and head down to Green Acres in the morning."

So it's settled, Ellen thought resentfully as she unlocked the car door and then handed the keys to Tommy. It made sense, of course. He was tired and hungry. She ordered her face to be blank as she settled into the passenger seat. The last time she'd sat there, Rayfield had been driving and she had mused on the symbolic significance of having someone else at the wheel of her personal vehicle. She glanced over at Tommy. When they were together, he always drove. It was assumed and understood by both parties, though she had no idea how it got started.

"Let's see if I remember the way to Karen's," he said as he backed out of the parking space. Tommy had an excellent sense of direction and a great memory for locations. Ellen had no doubt that he would proceed, without even one millisecond of doubt or one wrong turn, directly to Karen's door. She put her hand on his thigh as she always did, had always done, ever since that first drive to Truro twenty-five years before. A quarter of a century, she realized with an involuntary shudder.

"It's not really Green Acres," she said.

"Huh?"

"The place. My place. It's not really Green Acres."

Tommy laughed. "We'll see," he said. "Did you do something to your eyebrows? They look different. Sort of early Lauren Bacall."

"Everything about me is different," Ellen said mysteriously. She wanted to reveal herself slowly to her husband, but how was that possible when he knew her so intimately that even the curve of her eyebrow was familiar to him? She had so much to tell him, but she wanted to recite it like a poem. Tommy, a cut-to-the-chase New Yorker, preferred the headlines. He would want to skim the story, not listen to it with the respectful awe that poetry demanded.

"Well," Tommy said as he confidently changed lanes, "do we pick up where we left off or do we start over again?" Flirtatiousness put a scarlet edge on his words, creating a subtext that made Ellen feel pinned, like a monarch butterfly in a black velvet box. He moved his hand to her thigh and ran it up under her dress. Ellen didn't know whether to open her legs more or close them.

"I don't know you," she blurted out, and Tommy laughed and said, "All the better." He moved his hand to shift the car, and she clamped her legs together. They were already in the tunnel and would soon exit on Boulevard St. Laurent. Everything was happening too fast. Tommy was doing cartwheels and back flips around her, kicking up old bits of mental debris and making her feel defensive for no reason. She had waited a long time to see him, and she couldn't afford a single moment of distance or disharmony. Not only the weekend but life was too short. She replaced her hand on his thigh and made the choice to look at him with love.

"Go ahead, asshole," Tommy yelled impatiently at a driver who veered into his lane. "You fucking idiot." Ellen held her breath. Road rage was normal in the modern world and, in Tommy's case, completely harmless. He was just venting. But Ellen didn't see the point. The poor guy in the car in front of them probably needed to make a right turn. Was it a felony offense?

In front of Karen's building, Olivier, in the backseat, banged his little hands up and down and cooed like a pigeon. Grandmother Ng was standing outside the fruit and vegetable stand folding plastic vegetable bags into accordion shapes. "Look, he recognizes where he is," Ellen said as Tommy parked. As soon as Ellen lifted Olivier from his car seat, he ran to the old woman and hugged her about the knees. She squatted down to his eye level and smiled directly into his face. She was probably sixty-five but looked fifteen years younger. Karen had told Ellen that Grandmother Ng plucked out her gray hairs, one by one. In Vietnam, a neighbor child, too poor to go to school, had done it in exchange for arithmetic lessons. Here, her daughter, Ut, did it after they closed up shop each night. Grandmother Ng probably looked at Ellen's curls, with the beginning of a silver lining, and wondered how a woman could let herself go to pot like that.

Olivier detached himself and ran down the narrow aisle toward the back of the store, and Ellen tore after him. He scooted through the door to the storeroom just ahead of her. Ut gleefully picked him up and hugged him before she returned him to the floor to play with her own sons, Bao and Thanh.

"Cocho okay? Karen okay?" she asked, and Ellen shook her head slowly.

"We don't know."

"Bad thing," Ut said. Ellen knew that Ut, if anyone, was qualified to judge. Life before Canada, in Vietnam and then in a refugee camp in the Philippines, had been hellish for this family. Karen knew the details but had not passed them on to Ellen.

"My husband and I are going to spend the night upstairs," Ellen said. Remembering Tommy, she turned to look back toward the street where he stood, leaning against the car. He had removed his suit jacket, folded it neatly with the lining out, and laid it across the hood. In his sunglasses, he looked sexy, like a character actor shooting a foreign film on location. "Ut," Ellen said impulsively, "can I leave Olivier here for an hour?"

"Of course," Ut said, "we here all night, no problem."

"Thanks." Ellen kissed Olivier on the head and whispered, "Auntie Ellen will be right back." He hardly seemed to notice her, involved as he was in some esoteric baby game that involved a square sheet of bubble wrap and a cantaloupe.

"Ut is gonna watch Olivier for a while," Ellen said to Tommy with a lascivious raising of her eyebrows. "Let's go." On the way up the stairs, he pinched her rear several times. Her body felt ready to give in, anxious for the opportunity, and when she inserted the key into the lock and stepped in, her husband was right behind her. It was as hot as any sauna and took their breath away.

"Damn," Tommy said as he dropped his jacket on a chair, "this is worse than the city. Let's open the windows, not that it'll help." He crossed the room and began to push and shove at the swollen window frame.

"Moscow in the winter, Bombay in the summer," Ellen said, repeating something she frequently heard from Karen. She found two cold beers in the fridge and carried them to the bedroom, stretching out on Karen's bed and waiting for Tommy to arrive. When he did, he muscled the windows open and then downed half the beer in a series of swallows that made his Adam's apple flutter up and down, as if a small bird were trapped inside.

"Did you know that humans are the only animals who can choke to death?" Ellen said. Tommy looked at her blankly. "It's because of the position of the larynx in the throat. It lies below the esophagus, which puts it in the path of swallowed food. That's why food can get stuck. Of course, it also allows us to make vowel sounds, which probably made speech intelligible to hominids, and—"

"You talk too much," Tommy said, dropping onto the bed. "Shut up. Come here."

"I'm nervous."

"We're just gonna play. We've played together before," Tommy said. He kissed her.

Sometimes you wait for kisses, sometimes you avoid them, and sometimes they are thrust upon you. These particular kisses seemed to be happening to someone else. Tommy separated from her, unbuttoning his shirt and peeling it off. A second later, his trousers dropped around his ankles, like a tiny island upon which he stood like a male Statue of Liberty hoisting a bottle of beer to the sick and weary.

Ellen sat up. "Tommy! My God!"

Tommy clamped his arms in front of him like Mr. Universe or the Discus Thrower. His penis had extended downward, as if it were being filled from above with concrete. It was the state before it defied gravity and began to rise that Ellen particularly loved.

"The NordicTrack?" she sputtered.

"You betcha." He turned around so she could admire his newly toned ass.

"In just three weeks?" His love handles had almost melted away.

"I knocked off the booze and cut down on junk food, too."

"You stopped drinking?" Ellen wished she had not just given him a beer.

"I decided to make getting in shape a priority," he said.

"It worked. Jeez, Tommy, I'm totally impressed. You haven't looked like this in years."

"Yeah, it feels good," he said as he settled back onto the bed. "Now let's get this dress off you." Ellen cooperated by lifting her arms straight up so he could slip it over her head. He undid her bra and rolled her panties down off her hips.

Naked, she thought. Buck naked. Naked as a jaybird. The naked truth. Tommy propped himself up on one elbow and stared into her eyes. It provided a fixed point to focus on, and she actually noticed her life narrowing until Tommy became the only thing in it. When he leaned forward to kiss her, when his fingers pressed her nipples into tiny pyramids, when he used his knees to pry her legs apart, she ignored the pain created by lack of lubrication and called him "sweet honey" and "lover man." "Fuck me," she whispered because she knew it turned him on. "Oh baby, baby," he said before he suddenly howled. A joke from a movie in which Sally Field starred as a stand-up comic arrived in her mind. "My husband and I have been married so long that we just don't know where one of us ends and the other begins. The problem is, he's always ending when I'm about to begin." Ellen chuckled as her husband drifted away into the after-sex sleep that was so predictable. She listened with her head on his chest to the sounds of his body at work—his lungs and heart, breath and heartbeat, rhythms and snores and the periodic *puh, puh, puh* sounds that popped from his closed lips, and thought about how flat-footed and clumsy they had become in the big dance of human life. It was all probably normal. In a few years, she probably wouldn't even care about sex anymore.

Marriage would probably be smooth sailing after that. It was just the transition decade, the forties, that they had to get through. She closed her eyes, slowed her breathing, and forced herself to slip into a gentle sleep. Like a lightweight raft on a lazy stream, she drifted. But when she rounded a bend in her unconscious and saw Viola de Beer standing on the bank, she woke up as a way of avoiding her. Just that glimpse, though, reminded her that there was someone angry lurking in her shadows.

She looked at the clock. More than two hours had passed. "Shit," she said as she bounded out of bed and pulled on her dress. Tommy opened his eyes to the halfway point. "I've got to run down and get Olivier," Ellen said as she stepped into her shoes. Tommy rolled over. His shoulder and arm looked powerful against the background of Karen's delicate eyelet bedspread.

The vegetable stand was peopled with chic Montrealers, and Ellen nudged and sidestepped her way to the back room, where Olivier was squatting, Asian-style, eating a bowl of rice with his fingers as Grandmother Ng looked on. "I'm sorry I'm so late," Ellen said as she tucked a ten-dollar bill into the old woman's hand and hoisted Olivier up. She bowed, said "Thank you" several times, and left.

Olivier fussed and squirmed until Ellen finally put him down halfway between the third- and the fourth-floor landings. It was long past his bedtime, but he seemed to have his second wind. The stairs were steep and required Olivier to lift his knees almost to his chin with each step as Ellen helped by pulling him up by his spindly arm. It was a lot of work for him, but he seemed thoroughly determined to press on. It didn't even occur to her to wonder at his heightened motivation until he noticed that he was softly chanting, "Mama, Mama, Mama," in a voice warm with expectation.

"*Mama n'est pas ici,*" she said, summoning up her high school French and completely unsure if she had it right. "Mommy's not here, honey," she added in English. How could she have failed to foresee this possibility? "*Mama n'est pas ici,*" she repeated, hugging him, but when she opened the door, Olivier charged in yelling, "Mama! Mama!" The sound of his happy voice slit Ellen's heart to pieces, and she followed him, filled with deep dread, as he checked for Karen in the bathroom and then the bedroom. Seeing a lump beneath the covers, Olivier whooped with glee and scrambled onto the bed. When Tommy sat up, he began to scream. Within seconds, his face was purple and sweat had broken out across his little nose.

There was not a thing in the world to do. Olivier stiffened into a human plank. Tommy pulled the bedspread over his head and tried a few rounds of peekaboo but it didn't work. "What do we do now?" Tommy asked as he got out of bed and stood next to Ellen, watching in awe as Olivier thrashed about in a bona fide fit.

"I don't know."

"Make him stop," Tommy ordered.

"Let's just wait it out. This can't go on for long."

"Sooner or later, he'll pass out, right?" Tommy contributed.

"I should've realized that he would expect to see Karen here. We should've just gone back to Eagle Beak. Maybe we should go now. He'd calm down in the car."

"So I guess dinner's out of the picture." His voice sounded disappointed. "I'm starved."

"You can get something downstairs and eat it in the car," Ellen snapped, immediately regretting it. "Or you could go out and find a nice place and eat, and I'll stay here and try to get him to sleep," she added, hoping to soften the previous verbal blow. "Look, Tommy, I'm just as upset about this as you are," she tried again, but now she sounded cold. The noise level, with Olivier's screams, was far above the comfort level, and each sentence she yelled to Tommy felt like a grenade she'd lobbed into his foxhole.

"I'm gonna get in the shower," Tommy said.

"Mama! Mama!" Olivier screamed. Ellen tried to hold him in her arms but he bucked away. She considered tossing him, fully clothed, into the shower with Tommy just to snap him into a different reality, but that came perilously close to child abuse. She sat down in Karen's rocking chair and watched Olivier as if he were the main act in a talent show.

He kept it up in the car. Tommy, at the wheel, and Ellen, in the passenger seat, both stared out the windshield as if they were watching a suspenseful drive-in movie, maybe a horror film, with Olivier supplying the sound track. At red lights, people in neighboring cars shook their heads or looked suspiciously from the front to the backseat as if they were contemplating a citizen's arrest.

This was such an unwelcome intrusion into her precious time with Tommy. And since it was dark, there was no hope of distracting Olivier by pointing out the boats in the St. Lawrence River or the planes overhead. In desperation, she finally hung over the front seat and said, "Olivier! Where's Mutley? We gotta find Mutley. Where's Mutley?"

Like a small miracle, Olivier's screams ceased. A few seconds passed before the echoes stilled. "Let's find Mutley!" Ellen repeated enthusiastically. Suspicion accentuated the edges of each blotch on Olivier's face and he looked equally drawn toward calming down and revving up again.

"Mutley, we love you," Ellen sang to the tune of "The Farmer in the Dell." "Oh Mutley, we love you; Mutley, Mutley, Mutley, Mutley; Mutley, we love you." She could see she was winning Olivier over, but a sideways glance at Tommy's face told her that for him, between Olivier's screaming and Ellen's singing, it was a toss-up. Perversely, she launched into a new song. "Mutley, Mutley, had a farm, ee ii ee ii oooo," she sang. "And on that farm he had a boy, ee ii ee ii oooo; with a wah-wah here and a wah-wah there, here a wah, there a wah, everywhere a wah-wah; Mutley, Mutley had a farm, ee ii ee ii oooooo." She felt crazy, as if Olivier's temporary madness had jumped to her across the car seat. Now he was smiling, and without hesitation she belted out another chorus, poking him in the ribs on each "wah."

"I think I got to him," she finally said to Tommy.

"Thank fucking God," he said. "I couldn't take too many more choruses of 'Mutley, Mutley, had a farm.' " He sounded genuinely miserable.

"He'll be fine now." Ellen turned and resettled in her seat, worn-out.

"How much farther?" asked Tommy.

"Maybe forty-five minutes."

"Is there a place to get something to eat on the way?"

Ellen tried to think. "There's a *pommes frites* stand in Huntingdon."

"French fries. Great for the waistline. And nutritious, too. I wouldn't want to miss my daily quota of fry oil."

"Don't forget to order the poutine. It's like wallpaper paste that glues the french fries to the walls of your intestines forever."

"Just what I need for my cholesterol."

Ellen knew that he was just miffed because things were out of control. He wanted to stroll the quaint streets of Old Montreal, find a bistro, have himself a salade nicoise and a few glasses of a chilled *vin blanc sec*. Instead, he'd chomp on french fries seasoned in white vinegar and served in a paper cone covered with grease spots. No wonder he was disappointed. She wanted to say that she understood his mood and sympathized, but when she opened her mouth to speak, as if she were possessed, she said, "Look, one spoiled brat is about all I can handle at one time, okay?"

Tommy gripped the wheel and said nothing.

"Why did I say that?" Ellen said. "I don't think Olivier is a spoiled brat. He's a beautiful baby. And I feel terrible that you're hungry and tired and nothing is going right." Tommy did not respond. "At least Olivier is quiet now," she continued. In fact, when she looked over her shoulder at him, she saw that his head had listed to one side and he was about to fall asleep.

"It won't kill me to miss a meal." Tommy's voice tone and rhythm were both unnatural.

"I'll make you something good at home." She placed her hand on his thigh.

But when they finally got to Eagle Beak, Tommy said, "I'm beat. All I want is a bed." He didn't even comment on the house, which Ellen thought looked warmly inviting, its porch light burning serenely in the dark night and flowers everywhere inside. Ellen carried Olivier up the stairs and Tommy followed, bumping his head once on the door to the stairs and once on the door to the bedroom. He stripped and fell into bed, making no comment on the lousy mattress or the feather pillows, so packed they seemed like bags of concrete.

Ellen lay awake beside him. The Buddhists say that all problems begin and end with desire, but her desires were so minimal, such very small potatoes. All she wanted was a nice weekend with the man she loved, her husband of seventeen years whom she had not seen in twenty-one days. Was that so much to ask?

Both Tommy and Olivier were snoring, but Ellen could not relax. The illuminated face of her bedside clock said one thirty, two oh five, then two thirty. Tommy had rolled to the middle of the sagging bed, and Ellen had to exert conscious control to prevent herself from tumbling on top of him. As she clung to the edge of the mattress, digging her fingers in, it hit her that this might well be the very mattress Viola died on. From here, she had reached out to Rayfield Geebo, thinking he was Rodney, and said, "I'm sorry." She had probably died thinking that Rodney had deserted her, run out of the room and left her to face her fate alone. Had she gripped the side of the mattress as the circle of light closed, leaving her in the dark?

twenty-eight

When she heard Rodney in the kitchen and the aroma of coffee began to rise like vapor from the floor cracks, Ellen wished he wasn't there, which made her feel ashamed of herself. She had both begged and bullied him to be her breakfast partner, and now that somebody better had come along, she wanted him to get lost.

Quickly, she rose from the bed and put on her work clothes. Olivier was lying on his back, holding on to his feet and gurgling, when Ellen reached into his port-a-crib and drew him upward. Tommy needed sleep and she didn't want Olivier to wake him prematurely with his chatter, which often grew louder and more animated as he went along.

Rodney was already seated in his usual spot at the table with a fresh *Free Trader* spread out in front of him. "Hey, Rodney," Ellen said, she hoped cheerfully.

He looked up. "'Morning, Ellen. *Bonjour*, Olivier."

"What's new and good?" This had become her standard morning greeting.

"Well, they're getting ready for the Fireman's Field Day in town."

"This town?" Ellen could not quite connect Baldy's store and the pint-sized post office with the concept of a town, and as far as firemen went, she seriously doubted there was a professional one for many miles.

"Well, yaasss," he said with his North Country twang. "What're you taking?"

"Taking?" She felt mentally challenged and poured her tea to jump-start her brain cells.

"To sell."

"Sell?"

"Is there an echo in here?" Rodney asked, regarding her over the top of his drugstore reading glasses.

"What do you mean sell?"

"Everybody makes something to sell and the money all goes to the volunteer fire department and rescue squad."

"I'll write a check," Ellen said with a dismissive wave of her free hand, but then she felt a jolt of guilt. It was just like a city slicker to show up brandishing a checkbook while all the locals invested a part of themselves in what they offered. They probably baked pies, and an Eagle Beak honcho tasted them all and awarded the blue ribbon to some flour-coated housewife.

"What'd you make?" she asked as she put Olivier in his high chair and served him half a glazed donut.

"Same thing I make every year—a statue of an American eagle."

"Gee, Rodney, that's really generous."

"Well, think about it. Nothing stands between you and losing everything but the volunteer fire department. I was on it myself when I was a young man."

"I never even thought of it." She was used to the concept of fire stations with well-paid firefighters, state-of-the-art trucks, and polished poles that a fireman could slide down in a split second. "I wonder what I could give." She looked around the house, but nothing stood out as an appropriate donation.

"Money is okay," Rodney said. But now she wanted to do something more personal, something more folksy. She couldn't really offer anything from her organic garden because the only thing remotely pickable was her arugula and her romaine lettuce and who'd cough over big bucks for a green salad? And she couldn't sell kisses because who would line up at her booth? Her first chance to be of the people, and she was drawing a blank.

Her thoughts were interrupted by a bellow from above. "Caaawwwfffeee, caaawwwfffeee," Tommy called. A familiar ritual, but somehow she was not expecting it.

"I forgot your husband was coming," Rodney said. "I hope we didn't wake him up. You can hear every word all over this house."

"Let me take him his coffee. I'll be right back." Ellen fixed it exactly the way Tommy liked it: one level teaspoon of sugar, no milk. Tommy, shored up by pillows, had the covers drawn up to his hips, but Ellen could see the widest part of his patch of dark pubic hair. His body had shifted in the last few weeks, as if it were a lump of clay in the hands of a Nordic Rodin. She placed the coffee on the bedside table. Tommy put his arm around her hips and drew her to him. "I like to fuck in the morning," he said.

"Shhh, shhh. Rodney's here," Ellen whispered in Tommy's ear. He pulled the covers back to reveal a giant-size erection.

"Just sit on it, baby. Come on, it'll only take a second."

Ellen knew she could lower herself onto him, do a few deep knee bends, and it would all be over. It would feel good, sort of illegal, and Tommy would have a shit-eating grin for at least two hours. He tucked his thumb under the base and raised it up for Ellen to admire. Her breath quickened. She had always been a fool for a hard-on, and the legs of her work shorts were so wide she wouldn't even have to take them off. She could just shift them to one side, a technique she'd mastered in the hippie days when long skirts and no underwear combined to make public intercourse easy. All you had to do was sit on a guy's lap and keep the rocking and the screaming to a minimum.

"Come on, honey. We gotta make up for lost time."

"Wouldn't you like to have your coffee first?" Ellen stalled.

"No, I want pussy."

"I'm taking Olivier out for a little walk," Rodney yelled from below. Ellen was certain he had heard it all and had decided to make himself scarce out of politeness. It was somewhat embarrassing, but what the hell. This was, after all, the same man who had first met her when she was naked and hiding in a rain barrel. When she heard the screen door slam, she peeled off her clothes and slipped into bed beside Tommy.

It was useless to hope for foreplay when Tommy started out with a raging erection. The point, from his perspective, was not to make it last. He just wanted to come, and she knew it. The only way she could prolong it was to coyly order him, in the voice of a dominatrix rather than a nag, not to give in to his own urges. Then he would grimace and slow down the hip rotation so she could get a few more minutes out of him. But wait! This was no time to contemplate sexual justice, she knew. At their ages and after so many years of marriage, if you saw a rosebud, you gathered it gratefully and asked your questions later, while your husband snoozed and you amused yourself by counting the cracks in the ceiling above the bed.

Tommy rolled on top of her. Ellen winced as he centered himself and began his thrust into her. He hadn't even kissed her once, and his hand found its way to her breast only after his penis was positioned for his maximum pleasure and instant gratification. Suddenly Ellen started to giggle. She couldn't help herself. It was all so absurd in its way.

"Oh," Tommy whispered, "we're in for a laughing one, huh?" Rather than answer, she laughed louder. "Go ahead, baby, laugh your ass off." He did not change his rhythm, though he did bury his face in her neck and kiss her throat, her earlobe, her hairline.

"I'm sorry," she said between giggles. "It's gotta be a challenge to fuck a laughing hyena."

"I like to fuck you no matter what you're doing," he said in a husky whisper.

"Laughing, crying, happy, sad, mopey, distracted . . ." With every word, he moved deeper into her.

"I know I'm difficult," she said, her chuckles slowing.

"You're impossible."

Ellen kissed him with sudden passion.

"You sexy bitch," he said.

Ellen was less surprised to be called a bitch than to be called sexy.

"Say that again," she ordered, noticing that she felt hot, bothered, and turned-on like a teenager in a drive-in movie.

"You sexy, sexy bitch," Tommy repeated. His face was poised a half-inch from hers, his tongue tracing the outline of her lips. Ellen wrapped her legs around him and locked her ankles together. She rocked, she rolled, and she found herself suddenly on the rim of a huge, personal volcano, just wishing Tommy would push her in. And when he did, she tossed away every inhibition in the book and howled like a banshee.

It was beautiful, this union, even if the route to it was full of potholes and ruts. Once in New York, a whole section of the FDR Drive had collapsed and a car fell in. Amazingly, no one was hurt. The Channel 7 news had gotten there just as the car's stoic driver had been hoisted out of the crevice on a rope. How many times had she and Tommy lifted each other out of the great potholes of their marriage? Or driven, amid maniacal laughter, into one?

"I love you, Tommy," she said.

"Likewise, baby," he answered. In their relationship, this was a famous line. It had been uttered by one of her friend Lorraine's inarticulate ex-lovers in response to her first and only declaration of love. She had dumped the guy shortly afterward, when he gave her a gift certificate for a high colonic for Valentine's Day. Today, it wasn't good enough, though.

"Say it."

"I love you, Ellen." He was staring straight into her eyes, and she had no reason to doubt him. When he came inside her, she felt instantly happy, as if she had just received a lifesaving injection of trace minerals. Her breathing deepened, and when she extracted herself shortly afterward without waking him and collected her clothes from the floor, she was sure that the mere fifteen minutes that had passed, according to the clock on the nightstand, had expanded to the hallucinogenic proportions induced by a tab of windowpane acid, her personal favorite during her wild and wooly youth.

She looked out the window and saw Rodney and Olivier petting Mutley, who, now that his hair was growing back in, was just beginning to look like a dog and not a cartoon character. She tied her sneakers, unconsciously humming a chorus of "Mutley, Mutley had a farm" as she skipped down the kamikaze staircase.

At her age, it seemed ridiculous to allow self-consciousness to rear its head in the realm of sexual relations with one's own husband, but Ellen felt a twinge of embarrassment as she crossed the lawn. She made a conscious choice to brazen it out, and when Rodney said, "What? Done already?" she only smiled.

"Sorry to have chased you out of the house, Rodney, but I had no choice but to submit."

"That's okay," he said.

"Since we're on the subject, have you ever been married?"

"The right person never found me," Rodney said.

Ellen laughed. "Slim pickings in Eagle Beak?"

"Not so much that as . . . well . . . I got my problems." Ellen remembered the alcohol on his breath at seven in the morning. "What kind of problems?" she asked softly.

"Not everybody in the world wants to talk about their problems, you know," Rodney said. "Some things are personal."

"You might not believe this," Ellen said quickly, "but in New York, personal problems are public. Everybody either has a shrink or goes to an anonymous group so they can tell their most private stories over and over again, even if they have to pay someone to listen." She knew this was just fast talk. "Hey, you want to hear about *my* one and only night in group therapy?"

A therapy novice, she had allowed her shrink to talk her into attending a group session. When the first person spoke, a lumox who, in Ellen's humble opinion, seemed like a stick of dynamite searching for a match, he had complained in a soft voice about waiting for hours on line at the social services department. The therapist asked him if he wanted to express himself, and he had mumbled yes. Everyone rose to his or her feet, Ellen a half-beat behind. The Incredible Hulk, as she later referred to him, positioned himself directly in front of her, looked deeply into her eyes, and then screamed, *"I'm angry!"* into her face. At the time, she thought her eardrums might burst. Then he moved clockwise around the circle, yelling out his rage at the therapees who first mentally braced themselves and then just took it. Upon leaving, Ellen stopped at the first pay phone she saw and left a message on the therapist's answering service: "Group therapy is worse than reality. I quit." It made a great New York shrink story, and she had told it several times.

But Rodney didn't want to hear it. "I thought group therapy was strictly private," he said. "Whatever happened is none of my beeswax." Meanwhile, Olivier was sitting on Mutley, trying to make his ears flap down.

"Did you have your second cup of coffee?" Ellen asked.

"Not yet."

"Let's go in."

Ellen offered Olivier her hand and they all returned to their places at the dining-room table. No sooner had the coffee cups been refilled than the creaking of the floor overhead indicated that Tommy was up. Ellen set a place for him and they all waited as he made his way down the stairs.

"Damn, you could kill yourself on that staircase," Tommy said as he entered the room. "What kind of an idiot would build them like that?"

"That would be my grandfather," Rodney said, rising and extending his hand. "I'm Rodney de Beer."

Tommy shook. "Good to meet you, Rodney. No disrespect meant toward your grandfather. He must have had very small feet." Tommy's smile had a way of neutralizing any insult, though Rodney didn't seem the least bit miffed.

"This is my husband, Tom Kenny," Ellen said.

"I figured." Rodney sat down.

"Coffee and a donut?" Ellen asked, indicating the vacant chair. It rocked when Tommy sat down. Tommy looked around. "So this is it," he said, turning toward the window. "Pretty spot."

The green lawn stretched lazily to the line of dark trees, and the blue sky had only a few clouds in it, hanging like puffs of winter breath in the process of disappearing.

"I didn't realize this house had been in your family for generations," Ellen said.

"We built it."

"Rodney has a bigger place nearby," Ellen said for Tommy's benefit. But it struck her how fragile human roots were. They could be torn up so very easily. They could shrivel and rot away and mean nothing. Her roots were in White River Junction, Vermont, but she doubted she would ever set foot in that town again. Obviously, roots were an illusion. People did not have roots, no matter what they pretended. That honor and distinction belonged to the members of the plant kingdom. And most of them, sooner or later, were hacked off at ground level and eaten or burned alive in fireplaces.

"You came just in time for the Field Day. It's the biggest event of the year in Eagle Beak."

"What time does it crank up?"

"About eleven, and then it goes 'til midnight."

Tommy glanced at his Rolex watch. "Good. We have time to go buy a mattress before it starts. Ellen, I'm buying you a new mattress and box spring. How can you sleep on that one you've got?" He turned to Rodney. "Is there a local dump where we could throw a mattress?"

"There's one in Lamone. It'll be closed, but you could just pitch it by the gate. Take my truck. Make it easy on yourselves."

"But there's no car seat for Olivier."

"I can watch him. It'd give you two lovebirds a chance to see the town. We could meet up later, at the field day."

Ellen's heart leapt. A chance to be childless again, to walk at her own pace and have an uninterrupted adult conversation. They could stroll the elm-lined streets of Lamone, hand in hand. "What d'you think, Tommy?"

"I think we should hit the road before my man Rodney changes his mind." Rodney smiled. Tommy had a knack for making others, even the Caspar Milquetoasts of the world, feel like they were in charge. People liked him—men, women, and children. Even criminals liked him. They shook his hand at the end of their trials, regardless of the outcome, and said, "Thanks, man."

"Let's lug that backbreaker downstairs," Tommy said. As Ellen stripped the bed, she thought again of Viola, who had climbed into it to die. Perhaps it had psychic cooties that accounted for her Viola dreams. Still, she felt a moment of reverence was in order. Over the stained, lumpy mattress, she made a cross sign with her fingers. "Go in peace, Viola," she whispered while Tommy's back was turned. She had no urge to tell him all she knew about this bed, about the high drama that had unfolded in it, about the tragic ending and the final curtain. Usually, she told her husband everything.

"Let's take it to the top of the stairs and then just shove it," Tommy said. Ellen held up her end, and she gave it a good push at the appropriate moment. They carried the spring, so old it didn't even have a cloth cover let alone a pillow top, down step by step and hiked it into Rodney's truck. Then Rodney and Tommy exchanged keys. Ellen settled into the passenger side, and they took off, waving goodbye to Olivier with great gusto.

"Macho man," Tommy said as he hung his elbow out the window and steered down the dirt road.

"Nature girl," Ellen replied. "A woman who runs with the wolves." She did not add, even to herself, that running with the wolves was fine if you were a wolf or an adopted member of the pack, but if you were a tagalong or an imposter, secretly worried that they might turn on you and tear you limb from limb, the tension was exhausting.

"Me, Tarzan; you, Jane," Tommy said, obviously milking his moment in the wilderness for all it was worth. "Me, Adam; you, Eve."

Ellen wracked her brain for a couple in which the female was the mainstay and not the appendage, but nothing came to mind until she finally blurted out, "Me, Sheena; you, temporary playmate."

Tommy laughed. "You, Cleopatra; me, Marc Anthony," he said. "At least that way I get a name." He turned right at the end of her road without even asking for directions and sped down the mountain. Coming the other direction, up the Eagle Beak hill, Ellen spotted Rayfield's truck. She leaned forward and prepared to wave, but Rayfield never glanced in her direction.

"God, look at that! Did you see what that guy had on his truck?"

"No, what? Where?"

"Across the front."

Ellen had observed this North Country fashion statement. People put large printed announcements, such as "Mountain Man" or "Jesus Loves Me" on special bug shields that stretched across the front of the hood. She thought of them as advanced bumper stickers and had no idea where there were purchased. Somehow, though, she had never noticed Rayfield's, perhaps because of the number of splattered June bugs there. "What'd it say?"

"It said, 'I need a hummer.' "

"What does that mean?"

"It means, I need a blow job," Tommy said. "Now what kind of a guy would advertise that?"

"Maybe a guy who really needs one," Ellen answered reasonably. Again, she had a golden opportunity to tell Tommy Rayfield's story, all its chapters and verses including those in which she was featured, but she felt no desire to say a single word.

"Every guy needs one all the time," Tommy said.

"At least he didn't put it on a vanity plate," Ellen said.

"They have a hired guy at the DMV who researches all the requests for vanity plates to make sure there's no sexual subtext," Tommy said.

"As if sex is the worst possible thing," Ellen scoffed. "We're such a nation of puritans."

Tommy did not respond, but there was a subtle intensification of the atmospheric molecules in the truck's cab. Ellen could feel unsaid words suspended in the air around her head.

"What?" she asked after five seconds. In her heart, she already knew that there was something Tommy was not saying, and it had to do with sex.

"Are you reverting to free love in your old age?" Tommy asked.

"My old age?" Ellen repeated.

"Well, let's face it. We're not spring chickens anymore, are we, baby?"

"I guess not."

But could sex still cause trouble in their marriage? Ellen's reproductive system was going out of business, and Tommy was already worried about his prostate gland. Weren't they past the point where sex issues could rise up and wreak havoc? Why did Ellen suddenly feel so afraid?

"Tommy, is there anything you want to tell me?" She thought she sensed a slight hesitation before he said, "No, why?"

"I don't know. I just wonder if there's something hanging in the air."

"Not that I know of."

So Ellen let it go.

twenty-nine

So what do you think of the house?" Ellen asked as they sped away onward toward Lamone.

"It's rustic."

"Come on, Tommy. Humor me. Say a little more."

"It has the lived-in look."

"Does it feel cozy?"

"I guess so."

"Well, are you at all interested in thinking of it as *our* summer house?"

"Nope. I don't want a summer house, Ellen. I'd rather take a nice trip or spend my vacation at the beach."

"What're you doing this year?" It seemed unbelievably strange not to know. Tommy always took one week off in the summer, usually the first week of August. Last year, they had gone to Portugal.

"I'm not sure yet. I guess it depends on whether or not you're coming."

"Am I invited?"

"El-len," he said impatiently.

"Well, am I?"

"Of course you are."

"What about coming here?"

"No, thanks. Who wants to spend a week in the boonies with nothing to do?"

"Well, that's clear enough."

"I'm very clear on this point, honey."

"Okay." She couldn't hold it against him, though she did resent it. "So where are you thinking of going?"

"I'm considering a yoga retreat in the Bahamas."

"A *yoga* retreat?"

"Yeah. I started a yoga class. It feels great. I'd like to make it a habit."

"Geez, Tommy, when do you fit it all in? I mean, the ski track, the yoga?"

"The yoga class is at six thirty in the morning. I go before work."

"Really?"

"And when I get home, I work out on the ski track."

"That's great, Tommy. Jeez, I didn't know a fitness nut lurked beneath your lazy exterior."

"Neither did I. But when you left, I had to find something to do."

"I didn't *leave*."

"Yes, you did."

"But I didn't leave *you*."

"I know that, Ellen," he said, reaching for her hand, which he raised to his mouth and kissed. "You needed some space and you took it. Nothing wrong with that."

"Space? Have you been reading pop psychology, too?"

He ignored her question. "So how's it going, honey?" His tone was serious now.

"I don't really know. It's not what I expected." She felt miserable.

"Why don't you bag it and come home?"

Ellen thought carefully for a few seconds. "No, I want to stick it out for the summer. See what happens."

"Is anything happening yet? You've been here almost a month."

"Well," she began, "my garden's coming up, and I have Olivier . . . and Mutley. And I have two friends—Rodney and this guy Rayfield. And I'm seeing an acupuncturist who's helping me to open my heart for twenty-five bucks a visit."

"That's a bargain. It'd cost you five times that in the city," Tommy said facetiously. "How, may I ask, is he doing it?"

"With some tea. I don't know what's in it, but it's definitely doing something." Now was the time to tell him about her Viola dreams and her spontaneous love declarations. It seemed like so much and so little that she didn't know where to begin. But before she could even try, Tommy said, "Remember the dragon powder?" and Ellen giggled. Five years before she had consulted with a Chinese doctor who operated out of a storefront in Chinatown. She had felt listless and exhausted, and he prescribed daily doses of dragon powder. "Where does it come from?" Ellen had asked the teenage boy, probably a tong member, who was doing the interpreting. "Dragons," replied the doctor. Ellen took it anyway and was breathing fire within a week, but when she ran out and returned for more, the storefront was boarded up and the neighbors simply shook their heads and said nothing when she asked where Dr. Wong had gone.

"I still wonder what that was."

"I didn't know your heart needed opening."

"Neither did I. But it does. There's something wrong with me."

"Maybe it's the change of life," Tommy said.

"Maybe." She pondered that for a few seconds and then added, "I'm on an express train to an unknown destination."

"We all know the ultimate destination."

"Death?"

"The last stop on the subway line," Tommy said, and they both laughed nervously and turned their attention out the window toward the river, tumbling over the rocks on its way to Lamone. A fisherman wearing hip boots stood in the middle, his lightweight pole pointing upstream. "The closer it gets, the more you want to live," Tommy said. "The more you want to live fully and make it count."

"Poor Cocho," Ellen said, as if it were a natural transition. "Poor Karen, poor Olivier."

"And poor Ellen," Tommy said, reaching over to pat her lovingly on the shoulder. In the early days of their relationship, when Ellen felt that to be alive was to sit on a burning stove every moment, Tommy had often comforted her by holding her close and repeating "Poor Ellen" in her ear. They even invented a name for it: pooring her. "Come here and let me poor you," Tommy would say, and she would surrender to his embrace, listen to his words, and let the tears fall. Almost two decades ago. When had the pooring stopped?

"Why was I so unhappy when I was young?" she asked.

"Because you grew up unappreciated."

"What did you ever see in me?" She and Tommy were talking about her past as if it were someone else's. It was so far away now that Tommy could say anything and she would not hold it against him.

"I fell in love with you. Love at first sight."

"Why?"

"I don't know. When I saw you crying in that ice cream, I just knew I had to have you."

"Why?"

"You're one of a kind, Ellen." Usually at such a moment Ellen would burst into grateful tears. Today, though, she just took a deep breath and held onto Tommy's fingers. The road led them directly past a Furniture Weekend store having a Fourth of July sale. Tommy pulled into the parking lot.

The mattresses and box springs of the Furniture Weekend occupied half the length of the huge warehouse. Ellen and Tommy stretched out, full length, on several models, one by one. At first, it seemed odd to lie together on a display bed. In New York, they simply called 1-800-Mattress, stated a brand name and price range, and the next morning the mattress and box spring were delivered in protective plastic wrap to their door. Here in Lamone, they rolled from side to side, sat on the edge of the beds, and answered questions like "How's it feel?" from passersby. The name brands were costly, and Ellen felt guilty to think about Tommy paying big bucks for such a grand housewarming gift. "This is turning out to be an expensive weekend for you," she said.

"Don't worry about it," Tommy answered as he fluffed the goose down pillows and turned onto his side to face her. "This one feels great. Let's take it." But when Tommy found the salesman, he learned that the floor models were not for sale. The mattresses had to be ordered and took ten days for delivery. They did have a few mattresses in the storeroom, and Tommy ended up buying a high-priced queen set, sight unseen. Two teenage boys with elaborate haircuts muscled it into the back of the truck. Now two sets of bedware stood on edge, like a chorus line waiting for the music to begin and the kicking to commence.

When they got to the town dump, they faced a locked gate. "What do we do now?" Ellen asked as she stared at a mini-mountain of rusting refrigerators, household appliances, and general nonperishable debris in the distance, perhaps two hundred yards away.

"We dump it here by the gate like Rodney said and take off."

"What if we get caught?"

"Who's gonna catch us?"

"Let's do it and get out of here." But no sooner had they climbed into the truck bed than a police cruiser happened by, and seeing them at the gate, slowly turned into the dirt driveway leading to the dump.

"Shit, we're busted," Ellen said.

"Let me do the talking," replied Tommy.

The car stopped and a cop in his late twenties emerged from behind the wheel.

"Good morning, Officer," Tommy said in a cheerful voice.

"What d'you think you're doing? The dump's closed."

"We see that, but we need to get rid of this old mattress and spring, and, to tell the truth, Officer, we thought we could carry it to that pile of debris over there."

Ellen, anxious to contribute something, said, "We weren't going to *take* anything."

"It's trespassing on town property. You summer people?" He had probably hated the privileged summer people for his whole life.

"We're local taxpayers," Tommy said pointedly. "Property owners."

"Just here for the weekend?"

"My wife's here for the summer, but I'm only here for a few days. Can you give us a break?"

The cop leaned back against the hood of the car. "Okay. Go ahead." Clearly, he was going to watch the whole time, like the shotgun-toting, mirrored sunglass-wearing Southern sheriffs in charge of movie chain gangs.

"Thanks," Tommy said, adding to Ellen, "let's start with the spring." They lowered it out of the truck, hoisted it over the gate, and scrambled after it. Neither said a word until they neared the pile of junk. "I thought we were just gonna leave it at the gate," Ellen whispered, hoping they were out of earshot. Sweat was rolling down the side of her face and her hands hurt where the metal was digging in.

"I had to improvise. Besides, look at the plus side. You're getting rid of this lousy fucking bed." On the count of three, they pitched the spring onto the pile of debris and went back for the mattress.

"Where you folks live at?" asked the cop as Ellen and Tommy climbed back into the truck bed.

"Eagle Beak," Ellen said.

"I mean permanently."

"Manhattan," Tommy said. "New York City."

"Yeah? What do you do for work?"

"He's an attorney."

"A prosecutor," Tommy cut in, giving Ellen a sharp look.

"You got your hands full then," the cop said as Tommy and Ellen tipped the mattress over the edge of the truck and jumped down to drag it toward garbage mecca. The mattress had no handles, and Ellen kept dropping her end.

"Prosecutor?" she whispered.

"You should've said I drove a bus, for chrissakes."

"You think it matters?"

"Fucking A it does."

This time when they returned, the police officer was smoking a cigarette. "This your truck?" he asked.

"No, my neighbor lent it to me," Ellen answered.

"Inspection sticker's expired."

"I'll tell him. He's a responsible guy. I'm sure he just forgot."

"I gotta give you a ticket."

"All right, then go ahead and write one," Ellen snapped. Tommy got in the driver's side and opened the glove compartment to search for the vehicle registration.

"The man who owns this truck is a senior citizen. Maybe he's a little forgetful, you know?" Ellen was angry at this punk cop, and she couldn't let it go. "He's on a fixed income. He can't afford a ticket." She didn't even know if that was true.

"Registration and proof of insurance, please."

Tommy passed the paperwork through the window at Ellen, and she thrust them toward the police officer. "Here," she said. "Hope you get your quota."

"Ellen, get in the truck," Tommy said. "Let the officer do his job."

"What job? Protect and serve?"

"Get in the truck, Ellen."

"Shit," she swore as she climbed in, "I'm paying this ticket."

"You better cool it," Tommy said.

"Well, why does he have to be such an asshole?"

"You can't fight City Hall, Ellen. Just forget it."

When the officer handed Tommy the ticket, along with Rodney's various documents, Ellen stared straight ahead and silently fumed. The bed she wanted at Furniture Weekend was not available. The dump was closed, and now, thanks to her, Rodney had a blemish on his motor vehicle record. Tommy had abandoned his lifelong position as a public defender, gone over to the other side to humor a small-town cop on a power trip. And to top it all off, he was going to a yoga retreat in the Bahamas on his vacation. He'd rather stand on his head and sleep on a plank than spend his week off with her.

"I got an idea. Let's get the truck inspected."

"Fat chance on the Fourth of July weekend," Ellen answered.

"Okay. We won't bother. We'll just go to the Field Day and make like bumpkins."

"Nothing ever bugs you, does it?"

"Of course things bug me, Ellen. You know that."

"But kissing that little cop-twerp's ass doesn't?"

"Look, he yanked our chain. Get over it. It's not worth hanging on to."

"But I'm angry," she said. Her voice had risen in volume and was perilously close to yelling. And then it hit her. "My God, I've turned into that guy in group therapy!" She was incredulous. If she wasn't careful, Tommy would go back to New York and describe his weekend with his wife as worse than reality. "Tommy, I'm sorry. I don't know what's wrong with me."

"You should try yoga."

"Yeah. Maybe if Karen and Cocho get back in time, I'll go with you to that retreat."

After a slight hesitation, Tommy responded with a halfhearted, "Yeah."

Change the subject, Ellen warned herself. It seemed like all conversational roads led to dead ends today. It was impossible to believe they'd made love not more than two hours ago. The closeness it created had worn off quickly, which made her feel twice as lonely as she would have if Tommy had not visited her at all.

He reached for her hand. "Let's go back to your house and put the bed together."

"Good idea."

But the queen-sized box spring would not go up the kamikaze staircase. No matter how they twisted and shoved, it simply did not fit through the door and up the stairs.

"I see two possible solutions," Tommy said. "Tear out the door or sleep in the living room."

"There must be a way," Ellen said, her shoulder pressing against the box spring until it was firmly wedged in the doorway. "I will not accept defeat." She lay on her back on the living-room floor and shoved with her powerful legs, to no avail.

"Maybe we could hoist it up outside and take it in through a window. Let me go look." A few seconds later he was back. "Got a tape measure?"

"In the toolbox in the woodshed. Through the kitchen." Tommy left again.

This is definitely symbolic, Ellen thought as she studied the quilted box spring. Her potential comfort in life, jammed into the portal of the staircase to heaven. But symbolic of what?

Tommy returned. "Let's drag it back into the living room," he said. They tugged it free and maneuvered it this way and that. Tommy went to work, measuring the box spring from every angle. Then he went upstairs to check out the size of the window frame.

"Looking good," he called down. "I just have to pop the window out."

"Is it a big job?"

"It's not nothing." He came back downstairs. "But first let's go over to the Field Day and get something to eat. I'm starved."

"Okay. And we really should pick up Olivier."

"Let's go."

The closest place to park was a quarter mile from the field in which the festivities took place, across the road from Baldy's store. Ellen stopped to pet Useless and waved a hello to Baldy. Hand in hand, she and Tommy entered the cloud of smoke rising from red meat on the barbee. "It's a time warp," Tommy whispered as they passed a booth in which a local redneck was throwing darts at inflated balloons. There was also a table with sign-up sheets for the three-legged race. They naturally gravitated to the food stands and soon found themselves in a wonderland of fried dough, cotton candy, caramel apples, and hot dogs buried in chopped onions.

"See anything remotely healthy?" Ellen asked.

"There's gotta be potato salad somewhere. And corn on the cob. Personally, I'll be crushed if there's no root beer. Or should I say *rut* beer?" On they strolled, down the midway, where strangers milled everywhere. Many wore modified baseball caps to which two beer cans were fastened. Flexible straws, probably made of aquarium hosing, dangled from each in the vicinity of the wearer's mouth. "I wonder where you get those hats. I've never seen them in the city."

"In the city, you get hassled for having a visible beer. I wonder why they let 'em get away with it up here."

"What happened to America?" she asked.

"It's right here, at the Fireman's Field Day. Let's eat."

He stepped up to a food vendor and ordered two ears of corn and two Mountain Dews. When the woman passed them over the card table, the whole meal was color-coordinated. They sat down at a picnic table, ready to eat, but before either had taken their first bite, who should come ambling toward them but Rayfield. Naturally, he sported the indigenous headgear, but Ellen noticed that he had two caffeine-free Diet Cokes, not cans of beer, in his. In fact, even his beer belly seemed shrunken. Clearly, he was sticking to Dr. Yi's program.

"Hey, Rayfield," she said.

"Hey, Ellen."

"I'd like you to meet my husband, Tom Kenny. Tommy, Rayfield Geebo."

Tommy stood up and they shook hands.

"Rayfield's my friend," Ellen announced, like a kindergartner who was just becoming socialized.

"Slave's more like it. She's got me babysitting, washing clothes, mowing the lawn, driving her places. I ain't had a moment's peace since she got here."

"She knows how to crack the whip, definitely," Tommy said as he sat down again.

"How many jobs she got you doing?"

"Put it this way: there's a big one waiting for me back at the ranch."

Rayfield whooped. "Say no. Be the boss. Don't let her henpeck you, Tom."

"Hey, I'm not the one who insisted on buying a new mattress," Ellen interjected. "It's not my fault it won't go up the stairs and now you have to take the window out."

"See the thanks I get?" Tommy said, obviously entering into a conspiracy with Rayfield.

Ellen gulped down half of her jumbo-size paper cup of Mountain Dew.

Then she lowered her cup and stared at her tablemates. Tommy had his corn-cob in one hand and one yellow kernel was stuck to his cheek near his mouth, and Rayfield looked insane in his modified Viking helmet. Who were they to treat her like a nag?

"Did either of you two boobs ever think about the origin of the word *hen-pecker?*" she smugly asked. "Don't you think it's odd that the whole world uses it as a derogatory term for women, but in nature, in the barnyard, it's the males that peck the hens for no reason. They really hurt them, and the hens just have to take it. But in our world, if a woman speaks up or God forbid demands something, she's a henpecker. She's a bitch on wheels. It's not right."

Ellen shook her head at the unbreachable gap between men and women. If you needed them, they resented it and felt nagged. If you didn't need them, they resented it and called you a ball buster. If you asked them to do some-thing, even something simple like mow the lawn, they held it against you, but if you expressed a little independence, like buying your own house and moving there for a few months, they accused you of abandonment. It stunk.

"If you ask me," Rayfield shrugged, "it's no worse'n calling a man a boob." A belly laugh erupted from Tommy, and Rayfield smiled in triumph. Actually, Ellen was amazed that she had called Tommy a boob to his face. Name calling was rarely practiced between them, and when it was, it was usually for a good reason and no apologies were given nor expected afterward.

"Have you seen Rodney and Olivier?" she asked, just to change the subject.

"Not lately."

"Well, we gotta find them. Come on, Tom."

"Hey, I'm eating my corn here."

"Yeah, let the man finish his corn." Rayfield sat down and took a long sip of his Diet Coke using the straw that hung like grapevines near his mouth. Ellen was certain she detected an evil glint in his eye. The last time she and Rayfield had been together, she had wept on his shoulder. He had put his arm around her and then driven her car home so she could close her eyes. "So how do you like your new dog?" Rayfield asked.

"I don't have a new dog."

"What? You didn't tell him yet?"

"What's to tell? By the time I go back to the city, Mutley will be long gone. Back to you."

"I ain't taking him back."

"Okay," Ellen said. "Fine."

"Fine?" said Tommy.

"Don't worry about it," Ellen huffed, and then she continued on, sweetly, "Finished with your corn, Tommy?"

"Yeah."

"Then let's find Olivier, okay?"

"Sure." Tommy extracted his long legs from under the picnic table and stood up. "Nice meeting you, Rayfield."

"Same here." Rayfield stood up and they shook hands again, and Rayfield proceeded on slowly, like a water buffalo whose horns had mutated after decades of industrial pollution.

"Interesting guy," Tommy remarked.

"You don't know the half of it." Ellen knew she could drop Peyronie's disease into the conversation and within seconds Tommy's whole perception of Rayfield would go through a psychedelic transformation from interesting guy to tragic victim of cruel fate. But she didn't say a word. It was odd, holding back from Tommy. Usually, she told him everything, as if their wedding ceremony officially removed their skins and made them one entity. Maybe the upcoming crone phase would reinstate her boundaries. Maybe it would provide both the will and the way to resist further invasion.

Ellen had read that when traditional Japanese women reached menopause, all the bowing and kowtowing stopped. Obedience and passivity went south and suddenly they said and did exactly as they pleased, and not only the family but the whole world had to shut up and take it. Maybe in America, where liberated women felt obliged to say what they pleased, the process reversed itself and, after menopause, they were free to wall up their perimeter and post a NO TRESPASSING sign.

"What's with the dog?" Tommy asked when Rayfield was out of earshot.

"Forget the dog. Rayfield's just busting my chops. When I leave, I'll just take Mutley over there and dump him in Rayfield's yard. No problem."

Suddenly Tommy smiled. "Hey, honey, remember Merlin?"

"How could I ever forget?"

Merlin was Tommy's black cat, rescued from an alley a few months before Ellen and Tommy had gotten together in New York. He was old and extremely ornery, and the first time Ellen saw him, she knew his days were seriously numbered. Tommy had formed an immediate bond and considered himself somewhat of a feline hospice worker.

Perhaps two months into their affair, Ellen had made a trip to the Outer Banks of North Carolina. When she returned ten days later, she had rushed to Tommy's apartment to make love. Merlin was prone on the windowsill, obviously at death's door. In fact, Tommy had called in sick that day because he was certain that Merlin was in the final hours of his ninth life, and he wanted to be there for him. Ellen petted the cat and brushed him and even tried to lay healing hands on him, but nothing worked, and after a while the desperate need to fuck could not be put off another moment, and she and Tommy fell onto his futon bed.

A half hour into their passion, Merlin jumped down off the windowsill, came to the side of the bed, and let out a bloodcurdling howl. Ellen and Tommy ceased what they were doing and turned their heads in unison in his direction. He howled again. It was chilling.

"Should we stop?" Ellen asked.

Merlin collapsed into a heap.

Tommy remained still for a moment, and then he said, "No. That's death. This is life." So they turned back to each other and later, when they got up, Tommy held Merlin's body in his arms and cried while Ellen ran downstairs to the Korean market and got a box. They put Merlin into it and went out in search of a place to lay him to rest. Ellen suggested the Hudson River, since there was no patch of earth anywhere in Manhattan to dig a hole and bury a dead cat. But before they even made it to the corner, they ran into a casual acquaintance of Ellen's, a woman with whom she took flamenco dance.

"What's in the box?" she asked.

"My dead cat," Tommy answered flatly.

"We're looking for a place to bury him," Ellen said, and then the three of them laughed uneasily for a few seconds.

"Good luck," said the flamenco dancer as she hurried on.

In the end, they had dropped the box into a Dumpster behind a popular Italian restaurant. Ellen respectfully held up the lid while Tommy leaned way in to lay his kitty cat to rest. "Goodbye, Merlin," he whispered. Afterward, they had moodily strolled north on Thompson Street toward Washington Square Park.

"It's funny how a stray cat can imprint himself so indelibly in your memory," Tommy said.

"I can still hear those two howls," Ellen said, and she reached for Tommy's hand. For all the years since Merlin's death, Ellen had never been able to decide whether what they did was right or wrong. In her own defense, she had to say that it was extremely difficult for them at the time to turn away from Merlin and reconnect with each other, to make a conscious choice to express life even in the presence of its great opposite and natural enemy, death. On the other hand, it lacked compassion.

She couldn't help but compare it to Viola's final moments. She thought Rodney was too hard on Rayfield. Didn't Rodney know that it was difficult to steer a ship through crashing waves and impossible to make a good decision when the psychic surf was up? Mostly, you figured those moments out in retrospect, if at all.

"There they are," Tommy said, pointing off toward a swing set upon which Olivier sailed in a low-slung arc while Rodney gently pushed him. "Whee," Rodney was singing with each forward thrust. Olivier's face was lit with pleasure. His black curls alternately blew away from his face and then covered it as the swing moved in its back and forth trajectory.

Ellen waved, but neither noticed. "Don't they look cute?" she asked. "Giapetto and Pinocchio." The thought of the wooden boy come to life reminded her that she had not told Tommy anything about Rodney's great passion for chain saw sculpture. "I'm gonna make a documentary about Rodney," she said, shocking herself.

"You are? Why?"

"Because he's a great spirit," Ellen said, but she felt unsatisfied with that and tried again. "He's an original in a world full of copies."

Tommy watched Rodney for a few seconds. "I'll take your word for it. You know him a lot better than I do."

"Do you think I could do it?"

"Didn't I tell you for years to get out from under Reginald's thumb and go on your own?"

It was true. Every time Ellen reached her wit's end with Reginald Eubanks, Tommy would chant, "Dump that asshole, Ellen. Make your own goddamn documentary."

Yeah, yeah, yeah, she always thought. But now, out of nowhere, it seemed possible. All she needed, really, was a good movie camera and tape recorder and the will to do it.

"Of course, Rodney would have to go along with it."

"You mean you haven't asked him yet?"

"No, so don't say anything. And don't mention anything about the ticket, either. I'll take care of that." Meanwhile, Rodney straightened up from his swing-pushing position and waved. In his overalls, he looked like the quintessential old man of the earth. "Look at that face," Ellen whispered to Tommy as they walked toward him.

"Did you have any luck?" Rodney asked.

"Yes. Unfortunately, we can't get the new mattress through the stairway door."

"Well, I'll be goddamned. That's a shame."

"I'm gonna take the window out. Haul her in through there."

"Good idea."

"How was Olivier?"

"He's good company."

"Ready to give him up?"

"He's all yours. But you know something? Taking care of him made me think about Leland, about how he must've felt when he took me in."

"And how was that?" Ellen asked as Tommy lifted Olivier out of the swing and tossed him into the air a few times.

"Important," Rodney answered.

thirty

T he mattress-in-the-window episode was a personal disaster in the lives of Ellen and Tommy Kenny, married couple. First, the panes of glass shattered and the window frame fell apart. Then the casing, which seemed to be held in place by the pressure of the window itself, detached itself from the rotted wood behind it and fell to the ground. Mosquitoes filled the house, and Tommy, who was perfectly capable of repairing the window but lacked the necessary tools, sent Ellen on six different trips to the hardware store in Lamone. By the time he was ready to hoist the new bed through the window, Ellen had added more than $400 to her credit card debt and Tommy was swearing like a sailor on shore leave in Sicily. And when it was all over and he was ready to clean up, the water, probably from the bottom of the well as Ellen had just used the rest of it to give her garden a good drink, was dark brown, and Tommy refused to sit in it in the bathtub.

"I don't want any goddamn parasites in my asshole, if you don't mind," he said as he kneeled in the tub and used a cloth to remove the outermost layers of sweat and grime. They set off a bug bomb in the house and went for dinner at the Pizza Pie, which was packed full of cigarette smokers. Olivier, who had missed his nap, was cranky, and they had to return home immediately and put him to bed. Then, right at the moment when it looked like they might be able to salvage their sanity with a glass of fine red wine in the peace and quiet of the front porch, the fireworks started at the Field Day and Olivier woke up screaming.

Tommy poured the wine into his mouth and refilled the glass as Ellen ran up the stairs to try to comfort her distraught nephew. But Olivier was inconsolable, and ultimately Ellen put him in the car and drove off, hoping the motion would put him back to sleep. She left Tommy on the porch swing, alone, tying one on for the first time since he'd started his health and physical fitness kick. The enabler, c'est moi, she thought helplessly as a tear splashed onto the steering wheel.

She drove down the mountain as Olivier perfected his screaming routine in the backseat. Tommy would probably want to get away, back to New York where the blood blister on his thumb, which he had smashed with a hammer, could throb in private. And honestly, having him with her, feeling responsible every minute for how he felt, worrying if he was bored, what he might be thinking of her and her present crazy predicament—it was all more pressure than Ellen wanted. Fuck it all, she thought, turning on an oldies station loud enough to drown out Olivier's shrieks. In the sky behind her, in the rearview mirror, she saw explosions of colored light. Spirals of red, white, and blue fell from heaven toward the earth in the dark. The beauty was all too brief before it simply vanished. Ellen hit the accelerator pedal and imagined her husband falling into a drunken sleep. Her major regret was that he would no doubt polish off the whole bottle, and there wouldn't be any wine left for her when she finally got home. And the liquor stores of Lamone were all locked up. On she drove, through the dark countryside.

An hour later, she pulled back into her driveway. The house sat, darker than the moonlit night, as if a gloomy black drape had been pulled across the windows from the inside. Ellen remained in the car for several minutes and listened to the peepers. Her mind felt restless and nervous. After so many years of marriage, she could intuitively sense an oncoming high-pressure front, and they were definitely headed for one. Something was off, way off.

And the next morning, when Tommy put his coffee cup down on the night table and said, "Ellen, I have something I want to tell you," she knew the relationship winds were picking up and it was time to head to her internal basement and hunker down.

"What?" Her mouth was so dry that the tip of her tongue stuck to her alveolar ridge when she pronounced the *t*.

"I met somebody I like."

Ellen, prone in bed, folded her hands on her abdomen and crossed her ankles. "And?" she said, proud that she could even form one syllable.

"And I want to get to know her."

Secretly, Ellen had rehearsed for this moment many times over the years. All wives do, she had thought each time she had practiced. In her fantasies, she sometimes chose the high road and sometimes she rushed him and beat him about the face and neck with her fists. But now that it had actually happened, she simply crumpled, like a paper bag floating on an air current one moment and flattened by a passing public utilities truck the next. "Oh," she said. And as if a door to some locked closet in her intuition suddenly opened, she saw a blazing truth and said, "Your yoga instructor, right?"

"How did you know?" Tommy was clearly unnerved.

"For you to take a class at six thirty in the morning, it had to be more than the yoga." She felt trapped in a soundproof, glass box. "Don't tell me anything about her. Not one detail." Already, Ellen's imagination had coughed up a probable image: a Meg Ryan clone, complete with the "coupe savage" haircut. On the beach in the Bahamas.

"Nothing's happened yet," Tommy said. "I wanted to tell you first."

"What? To get my blessing? My permission?" Her words were heating up and felt like lava oozing out the fissure in a volcano.

"No, I'm not asking for permission. You're not in any position to give it anyway."

"What does that mean?"

"It means I don't answer to you." He placed his cup on the table. "Any more than you answer to me," he added.

Ellen scooted down and pulled Viola's quilt up over her head. The new bed was so large and so firm that she wasn't even touching Tommy. In yesterday's bed, they would have been thrown together in the dip. She preferred to have these crisis conversations with flesh to flesh contact.

I hate this bed, she thought. She had no sheets that fit it, and it took up almost the whole room. It smelled of some new oil-based fabric. Given the choice, Viola's bed, in which she had lived and died, or this bed, in which her husband had announced the possibility of having a fling with a Meg Ryan look-alike in a leotard, she would definitely have taken the popping springs and the center sag. She felt like a little island, all alone in the middle of the deep blue sea, and she held her breath and drew her knees up to her chest. When Tommy placed his hand on her hip, she moaned. Even to her own ears, it sounded like the growl of a mother bear prematurely disturbed from a beautiful winter's hibernation. He patted her again and she growled louder. And then it hit her that she was being poored, and she sprang up, not like a sleepy bear but like a trapped wildcat, sending the covers flying into a heap on the floor. Her face contorted and, on her knees now, she raised her hands like claws ready to strike out at Tommy and hissed into his face. She could even imagine having whiskers that extended from beyond her cheekbones.

"Hiss, hiss," she said, her fantasy claws shredding the air between them. "Hiss. Don't you dare poor me after all this time, you son of a bitch," she said.

A look of wariness intensified Tommy's beautiful brown eyes. "I see you're upset," he said.

"Hiss," Ellen responded, swiping near his face with her paw.

"I still love you," Tommy said, his eyes fixed like a hypnotist's on hers.

Ellen sat back on her haunches and lowered her arms.

"Come here," he said.

She moved toward him and felt the warmth of his body like a halo around her. He held her close, her cheek pressed into his chest and the hair there tickling her nose. She began to cry in earnest.

thirty-one

What was I gonna say?" Ellen asked, shaking her head to fend off intense bewilderment. "No? You can't?" She sat at the dining-room table with Rodney, halfway through a jelly donut. It oozed berry juice like thick blood onto her plate and she wiped it up quickly with her finger and extended her hand to Olivier to lick it off. "To tell you the truth, I'm surprised it hasn't happened before."

"Why don't you hightail it back home where you can watch him like a hawk?"

"What would I do? Trail him to the yoga class and punch out the yoga teacher when he's not looking?" She shook her head no. For the forty-eight hours since Tommy had dropped his romantic bomb into her lap, she had shaken her head no so constantly that the muscles in her neck ached.

Rodney cut his Boston cream down the center. "Maybe it's nothing. When the cat's away, the mice will play, you know," he said.

"Yeah." Ellen sighed. She wanted to say more, to protest, but the specific words she needed had turned to crust on her vocal chords and were choking her. She could neither bring them up nor swallow them. "I feel so threatened. Seventeen years of marriage doesn't stand a chance against a fling with a yoga girl." Ellen could just imagine the new sex positions Tommy could try with her. She could probably fold herself into a pretzel if he wanted her to. The missionary position paled by comparison.

"Well, that's not true," Rodney said. Ellen could not even recall what he was talking about. Olivier, banging his plastic cup on the high chair tray, did not help, either.

"What isn't true?"

"That you would lose."

"Oh, I know," she said listlessly, "but I've got this image in my head of Tommy as a swinging single. A swingle."

"It's not like he's after a Playboy bunny, Ellen."

"It would be better if he was. Then I could chalk it up to a midlife crisis. He would seem like a helpless fool to me and maybe I could just ignore it." In the late sixties, her own father had unexplainably gone through a phase of wearing love beads and her astonished mother had never, not even once, suggested that he remove them. Ellen had her mother's genes, after all, and if Tommy's behavior were far enough out in left field, she could step back and possibly even enjoy it. But yoga teachers were seriously real people involved in a spiritual pursuit, not sex bimbos who wore spiked heels and went to work with a cottontail sewed onto their ass.

"It'll blow over," Rodney promised.

"Yeah." Ellen took a sip of open-the-heart tea. It was an act of courage flung into the face of her fears.

Rodney got up and carried his plate to the kitchen sink, where he rinsed it and put it in the dish drainer. "I've got some errands to run downtown. Want me to take the little one with me? Give you some time to yourself?"

Ellen perked up. "That'd be great. You sure you don't mind?" she asked at the same time she handed him the keys to her car.

"I'd enjoy it. Come on, Little Man. Let's go to town." Olivier raised his arms and Rodney lifted him out of the high chair. Ellen didn't even get up until they had disappeared down the dirt road.

After her hissing fit, Ellen had lain in Tommy's arms and sobbed for a good half hour, but she refused to discuss anything at all. Tommy's possible affair was not mentioned again. It hung like smog between them, and when Tommy suggested that he take an earlier flight back to New York, to catch up on work, he said—not to be fresh for yoga in the morning—Ellen did not protest.

At the airport, he had kissed her deeply and said, "I can't wait for the summer to end. I want you to come home." But she couldn't help but wonder if she would ever find her way back. Or if Tommy would be there, waiting. She felt as if she'd taken a wrong turn and was now lost. A goner. With Olivier on her hip, she'd made an about-face in the airport and driven home to Eagle Beak to feed Mutley. It wasn't until she stood up after filling his bowl that she caught sight of her garden and realized that Tommy had not even looked at it once.

And why should he? He didn't care about it, and Ellen might just as well face it. Tommy could afford to buy the best organic produce in the city. Why make a fuss about his indifference to her sorry-looking greens? She herself was barely holding onto her own organic farmer fantasy. The next morning, as she had moved along the rows of vegetables, the tomatoes and the peppers had seemed unimportant in the big scheme of things. She had put some seeds into the earth, and they had grown. Big deal. When they reached their full self-expression, she would eat them. So what?

In a way, she had even grown Tommy's fascination with the yoga instructor. She had neglected the patch in which their marriage grew, and now a weed had taken hold. There was no way to pull it up, no way to know if it would take over and ultimately crowd out the old growth.

Of course, Ellen knew that her own mind was exactly like the fertile earth of her garden. Put an idea in, and it flourished. Jealousy, fear, feeling threatened by this yoga teacher—these ideas could multiply like plants in a rain forest jungle. They could take over her life, insert themselves between her and every passing minute. She could easily imagine Tommy and the yoga girl with a baby carriage. She could imagine them side by side on a tropical beach doing the sun salute in perfect choreography. She could imagine them flipping together through the pages of the Kama Sutra and practicing tantric sex.

The problem was not indulging in the possibilities; it was refusing to. Turning her mind off was imperative, she thought as she sipped her open-the-heart tea. She needed to put her attention elsewhere. It was her attention and nothing else that made the terrifying figments of her imagination grow to unruly proportions.

She had, just two days ago, announced to Tommy that she was going to make a documentary about Rodney. Those words had sprung from her lips, unbidden, but it had sounded like a fully formed idea. Maybe she could give Rodney his fifteen minutes of fame and enjoy her own, too. She went into the dining room to get a yellow legal pad and a pencil. It was time to make a list. Ellen even knew how she would begin the film: a close-up on the blade of a chain saw ripping through dark, grainy wood. A racket on the sound track. Viewers might think for a moment that this was a film about the Northwest logging industry, an environmentalist stance. Then pull back to reveal Rodney, shaping a figure—maybe one of the hanging Jesuses. And then a voice-over: the story of how he took up the chain saw to keep from killing his mother. Quickly, she jotted down notes and soon the page was full and she had to flip it over. It was like being God, putting ashes into a pile and blowing life into them. Maybe she would take a trip to Boston with Rodney—film him against the rail of "Old Ironsides" reenacting the moment when he chucked Viola's urn into the murky waters of Boston Harbor. She listed all the points she would accentuate: Rodney had wanted to join the Ice Capades but chose to take care of Leland instead. He transformed his filial frustration into odd works of art and covered his acres with the figments of his imagination, all created with his own two hands. He never had children because he feared the genetic makeup of his own sperm. Could she ever do him justice? She rocked gently on the porch swing, absently staring over the green lawn. The lilacs had passed, leaving brown skeletons behind.

She thought of Cocho. She was desperate for word from Karen, desperate to know if Cocho had fought his way back into this world or was sliding into the next one. It broke her heart that Karen and Cocho were missing so many days and weeks in Olivier's young life. Every day he changed. He could say *bird* and *house*, *truck* and *car*, *water* and *blanket*. Rodney had become his stand-in grandfather, and Mutley had become his dog. His hair spiraled farther from his scalp and his skin grew darker in the sun. Olivier seemed to have jumped from baby into boyhood in a few short weeks. She looked toward the south. "Breathe on, Cocho," she whispered. "Breathe on." Of course, her doubts about Cocho's chances burst forth like brushfires that she had to stamp out quickly. So many fears to suppress, she thought. She needed blinders just to keep them all out of her peripheral vision.

The phone rang. "Ellen? Rayfield."

"Yo, Rayfield," she said.

"I'm on the horns of a dilemma," he announced. Ellen felt a buzz of interest. "Yeah? What?"

"It's about Wide Load."

"What's she up to?"

"She's getting married next Friday."

"So soon!" Ellen stalled for time. "I wasn't sure if you two were divorced yet."

"The divorce papers are final on Wednesday."

"Jeez, she doesn't waste any time, does she?"

"Old Wide Load's never in doubt about what she's doing," Rayfield said.

"So what's your dilemma?" Ellen hooked the phone between her shoulder and her jaw, freeing her hands to make a cheese sandwich at the kitchen counter. She felt far away from Rayfield and his problems.

"Whether or not I should try to bust up the ceremony."

"Why do that?"

"What've I got to lose? She already thinks I'm an asshole. Besides, you told me I should fight for her."

Ellen rotated the receiver so she could chew without it being obvious to Rayfield. It was never pleasant to be reminded of her own advice. "Well, what do you hope to gain?" she asked.

"Maybe I can save her from making a big mistake."

Ellen moved the wad of cheese in her mouth to her cheek. "I don't believe you'd get off your ass and crash a wedding ceremony unless there was something for you in it, Rayfield."

"Shows what you know," Rayfield said, sounding wounded.

Ellen felt immediately penitent. Why was she going on the offensive when he'd turned to her for help? That was the worst thing to do in someone's hour of need. "Do you have a VCR?" Ellen asked.

"Yeah. Why?"

"I'm gonna come over this afternoon with a video."

"What for?"

"Don't worry. It's on the subject. See you in a couple hours."

Acting on a surge of inspiration, she hopped into Rodney's truck and drove downtown, joined a video club, and rented *The Graduate*. It had a scene in which a regular guy, just like Rayfield, rerouted the romantic fate of his beloved. Ellen had mysteriously swung from doubting Rayfield to jumping onto his bandwagon. She bought some Jiffy Pop to take along to help establish the movie theater atmosphere. Then she had the truck inspected for Rodney and drove it home.

When she got there, Rodney and Olivier were in the middle of lunch. Rodney had heated up a can of soup and was feeding it to Olivier using the "Here comes the airplane, open the hatch" method. Olivier clutched mangled jelly sandwiches in both fists.

"Rodney," Ellen said as soon as she opened the door, "I want to make a movie about you. What do you say?" Clearly, her inner time belt was fraying. She had fully intended to butter him up first.

"Why would anybody want to see a movie about me?"

"Because you're interesting. Come on, Rodney, what do you say?"

"Let me think about it."

It hadn't occurred to Ellen that Rodney would thwart her plan, and she felt compelled to lobby for what she wanted like some Washington sleazeball, but she held her tongue. Rodney needed room and time to make a decision, and she had to give it to him. It was the weight of responsibility, of relationship, upon her, like a heavy knapsack that dug into her shoulders after a long hike—necessary but uncomfortable.

Ellen looked around the dining room. There sat Olivier, his mouth so covered with jelly that he resembled a clown made up for a circus performance. Rodney was staring out the window, his expression unreadable. Out in the yard, Mutley snoozed. Her garden grew, depending on her for water and weed control. Her house, if she planned to keep it, needed some tender loving care. Rayfield was capering around Porkerville, expecting her to show up to guide him through the thorny terrain of Wide Load's imminent wedding ceremony. Meanwhile, her whole marriage hung in the lurch, as Tommy practiced yoga and fantasized about putting the wood to the teacher. And to top it all off, Cocho was in a coma and Karen was in Peru, checking to see if he was still alive several dozen times a day.

Her life was a mess. If she could peel off all the responsibility, like an old coat, she would. Responsibility made her feel overheated, and she mopped her brow. In New York, she often ate at a Chinese restaurant whose walls, for decoration, were covered with framed koans, written in graceful and mysterious ideograms. Whenever she went there, Ellen always sat at a table under the one that said "The joy from lack of possessions makes the whole body light," the translation typed and taped to the wall below it, because she found that message particularly uplifting. She prided herself on her detachment. She didn't own one item that she would particularly miss if it disappeared, not counting, perhaps, her wedding ring, which had only cost thirty-nine dollars new. But now things were starting to stick to her—big things, and many of them were living. Maybe Rodney had the right idea. Carve statues for company.

"Would you call yourself a hermit?" Ellen suddenly asked.

"Me? Heavens no," Rodney answered. "I see people every day."

"But you spend most of your time alone."

Rodney folded his hands on the table as if he were in church. "Are you feeling lonely today?"

Ellen laughed. In fact, she was feeling crowded and overwhelmed. "I don't think so," she said.

"Because even if your husband does take off, you'll be okay in the end." Rodney said this softly. Ellen looked up into his eyes, which matched the sky out of the window behind him. The drooping skin of his brow dipped across the top of each iris, but even without their full circumference, Rodney's eyes had the power to soothe. What makes him such a port in the storm, Ellen wondered, never turning her gaze away from him.

Shortly afterward, Rodney left and Ellen bundled Olivier into his car seat for the short hop to Porkerville. Armed with her inspirational video and her popcorn, she set out on a sacred mission: to convince Rayfield to push the romantic envelope. When Dustin Hoffman storms into the church to drag his beloved, in her white wedding dress, out into the street, when he locks the doors behind him by shoving a crucifix through the door handles and hustles her onto a passing bus, he becomes every woman's hero. Rayfield could join the ranks if his shenanigans were choreographed in advance. What it lacked in spontaneity could be made up for in style.

Ellen knew, of course, that her willingness to become his coach and dramaturge was simply a manifestation of her own displaced desire to do something similar—or better yet, have Tommy do so. She could see it all: herself tumbling like a trained acrobat into the yoga studio, disrupting the peace and forcing all the students, scattered about the floor on their mats performing the corpse pose, to open their eyes and stare as she did handsprings around them, ultimately landing in front of the teacher to howl "Back off!" Or Tommy, showing up with no notice at her door with seventeen bloodred roses, one for each year of their marriage, and two tickets to Tahiti.

Rayfield wasn't in the yard, parked in the bucket seat like he usually was, so Ellen freed Olivier from his car seat and held his hand as they approached the door to Rayfield's trailer. For the first time, she noticed a hand-lettered sign above his door that read IF YOU DON'T SWING, DON'T RING. Shades of Hugh Hefner in the Porkerville version of the Playboy Mansion. It's better than "Abandon hope, all ye who enter here," she thought as she knocked. A moment later, Rayfield opened the door.

"This doesn't apply to me, I'm assuming," she said, pointing skyward to the sign above the door.

"Nah," Rayfield said, "it's an old sign." He seemed rather subdued.

Ellen held up the video. "You need inspiration. Let's watch this."

Rayfield loaded it into his VCR, popped the popcorn, and settled into the orange bucket chair. Olivier, tired, climbed onto the love seat and fell into a deep sleep with his head in Ellen's lap.

When the movie had progressed to the all-important wedding scene, Rayfield leaned forward, entranced. "Shit," he said as Dustin Hoffman fearlessly brandished the crucifix. Meanwhile, Olivier was just sitting up in his post-nap daze. As soon as he got his eyes focused, though, he went for the popcorn like a starving orphan—a gentle reminder to Ellen that her management of his diet left much to be desired.

Ellen waited for the final credits before she said, "Well? Does it give you any ideas?"

Rayfield remained uncharacteristically silent for a few moments.

Suddenly, Ellen felt impatient with the whole freaking topic. Her own marriage was in an uproar and she had no business butting into Rayfield's. Abruptly, she stood up.

"Look, Rayfield, don't listen to me. Don't storm Debbie's wedding just because it worked in *The Graduate*. It's just a movie. It's a myth." Rayfield sat back in the bucket chair and observed her curiously.

"You're fucking nuts, Ellen," Rayfield then said.

"Guilty! Guilty!" Ellen whooped, and then a laughing fit began and popcorn exploded from her mouth like fireworks. "Nuts! It's so simple!" she exclaimed. Ellen gasped for breath as tears formed and began their customary cascade down her cheeks.

"If I tried to drag Wide Load out of church, I'd get a hernia," Rayfield said, and now he was laughing too. It always happened. Hilarity was catching. "She'd deck me," he added.

"Oh, Rayfield, what are you gonna do?"

"Oh, Ellen, what are you gonna do?" he countered.

Suddenly they were both silent. They locked eyes as the merriment vanished and the dread took over.

thirty-two

It was much later, after she'd returned home, after she'd finished her watering and weeding, that she realized she had not told Rayfield about Tommy's confessed interest in another woman. So he had not asked her that final question—"What are you gonna do?"—in response to anything that had happened on the surface. Rather, he had intuited that she, like he, was in the midst of a marriage meltdown. How did he know? Was she an open book? Or was Rayfield just unusually adept at reading subtext?

She moved so she could rest her back against the bark of the maple tree at the end of the driveway. Mutley, his head resting on her thigh, gazed deeply into her eyes. She pressed lightly along his browridges and ran her fingers along the length of his nose. Olivier, squatting like a rice paddy worker, played in the grass several yards away.

Suddenly, Ellen felt the air pressure shift, as if her ears needed to pop. The afternoon sun on her neck, the softness of Mutley's fur coat, the rhythm of Olivier's babbling—it seemed so precious. It was like being on acid and seeing each tiny detail in all its throbbing beauty.

In her hippie daze, Ellen had once insisted that a friend drive her out into the middle of the country at midnight and drop her off. Fortified by magic mushrooms, she wanted to walk around in the dark and listen to the sounds of nature. Walden Pond seemed an obvious choice, and when Ellen stepped out of her friend's VW van, she felt like a spiritual anthropologist. She watched the taillights on the van disappear and then tiptoed down to the lake. Every tree was her brother, and every rock, her sister, and she experienced indescribable bliss when she stripped off her clothes and plunged into the water. The frogs sang for her and no one else. She thought she could feel moss growing on her, and by the time the drugs wore off, near dawn, she was convinced that she was invisible among the greenery.

This moment, under her own maple tree, had some of that magic.

I have to write a mission statement, she suddenly realized. Now, when I'm in this altered state. But if she moved, ran into the house for a pen and paper, she would disturb Mutley, who seemed supremely happy.

Ellen didn't like to think unless she had a pen in her hand. Important thoughts got away, like wild animals, unless they were tied down with ink. But today, for the preliminary work on her personal life mission statement, she would have to wing it. She was certain that crafting a mission statement, one that not only reflected her past values but also required her to be, in the future, more than she already was, would put her life back on track. It would clarify her essential essence and allow her to eliminate all unproductive, useless activity. A mission statement was like a lucky charm, a talisman, or a medicine bag.

But when she tried to think forward, a curtain was stretched across her field of vision like the thick velvet drapes of a Broadway stage. In Ellen's youth, even the neighborhood movie theaters had such a curtain—two curtains, actually: a heavy outer one and a translucent inner one. Each separated and pulled away from its other half, the bottom gracefully fluttering like a party dress. Watching the curtains part had symbolic significance. It meant that real life had been beaten back, surrendered to an alternative world.

If her future were a movie, though, Ellen had no idea of the genre. She had bought her ticket blindfolded. She felt the ultraviolet rays of the sun penetrating the layer of skin that was beginning to sag off her cheek- and jawbones. The warmth seemed to open her mind, and suddenly she realized that, throughout female stages one and two, the first and second movie features of her life, she had held the image of *ipsissimus,* she who is most herself, in her mind as her goal. Obviously *ipsissimus* had been the nutshell version of her unconscious mission statement. But because she had not formalized it, because it had been more of a philosophical musing than a practical battle plan, she had often strayed. She had forgotten about it for days, months, and years on end. Mission statements, like posters demonstrating the Heimlich maneuver, had to be posted in a prominent place and reread daily as a practical reminder.

"Sorry, Mutley," she said as she extracted herself from underneath him and ran to snatch her stenographer's notebook from the car seat. When she returned to her spot under the tree, Mutley had not even lowered his head and she was able to slip right back into her previous spot.

She flipped open the notebook, wrote "Mission Statement" across the top of a blank page, held her pen poised at the left margin, and gazed out over the

vegetable patch, expecting inspiration. The blank page had never been a problem for Ellen. Words wanted to form themselves and jump onto paper for her.
She could no more avoid them than the *Titanic* could have avoided the iceberg.

But like the iceberg, much of the self she was headed toward was submerged.
She could sense its presence in the waters of her unconscious, but she wasn't exactly sure where it was or what it would look like when she finally crashed into
it. Her mission had something to do with love, she knew, though maybe that was
only the temporary side effect of Dr. Yi's tea. To do good work fit in somewhere,
but Ellen wasn't convinced that that originated inside of her. It could be a legacy
of her Catholic upbringing—something that was pounded into her head by
nuns in black habits before she ever knew that extreme selfishness was the option of choice for most people who accomplished anything in life.

She looked down at the notebook in her lap. And then, as if it were written there, a memory asserted itself. For Ellen, it was like watching a home
video, twenty years old. She was sitting at her kitchen table in her apartment
on Thompson Street in the city. The clock she could see in her mind read
1:05. Fifty-five minutes until her psychotherapy appointment. In front of her
was a legal pad, and she was in the process of making a list of all the ways she
hated herself. She had taken on this bizarre task because, the previous week,
amidst her sobs about the state of her life, she had blurted out a sentence she
had lived to regret: "I should be looking for a job," she had confessed to her
therapist, "but instead, I'm making a list of all the ways I hate myself! It's already five pages long." Carried away with the drama of the moment, she had
exaggerated quite a lot. In fact, under the influence of a Thai stick, she had
undertaken the chore of listing her worst traits, but had run out of steam after
the first five, which were hardly hot news to her: financial fuckup, slothful, di-
rectionless, promiscuous, oversensitive.

"Why don't you bring your list in next week?"

"What?" Ellen had asked, busted.

"Your list."

"Okay," she'd said blankly as she watched Marcia, her shrink, trace small
circles on her kneecap with her fingers. Ellen, a deep-sea diver exploring the
subconscious world of her psyche, had thought of Marcia as her buoy on the
surface. Twice a week, she'd seen her. Ellen had relied on it.

Not wanting to be caught in a fib, Ellen had worked hard on her self-hatred
list. Her tendency to decorate the simple truth to make it more entertaining
was a trait she was trying to discourage. She called her little lies phantom
facts, creative amplifications, or permutations on the original. Ellen had a
whole vocabulary of euphemisms, but in her heart, she knew they were lies
and she gave herself no credit for her rich imagination. "I'm a liar," she added

to her list, bringing it one line closer to the bottom of page one. I waste time. I am resentful of people who have it easy. I do not live up to my full potential. I bear grudges. I drink too much. I am petty.

On and on she went, flinging every insult she could think of into her own face. She even tried to recall the Ten Commandments so she could document the ones she routinely broke. Because it was essentially a mental exercise, she didn't cry. But when she reached the middle of page three, she threw her pen across the tiny apartment and abandoned the task.

A half hour later, she had told Marcia the truth. "So there I am, sitting at my kitchen table, trying to come up with five pages of things I hate about myself. There are thirty-five lines per page, you know, so that's a hundred and seventy-five separate things. I got to a hundred and I said, 'Fuck it.'"

"Congratulations," said Marcia. "Did you bring the list?"

"No, I threw it in the garbage." Another phantom fact. It was laying in wait on the table, exactly where she'd left it when she had fled to her appointment. Ellen went directly from therapy to her waitressing job and didn't arrive home until midnight. She was slightly tipsy, as usual, and had forgotten all about the legal pad and list. She swept it onto the floor, the Jack Daniel's she'd consumed in a bar on the corner temporarily bringing out the swashbuckler in her.

But something made her pick it up again. She turned out the lights and lit a candle. She placed her boom box on the table, and put on her most beautiful nightgown, ice green with spaghetti straps that crossed in the back, worn only on the most special of occasions. She pressed the record button and read her list. At the end, she burned the three pages to ashes, leaving the recorder going until the last crackle of the fire had ceased and only the honking of horns on the street below could be heard in her apartment. She labeled the tape "Adios, self-hatred" and hid it among her most private papers. She had never listened to it again.

The memory made her sad. There was no way to measure suffering, and compared to the starving people in Africa and the children from war-torn countries in Eastern Europe who had seen their parents blown apart before their eyes, hers had been minimal. But at that moment, her heart ached for her younger self, for all the pain she had had to bear. The intensity of her suffering, necessary or not, had brought Ellen to her knees to beg for mercy many times in her twenties.

When she was younger, she tended to define herself by the "nots." I am not disciplined, not confident, not rich, and so on. In its inimitable way, even her unconscious cooperated, offering her nightly dreams of knots in her hair (and Ellen, without a comb) or knots in her stomach (and Ellen, with no supply of Valium). Somehow the creation of the list she now remembered, her list of flaws that she later burned to ashes, had initiated the "not phase." It was as if her refusal to scorn herself, as symbolized by the burning, had gone haywire and suddenly she'd become the negative of her former self.

Now, she suddenly realized, she was transitioning back to a positive image, like a photographic print submerged in the waters of a chemical bath. She was thinking in terms of "I am" instead of "I am not." Her notebook was in her lap, a patch of white in a sea of green grass. Without thinking, she wrote "To do good and be love."

Her writing hand fell to her side and she stared in shock at what she had written. The simplicity of the mission statement left no room for misinterpretation, but where had it come from? She had expected something more of herself, perhaps along the lines of "To see my documentary on Rodney at the Cannes Film Festival" or "To remove the slugs from under the rocks of my personal psyche." Quickly, she closed her notebook.

In the sixties, she'd proudly worn a "Make Love, Not War" button on her fringed leather vest. Perhaps, all things considered, she hadn't changed that much, though there was a certain aggressive resistance to the "make love" statement that had evaporated from the words she had written inside her closed book.

She opened it again and found the right page. Could that really be her mission statement as she approached the portal of the crone phase? Be and do, do and be, she thought: the two big verbs of everybody's native tongue. Essence and action. She could certainly handle the "do good" half of her mission statement. She simply had to choose the righteous path in each moment. Each action had to be held up against an image of unselfish goodness. She looked down at Mutley. She had saved him from life in the dog pound. That was good. And she had taken Olivier without a split second's hesitation. That was the right and good thing to do in that moment. She was growing organic vegetables, tending to Mother Earth, pulling weeds with her bare hands and lugging water back and forth across the lawn with the cheerfulness of a Zen monk. She was helping Rayfield cope with his donut dick, saying short prayers on behalf of Cocho, and preparing to bring the down-home sweetness of Rodney de Beer to a wider audience. In a way, she felt that she was even doing good on behalf of Viola. She was getting people to talk about her, draining the swamp of unsaid words that festered and stunk. At the present moment, she was a veritable ambassador of goodness, even by her own objective standards.

But being love? That was a different ball game. What did it mean? Ellen didn't even know how to think about it. Maybe it was like being a radio transmitter. You just pulsated in private, there for anyone who wanted to tune in. But what did you transmit? What was love anyway?

An old boyfriend, rarely brought to mind for a guest appearance, had defined it as being totally hungry and totally satisfied at the same time. But that was genus love, species sexual. That was lust and passion, which figured prominently in making love but had nothing to do with being love. Loving Olivier, loving Mutley, loving Rodney—in all these examples, Ellen thought, the love had pressed on her from the inside out, giving her a physical sensation she couldn't ignore. It was too powerful to contain, so saying the words "I love you" was like begging for mercy. But being love, that was different. It relied on neither a recipient nor a possible payoff. It was a paradox: to remain in that state would require total concentration but maintaining the focus was something that you *did*. And *be* was not *do*. Maybe if you did long enough, though, it was possible to just *be*.

Ever since Tommy had lowered the love boom, Ellen had avoided thinking about him. If she turned her mind in his direction, she saw Tommy in the lotus position with the yoga teacher in his lap—and the blissful look on her face, Ellen was certain, had more to do with the G-spot than with any of the seven holy chakras. She was terrified to widen the angle of that image just in case pulling back would reveal the four walls of her apartment on Tenth Street. Ellen didn't want the yoga teacher in her sacred, private space, but she knew there was a possibility that Tommy might bring her there. Many of her married friends had affairs, and when they did the concept of the inviolability of home was the first thing out the window. And she had to face it.

Did being love mean that she should let Tommy go? Release him once and for all from her psychic handcuffs? And if he did move on, what would she have of the last seventeen years? Nothing, really. There was no way to hold on to time and once it was gone it left a void. A blank slate upon which nothing could ever be written again.

It felt strange to calmly consider the possibility of life without Tommy. What would she do if he left? Fight him for the apartment? Join the Peace Corps? Carry the banner of do-goodism to the four corners of the known world? Become a nun?

She glanced at her house.

Live here?

"No," Ellen said in a loud voice. "Let it be known, I do not want to end up here, starring in the Viola sequel. I am making this clear to all the forces of the universe." Both Mutley and Olivier turned toward her with curiosity. "I won't do it," she added belligerently. "I refuse. Amen." She stood up and shook her fist at the sky, and she would have launched into a war dance but just then the phone rang and she sprinted toward the house.

"House of laughs," she said into the phone.

"Ellen?" It was Tommy's voice.

"Hi, Tommy."

"Long time, no phone call."

"Just a couple days." She said defensively. Ellen knew she had withdrawn from him, as if she were in rehearsal for being dumped when he ran off with the yoga instructor. "Anyway, my phone rings, too," she added. Her voice was cool, and in an effort to warm it up, she added, "Where are you? Work?"

"Yeah." There was a short, painful pause.

"So how's it going?" Ellen asked, just to end it.

"Not too bad. How about you?"

"Fine."

"You don't sound fine."

"I don't?"

"No. You sound pissed off. So what gives?"

Ellen moved to the window to check on Olivier. "Nothing," she said. "So how's yoga?"

"Oh, so that's it."

"Of course that's it," Ellen snapped. "Why'd you tell me anyway? You could've just done whatever you wanted and I'd never have known."

"Ellen, ever since we've been married, you've said you'd want me to tell you if I was considering having an affair. How many times have I heard it? How many times a week do you say, 'Honesty is the best policy'? How many times have you gone on and on about how deceit and sneakiness are worse than infidelity and—"

"All right!" Ellen snapped. "Enough! *Basta!* I changed my mind, okay? Now that it's upon me, I can't handle it, okay? I give you permission to lie to me. Lie to me about everything from now on, okay, Tom? Because the truth hurts."

"Am I supposed to feel sorry for you?" There was a tone in his voice that Ellen loathed. "Because guess what? I don't. Every guy I know fucks around on his wife. I never have. And now, after all these years of your 'You're a free agent, Tommy' crap, I actually consider it, and suddenly you're playing 'Queen for a Day' and . . ."

Ellen was hardly listening. He had said he was considering, not doing. He had always said "considering," and it was she who jumped to conclusions and then suffered for it. If she could just stay calm, perhaps this whole interlude would just blow over. Besides, though she didn't want to admit it, in her heart she knew he was right about the rest of it, too. Who did she think she was to carry the banner of truth and then pitch it into the mud in her first personal skirmish?

"Look, Tommy—"

"I'm not finished!" he yelled. "All these years it's been the same damn thing. You run your mouth in one direction but it means nothing because your mouth runs directly opposite what everybody but you knows is true about you."

"Hey!" Ellen cut in, not knowing what else to do. It was her equivalent of a karate chop, but it did nothing to intimidate or distract him.

"You think the whole world revolves around you. Well, I've got news for you, Ellen. It doesn't. There's such a thing as consequences. You ever heard of that? Cause and effect? You decided you were going to buy that fucking house, and you didn't even talk to me about it. You sailed off on your quest for whatever the fuck it is, and I'm supposed to sit here and twiddle my thumbs. Well, it doesn't work that way."

Ellen felt as if she'd been picked up by a mental tornado and was whirling around in a circle above her own life. Tommy's voice, which had not decreased in volume, seemed to be fading and she held the receiver to her ear for the sole purpose of having a grip on something familiar. "I'm not gonna put up with it anymore," Tommy was saying.

Ellen held her breath. Tommy stopped talking. She felt as if she'd been stuffed into a vacuum bag where both sound and movement were impossible. I'm dying, she suddenly thought. "So, are you finished?" she finally murmured, putting a lid on it, though she had no idea what she was trapping in—or out.

"Yeah, I'm finished," Tommy said. "Christ, is that all you have to say?"

"Well, I'm also toying with, 'Go shit in your hat.'"

"I'll talk to you later, Ellen," Tommy said tightly. "Bye."

"Bye, Tom," she responded as he clicked off. Ellen sat down. Outside, Olivier had toddled over to Mutley. She had almost forgotten them both. She quickly got up, crossed the kitchen, and took an orange Popsicle out of the freezer. She broke it in half and then unwrapped it, carrying half to Olivier, who said, "Thank you," in English as he accepted the stick.

Her notebook was still lying under the tree where she'd left it, and she opened it to the page where she had written "Do good and be love." Within seconds of forming her mission statement, she'd had her first test and all she could recall of it were the words, "Go shit in your hat." Not much of a start, really. She flipped the book closed and held it pressed against her chest. She sucked hard on the orange Popsicle, running her tongue around its edges to catch the drips before they could fall onto her notebook, thereby staining its cardboard cover.

thirty-three

When the phone rang at seven thirty in the morning on Friday, the day of Wide Load's nuptials, Ellen knew it would be Rayfield and she considered not answering it. Rodney, halfway through his cup of coffee, regarded her curiously over his drugstore glasses.

"Ain't you gonna get it?" he asked as the fourth ring reverberated in the dining room.

"I guess so." She sighed, reluctantly reaching. "Hello."

"Yo, Ellen. Today's the day," Rayfield said.

"What're you gonna do?" No matter what Rayfield decided, Ellen would feel personally responsible, which she resented.

"I'm still debating."

"Look, Rayfield, just do something you won't regret afterward." Rodney, having heard the name Rayfield, had returned his attention to the morning paper.

"That's the problem," Rayfield said. "No matter what I do, I'm gonna regret it, so I might as well go for broke."

"Which means . . . ?"

"I want you to drive over to the church with me."

"What?" Ellen shrieked.

"I'm calling in my chips," Rayfield said. "You owe me, big-time, and this is where I collect. You drive."

"Rayfield, wait a minute. I don't owe you big-time." Sure, weeks ago he had loaned her a lawn mower and even cut the grass, but what had he done lately?

"You're the one who got me into this."

"I did not!" Ellen protested. "You called me and said you were thinking of busting up Wide Load's wedding. All I did was . . ." She hesitated. What had she done? "All I did was show you an old movie," she finished. It was the truth, with her responsibility surgically removed.

"I'll be over there in an hour. Get ready to rock and roll," he said and hung up.

Ellen stared at the phone. "Rayfield's coming over, Rodney. If you don't want to see him, you better clear out soon," she said flatly. Then she replaced the receiver in its cradle. "Shit." She could just imagine it: herself behind the wheel as Rayfield shoved an irate Debbie into the backseat and Ellen drove off, accessory to a felony kidnapping charge. "Shit," she said again. She should probably stand up to Rayfield, refuse to participate in his madness, but some part of her also wanted a front-row seat for this show, whatever it was. She turned to face Rodney. "Rayfield's planning to crash Debbie's wedding and he's trying to drag me into it." Secretly, she was gathering her courage to ask Rodney to babysit Olivier. She could hardly allow her toddler nephew to be involved in a romantic fracas.

"Who's she marrying? George Robideaux?"

"I have no idea. Who's George Robideaux?"

"Her childhood sweetheart. We all thought they would get married and live happily ever after. When she paired up with Rayfield, poor George almost threw in the towel."

"Jeez, it's worse than Peyton Place up here," Ellen said as she refilled her tea. "Do you think George has waited all these years for her?"

Rodney looked at her slyly. "Who said he waited?"

"You mean she's been involved with him while she's been married to Rayfield?"

"Let's just say there was enough of her to go around." It was the closest thing to a cutting remark she'd ever heard out of Rodney's mouth.

"Did Rayfield know?"

"I imagine he got good at looking the other way when he had to."

When she and Tommy were just starting out, Ellen had asked their downstairs neighbor, an elegant woman from Virginia who had been happily married for fifty-two years, to share the secret of her marriage's success. "Look the other way when you have to," she had said. At the time, Ellen had felt hugely cheated. If that was the secret of marital longevity, it was truly depressing. That couple had lived on the second floor of the building on Tenth Street for eleven years before they both died within a month of each other.

"God, everything is so complicated," Ellen huffed. "So should I tell him to go piss up a rope?"

"Why not follow your own advice?"

Ellen found Rodney very vexing today, and it showed in her tone. "And what advice might that be?"

"Don't do something you'll be sorry for later."

"Damn it, Rodney, I hate it when my own words come back to haunt me."

Rodney chewed his donut and did not respond. He seemed so completely balanced, so totally centered and sure of himself, that Ellen felt an irresistible impulse to knock him for a loop. "Rodney, why don't you and Rayfield bury the hatchet?"

Rodney sat up straighter. His mouth froze, leaving a wad of half-masticated mush in his cheek. The shock in his blue eyes brought Ellen to her senses, and she distinctly remembered promising Rayfield that she would never reveal the secret he had shared with anyone, let alone Rodney himself, and she began to backpedal. "I don't know what's going on between you two, but something's not right," she said in a hurry. "What is it anyway? You didn't put the moves on Debbie, did you?"

Rodney looked like he'd been socked in the stomach.

"Oh, Lord, that's not it, is it?" She knew she was laying it on too thick but she couldn't help herself. Onward she blundered. "It's none of my business. I'm sorry I ever brought it up. Just forget it, okay?" The silence from Rodney was Ellen's enemy, and Olivier's chatter meant nothing. Finally, though, she gave up and closed her mouth. Rodney's jaw reactivated and he chewed his food a few times and swallowed it. As soon as his Adam's apple returned to its normal position in his throat, he spoke.

"He told you what happened, didn't he?"

Ellen felt ill. "Yes," she whispered. "I pestered him until he told me." Impulsively, she got up and ran around the table to Rodney's chair. Squatting down beside him, she reached for his hand and said, "Rodney, please don't cross me out of your life for this, like you did Rayfield. I'm begging you, please, just let it go."

"What do you get outa poking your nose in other people's business?"

"Trouble," Ellen answered. "Trouble and grief."

Rodney's hand was cool in hers, as if no blood flowed through it. "I think I feel like . . . like . . . like there's some answer out there, some ultimate explanation, and the more I know—about everything and everyone—the better chance I have of finding it. I guess that's why I ended up a researcher when I always wanted to be a backup singer." It felt truthful, though she had never articulated this before. In life, she could listen to each of the million stories in the naked city and still thirst for more; doing research, she always pressed on to find one more book or one earlier newspaper to view on microfilm. "For the record, Rayfield said that what happened with Viola was one of the most significant events of his whole life. He understands why you're mad at him, but there's nothing he can do."

"He could stop talking about it to every Tom, Dick, and Harry, for one thing," Rodney said in obvious irritation.

Abruptly, Ellen dropped his hand and stood up. Her knees creaked loud enough to hear. "You're not being fair, Rodney," she said. "He's lived with it all these years, just like you have, and he never told anybody but Debbie until I pried it out of him." Rodney didn't speak. She barreled on. "Rodney," she said, "I know you're mad at me for prying and you have every reason to be. And I know you're disgusted with me. But before you go away mad, I want to tell you one thing. I think you're a great person." She returned to her chair and sat down, accepting that the various chips of friendship would fall where they would. Olivier was having a heyday with a sticky bun, sweetly oblivious to the tension in the room.

"So are you gonna go along with Rayfield?" Rodney finally asked, his words clipped.

"You know, Rodney, I'm past trying to predict what I'm going to do. I'm no longer in charge. I am a spectator in my own life."

"Hmmm." For at least thirty seconds, they sat in silence. Out the window, Ellen watched a black and white woodpecker bash his head into a tree trunk. "Must be weird to be a woodpecker," she said. Rodney followed her glance.

"All that beak banging, and alls you get in the end is to eat a bug."

"Ain't nature grand?" Ellen said as she turned to look at Rodney. He seemed, she thought, about to say something. "What?" she prodded.

"Nothing, really. It's just that what you said about being a spectator in your own life? That's the way I feel when I'm working on wood."

Ellen perked up. "Really? You know, it would be worth it to me if it actually resulted in a product."

"Well, you have your garden. And this house."

"Yeah, but I don't know what I'm doing here."

Rodney took a long drink of coffee. "You know what's wrong with you smart people?"

"What?"

"You always think things make sense."

"You don't think so?"

"Nope."

"Well, a lot of scientists wouldn't agree with you, Rodney. It's called chaos theory. They assume there's order in everything, including chaos."

"Believe me, they'll find it even if it ain't there."

"There's gotta be a bigger picture, Rodney. There has to."

Rodney swallowed the last of his donut. "Want anything in town?"

"No, thanks."

"Okay. I'll see you tomorrow. Same time, same place."

"Same time, same place," Ellen repeated. It had become their daily parting pattern and Rodney was leaving at the same time as always, yet Ellen felt he was vacating the premises to avoid any chance of crossing paths with Rayfield. She lifted Olivier out of his high chair. "Ready to water?" she asked, kissing the top of his curly head. "Let's put shoes on." Soon, they were at the faucet filling the watering cans with Mutley in attendance. Olivier pounded Skin-So-Soft into Mutley's cranium, and the dog submitted with cheery patience. A dog and his boy, Ellen thought as she watched their two heads bob along through the tall grass at the edge of the yard. Mutley outweighed Olivier by ninety pounds and clearly considered himself the being in charge. Ellen even suspected that his dormant herding instinct was kicking in by the way he subtly directed Olivier toward the garden.

On their third trip to the faucet, Rayfield pulled in. He hopped out of his truck wearing a navy blue sport jacket, a white shirt and tie, and a pair of khakis with a sharp crease. His hair was pulled into a ponytail and he had shaved.

"Rayfield, is that you?" Ellen asked, rubbing her eyes in disbelief. "Jeez, you clean up good."

"I ain't been able to button this jacket in ten years," he said, but now the brass buttons were closed with room to spare. Rayfield's beer belly had shrunk, making his shoulders appear wider. Ellen shielded her eyes against the sun for an even better look. Only then did she notice that Rayfield had also shined up a pair of black oxfords for the occasion.

"I take it you're going to a wedding."

"Correction. *We're* going to a wedding," Rayfield answered.

"Rayfield, I'm not up for this. I want to start minding my own business. Besides, I've got Olivier here, and I've got to think of him."

"Cop-out, cop-out," Rayfield chanted. "Look, Ellen, I got this all worked out. You don't need to go getting no stage fright. You only got a bit part."

Ellen put down her water bucket. "Well, what is it?"

"Getaway driver."

"I knew it," she said. She glanced at her watch. Eight twenty. "What time is the wedding?"

"Ten, but it takes almost an hour to get there. Besides, I wanna see who shows up."

"The plot thickens," Ellen said. "Is she marrying George Robideaux?" The instant the name was out of her lips, she felt sorry. But Rayfield didn't even notice.

"Nope. A guy named Jake Gokey."

"Do I need to dress up?"

"For chrissakes, Ellen, you ain't invited. Stop stalling."

"Okay, okay, just let me change Olivier's diapers and we'll take off." As she wiped and powdered her nephew's tiny rear, Ellen marveled at the fact that she was going along with Rayfield. The cycles of change were spinning too fast to hold onto anymore. She had made a mistake by butting into other people's business, learned her lesson, and forgotten it before she'd even finished watering the garden. It was truly surreal. Maybe Rodney was right: there is no order, no greater truth, no overall pattern of positivity to fit into. She combed her hair and smiled warmly at herself in the bathroom mirror. Out the window, Rayfield waited in his Sunday best. From her second-floor vantage point, she noticed that he had moved a bouquet of wildflowers from the passenger seat of his truck to the backseat of her car. His hand had been dealt in the big game of love, and he was ready to play it. Would he win or lose?

On the drive to Skerrie, Rayfield was silent and Ellen nervously hummed along with the radio. She wondered if somehow his thoughts were being transmitted to her because there seemed to be no other explanation as to why she was suddenly viewing Debbie as a trophy wife and visualizing Rayfield's triumphant return to Porkerville with Wide Load in tow.

"Debbie's not going to be thrilled to see me, you know," she said.

"Don't worry about it," Rayfield answered, and then he didn't speak again except to give directions. The road to the chapel of love curved between woods and farmland, and green plant life pressed in from both sides. Occasionally, grass even sprouted defiantly through cracks in the pavement. But within a few short months, a thick layer of white snow would kill off the plants and transform the meandering road into a treacherous, icy deathtrap. The violent growth of summer would be overthrown, buried alive, and ice would reign for a while. Then the sun would return and wipe it out, changing the plow piles by the side of the road into rivers of snowy tears. Every lesson of nature warned against holding on to the present, she thought, but it never provided instruction on how to let go. Instead, it tore away the illusion of control and left a trail of stunned, and sometimes pathetic, survivors in its wake. It was all so overwhelming. She glanced at Rayfield, in his shiny shoes and Yale blazer, about to step into the fray.

Ellen looked at her wristwatch. It was nine thirty-two, twenty-eight minutes to showtime. She took a left into the parking lot of a small chapel painted white. There was only one car in the lot, a dented Chevy Impala, and Ellen pulled in next to it and shut off the ignition. In the backseat, Olivier snoozed with his head braced against the side of his car seat.

"Rayfield, I'm not trying to undermine you, really, but I'm just wondering why you want Debbie back so much."

"Shit, Ellen, cut it out. I'm nervous enough as it is without you going philo-sophical."

"I'm not being philosophical. I have my own reasons for asking. I'm trying to figure out what makes a man want a woman so badly."

"Chemistry. There ain't no other word for it."

Did she and Tommy have any chemistry left, she wondered. They certainly had had it in the beginning, but that was twenty-five years ago, when passion ruled. Now they had to blow hard on the romantic embers to get a spark, and all the fanning in the world couldn't keep their fire burning for more than an hour. Chemistry wore off in time. But maybe not for everybody, if Rayfield was any indication.

A car pulled into the lot, and a couple emerged and went into the chapel.

"You know them?"

"Never saw 'em before." Within seconds, two more cars arrived, and Ray-field slumped low in his seat to avoid being recognized by Debbie's brother and sister-in-law. At ten to ten, Debbie herself arrived in a rented limo that looked completely incongruous in the setting.

"She's here," Ellen said as Debbie lumbered from the backseat. She wore an off-white brocade sheath and a beaded headpiece with a starched shoulder-length veil. Her hair was pinned up in front but extended in long crinkles down her back. On her feet, she wore gold flats.

Rayfield raised himself enough to peek over the dash. "Damn, that's the same dress she wore when we got married," he said.

"Really?" Ellen was shocked. It was sacrilegious, even in the age of recycling.

Debbie hiked up her skirt to ascend the concrete steps, and Rayfield raised himself to watch, now that her back was to him. "Brings back memories," he said.

"Did you two go on a honeymoon?"

"We went to Niagara Falls."

"How was it?" Ellen's only reference point to the Falls was a Hitchcock movie.

"How would I know? We never left the room. We was in one of them hon-eymoon motels with a vibrating bed and a Jacuzzi shaped like a heart. Real high-class. Wide Load loved it."

"Who wouldn't?" Ellen asked. Debbie had vanished into the gray light in-side the chapel. It was almost ten. Including hers, there were only six cars in the lot, but at two minutes to ten, a shiny new pickup with an extended cab screeched to a stop a few feet away and two men, both in tuxedos, emerged, one from each side.

"Which is the groom?"

"You got me. They're twins."

Ellen looked closer. The two men were indeed carbon copies of each other. They even jogged in near perfect coordination toward the door.

"Freaky," she said, imagining the fun Debbie would have if these twins ever took it in their heads to pull a fast one on her and trade places in the middle of the night. "What're you gonna do?" she asked.

"Just what the system's already set up for. When the minister says that bit about 'If there's anyone here who knows a reason why this wedding should not take place,' I'm gonna stand up and say what I've got to say."

"You nervous?"

"Hell yes. Quit asking me."

Just then, the first organ tones of "Here Comes the Bride" wafted through the heat toward the car. Ellen was certain she could see the whole building tremble slightly with each of Debbie's footfalls. Rayfield turned toward Olivier, who had just opened his eyes, and said, "Wish me luck, my man." Olivier slapped him a highfive, a new trick, and Rayfield climbed from the car. "Pull up to the front door and keep the engine running," he said through the open passenger window as he straightened his jacket and smoothed his ponytail. "Here goes nothing."

Ellen felt a wave of admiration as she watched him waddle toward the church on his love mission. Rayfield, an aging Cupid, was about to shoot his arrow toward Debbie's heart after only two days of divorce. Would she be susceptible so soon after she'd written him off? Or would she grab the candlestick off the altar, swinging it like a country scythe, and chase him out of the church?

Slowly, Ellen drove the car to the door. She peered into the gloomy interior but a pair of swinging doors across the foyer blocked her view. "Damn, this is just too good to miss," she said to Olivier. "I'll be right back, honey. You wait here." She crept out of the car, moved toward the chapel, cracked the swinging door, and maneuvered herself around until she had Rayfield squarely within her sights. He sat quietly in a rear pew as the preacher droned on with the generic wedding spiel.

A few moments into it, she heard the sentence Rayfield was waiting for. "Speak now or forever hold your peace," the preacher said, and Rayfield jumped to his feet. "Objection!" he yelled out as if this were a *Perry Mason* episode. The entire congregation turned toward him in shock. Ellen crossed the fingers on both hands and held her breath. "I'm basically talking to Debbie here," Rayfield said. "The rest of you can listen, but this don't have nothing to do with you."

Ellen opened the door two more inches so she could see Debbie, who had pivoted completely around on the altar. "Rayfield, get the hell outa here!" she ordered.

"Debbie," Rayfield calmly began in a loud, clear voice, "Please don't do this. Don't get married again. Don't make the same mistake twice."

Jeez, thought Ellen, that was hardly the lead-in she would have advised. Rayfield obviously needed intensive tutoring in the art of rhetoric.

"Nobody knows you better than me," he continued, "and I can tell you straight out that you're not thinking clearly. Getting married two days after getting divorced is like climbing out of the frying pan and landing in the fire. I'm not saying nothing against Jake Gokey. In fact, I'm asking him politely to give you some time to come to your senses. If he really loves you he should be willing to do that." Rayfield took a deep breath. "I love you with all my heart, and I'm saying it here, in front of all these people." He swept his arm to cover the group, which was sparse. "I'm begging you to take your time. I know you for a long time, Wide Load, and I'm here to tell you that you're going off half-cocked."

Tears stung Ellen's eyes as Rayfield stood there, alone. What honor! What courage! What romantic bravery! Ellen, along with everyone in the audience, turned to Debbie as if they were watching a tennis match.

"The only one who's half-cocked around here is you, Rayfield," she said, and Ellen winced. Low blow, she thought. Out of bounds, mean-spirited and unnecessary! But Rayfield didn't make a peep. "I'm moving along in my life," Debbie continued. "Don't you dare try to stand in my way."

"I'm gonna knock him into the middle of next week," the groom chimed in, taking a step off the altar. Debbie reached for his hand, stopping him.

"Wide Load, just look at what you're doing," Rayfield persisted.

Debbie turned away from her so recent ex-husband. "So what do we do now?" she asked the minister, who looked like an Elvis impersonator. "He can't make us stop, can he?"

The minister snapped to life. "Sir," he said, "your objection is duly noted."

"Don't come crying to me when this blows up in your face," Rayfield said to Debbie's brocade back. "If you go through with this now, that's it for us."

Suddenly the best man, clone of the groom, burst off the altar down the center aisle. Ellen charged away from her hiding place, making it into the car a half second before Rayfield crashed through the swinging doors and yanked the car door open. "Go!" he bellowed. The best man and groom, too, were right on his heels.

Ellen stepped on the gas, and the Honda peeled through the dirt lot. Rayfield's pursuers hovered in a cloud of dust, like mythic figures representing the wrath of the overcivilized, tuxedoed male. She zoomed onto the paved road and gunned it around the first curve while Rayfield slumped in the front seat, a defeated man.

"I take it Debbie didn't go for it," Ellen finally said.

"Nope."

"Why were they chasing you?"

"They got a short fuse. What can I tell you?"

"Well, I'm glad you made it out in time," Ellen said. Even with his trimmer body, Rayfield hardly seemed prepared to go a few rounds with a set of identical twins.

"What you just did took a lot of courage," she said, mainly to compensate for her own doubts.

"Foolish is more like it."

"Do you want to talk about it?"

"Hell no."

Ellen turned her attention to her driving, noticed she was doing seventy in a fifty-five, and eased up on the accelerator pedal. She had no idea where she was, and the dense forest on both sides of the road left no place to turn around and no option for rights nor lefts. "You know, Rayfield, it's hard to take a step off the beaten path in life."

"Now what're you talking about?"

"This road. It's like a metaphor for life. There's so much pressure to stay on the straight and narrow." She gestured toward the woods. "Step off it, and you could wander, lost and alone, forever."

Rayfield stared at her with a slack lower jaw. "Cripes, Ellen," he finally said, and then he shifted his shoulders and looked out the window.

Just then, Ellen rounded a curve and saw a sign for Lamone. Rayfield never spoke again the whole way home, and the flowers he had picked wilted on the backseat. She wanted to probe Rayfield's romantic wound, to pick it clean before he returned to his trailer and shut the door behind himself to heal in private. Any unexpressed emotion, she thought, was a potential infection. If romantic gangrene set in, Rayfield might abandon his Peyronie's treatment and return to a diet based on beer and cigarettes. Worse, he might become cynical, embittered, and romantically disabled. Yet she knew it wasn't pure altruism that compelled her. She also wanted reassurance that there was a will to go on even at the precise moment when a long-term marriage took its deathblow.

Somehow, she contained herself and just let Rayfield be. Absentmindedly, he peeled off his blazer and tossed it into the backseat, along with his tie.

Then he untucked his freshly pressed shirt and undid the buttons on both wrists and the neck. She glanced toward the floor to see if he had shucked his shoes, but he hadn't.

"I'll call you," she said as he climbed out of the car.

"Gimme a couple days." He reached through the open back window to pat Olivier's head. "Never fall in love, my man," he said, and then he walked, round-shouldered, toward his truck.

thirty-four

That night, after Olivier had slipped into deep sleep, Ellen was seized with a desire to tear the pea-green slipcover off the wingback chair in the living room to see if the original upholstery was more aesthetically pleasing. She started with the back panel, yanking out the long tacks one by one. Each one that came loose sounded like a pistol shot in the distance. When one corner was slack enough to fold back, she knew she was on the right decorating track because a lovely pattern of red-and-white mystery vegetation covered the chair. Just the sight of the feathery design cheered Ellen, and she pulled at the sickly green fabric with renewed vigor. Soon the whole back of the chair was set free, and Ellen sat back on her heels with satisfaction.

"Much better," she said out loud, wadding up the soon-to-be-discarded slipcover as if its mere presence were a personal insult to the more beautiful upholstery fabric underneath. But as she prepared to toss it into a pile, she felt a strange rigidity in the seam, and she carried it to the light where it became obvious that Viola had sewn something circular along the edge of the material. Ellen ran up the kamikaze stairs to get her manicure scissors and was soon snipping the hand-done stitches at the side of the panel.

Inside, she found nine gold coins, each worth a face value of two dollars and fifty cents. She used a magnifying glass to examine the Indian chief in full headdress on the coins, all of which matched one another except for the dates, which ranged from 1897 to 1928. Her immediate impulse was to call Tommy, but a glance at the clock revealed it was close to eleven P.M. and she didn't want to wake him. She didn't want to listen to the phone ring unanswered either, or, God forbid, hear the melodious voice of the yoga instructor. So she abandoned that idea, spread out the coins on the dining-room table, and reexamined each one like a world-class miser. She assumed they would be worth more than their face value, but how much more? She would hit the library first thing in the morning and find out.

Ellen returned to the chair and ripped the rest of the fabric carefully off the sides. She didn't expect to discover more gold, but it didn't stop her from hoping. And then, taped against the front of the chair, inside the slipcover, she found treasure of a different sort: three handwritten letters to Viola de Beer. Ellen examined the postmark, which was the same in all three cases: Syracuse, New York, and the dates all fell within the month of July in 1932. The return address was faded to a blue color only slightly deeper than the shade of the envelope and Ellen had to carry it to a better light to read it. Her heart began to palpitate when she saw the name Rodney L. Murphy in the upper left. Obviously, Viola had named her bastard son for his father, and here was the proof. Ellen had both the researcher's technical interest in the content of the letters and her own personal curiosity, a powerful combination, and usually she would not have hesitated to indulge herself in the joy of snooping, but being that this involved Rodney and she was already on thin ice with him over privacy issues, she put on the brakes. Was there a right and a wrong here? Did squatter's rights, or, for that matter, a legally transferred deed, bestow upon her the freedom to open Viola's personal mail? But what if there were something in the letters that would hurt Rodney? By merely reading them before she handed them over to him, she reasoned, she might prevent a psychological trauma to a senior citizen.

Normally, she would talk it over with Tommy. She glanced at the clock again, but in her heart she knew it was not the hour that prevented her from dialing his number. She and Tommy were officially alienated, which happened periodically in their marriage. Usually, it escalated into a fight that cleared the air and set both partners back on the road to togetherness. But if you were far apart, each in a separate corner, you swung your punches in private and never experienced the relief of formal confrontation. Ellen missed her husband, but all the missing in the world could not negate the gulf between them, which grew wider with each passing day. As if by mutual consent, they had stopped calling each other, and, though she couldn't speak for Tommy, for herself "out of sight, out of mind" stood a fair chance of leaving "absence makes the heart grow fonder" in the dust. It was all too disturbing, too confusing, to do anything but climb into bed and pull the covers up over her shoulders. This, she did, and after some basic tossing and turning, she fell into a light sleep that ended with the first chirps of the morning birds.

When Rodney arrived for breakfast, Ellen was already on her second cup of tea.

"You look like the cat that swallowed the canary," Rodney said as he came through the screen door.

"Not guilty! Not guilty of anything for once!" Ellen exclaimed, happy that it was true. "But guess what!"

"What?"

She told him the whole story, sweeping her hands grandly over the visual aids—the three letters. She had tucked the gold coins away. They were just filthy lucre, and she felt no duty to share them.

"Well, I'll be goddamned," Rodney said as he put on his glasses.

"They're from your father, aren't they?"

"I wouldn't know. My mother never said word one about him."

"It's gotta be him." Ellen picked up the nearest letter and thrust it under Rodney's eyes. He moved his head back, trying to focus. "The return address is Rodney L. Murphy. She must've named you for your father, Rodney."

"The date is six months before I was born."

"Viola must've figured out she was pregnant and written to him."

"Did you read 'em yet?" Rodney dropped the letter on the table and went to the kitchen for his morning coffee.

"Nope. I'm a reformed busybody."

"Maybe we shouldn't read 'em," Rodney said as he sat down with his chocolate eclair. "They're my mother's private property."

When their parents had died, Ellen and Karen had sifted through their entire collection of worldly possessions and not found one unexpected item. Had her parents been Communist spies under cover as just plain folks, their stories would have been 100 percent convincing.

"Aren't you dying of curiosity? Jeez, Rodney, this is the story of your life. Most people would jump at a chance like this. I have a friend who was born in a taxicab, delivered by the driver, and she *still* asks her mother to tell her the story every time she sees her."

"That's different from prying into letters that were hid away."

"Maybe she hid them because they were precious."

"Or evidence," Rodney cynically added, "in case she decided to blackmail him. That would've been right up my mother's alley."

"Maybe he's still alive. Maybe I could help you find him."

"I'm sure he knows where I've been all these years if he wanted to say hello."

Ellen, having come up against Rodney's formidable resistance in the past, decided there was no point in hoping that he would cooperate with her and simply rip open the letters so she could read along over his shoulder. "Well," she said, "I think they're rightfully yours, but if you don't want them, just leave them here."

"Would you read them if I did?"

"Yes."

He stared pensively at his eclair for a full minute as Ellen served Olivier a glazed donut and some dry Cheerios in a bowl. Do good and be love, she reminded herself in an effort to sidestep any attempt at manipulation.

"I think I'll leave them with you," Rodney finally said. "If she says anything hateful about me, don't tell me."

"You weren't even born yet. How could she have anything bad to say?"

"I was in the womb."

Some women did hate their babies in the womb, which was a very troublesome thought. Surely, waves of hostility and rage polluted the waters of the amniotic sac. It could so easily have happened to Rodney, yet, other than one crummy morning of booze breath and a couple snippy comments, he was one of the kindest, gentlest human beings she had ever known. Ellen reached for the three letters and dropped them into the drawer of Viola's old china hutch. There, in the corner, sat the cardboard box in which she had stashed her newfound gold. It was pure greed, she suddenly realized, that had kept her from mentioning the coins to Rodney. But technically, she owned everything in the house. Maybe she could cash in those gold coins and pay off part, or even all, of her recently acquired credit card debt. Besides, finders keepers was the rule. Finders keepers.

She glanced at Rodney.

Losers weepers.

"There's more," Ellen blurted out. "I was saving the best for last." She all but flung the box of gold coins onto the table. "Check it out! I found these sewn into the seam of the slipcover I took off the chair."

Rodney lifted the lid off the box. "I'll be goddamned," he said. "Gold coins."

"Did you know your mother had them?"

"I never saw 'em before. I wonder how long she had 'em."

"Well, the newest one was minted before you were born, so it had to be at least that long."

Rodney picked up one and stared at it from a distance of three inches. "When I think of all the times we went without, practically starving or freezing to death, and then I think that she had these coins that could've been cashed in, I could flat-out crown her."

"Who knows why she kept them," Ellen said as the whole interlude skidded offtrack. Rodney was clearly upset, which was the last thing she had expected.

"You have no idea what it was like," Rodney said. His eyes teared up, but he clamped his jaw shut in a way that Ellen recognized as his signal that the subject was now officially closed.

"Rodney, I'd like to give you the coins in Viola's name. To do with what you want. I'm sure she meant for you to have them."

"I don't want 'em. It's very nice of you, but when I left this house as a boy I didn't take one thing except the three changes of clothes and the two pairs of shoes I had to my name. And when she died I didn't take nothing out of here. And I don't want nothing now—not her stinking letters or her gold coins." He stood up. Olivier raised his arms, hoping Rodney would free him from his high chair. Rodney, too preoccupied to notice, stepped away and Olivier began to scream and pound his little fists on his tray table. Ellen leaped up and pulled her nephew out by his underarms and placed him on the floor. His bare chest had bits of donut glazing cemented onto it like Mardi Gras decorations.

"Oh, Rodney, I didn't mean to upset you."

"You didn't. Remembering the past did."

"But I'm sorry. I wish I'd never found the letters or the gold coins."

"Just don't mention them to me again," he snapped. Then he took Olivier outside. Ellen stood at the screen door watching them cross the yard, hand in hand, and tears flooded her eyes. What would make a woman hoard gold while her son went hungry, she wondered. What would make her sew nine gold coins into the fabric of a slipcover and never tell a living soul they were there?

The obvious answer was insanity. Viola De Beer was nuttier than a fruitcake, and poor Rodney was her victim. She had tormented him in life, and now that he knew she had a secret, unused stash of gold, she was throwing one more punch from the grave. Sometimes, it all seemed so relentless, as if life itself were a blowtorch with an endless supply of fuel that mysteriously remained trained on each and every individual. Long ago, her hippie friend Nelson had coined a term for surviving the daily grind: "Doing the whole life shuffle." There, in the yard, was Rodney, shuffling away.

Moodily, Ellen brewed a new pot of open-the-heart tea. The twigs and berries moved crazily through the bubbles, and she watched for a long time. The problem with opening the heart, she thought, was the pain it forced you to feel. If it were only open to joy, it would definitely be worth it, but considering that she couldn't make any stipulations, it was a toss-up. She had started this whole tea rigmarole to get over the pressure of semidespondency. Had it lifted? Or was she actually more immersed in it now that she had begun to feel more for herself and others?

If you looked at it technically, the major positive effect was that she was now grinning at herself in the mirror, which was probably a preferred pastime of individuals incarcerated in mental hospitals all over the country. She was shooing deerflies away from Mutley and respecting Rodney's privacy by not immediately reading Viola's hidden letters. But all in all, it didn't seem to add up too high in the profit column.

She pushed out the door, tea in hand, and sat on the crumbling front steps.

thirty-five

The phone rang in the middle of the night, slicing through Ellen's dreams like a butcher knife. She ran down the kamikaze stairs, the balls of her feet barely touching the creaking wood of each step, and through the dark living room with the assurance of a blind person on home turf. She reached for the phone on the fifth ring.

"Ellen?"

"Karen! I've been worried sick about you."

There was a silence that took Ellen's breath away. "Karen?" she finally whispered.

"Cocho died," Karen said.

"Oh, honey, where are you? Are you alone? I'm so sorry." In her heart, Ellen had feared it would come to this. Her "breathe on" mantra was not a magic bullet after all. "When?"

"A little while ago."

"Were you there with him?"

"I was, but he wasn't."

An involuntary yelp erupted out of Ellen, and she felt ashamed.

"I mean, his spirit had drifted so far away while he was in the coma. He started not to even look like himself. And then it just drifted one more inch, and he died."

"He never regained consciousness?"

"Never."

"Karen, come home. Come home." Tears blinded Ellen. The dining room blurred, as if she were staring at it through a downpour. "Come home."

"I'm going to go with Cocho's parents. With Cocho. They're going to bury him in his village. And then I'll be home."

"Karen, I love you. Olivier loves you. I know it doesn't help right now, but . . ." She had no idea how to continue.

"I know, Ellen. Thanks."

"Is there anything I can do?"

"No. There's nothing anybody can do."

"Come home."

"I miss him so much."

"Come home."

"As soon as I can."

Ellen wished, selfishly, that Karen would cry, fill the phone lines with sobbing that would smother the need for words. She wanted good words, comforting words for her sister, and she had none.

"Do you know when that will be?"

"Maybe three or four days. Cocho will be buried on Tuesday. Then it'll take me a day to get back to Lima."

"Olivier and I will be waiting at the airport. Do you want me to call anyone? Regine-Marie?"

"Would you?"

"I'll go there in the morning and tell her in person."

"Thank you. I just can't talk to anyone else tonight. I have to go now. To sit with Cocho."

"You have the strength and courage to get through this," Ellen said.

"I hope so. Kiss our little boy for me. And for Cocho."

"I will, I will," Ellen cried, clutching at her cramping throat. "I will."

Karen hung up, and Ellen held the receiver in her hand but could not replace it. Cocho's life was over. Cocho was gone. He would never be back, never see his boy again, never play the wooden flute in Place Jacques-Cartier on a summer day. She felt dizzy and collapsed onto the floor. The wide pine boards felt like the smooth face of a high cliff, and she could not grab hold of anything.

Cocho was gone. Her sister's true love, gone. Olivier's father, gone. His spirit had floated farther and farther away from his body, Karen had said, and then detached itself and floated on, out of human range. Even Karen's grip on his hand could not hold him.

In her hippie days, Ellen had selected a metaphysical reading for her own funeral and made sure all her friends knew it was what she wanted in case she overdosed, got murdered, or died in a car wreck. Now, she could not even remember the name of the Indian swami whose words she loved, but the first line was "I am flying home." Cocho, the air spirit, was flying home now, well on his way into the big nothing. His body, like "The House With Nobody in

It," the poem she always recited to Tommy at the Suffern exit of the New York State Thruway, was already decomposing, returning to a pile of rubble. A state, Ellen thought, that we all, each and every one of us, are just one short breath away from every second. Karen, left without her lover, was sitting by his corpse somewhere in the city of Lima, Peru, alone. Ellen cried and cried. When she finally felt capable, she called Tommy. He answered on the third ring, sounding gravel-voiced.

"Tommy, Cocho didn't make it. He died a little while ago."

"Oh, no."

Ellen could imagine him standing in their kitchen. He slept nude in the summer. He was leaning against the doorjamb, the phone held to his right ear.

"Karen sounds like she's sleepwalking."

"Should I go down there and get her?"

"I don't think you'd be able to find her. She's going back to the town Cocho's family lives in—way up in the mountains." Ellen could barely breathe. "Oh, Tommy, this is so terrible."

"I know," he whispered. "I'm so sorry. Can I call her?"

"I have the number of the hospital here," she said as she scanned the slips of paper thumbtacked to the wall, "but I've never been able to get through to her there." Tommy took the number anyway.

"Why don't you and Olivier come down here?" he asked. "You can even bring Mutley if you have to."

Ellen was silent, though touched.

"Maybe we could enroll him in the day care center," Tommy said. There was a private preschool on the ground floor of their building. "Resident dog-mat." Ellen forced a halfhearted giggle and then said, "I'd love to come, but I think I should hang around here in case Karen calls or comes back suddenly. She'll need Olivier."

"She'll need you, too."

"You think?"

"I know."

She wanted to say, "What about you, Tommy? Do you need me?" But she refused to be self-centered at a moment like this.

"Is she going to have a service for him?" Tommy asked.

"We didn't get that far, but I suppose she'll need one. We all will."

"I'll come up for that."

"Are you really busy?" The question sounded almost wistful in her own ears.

"Very. Big case."

"Have you decided about your vacation?"

"I haven't been thinking about it."

Ellen was afraid to know what Tommy was thinking about instead. A small silence resonated between them.

"Well, I should let you get back to sleep." She did not add, "Only four hours until yoga," although it crossed her mind. "I just needed to hear your voice."

"Oh, honey, I would've been very upset if you hadn't called me at a time like this. I wish I were up there with you."

"Thanks for saying that, Tom."

"I love you."

"Likewise, baby," she said.

Ellen felt unequal to the task of climbing the stairs to check on Olivier, asleep in his port-a-crib. She had to brace herself against the stairway wall on each step to keep from tumbling backward into the living room.

She sat on the edge of her bed, with its firm new mattress, and watched Olivier breathe. In the pale moonlight, his skin looked bronze and his black curls spread out over his pillow like a map of the state of Texas. Ellen leaned into the crib and lifted him out. She held him in her arms and kissed him once for Karen and once for Cocho, as she had promised. Then she stretched out on the bed, his little body pressed close to hers, and pulled Viola's old comforter up over their shoulders. She counted his breath in sets of four through the darkness, through the first hint of dawn that eased through the east-facing windows, through the half hour that it took for the room to lighten up, until Olivier finally opened his eyes.

"*Bonjour*, Olivier," she said from three inches away.

Olivier giggled and sat up. "Wet," he said, tugging at his pajama top. Ellen noticed it was soaked.

Her tears.

She peeled it off him, taking huge breaths to prevent herself from sobbing at the sight of his narrow chest, so like Cocho's. She dressed her nephew, fed Mutley, watered her plants, packed up the car for a day trip, and left—all before Rodney showed up at his customary eight A.M. She left the door open and a sad note for him on the table.

On the drive to Trout River, Ellen sang nonsense songs to Olivier, with "Supercalafragilisticexpialodocious" the headliner tune. Once, she glanced at him in the rearview mirror and saw that he was watching her curiously. The poor kid should not have been subjected to her imitation of Ethel Merman doing "There's No Business Like Show Business" either, but she could feel herself heading to it, as if her vocal cords were preprogrammed to segue into show tunes as soon as she wrapped up the Jiminy Cricket number "Get Your Encyclopedia" that she had learned while watching the Mickey Mouse Club and sung periodically ever since.

Besides, really, it was all show business. Here she was, driving to Montreal singing her head off when what she actually wanted was to drive into the cave in Eagle Beak Mountain and never come out again. She wanted to hibernate, like a big black bear, and dream of paradise.

The customs agent had seen them before, and to Ellen's astonishment, remembered them. "Still babysitting?" she asked cheerfully in English.

"For a few more days," Ellen answered.

The agent waved her on. Until that precise moment, Ellen had not faced the fact that life with Olivier was about to come to a crash landing. He had been her companion and her joy from almost the beginning of her Eagle Beak sojourn. He distracted her from having the deep meditation she'd expected, but he, like Dr. Yi's tea, also pried open her heart and filled it with love. She would miss him. Nothing would be the same without him.

Ellen entered Montreal with a feeling of dread. The cobblestone streets of Old Montreal rattled the Honda until her teeth ached. Everywhere, window boxes dripped with bright flowers and slim young women carried mesh bags from which thin loaves of bread protruded, but no pleasant visual could lift her tired spirit. On a whim, she decided to take a stroll around Place Jacques-Cartier before they went to the café to look for Karen's dearest friend.

In the square, they meandered slowly by the caricature artists, most of whom looked quite hungover as they committed their sugarcoated insults to oversized drawing pads. The cafés along the edges were peopled with tourists in baseball caps, and a black man played Sonny Rollins tunes on a gleaming saxophone. His case had many two dollar coins resting in its plush fake fur. Blankets were spread out along one wall and beauty entrepreneurs wrapped colorful threads around thin strands of hair as their customers sat with the sun beating down on their heads. Henna artists busily painted snowflake patterns onto the hands and feet of tourists, and a juggler who had attached a red ball to his nose threw bowling pins into the sky. To Ellen, it felt like a Renaissance Festival, a staged event, but she knew it wasn't. This was everyday life when the weather held. At some point, the caricature artists and the henna painters packed up and went home to charming old buildings, like Karen's, where they probably fucked each other silly into the wee small hours. They probably still grew pot on their little balconies and considered seven A.M. the middle of the night.

Ellen sat on a bench and hoisted Olivier into her lap. Sometimes Cocho and three of his Peruvian friends had come here to play. Ellen had witnessed it herself. They would drop their backpacks at their feet and spread out their CDs, which sold for eighteen dollars Canadian, on a woven blanket, and soon the sounds of the Andes mountains would drift above the pavement of Place Jacques-Cartier. A crowd would gather in a horseshoe shape and, if there were little children present, they would often start to dance. Cocho, with his narrow chest, hardly appeared to have the wind to keep going, but he was the spine of the band. Women of all ages would stare at him quite openly as their hips began to gently sway and their shoulders and necks loosened.

Would the band stay intact, find another flute player to channel his breath through the zampoñas? Would Ellen return here next summer and see the revised group with CDs for sale, Cocho's image gone from the group photo? Or would Cocho's death send them all off in different directions, like the wind that sang through their fragile instruments?

"Your daddy played his flute here," Ellen whispered in Olivier's ear. "He would play, and all the people in the square would forget their cares and worries. It was beautiful. I wish you could have grown up seeing it."

Olivier felt so tiny and inconsequential in her arms. Now he had no father to watch his back as he negotiated the mean streets of childhood. It seemed incomprehensible and unfair. Ellen stood up and started across the cobblestones, trying to outrun her tears, and soon she stood in front of the Café L'Alibi. The petunias and pansies in the barrels by the entrance and in window boxes along the railing of the outside patio created a riot of color, and Ellen felt, as she stepped forward, that she was entering an Impressionist painting.

Regine-Marie had just delivered a tray of coffees in sturdy mugs to a table in an alcove to the left of the door. Ellen could see her right hand resting on the shoulder of a tall blond woman who wore fifties-style cat's eyes glasses with rhinestones in the corners. Ellen remained perfectly still, savoring the last few seconds before she had to deliver her terrible news.

When Regine-Marie stepped away and started back toward the counter where several variations of coffee mugs and teapots steamed, she glanced once toward the door, the practiced assessment of a café owner, and saw Ellen standing in a triangle of sunlight with Olivier in her arms. Ellen saw a smile start to form and then freeze. Inquiry entered Regine-Marie's eyes, lighting them in the same odd little squares that animate the eyes in a paint-by-number set.

Ellen shook her head no.

Regine-Marie's hand rose to her throat. Olivier, meanwhile, with a gleeful *whoop*, squirmed out of Ellen's arms and ran to Regine-Marie, throwing his arms around her legs like a surfer clinging to a piling in an unexpected storm. She lifted him up high, hugged and kissed him, and then moved toward Ellen, whom she embraced with her free hand.

"When?" she said.

"Last night."

"Oh, God." She led Ellen to a table and then sat down. "Oh, God." She put her head down on the table and sobbed.

"I probably shouldn't have come here to work to tell you, but I didn't think I could find your house, and . . ."

"Of course you had to come. Just let me cry for a few minutes."

"Yes."

Olivier, on Regine-Marie's lap, seemed thoroughly mystified by the crying woman who held him. He slapped the tabletop and made a grab for the sugar dispenser. "Poor Karen," Regine-Marie moaned. "She loved him so much."

"She was with him at the end. She's going with his parents to bury him. Then she's coming home."

"Good. She needs to be here."

A waitress wearing a batik sarong, seeing that Regine-Marie was in the midst of a meltdown, delivered coffees and served toast and croissants to various waiting customers. Karen has a beautiful life here, Ellen was thinking as she looked around. She and Regine-Marie donated 10 percent of their net income to charities devoted to fighting world hunger, and the café, at any given moment, was like a miniature United Nations, minus the tension and hidden agendas. Surely there was someone here to speak Spanish to Olivier, to tell him tales of llamas and supply alpaca sweaters and ponchos in the earth tones of Peru as he grew. Karen and Regine-Marie and the other Peruvian men who played music in Place Jacques-Cartier would keep Cocho's memory alive. They would talk about him, and Olivier would sense his father's presence in his life. One day, years from now, Ellen would tell him the story of Eagle Beak, how he lived with her when his mother rushed to Cocho's bedside. She would tell him about Rayfield, Rodney, and Mutley. Maybe someday, Olivier would have a son and name him Cocho.

Ellen reached out and placed her hand on Regine-Marie's head, stroking it like a puppy dog. Olivier took the clue and began to pat her face and soon Regine-Marie giggled through her tears and used a paper napkin to remove her smudged mascara. "Let's take a walk," she said. She called out something in French to the waitress in the South Seas ensemble and waved goodbye.

They started down the street, each woman holding one of Olivier's hands. Soon he was lifting his feet and merrily swinging. "Did you know I introduced Cocho and Karen?" Regine-Marie asked.

"Really?"

"Uh-huh. I met him when I was playing at the jazz festival four years ago. I knew instantly that this was the guy for Karen. I've always felt like their sponsor."

"What was it that you knew she'd be attracted to?"

"His dreaminess. Karen feels so inhibited by her practical nature."

"She does?" Ellen wasn't certain that she knew this about her sister.

"Cocho lifted her out of herself and let her fly. And she gave him roots."

"But how did you know they would work together?"

"I just did."

"They made a beautiful couple."

"They made a beautiful child."

"Thank God she has Olivier."

They came to the end of the block and turned right toward the river. Olivier grew excited at the sight of a huge ship, and they strolled toward it and then sat down on a bench. Olivier ran to the fence that prevented entry into the boat slip and peered through the chain-links like a youthful offender in a trendy B movie about prison life.

"Did you expect Cocho to die?" Ellen asked.

"More, as the weeks passed. It's probably a blessing. He couldn't possibly have been normal and healthy after being in a coma so long." Regine-Marie started to cry. "Could he?"

"I don't know. I don't think so."

"I'm going to miss him so much."

"Did you know him really well?" Ellen asked wistfully.

"Yes." Suddenly the air between them seemed charged, lit by invisible lightning. It only lasted a second, and after it passed Ellen couldn't be sure what was illuminated in the flash, but she thought it was trouble. After the briefest pause, Regine-Marie added, "He was one of my closest friends."

"Oh, Regine-Marie, I'm so sorry for you," Ellen said, feeling that she was slamming the lid down on Pandora's box. "I didn't know you were so close. I'm just realizing, in all of this, how little I really know about the people Karen loves." Except Olivier, she thought, I'm learning about Olivier. "Tell me about Cocho," she said.

"What do you want to know?"

"Anything. Everything."

Regine-Marie reached into her huge canvas bag to find her sunglasses and a pack of cigarettes. She lit one and blew a long stream of filthy smoke into the white clouds before she spoke.

"He wanted to be a doctor when he was a little boy," she began. "He came from a big family—seven kids—and one day his next older brother got bitten by a poisonous snake and the whole family thought he was going to die. There was a doctor in the next village, an American guy in the Peace Corps, and he came over with antibiotics and saved him. The doctor was like a god, Cocho said. He dreamed of being like that—having a magic black bag and curing snakebites and speaking English. When the doctor left, Cocho walked him out to his truck and the doctor shook his hand. Cocho said he felt initiated into the healing arts in that moment. He said he could still feel the size of the doctor's hand. It was the first time an adult had shaken his hand, he said, and when he looked up, he said the doctor's eyes were as blue as the sky and he felt like he'd been gently drawn out of being a child, sort of placed in his own future, and he knew that someday he would do that for other people. Touch them and transport them somewhere else. Somewhere where the skies were very, very blue."

"The music doctor," Ellen said with a sense of wonderment.

Regine-Marie nodded. She stared up the river for a few seconds, perhaps watching the traffic on the faraway bridge. "He was passionately in love with his lungs. Every morning when he first opened his eyes, he would put his two hands on either side of his chest and imagine his breath and his fingers in deep communication. And then he would get up and play."

Ellen felt a little dizzy. How could Regine-Marie know such intimate details of Cocho's life? She looked sideways at Karen's best friend, who wiped a tear away from under her sunglasses. Ellen closed her eyes for a second, remembering the early-morning sound of Cocho's flute, which she heard whenever she had visited Karen. Cocho was an early riser, and several times his music had lured her gently awake. Once she had confusedly thought that she was with a shepherd on the hills of Greece; another time, she thought she was back in Paul's Mall, waiting tables while Charles Lloyd played solo onstage, perched on a three-legged bar stool.

"I wonder if Karen held his hands or hers to his chest in the mornings in the hospital," Ellen said.

"I'm sure she did," Regine-Marie answered.

Ellen wanted to prod Regine-Marine on, bug her for more stories about Cocho. At the same time, she felt bowled over by the intensely intimate peek Regine-Marie had already given her. "You know what's strange?" she asked. "That something as nebulous as air, something without weight or color or substance, can be harnessed by mere humans and the result is music."

"It's all music, Ellen," Regine-Marie replied.

thirty-six

Ellen spent the afternoon scrubbing every square inch of Karen's loft. Her sister would return in a few days, and Ellen wanted all depressing dust motes and unidentifiable city grime banished. She put the houseplants in the tub to rinse their leaves, and she washed the sheets and vacuumed behind the couch cushions. Olivier occupied himself by tossing toys in high arcs from the old trunk by his bed. When he finally climbed into her lap and fell asleep, Ellen placed him in his crib and then rubbed each window with white vinegar-soaked pages of the *Montreal Gazette*. Then she picked the dead petunias and pansies from the window boxes and gave all the plants fresh fertilizer sticks and a long drink of Miracle-Gro.

In her heart, she knew that all the cleaning in the world would not reduce Karen's grief by even the tiniest fraction, but she hoped that it might subliminally suggest to Karen that order was still possible. With the sun streaming in, warming the old wooden floors and creating rainbows through the prisms in the windows, the loft seemed like the most peaceful place in the whole universe. It made Ellen sleepy, and she climbed into a convenient hammock and closed her eyes.

Hypnogogic images of purple and green halos appeared behind her eyelids, leading her away from this world into the place she called Alphaville. She hurried on, rushing toward sleep. The feeling of suspension in the hammock, perhaps the shallow curve of her spine, sent her floating along a neural pathway into a quiet cove along the shore of some nameless lake. Sleep logic presented the possibility that it was Peak Pond, with its ring of rustic camps and its tiny public beach. Ellen felt as if she were in a canoe, as if she herself were a canoe, moving silently across the surface of the water. On the shore were tall spruce trees, their long trunks bare of branches with only a spray of greenery at

the top where the sun touched them. Ellen thought she could see benign animals among the trees—deer and rabbits, beavers and foxes, camouflaged by the
colors of nature. Onward she paddled around a bend, which opened into a
wide vista. There was a huge rock, similar to the one in the middle of the Aca-
pulco Bay, and, at its top, a man was standing dangerously close to the edge. A
cliff diver meditating on the waves.

"Cocho?" Ellen said in the dream. She paddled speedily toward him, but
Cocho, a sleepwalker, extended his right leg into the air. "Wait!" Ellen whispered. "Wait!" Then, before her eyes, he stepped off the edge and plummeted
toward the water. "Wait!" she hollered as she watched his body drop through
the air and then straighten itself into diving form to pierce the dark water like
a bullet from the sky. Within a second, Ellen, in her little boat, arrived at the
place where he had disappeared, but already the ripples had stopped and there
was only the ghoulish sea. She peered into its shadows and saw no sign of Cocho. "No, no!" she screamed, her heart thumping in arrhythmia.

Ellen woke up flailing in the hammock with such vigor that she actually
pitched herself out of it onto the floor. She raised herself to her hands and
knees, feeling like a boxer who needed to rest as much as possible before the
count of ten made it obligatory to stand up and start fighting.

Though she assumed she had yelled out loud, Olivier was still sleeping
peacefully across the room, and Ellen was grateful. She climbed to her feet and
tiptoed toward the refrigerator where she cracked a cold beer. Her hands shook
as she poured it into a glass mug and carried it to the kitchen table. Her dream
had put her in a bona fide panic. But why? Cocho, with the precision of Superman, had simply disappeared into another world. Why couldn't she ap-
plaud his airborne theatrics instead of wishing to stop him in midair? He was
flying home, after all.

He was flying home.

Ellen gripped the side of the chair as if it were an ejection seat. She felt
breathless. Was there any such place as home? Birds made their nests and bees
made their hives, bears found their personal caves and salmon swam against
the current by the millions to return to the waters from whence they came.
Was it possible that shelter, in all its many forms, was a foreshadowing of some
big, cosmic home beyond the pale? Or was the concept of a home on the far
side of the gates of death just a way for the terrified human mind to cope with
the fear of dying?

According to the old saying, Home is where the heart is. In the jazz club
where she had worked, the great Esther Phillips had sung a spine-chilling version of "Home Is Where the Hatred Is." Stephen Foster felt home was on the
range, where the deer and the antelope play. But perhaps home was where you

were, moment by moment, but one had to cross over to the other side to un-derstand exactly what that meant. Ellen mulled it over later, as she sat in the homey atmosphere of the Café L'Alibi with Olivier for an early dinner. The staff glanced sympathetically at Olivier, who had just lost his father though he didn't understand that, and expressed sympathy for Karen. Ellen, her back to the wall in a tiny corner booth, felt nurtured in every way: by the healthy yo-gurt and fresh fruit, by the repetitive reggae music, by the melodious French language all around her. Regine-Marie was not working, but she came into the café when Ellen was halfway through her meal. Her eyes were swollen and lines that Ellen had never seen before had suddenly appeared between her eyebrows. She drank a double espresso in small sips with Olivier seated in her lap.

"How's your garden doing?" Regine-Marie suddenly asked.

"Good," Ellen replied. No one had ever asked her about her garden, and she felt oddly emotional. "Sometimes the plants grow inches in a day." She wanted to go on, to relate tiny details, perhaps about her irrational fear of po-tato bugs and tomato worms, but she didn't dare bore Regine-Marie to death after she'd been polite enough to ask.

"You ought to invent the Auntie Ellen salad, made only of things from your garden. We could put it on our menu as a summer special."

Ellen laughed. "I don't deserve such glory." But driving back home, through the psychedelically green landscape, Ellen waxed philosophical. She had claimed a little patch of land, fought back the wild proliferation of weeds, selected the best organic seeds, and grown vegetables that were both thor-oughly health-promoting and borderline decadent in their association with the privileges of upward mobility. She had carried water and pulled weeds. She had been the personal trainer and bodyguard to each shoot, stem, and leaf.

But was she doing the same thing for her psyche? If her life, at age forty-six, was her garden, was she doing her mental weeding? And if she was growing herself into some new, more mature hybrid female form, which, she thought she was, then who and what was she in the process of becoming? Was she growing away from New York? From Tommy?

When she thought of leaving Tommy or leaving New York, the picture changed. It depicted failure, not joyous growth. The idea that discontent had taken root below the surface and grown unchecked made her feel sad. Anyway, it was impossible to be anything but sad with Cocho dead and soon to be six feet under. Ellen only knew one thing for sure about dying, or, more precisely, about the phase of life that immediately preceded death. She had seen it with her own eyes and had heard about it from countless others. As time ticked down, or perhaps got yanked away as in the case of an accident, just as life itself tightened like a noose around the dying person's neck and the future suddenly became as confined as the coffin that would enclose it, there, in the midst of perhaps the utmost possible constriction, there was space and amaz· ing things happened in it.

Her own father, a man who pooh-poohed the mystical, had nearly died at age eleven when his foot got caught in a submerged tree root while he was swimming in the White River on a hot summer day. During the few minutes in which his fingers tore at the slimy tendrils, he had seen, he said, in minute detail, every single second of his life. He said that for years afterward he would comment on events of the distant past and his mother, completely unnerved, would mutter, "You can't possibly remember that! You were only two years old!" But he did remember, and he said that when he had finally hoisted himself onto the riverbank, gasping for breath and unsure whether he was safe or drowned, he knew for a fact that time was as elastic as a rubber band.

Knowing that death was near, people found the will and the way to speak directly from the heart, to say words like, "I love you," to those they had struggled with all their lives. Words that had never been said, could never be said, suddenly gushed out like oil from a rich strike. That emotional space was probably always there but it was inaccessible for some reason.

The point was, if both time and space could disappear so easily, all the hanging on was a waste of precious energy. Still, Ellen felt like a pilot in a cloud with zero visibility and no radio contact. There was nothing to do but speed on and hope there was no debris ahead. It was strange to be so alone in it, not even a blip on anyone's radar screen. Life and death were beyond comprehension, so she might as well give up trying to make sense of them.

"I let it go," she said in a whisper. She had driven to Montreal and delivered the sad news about Cocho in person to Regine-Marie. She had scrubbed Karen's loft until it begged for mercy. Now she was driving back to Eagle Beak, where she would feed the dog and listen to some music, probably Motown.

And then it came to her that somehow, in the midst of all the turbulence, she had not read the letters that she had liberated from Viola's pea-green wingback chair. Rodney's reaction had left her confused, but now a new attitude was surfacing. The letters were merely documents, and she was just a witness to history. Nothing in the letters could rock the status quo, or if it could, then the status quo obviously needed some readjustment.

She turned on the radio, softly, so as not to disturb Olivier, who typically conked out within minutes of being buckled into his car seat. She tuned into a French station in which the male announcer spoke in a serious voice. It was a talk show, and Ellen concentrated on recognizing a word here or there that would give her a clue to the subject under discussion.

I have to learn to speak French, she thought as she identified a few phrases, such as *bien sûr* and *vous êtes*. Humans needed every edge they could get, and being multilingual was probably an evolutionary necessity in the modern world—even if half the world's languages disappeared as predicted during the first century of the new millennium. As soon as I get settled, I'm signing up for French classes, she promised herself. She simply did not want to be on the outside of anything, especially understanding.

thirty-seven

Olivier never even altered his breathing pattern when Ellen lifted him out of his car seat and carried him into the house and up the stairs. He lay in his port-a-crib like an exhausted angel, his face expressionless. Ellen quietly left the room, though she was quite certain that she could have trampled down the stairs like a wild horse and it would not have disturbed her nephew. She put her open-the-heart tea on to boil and collapsed onto the porch swing. It was dark and the frogs were harmonizing in the wetlands nearby, creating a kind of sorrowful music. The Adirondack lakes were dying of acid rain and the practice of killing beavers had forever altered the size and shape of the swamps that were their habitat. Were the mammals and amphibians chanting, "All is lost!" she wondered. Even so, it beat the sounds of car alarms, police sirens, and ice-cream trucks that circled the block with "Camptown Ladies" or "I'm a Yankee Doodle Dandy" blaring from their loudspeakers.

Soon the teapot started to whistle. As she went into the kitchen, Ellen glanced at Viola's letters, on the dining-room table, waiting to be read. She returned with her tea, sat down, and arranged them in chronological order, but suddenly she felt a tremor of fear. She definitely didn't want to draw the postmortem wrath of Viola de Beer down upon her head. "Viola," she said, "if there's any reason you don't want me to read these letters, give me a sign. Any sign will do." Nervously, she held her breath and looked from side to side, but no floorboards creaked and no window shades snapped upward. "Going once, going twice . . ." She listened carefully. "Gone."

She reached for the first letter, turned it over, and studied the back flap, which had remained sealed during all the years in the chair, perhaps due to the weight of Viola's legs against the front panel. Or maybe Viola had never opened these letters at all. That would cast a different light on their contents.

She got the magnifying glass out of the drawer of the treadle sewing machine and examined the flaps of all three letters. She could not discern whether they had been previously opened, though she was certain a forensic lab in the city could. She tapped the first letter down into the envelope and cut off the end. Maybe she would want to have it tested later for some reason.

The letter was written on lightweight paper that matched the envelope. Carefully, she unfolded it. The writer had obviously been schooled in the Palmer penmanship method. Ellen vaguely remembered her mother showing her how to place a sheet of heavily lined paper behind this translucent tissue stationery to keep her handwriting from slanting up or down along the line. Rodney Murphy had probably used such a technique himself. His lines, aside from the fancy loops and tails, were as uniform as humanly possible. Ellen leaned forward over the paper and began to read.

July 8, 1932

Dear Viola,

    I am praying that you collect this letter out of the mailbox before your father sees it, for I know he would be very angry with me if he knew or even thought that I am writing to you. He told me in no uncertain terms that he didn't want me anywheres near you. In fact, he all but ordered me to stay away from not only you but the hamlet of Eagle Beak. Needless to say, I can't do that. I have to go where the hops are. I am sure your father will accept this as time passes. He is hotheaded but in the end of it all, he is a reasonable man. However, I know the risk of writing to you, and my great worry is that he will take it out on you if he sees this note. Please let me know right away if and when you get this. I am enclosing a stamp for you to use in your reply.

This opening paragraph took up three-quarters of the page. Obviously, Rodney, Sr., had either been in the hop-picking or the hop-buying business. Baldy had mentioned that Eagle Beak had once been known for its hop fields, but they had all disappeared and now only a few clear pastures remained in the whole area. The entire plateau at the base of the mountain was overgrown with brush and essentially impenetrable.

    I am totally throwed off balance by your news. I don't have the education to know the words I should use to tell you how much I wish things were different and we could get married and live happily ever after with a bunch of little Rodneys and Violas. If all the girls looked like you, I would be one happy man.

    But the only way I can see we could do it would be if we ran away, maybe out West, and changed our names and started over from scratch. I have

enough money saved to get us going but I don't think traveling in your condi-
tion is the best thing to do. And I honestly don't know if I can do it to Marion
and Eva. I don't love my wife, but I do love my little girl and it would crush
me to break her little heart. Sometimes I think of just taking her with us, but
Marion would have the Pinkerton men on us right away, and I would proba-
bly end up put right in jail.

Viola, I am between the devil and the deep blue sea. What should I do?
What do you want me to do? Every time I think of our stolen hours I get a big
grin on my face that just don't match my broken heart. Please write me back
right away. I am far away from you, and the truth is, it don't feel good at all.

Love,
Rodney

Ellen finished the letter with a mixture of cynicism and girlish delight. On
the one hand, it sounded as if Rodney L. Murphy genuinely cared about Viola,
but on the other, his bottom line was quite clear. He was not rushing to her
side. Over the years between 1932 and 1995, Ellen thought, men and women
had stopped pussy-footing around like this. Now women sued for child support
and deadbeat dads blatantly ignored both the court orders and the needs of
their offspring. Men felt that women who got pregnant were trying to trap
them and felt free to disappear, while women had successfully shucked the unwed mother stigma and proven that families can thrive without fathers anyway.

Rodney, Sr.,'s letter had let-her-down-easy written all over it, Ellen
thought, but if she herself had gotten it in her youth, she could easily have
wound up feeling sorry for him instead of herself. Poor, poor Rodney, she
might have thought, he wants me but there isn't a thing he can do about it.
Did Viola feel like that? Had she let this man off the hook only to go off the
deep end herself?

The second letter was dated just eleven days after the first. It consisted of
two sentences.

Dear Viola,
You have to let me know if you got my last letter. Please, I am losing my
mind and have to know.

Love,
Rodney

It was clear to Ellen that it was Viola and not her father who had snagged
Rodney's letter from the mailbox sixty-five years ago. Otherwise, she would

not have had it to hide away. Irate fathers waved such things in their daughter's faces and then tore them to shreds. Clearly, Viola had chosen not to answer, despite the free postage stamp that Rodney had purposefully enclosed. Ellen moved to the armchair and sat among the doilies Viola had crocheted with her own hands. "Why didn't you answer him, Viola?" she asked. It was easy to speculate upon the possibilities and impossible to know the truth. This was the mystery of all written documents. They hid as much as they revealed, and the reader's imagination automatically started to fill in the blanks. It was strange for Ellen, being in Viola's house and being a personal friend to her child, who was now a senior citizen. Viola had not run off with Rodney, Sr., had never mentioned him to their son, had not answered her lover's frantic letter for at least eleven days.

Ellen got up and moved to Viola's chair. There was a deep groove, no doubt left by Viola, that was too narrow to accommodate her ass. Did Viola sit here, decade after decade in this chair, just to absorb the subtle vibration of her youthful passion? And what had possessed Ellen to tear the slipcover off when she had never done such a thing before in her life? She looked around. There were four more god-awful chairs in the living room, yet she had not attacked them at all.

She held the third letter in her hand. It seemed reasonable to assume that this might be the last letter Viola received. The postmark was a full month after the last one—a long time within the framework of a pregnancy. She tapped the contents of the envelope to one end, slit the other with scissors, and opened the tissue paper with reverence.

Dearest Viola,

The road of true love is never easy. Sometimes you can't see around the curves, but true love makes it all worthwhile.

I thought you and me were on that road together, but now I am beginning to wonder. You still have not answered my two letters and I know you know I was in Eagle Beak last weekend, yet for some reason you avoided me. Why, Viola? Why would you ignore the man who loves you so much? You are an impossible woman to understand.

I have been over and over this in my mind and this is what I can come up with. I want you to run away with me. You, me, and the baby will be a family where nobody knows us. Somehow it will work out.

When I was up there last week, I went to the cave where we have passed so many wonderful hours. I put a little burlap bag under the flat stone we use for a table. I put my gold coins in it. I want you to go there and collect them. Cash them in, and get on the train to Syracuse. When you get there, go to the

Stanhope Hotel and wait for me. I will check in every afternoon at six to see if you have arrived. But after one month, after September twenty-fifth, I will not check anymore because that will mean to me that you're turning your back on me.

I'm begging you, Viola, and it ain't easy for a man like me to beg, but I'm begging you not to turn your back on me. I love you even if you are mean at times, and I want to get you away from your father. I want to go to California with you and start over.

I will not be writing to you again after this.

I am waiting for you.

He had signed it "R." Ellen had to move the letter quickly because suddenly she was crying and she didn't want to blur even one of Rodney, Sr.,'s words with her emotional waterworks. She could just imagine poor Rodney, Sr., receiving a no at the reception desk of the Stanhope Hotel as the days ticked down from thirty to one. Ellen felt a convulsion in her chest, as if her heart had cramped first and then opened to allow one more person across its borders. Here she was, sobbing for this poor unknown schlub who had had a broken heart more than sixty years before. Why had Viola rejected him? Why had she chosen to stay in Eagle Beak when she could've gone to California and, perhaps, settled in Big Sur or San Juan Capistrano? Rodney, Jr., could've had a normal life, as part of a nuclear family, instead of being cast as the local bastard, the no-goodnik, the son of a bitch-on-wheels. She ran to the drawer, drew out the box of gold coins, and pressed it to her heart.

It was all so sad.

We are all helpless sheep, Ellen thought as she cried on, thinking now of her sister and Cocho and poor little Olivier who would never know his father. Helpless sheep, heading for the slaughter.

thirty-eight

For the next twenty-four hours, Ellen lived as if she had been cracked over the head with a beer bottle in a barroom brawl. Olivier came down with diarrhea, which made him uncharacteristically cranky, not to mention smelly, and Rodney simply didn't show up for their breakfast meeting. Ellen's thoughts ping-ponged between Karen and Cocho and Rodney and Viola. Broken hearts and broken lives seemed to whirl around her and even though she was a mere observer, she felt centrally involved. Viola was dead, Cocho was dead, and Rodney, Sr., would have to be at least in his mid-eighties if he were alive at all, but Ellen felt their presence as if they had moved, en masse, into her spare bedroom under the eaves. She didn't dare ask them what they were doing there, but she felt the pressure of a hostess in a houseful of demanding guests. It made her despondent, but she felt guilty about sobbing constantly in front of Olivier, so she controlled herself as best she could. "Dirty," he said several times a day as he pointed to his diaper. "Tinky."

"Ain't that the truth," Ellen would say as she changed him again. Disposable diapers built up like a stash of snowballs in her garbage can, and she wondered if she should look for a local pediatrician. Was Olivier becoming dehydrated? She'd had a few attacks of turista during her trips to Mexico, and she knew that dehydration happened fast. The workings of the physical body were very complex. Was she taking an unnecessary risk with her nephew's health?

And at the moment when she felt, perhaps, most confused, who should squeal into the driveway but Rayfield Geebo of Porkerville. His "I need a hummer" bug guard suddenly irritated her, as did his noisy muffler and the way he slammed the truck door when he got out. Ellen stood at the screen door, her arms akimbo, refusing to surrender to an urge to insult him for no reason.

"Yo!" called Rayfield. Today he wore a T-shirt that read "Workers of the world . . . UNTIE."

"Yo yourself," Ellen answered civilly. "How goes it?"

"It goes damn good," Rayfield said. "I come over to tell you all about it."

"Great. I could use a little good news." She opened the door for him. She didn't want to tell him about Cocho—at least, she didn't want to blurt it out immediately. It seemed like a violation to even think it. He moved past her and dropped into a chair. "Guess who woke up this morning with a hard-on?"

"Jeez, do I really want to know?" Ellen replied. "It wasn't you, was it?"

"Goddamn right it was me," Rayfield beamed.

"I'm at a loss for words."

"Damn, Ellen, you just don't get it! Ever since I got this goddamn disease, if I started to get a hard-on it would hurt so much that it wasn't worth having it. I was snapping them away left and right." Rayfield demonstrated this snapping procedure in the air, flicking his pointing finger off his thumb to beat the band. "But today I must've got one in my sleep and it didn't wake me up. So when I woke up, there it was! It's a goddamn miracle."

Ellen played along. "Hurray!" she cheered.

Suddenly Rayfield leaped to his feet. "I owe it all to you," he said, and before she could dodge him, he bounded to her, took her in his arms, and kissed her smack on the lips. She was too shocked to protest, though she hung like a rag doll with her back slightly arched over his arm, which circled her waist.

"Don't mention it," she mumbled. Rayfield's face was less than an inch from hers and she could feel the wiry brush of his beard against her chin. She knew it was time to squirm away from him and make a joke of his display of passionate gratitude, but she felt frozen. The male gaze, which has objectified women and thrust them into second-class citizen status for centuries, has its mysterious power. She could feel herself getting lost, as if she were one of those young women in long white dresses romping through a field of wild lavender that so often appear in commercials advertising vaginal deodorant. She might have luxuriated in her purely feminine moment, but a convenient mosquito circled and landed on Rayfield's forehead in the approximate position of his third eye, and Ellen smacked it. It remained there after it was squashed, a tangle of legs and wings, like a Rorschach blot of fresh blood or a caste mark on a cross-dresser from the black hole of Calcutta.

"You sure know how to break the mood," Rayfield said, releasing her.

"We weren't having a mood, Rayfield," Ellen said. "By the way, you've got a bug stuck on your forehead." She went into the kitchen and tore a square of paper towel off the roll sitting on the counter and handed it to him. "Look, Rayfield, it's not like I mean to diss you. You're just feeling your oats today because you had a successful erection." She said this matter-of-factly, using the tone that a registered nurse might use to reassure a modest patient that there is absolutely no reason to feel self-conscious while handing over the bedpan.

"You're probably right," he agreed.

Now, irrationally, Ellen felt insulted. It was fine if she chalked up an amorous moment to Rayfield's long dormant oats, but she certainly didn't want him to. Even if it was only Rayfield, she still liked to think that a sexual moment had something to do with her and wasn't just free-floating, hormone-based electrical charges. "Anyway," she said, "do you think it's the acupuncture that helped?"

"It's got to be, unless . . ."

"Unless what?"

"It's stupid."

"Don't worry, Rayfield, I expect stupid from you." Ellen nearly covered her mouth with her hand. But Rayfield, who didn't seem to notice, simply carried on.

"In a way, it kind of gives me the creeps the way it happened right after I finally cut the ties with Wide Load."

"*You* cut the ties?"

"Well, she cut them first, but after she knocked me out of the ballpark, I finally got the message to let her go out of my heart. And I did."

"When did this happen?"

"Since I last saw you."

So much had happened in those last few days. So much.

"So what do you think?"

Ellen had drifted. "About what?"

"About my theory."

"What theory?"

"For chrissakes, Ellen, pay attention." Rayfield was clearly exasperated. "My theory that hanging on to Wide Load was what kept my dick rolled up."

"Hey, I'd be the last to doubt you."

"Gives me the creeps," Rayfield repeated.

"What's so creepy about it?" Ellen asked, suddenly interested.

"It's like she put a hex on me."

Ellen remembered how, when she had first seen Debbie at the lake, she thought she looked like an ancient goddess with a vindictive bent. "Well, if she did, you managed to shirk it off," she comforted him. "Besides, there's probably a scientific explanation. Like your stress level got reduced when you finally accepted that she was gone. Peyronie's disease is stress-related, remember."

Rayfield looked thoughtful. "I guess I'll never know," he said, and then, as if he had just remembered his manners, he added, "So what's new with you?"

Ellen stood very still.

"What's the matter?" Rayfield asked.

Ellen sat down. "My brother-in-law, Cocho, died. Olivier's father."

Rayfield stole a sideways glance at Olivier, who sat happily on the kitchen floor in the midst of his pots and pans. "Poor little fella," Rayfield said, and then he collapsed into a chair, put his head on the table, and commenced to weep. His shoulders shook so violently that Ellen feared they might break away from his body and fall to the floor. She was so shocked she almost put her arms around him, but given his recent return to virility she didn't want to set off some crazy chain reaction that might sweep them both away on an emotional tidal wave. So she just sat there and waited.

Rayfield raised his head. "It's the saddest goddamn thing I ever heard," he said as tears rolled down his face and disappeared into the jungle growth of his incoming beard. He wiped them away, leaving a little streak of mud behind. Sometimes seeing another person sob catalyzed her own tears, but seeing Rayfield blubber had stunned her tear ducts into a dry state rare in the past few days. Snot had started to run out of Rayfield's nose, and he used his bug-wiping paper towel to remove it.

Olivier, alarmed in a toddler way, came waddling over and put his hand on Rayfield's knee, and Rayfield picked him up, which seemed to restore his equilibrium. "Let's mow the lawn, my man," he said in a gravelly voice. "That grass is out of control." He got up and carried Olivier out the door. Ellen watched as he took a gas can from his truck, filled up the mower, and climbed on. He fired it up and soon he and Olivier were chugging back and forth across the front lawn in ever-narrowing rectangles. Ellen's mind was a complete blank. Observing the lawn mower moving in and out of her field of vision was quietly but completely fascinating.

It was such a strange event when a grown man wept. Ellen could count on one hand the number of times she'd seen Tommy break down and bawl, and he always apologized afterward, as if he had somehow let her down. She had told him that, far from alienating her, his tears only increased her love for him, but he didn't believe it. Rayfield was obviously an anomaly in the gene pool of gender, though perhaps, she thought charitably, his surprise meltdown was a once in a lifetime event. It had its own integrity, and it made her respect him neither more nor less.

She got up and washed the dishes. The yellow-orange tinge of the water seemed totally acceptable now, and she no longer worried that it left a film of amoebas and paramecia behind. Beyond the wavy kitchen windowpane, the green and blue of earth and sky looked smeared on with a palette knife. Her special tea boiling on the stove filled the room with a swampy smell that went right along with her general mood, and she found herself humming. When she realized it was one of Cocho's compositions, she felt a surge of happiness to hear his voice again, and she sang a little louder as if to spread his words past the limits of this house, down Eagle Beak Mountain, along the Salmon River.

But that night, she had a monumentally disturbing dream, which dredged up images of Rayfield sobbing at the table, Viola bolting through the pasture on her manly legs, and Tommy skiing over the Alps on his NordicTrack wearing a thong bathing suit. She tossed and turned and soon found herself sitting up in the center of her bed, glistening with sweat. The covers were thrown onto the floor, and the sound of the frogs was intense, as if they were being broadcast over a high-tech public address system. Ellen crawled out of bed, stole down the stairs, and put on a pot of open-the-heart tea, just for something to do.

The phone rang before it even started to bubble. Ellen, who happened to be standing beside it, yanked up the receiver before the first ring reached its crescendo. "Karen?" she said.

"Ellen? Were you sitting on the phone?"

"Something like that. How are you?"

"I don't know. I want to come home."

"Good."

"I can get a flight in a couple of hours that gets me to New York in the middle of the night, but I can't get one from there to Montreal for ten hours, unless I go to Newark, but the connection there is really tight and I might not make it. Or I can get one to Boston with a good connection to Montreal, but it doesn't leave here until late tomorrow. I just want to come home." She was crying like an overtired child. "I can't decide what to do."

"Get on the plane to New York. I'll come pick you up."

"It's so far."

"Nowhere is too far. Just give me the flight information and then get on that plane."

"Really?"

"Really."

"Okay." Karen was almost wailing as she repeated the flight number and the arrival time.

"Is Cocho buried?" Ellen asked, wishing there were a more polite way to say it.

"Yes. In his village."

"Oh, Karen . . . I'm so sorry. You must be devastated."

"I am."

"You get on that plane."

"Thank you."

"I'll see you in New York."

Ellen hung up. She was going to the city.

thirty-nine

Ellen packed up the Honda with the efficiency of a professional mover. At the last moment and for no logical reason in the world, she called Mutley into the car and then made one more dash into the house for his water and food bowls and a two-day supply of kibble. It was insane to take him, but suddenly, seeing him nodding off under the maple tree, she thought that the bright lights of the big city might jump-start his canine battery. She left a brief note for Rodney, though she had no idea whether or not he would show up at their usual time an hour later. Something had gone screwy in their relationship after she had found the letters, and it was probably her fault, but she couldn't fix it right now.

A drizzle required the interim use of her windshield wipers, and Ellen mused on the symbolic nature of the periodic clearing of her vision. Moments of clarity are short-lived and then we re-enter the fog, she thought, though she was certain that she was doing what needed to be done—driving three hundred and fifty miles to New York to meet her sister. Being there at the airport for Karen was her lighthouse beam in the mist, but she couldn't really see much in the shadows beyond its glow.

She had not expected to walk the streets of the city for another five weeks—until Labor Day—and her sudden return was slightly unsettling. Her key ring, with its four apartment keys, seemed cumbersome in her jeans pocket and she removed it and placed it on the dashboard. And she had not called Tommy, though she planned to as soon as she arrived on Tenth Street. He would be at work. She would rest a little in their apartment, and then phone him to inform, or warn, him that she, Olivier, and Mutley were there and waiting. Karen's plane came in at two A.M., and Ellen was prepared to do whatever

Karen wanted, including making a U-ey and heading directly to Montreal. Karen was a homebody, a person who felt best in her own little world, though Ellen worried that the loft in Montreal would harbor more hurt than comfort. Cocho's clothes still hung in the closet and for all Ellen knew, there were calls for him on the answering machine. Would all those reminders break Karen's heart or heal it? Ellen had no clue.

Downstate she drove, backtracking through the towns she remembered from her first trip through the North Country: Saranac Lake, Lake Placid, Keene. She stopped in a rest area in which a pipe emerged from a natural spring, offering weary travelers a taste of honest mountain water. Of course, the smell of the pine trees and damp earth was overpowered by the odor of hot dogs rolling on the portable grill of the Sabrett's truck that was parked there. Mutley peed in the bushes and took a long, slurpy drink from the puddle near the car, then climbed back into the seat and got comfy. Ellen bought Olivier an orange juice and a buttered bagel, and they took off, up the ramp onto the Northway. And five and a half hours later, at two thirty P.M., Ellen pulled next to the fire hydrant in front of her apartment building on Tenth Street. Quickly, she unloaded the car, stashing everything that was stealable, including Olivier's car seat, behind the locked street door. She didn't even speculate on how she would schlep it all up the stairs while simultaneously keeping an eye on Olivier and Mutley. She simply blocked that future challenge from her mind and carried her nephew back out, holding him in her lap behind the steering wheel—a motor vehicle crime—and circled the block in search of a parking place.

She finally found one on Avenue B between Ninth and Tenth, which placed the dog run in Tompkins Square Park directly in the path of her return to the apartment. What the hell, she thought, why not stop? If Mutley saw the city dogs frolicking and capering around their little patch of dirt, he might get a grip on his own glorious canine heritage. She left him sleeping in the backseat and ran into the Korean market for a collar and leash, neither of which were among Mutley's worldly goods. Then she dragged him out of the car by the neck and pulled him toward the park. Never, in all her life, had Ellen felt exactly as she did in that moment. A woman with a baby and a dog, heading into the neighborhood park for a little mid-afternoon relaxation. It seemed so normal.

Ellen opened the gate to the dog run, settled on a bench, and undid the leash. "Go play with the other dogs," she said to Mutley. He started to sink down onto his hindquarters, stage one in his descent to slumberland. Peeved, Ellen propped her foot, toes pointed skyward, under him. Mutley felt it, hesitated, and stood up. And then, totally out of the blue, his ears perked up and turned like radarscopes, his head snapped around, and, wonder of wonders, Mutley started to run.

Ellen jumped up, the better to see Mutley's muscles ripple under his sleek new fur. And when he leaped—up, up, up through the air, like an ancient god who had no use for gravity, his four paws off of Planet Earth at the same time, his spine twisting as if a spiral of kundalini energy were shooting through him, the sun bringing out the purples and blues in his coat, Ellen, and possibly Olivier, forgot to breathe. And then she saw a flash of fluorescent pink, a disk moving through the air like a flying saucer, and Mutley, with a powerful though silent roar, opened his mouth and snagged it with his teeth.

A Frisbee! Ellen realized. And her mind whirled back to Rayfield's second *Free Trader* ad. "Can catch Frisbee," it had said. How had it happened that she had never grilled Rayfield about this? That Mutley, a Frisbee lover, had languished for weeks under the maple tree when he could have been bounding, leaping, spiraling toward the stars, and then snatching the flying Frisbee from the air with the jaws of life?

"Hey, whose fucking dog stoled my Frisbee?" screamed a Nuyorican youth with a shaved head, no shirt, and a pair of pants that resembled a long skirt from the 1890s. Ellen didn't answer instantly and he followed up with, "I want my fucking Frisbee back *now*."

"It's my dog," she called, waving him over. Mutley was on his way back to her anyway, cantering as proudly as a Vienna stallion. The young man shuffled toward her. "Sit down a minute," Ellen said when he arrived at her bench. She patted the wood beside her.

"Come on, lady. Alls I want is my fucking Frisbee. I ain't in the mood to conversate."

"I'll give you ten bucks for it," Ellen said.

"Why?" He looked suspiciously at Mutley, who had just deposited it in Ellen's lap. She jumped up and flung it.

"Hey!" protested the kid as Mutley scampered away.

"Look, my dog's depressed. This is the first time in two months that he's shown any interest in life."

"That is so honky," the shirtless boy sneered. "What's he depressed about anyway? The stock market? Shit, I didn't know dogs got depressed."

"Sure they do."

"My dog don't."

"Which one is yours?"

The boy hollered, "Fidel!" and a Doberman pinscher that had somehow been genetically altered to fit into a Chihuahua's body tore across the dog run to the bench and leapt up as if he were spring-loaded. He bounced around like a jumping bean, delighting Olivier and covering him with sloppy dog kisses.

"He does seem jubilant," Ellen said. "Full of joy," she added when a look of suspicion seemed to shadow across the kid's face. "So what do you say? Ten easy bucks?" She reached for her wallet.

"Twenty."

"Twenty? You're mugging me in broad daylight. Fifteen."

"Twenty. Take it or leave it."

"Shit." On principle, she wanted to refuse, but Mutley, his eyes sparkling, had returned again and was watching her with a look of thrilled anticipation. "Okay, but you ought to know that you're intentionally screwing a nice person who doesn't deserve it."

"I can handle it," he said, extending his hand. He pocketed the money, placed Fidel in the crook of his elbow, and strolled out of the dog run. Probably going to score some crack, Ellen thought, but then she was ashamed of herself. He was just a city kid who saw an opportunity and took it. More power to him. This was New York, after all.

She threw the Frisbee and off went Mutley. It was a freaking miracle. When she returned to Eagle Beak, where her personal yard stretched for fourteen acres, she would give that dog a major daily workout, get his juices flowing again, and cure his narcolepsy once and for all.

Mutley showed no loss of interest after one half hour, but Olivier had started to squirm. She didn't want to let him down into the germs and bacteria of Shitville, as it was affectionately called by the inhabitants of the neighborhood. Even though the dog owners cleaned up almost immediately, viruses swept through the canine population like the Black Plague. She would not expose her beloved nephew to it on the last day of her guardianship. The last day! She clutched little Olivier to her bosom and fought off an attack of possessiveness. Her dear nephew, hers no more.

"Come on, Mutley," she said, standing up and stowing the expensive Frisbee in her bag. Mutley eyed it with regret. Quickly, she attached his new leash around his neck and proceeded to pull him out of the dog run. As she secured the gate, she glanced up at the long list of rules: No person without a dog, No dog without a person, No toys of any sort. No this, no that, no, no, no. Suddenly, Ellen felt cramped and inhibited. Of course, individuals needed to be managed in a city of ten million, but it felt like a personal assault. Plus, it stunk, obviously because the trash can into which all the dog lovers deposited their dog-do stood just to the left of the gate.

Ellen hurried away, down the paved paths of Tompkins Square Park. It was peaceful if she discounted the agitated auras of the men who lay on the benches, their worldly possessions tied onto shopping carts or piled beneath their heads. One man, whose clothes were encrusted with grime, had removed one of his shoes and was using it for a pillow. This park had a long, glorious history as a haven for the dispossessed. Tent City, the ill-fated land claim of the homeless, had sprung up here, like a frontier town in the Old West, and then been destroyed by New York City police in riot gear. Every Labor Day, transvestites that looked like *Vogue* models flooded into the park for Wigstock. Bowery bums staked out personal turf and spent nonshelter hours dozing, begging, and often ranting and raving to nonvisible antagonists whom Ellen and Tommy termed "the air people."

It was strange to see the city as a person from outside of it. Ellen knew, from long experience, that it captured you with its magic, seduced you into believing that it was the center of the universe and you were a vital cell in it, challenged and rewarded you and left you breathless. But today it looked dirty, as if exhaust fumes had stagnated in the air. The gutters had iridescent puddles, and old newspapers and brown bags had blown up against the wrought-iron fences and stuck there, like Tibetan prayer flags run amok.

Please don't let me fall out of love with the city, Ellen fervently prayed as she crossed Tenth Street. New York was a jealous lover. If you questioned your commitment, it had a way of spitting you out, like a watermelon seed. Ellen didn't want any such thing to happen to her, and she shushed a small voice that whispered, "Montreal," in her ear.

Her building was cool and dark, and the terrazzo tiles on the walls, with their intricate Italian pattern, seemed to beckon her in. She unlocked the second door and slowly, slowly, they began their trek to the fifth floor. Olivier climbed each step as if it were a separate event in his life, and Mutley managed to get all four legs coordinated enough to make progress. Ellen was grateful for this because if Mutley balked at stair climbing, she had no idea what she would do. On the fourth-floor landing, Olivier turned to her and, raising his little arms, said, "Up, up." Ellen lifted him.

Finally, they arrived at the door of apartment 5A. Ellen inserted her key and undid the police lock. Then she unlocked the dead bolt and finally the original lock, the one that had been quite enough back when the house was built so many decades ago. She gave the door its customary summer shove, necessary when the humidity had swollen the wood, and reentered the life she had run away from after she'd been fired, after she'd bought herself a country estate, after she had surrendered to the voice in her head that kept repeating, "Just get out."

Ellen was glad that Tommy was safely at work because she always reacted badly to his bachelor habits, such as leaving his clothes on the backs of all the chairs, allowing dishes to molder in the sink, and refusing, or at least not bothering, to make up the futon bed. Whenever she returned from business trips with Reginald, she and Tommy got into an argument before they even said hello. Ellen would resentfully do the dishes, collect the laundry, and scour out the tub, and eventually her wrath would pass. Today, though, she didn't feel up to resurrecting her latent inner housekeeper. Let Tommy live in a pigpen if he wanted. As of today, the pattern was smashed forever.

The NordicTrack, with its complicated assortment of ropes and wood, stood dead center in the living room, consuming, basically, the whole room. Tommy had pushed back the furniture against the walls so the comfortable chairs and the antique tables formed an admiring circle around the alien from the world of physical fitness. It certainly was not their living room anymore, though the newspapers piled by the side of the sofa looked familiar, as did the coffee cups that littered every possible horizontal surface. Ellen dropped her heavy bag and put Olivier down, unsnapped Mutley's collar, and closed the door behind them.

Surrendering to a perverse need to face the worst, she went to the bedroom and peeked in. A yoga mat was spread out on the floor and a book of complicated yoga poses was held open with a brick. Curious, Ellen took a few steps and peered down at the page. On it, a turbaned swami in double-knit bathing trunks sat, his legs, arms, and spine in a tangle, with his eyes crossed and his tongue extended full length. Ellen laughed outright, just imagining Tommy diligently practicing this particular pose. If this is what turned on the yoga teacher, she must be very kooky.

She went into the kitchen, found it as expected, and opened the fridge to see what was available for the hungry traveler. To her surprise, it burgeoned with fresh fruit and vegetables. In the freezer, the Ben & Jerry's Chubby Hubby had been replaced with tofutti, and four different flavors of vegeburgers were stacked in a neat pile. Obviously, Tommy had transformed into a health nut without her, though she certainly approved. In the bathroom, he had posted a chart with all the pounds from 205 to 170. Big, black x's were drawn through all the numbers higher than 188. Ellen looked down at the new digital scale that had replaced her ancient seafoam green model, which had a dead cockroach stuck on pound number 151. She wanted to step on, but she felt somehow vulnerable in this apartment, squeezed out. She knew she would promptly lose her mind if she had gained a few pounds, too, so she backed away, her reconnaissance tour of the apartment complete.

"Want a drink, Mutley?" she asked as she dug his bowl out of her bag and filled it. "You must be thirsty after all that exercise." Mutley lapped away like a normal dog. Then he wandered into the bedroom, stepped unapologetically onto the futon, and lay down for a nap. Olivier, whose eyes had begun to droop as he climbed the Mount Everest of staircases, flopped down beside him and soon joined him in dreamland. Ellen glanced at the clock. Three thirty-five. A good time to call Tommy, though she felt an undeniable wave of self-consciousness as she waited for his secretary to answer.

"Thomas Kenny's office," Edna said, oozing efficiency.

"Hi, Edna, it's Ellen."

"Ellen! Long time no talk to."

"Yeah, I've been up in the boonies."

"So I heard. How *is* life in the provinces?"

"Different," Ellen said. She was tempted to list the ways, but she knew that prolonged conversation would be inconvenient for Edna, no matter how friendly the tone, no matter how many gold earrings and leather bags she had selected for Tommy's annual Secretary's Day gifts. "Is Tom in?"

Edna hesitated. "He's in D.C. doing a deposition. An overnight. Didn't you know?"

"Oh! I forgot," Ellen said, covering. "Guess I should make a point of look-ing at the calendar once in a while."

"He's booked back on the six o'clock shuttle tomorrow. Any messages?"

"No, I'll just call him there," Ellen said, although she had not the slightest idea where Tommy would be staying in the capital. She hung up. So, she thought, she wouldn't be seeing Tommy after all—unless, of course, Karen wanted to stay in New York for a few days to catch her breath. It seemed smart to join her boy and her dog in a siesta, and she crept into the bedroom and stretched out on the free side of the futon. She noticed that Tommy had propped up an index card against the lamp on which he had mysteriously writ-ten "noni juice."

Hmmm, thought Ellen. This was a new one for her, though she usually led their brigade of two into the realm of exotic fruit drinks. Maybe noni is a veg-etable, she reasoned as her mind began to dull. Her body was tired and the long drive, the Frisbee throwing, and the five-story walk-up had done her in. Outside, she could hear the racket of a pick-up basketball game in the park under her living-room windows and the sirens and the ice-cream truck on the corner. The sounds of the city pressed in on you, as if they altered the atmos-pheric pressure. Suddenly Ellen became aware of her own heartbeat. She placed her left hand on her chest and experienced the subtle vibration that rattled through her bones. "I love you, heart," she whispered, not even think-ing that she was co-opting Cocho's morning rite. Much later, though, after she had walked Mutley again and taken Olivier to a vegetarian restaurant for din-ner, the moment returned to her and she recognized its source. Cocho had loved his lungs and had used them to produce music that transported listeners into the wild blue yonder. She loved her heart and could use it to produce . . . what? Love, she thought. Love, love, love.

Whenever Tommy had sodium Pentothol, basically for the purposes of tooth extraction, he was chemically delivered to some free love zone in which he gushed with goodwill. "Honey," he had once said, "I want to send flowers to every dentist in this building." Another time, tears had filled his eyes and he had whispered, "The Beatles were right, you know. All you need is love." And, in the grand finale of altered consciousness, he had once found incomparable beauty in the Muzak rendition of "Love Is Blue," which was being piped into the recovery room after two of his wisdom teeth were pulled. Ellen had burst out laughing when he said he hoped it would sweep the Grammy Awards, which hurt Tommy's feelings a lot. He simply didn't fit the flower child profile. But did she? She had in the sixties, but what about the nineties? Only time would tell.

At midnight, Ellen pulled into the short-term parking at JFK International Airport. She had misgivings about leaving Mutley alone in the car, but she knew he would soon stretch out on the backseat to catch some z's. Besides, who would break into a car that was guarded by a ferocious German shepherd? She left each window cracked one inch, so Mutley would get his fair share of exhaust fumes, and carried Olivier into the airport.

"Mama's coming!" she whispered over and over again. Had she been asked, she would've said that her main wish in life was that Olivier would fall into Karen's arms with glee, but she was secretly afraid that he would pull back from her, perhaps not recognizing her after so many weeks or feeling too wounded by her abandonment to trust her now.

Even at this hour, the airport throbbed with activity. People read newspapers in all the languages of the earth; they munched on junk food or slept with their chins on their chests in molded plastic chairs. Ellen longed for the days, before the Lockerbie terrorism, when you could meet your loved one at the landing gate. It was so much more civilized and trust, rather than fear, centered. But what was the use of crying over spilled milk? She settled into a seat next to a clean-cut man who madly pounded the keys on a laptop computer. Ellen peeked over at the screen but the angle made it impossible to read.

"Commodities market," the man said with a glance at her.

"Oh," she replied, shifting slightly away from him to compensate for her initial invasion of his space.

"*Où est Mama?*" she said to Olivier. "*En un moment . . . ici!*" She bounced him on her knees, and Olivier rested his head against her. He was a little sweaty, but he looked adorable in his overalls and muscle T-shirt. Ellen circled him in her arms and cherished her last few minutes as his primary caretaker. She hated sad endings, and, for her, this certainly qualified.

Thirty minutes later, Ellen, with Olivier in her lap, was dozing to the click of the computer keys and the occasional garbled PA announcement. She felt a slight tap on her shoulder, opened her eyes, and there was Karen. She looked waxen beneath the fluorescent lights, as if the weeks in Peru had deposited a smooth alabaster coating on her skin that made her both impossibly beautiful and almost unreal. Her strawberry blond hair was pulled into a ponytail, and, aside from a river of weariness in her eyes, she had a certain serenity that Ellen did not expect.

Karen smiled and said nothing.

Ellen rose to her feet, jostling Olivier, who half-opened his eyes, lazily took one look at his mother, and, in an adrenaline rush, dove into her arms, and hollered, "Mama! Mama!" Ellen surrendered him with a wide-open heart. Even the commodities nerd stopped what he was doing and watched for a few seconds with a big grin on his face. Karen kissed Olivier's neck and threw him high into the air. She hugged him and roughed up his curls.

Thank God, Ellen thought, though now it seemed ridiculous that she had ever doubted that Olivier would remember his own mother. A few seconds later, Karen opened her arm for a hug from Ellen, and Ellen stepped forward into it. "Welcome home," she said for lack of better words, for Karen was not home. Not really. This was not her city, not her country. Not her.

"I missed you both so much," Karen said.

"We missed you."

"I don't want to cry," Karen announced.

"No," Ellen agreed. "Later." Karen nodded and looked as if she were struggling to get an internal grip on something slippery. "Do you have bags?"

"Just this." Ellen had not even noticed the knapsack on the floor.

"Then let's bug out of this creep joint." It was a sentence from the sixties, employed by Ellen's friend Rebecca when she'd gotten fed up during a dinner party at her boyfriend's disapproving parents' Boston townhouse. Karen giggled. She had bugged out of many creep joints with Ellen over the years. In a pit stop in the ladies' room, while Karen was in the stall, a late-night traveler asked Ellen how old her grandson was.

"G-g-g-grandson," she stammered, reaching back to grip the sink for balance. "Nineteen months," she answered once she got her wits about her.

"Adorable," the woman said as she left.

Of course, Ellen knew she was mature enough to be a grandmother, but no one had ever used that word on her. Next thing you know, she thought in a panic, the cashier at the Super Duper would be asking to see her Senior Citizen card. It was horrifying. Her life was winding down, and strangers who flew the red-eye were unceremoniously placing her in the "past the prime" category.

Oh well, she thought, as millions upon millions of women had thought before, oh well. She had arrived at the crossroads, and ultimately she would have to choose her position: hormone replacement therapy, plastic surgery, sun hats with neck scarves attached, an exercise regime, and a rigid diet to maintain some pseudo-semblance of youth, or don't bug me, I'm busy going to pot. Which one was more personally correct for her? Self-preservation was a myth, but giving up also carried a stigma.

"Somebody called me a grandmother," Ellen commented when Karen emerged from the stall.

"An honorable title," Karen said, absentmindedly, as she washed and dried her hands.

"Actually, I was insulted."

Karen laughed. "Oh, Ellen, you'll never lower your colors, will you?"

"I'm letting my freak flag fly," Ellen responded, though she hardly looked like a hippie freak. But I am living like one, she reminded herself as they schlepped toward the parking garage. Had she been who she was now, doing the same thing, homesteading on an organic farm, way back in the sixties, she would've been regarded as very, very groovy. A beautiful person.

"Karen, meet Mutley," Ellen said as she opened the rear door of the Honda. Mutley opened his eyes but didn't bother to raise his head from the seat.

"Olivier's best canine friend," Karen said as she strapped her son into his safety contraption and then paused to scratch Mutley's ears.

Ellen put the keys in the ignition. "New York, Eagle Beak, or Montreal?" she asked. "Wherever your heart desires."

"Really?"

"Really."

"Okay. Let me think and feel." Karen closed her eyes lightly. Given the same situation, Ellen would have jammed her lids shut until her forehead and cheekbones nearly met over the bridge of her nose. Karen was delicate in every way, while Ellen was Brunhilda, a Brahman bull, a sumo wrestler. "Tommy's away overnight," Ellen said, just to provide complete information.

"Oh, too bad," Karen said, obviously disappointed. She returned to her trance and Ellen waited. "New York," she finally said. "Eagle Beak tomorrow, and Montreal sometime within a few days."

Ellen turned the key, parted with eight dollars at the gate, for which the attendant didn't even say thanks, and sped toward Tenth Street. She dropped Karen and Olivier at the building and circled the block with Mutley in search of a parking space. The neighborhood was both familiar and unfamiliar at this hour. Visuals she took for granted, from the phone wire with a hundred pairs of sneakers hanging from it to the shrines to the Virgin Mary that overlooked the street from various window guards, now seemed somehow odd and even threatening, and Ellen was glad she had Mutley with her, even if he was all bark and no bite. And maybe not even bark.

She squeezed into a space on Twelfth Street, happy to have found a spot even though the car had to be moved in five short hours. Then she walked down Avenue A, purposefully, like the antivictim literature suggests, toward home. Mutley sniffed at every streetlight and ate a soggy french fry off the street before Ellen could yank him away. He peed twice and then climbed the stairs, as was expected of him.

The door to the apartment was ajar, and Karen was sitting in Ellen's an-tique bentwood rocker with Olivier in her lap. The beauty of the image stunned Ellen, and she watched as Karen wound Olivier's curls around her fin-gers, shaping them into slender ringlets. He had fallen asleep with his cheek pressed against her. It was a private moment, and Ellen wished she could avoid altering and therefore destroying it. Then Karen looked up. "He seems so much bigger."

"He grows overnight."

"He's speaking English."

"Yeah."

Karen rocked in silence, seeming distracted.

"Tommy's taken up the Nordic ski track," Ellen said.

"So I notice. What're you going to do with it when you come back?"

"Who knows? Maybe move it into the bedroom, next to the yoga mat."

"Yoga too? What got into Tommy?"

It was the perfect opportunity to tell her about the yoga instructor, but in-stead Ellen waved her hand. "Who knows? Let's just pray he doesn't take up tumbling." She sat down. "You tired?"

"Exhausted."

"I have to go down early and move the car. You and Olivier take the bed-room."

Karen stood up. "We'll have lots of time to talk tomorrow," she said as if reading Ellen's mind.

"Get some rest."

Karen disappeared into the bedroom and shut the door. Ellen felt intensely aware of sacrificing her own need to tell Karen everything, to hear everything. They had not even said Cocho's name. She had not mentioned that she and Tommy, aside from the little burst of intimacy inspired by Cocho's passing, were barely speaking, drifting in separate directions, caught in a marriage riptide.

She went to the window and looked down at the street. Cars and taxis gunned it along Avenue A, and the windows of the all-night deli were full of trendy customers. Ellen sat down on the wide windowsill, leaning back against the casing and raising her legs to fold them into what was probably no longer called Indian-style, now that political correctness had arrived. Over the years, she had logged up countless hours in this position. She had felt lonely, bored, content, restless, peaceful, and ravaged here. It was both soothing and meditative. Between the windowsill and the deep bathtub, under a skylight, no less, she had always had a haven to retreat to when the pressure or pleasures of the city were upon her.

But obviously, she thought, it hadn't been enough. Trouble had built up, and now she was living three hundred and fifty miles away and feeling like a New York imposter on her own block. And if this *was* her home, why was it full of gym equipment? And where was Tommy? For that matter, who was Tommy? He had turned into a stranger who scribbled "noni juice" on an index card and sat on a purple mat with his eyes crossed and his tongue hanging out like a dog.

It was only denial that made her assume everything would work out soon, that the summer would come to its inexorable end and she would return to her husband's open arms. When she'd left, she knew only one thing for certain: she desperately needed a break. She might have been running to something, away from something, or around in circles. She had felt weary and probably clinically depressed, if tears, sighs, and glimpses of mental desolation row were its indicators. Yet she couldn't say if something had been building up or emptying out ever since. Buying the house in Eagle Beak was a mighty big move, but she had done it without a trace of indecision. Moving there for the summer had seemed totally benign, but now it felt as if she had torn a hole in the fabric of her life and squirmed through it into a new, but not necessarily better, world. Was there any going back?

forty

The infamous New York humidity lay over the city like a bad spell, and even at seven forty-five, when Ellen went down to the street to move the car, people were navigating slowly, like sleepwalkers. Conversation was limited, and bags of garbage set at the edge of the curb for pickup had begun to emit sickening odors. Ellen stopped in the deli for a coffee to go and then unlocked the door of her car. She started it up and didn't notice, until she turned to look over her shoulder as she backed up, that the rear window on the passenger side had been smashed to smithereens. Shards of glass glittered from the dark upholstery like beads of sweat.

"Shit," Ellen swore. "Great timing." Her car had never been broken into before, probably because she and Tommy purposely made it unappealing. The radio-tape player was hidden in the glove compartment, leaving a gaping hole in the dashboard; an assortment of empty bottles, cans, and coffee containers littered the floor, giving off the "poorly cared for" message; and dirt and crud covered the outside until some local prankster invariably wrote "Wash Me" in the grime on the rear window. Now, a whole new range of possibilities presented themselves. If she simply drove across the street and parked as she would have done, drug dealers might open the back doors and conduct business there, smoking crack or whatever new designer drug had worked its way to Alphabet City. Or one of the many homeless, maybe a psycho, might climb in for a snooze. He might pass out, urinate, or throw up in her backseat. She glanced at the patch of sky visible through the buildings. It might rain. And at any rate, she couldn't make a seven-hour drive with a missing window.

Ellen shifted into drive and at the corner of Avenue B, she turned south toward Chinatown. Many times she had noticed a car window replacement business on Canal Street just before the entrance to the Holland Tunnel. It was run by tiny Chinese women who operated hydraulic lifts and clambered over car hoods wearing burgundy jumpsuits that would've warmed the heart of Chairman Mao. Ellen, while gridlocked, had often watched these workers with fascination. Their shop buzzed with cheerful efficiency, like a human anthill. With their ear protectors, they looked a little like city mice, too, and Ellen, bleary-eyed with tunnel impatience, had once thought she saw the line between humans and the so-called lesser kingdom of animals blur right before her eyes.

Today, a young woman, perhaps a teenager, with platinum blond streaks in her jet-black hair and platform boots waved her into one of five work stations. Ellen had already decided that, no matter what, she wouldn't haggle over the price. Just pay it and be gone was her M.O. With any luck, she would be back on Tenth Street before Karen and Olivier even got rolling.

"I need a new window," she said, pointing. "Passenger, rear."

"Okay. You leave car. Forty-five minute, tops. Ninety-nine, ninety-nine. We clean up car good. Free for you."

"Okay," Ellen said as she got out.

To kill time, she moseyed along Canal Street, naturally slipping into the New York City sidewalk weave in the pedestrian traffic. This was the New York she loved. Every building held its mystery and every corner had its secrets. Even now, she glanced up and noticed a small sign in a second-story window: DEPARTMENT STORE. ENTER THROUGH LUGGAGE SHOP. Impulsively, she headed into the storefront shop, climbed a dingy, wooden staircase, opened a nondescript door, and crossed the threshold into a room that seemed to stretch in more directions than was architecturally possible, given the shape of the building. Ellen wandered through a wonderland of material goods—everything from pottery to bottles of Siberian ginseng, cleavers to silk screens, exotic wrapping paper to carved or gilded Buddhas. But when she came upon a display of satin bathrobes, she stopped in her tracks. The rack shimmered with all the colors of the rainbow and every variation thereof. On the lapels were embroidered Chinese ideograms, translated for the benefit of the illiterate on a piece of cardboard and attached by a string to the label. These beautiful symbols embodied the concepts of harmony, peace, joy, prosperity, and many other foundations of sanity. On the back of each robe were stunning embroideries—dragons, houseboats, terraced gardens, warriors. She noticed a black robe with a shimmering pouncing tiger that was just Olivier's size and she pulled it from its hanger. Then she saw one in ice blue with a pastoral scene featuring herons standing on one leg that would fit Karen and she took that one, too.

By the time she approached the register, she had robes for Olivier, Karen,

Tommy, Rayfield, Rodney, and herself. They weren't cheap, either, but for some reason, Ellen didn't care. Out came her credit card, *whirr* went the machine seeking its approval, snap went the catch on her purse as she closed it up with the Visa safely back inside. She hoisted the car seat with one hand and the bag of robes in the other and started back down the creaky staircase. On the corner, she hailed a cab for the short hop back to the car repair shop. Comfortable in its backseat, she devised a plan to hang Tommy's robe on the bathroom door with a note that said, "May all your meditations be fruitful" in her best handwriting.

Ellen hardly recognized the Honda. Not only was the window repaired, but all the others sparkled and the whole car gleamed. Even the tires appeared to have been treated with Armor All. The garbage inside had been tactfully removed, and the repairwoman with the platform boots smiled. "Wow," Ellen said as she handed over the cash, "my car never looked so good in its life," but the woman was already headed out into the street to signal to Ellen when a break in the near continuous stream of cars and trucks made it possible for her to back out. The moment came, Ellen gunned it backwards, shifted, and entered the flow of traffic. Driving in New York was second nature to her, and she swerved between lanes and ran newly red lights with glee.

Once, shortly after she moved to New York, she was in a Lincoln Continental with her friends Rusty at the wheel and Valerie and Margie as fellow passengers. In the middle of rush hour, on Third Avenue in the Fifties, heading downtown, the car had stalled, causing a cacophony of blaring horns and screeching brakes. "Vapor lock," Rusty calmly announced as he propped the hood open and disappeared around the corner.

"Where's he going?" they had asked one another, feeling stranded and abandoned on a tiny island in the middle of a raging sea. They were stoned, of course, which added to their sense of vulnerability. Ten minutes later, Rusty reappeared carrying a jumbo-size pizza in a warming bag. Soon, the aroma of black olives and onions filled the car, and they all ate with marijuana-inspired gusto, happy to be well fed and together. When the last slice was consumed, the Lincoln had had sufficient recovery time and they tooled on, dropping off the quilted pizza bag for which Rusty had left a five-dollar deposit. Ellen laughed, remembering.

It was another life, really.

How many lives did one person have, she wondered as she sped around the corner onto the Bowery. Aside from the fact that she had memories, there was really nothing left of that former Ellen. The idea of scarfing down a pizza pie while disrupting the rush-hour traffic evoked fear of road rage. And she hadn't seen or heard from Rusty in more than a decade, though she did cherish the memory.

When she did a mental scan, she noticed that many of her treasured memories were her private Dionysian moments. The common thread that pulled them together, like precious beads on a cosmic string, was a willingness to kick back and party, no matter what was happening. Nero got a bad rap in history for playing his violin while Rome burned, and he no doubt deserved one, but when powerless people like her laughed in the face of trouble or conflict or gloom and doom, or even the status quo, it was a beautiful thing.

Back on Tenth Street, Ellen circled the block like a vulture and finally squeezed into a not-really-legal space that partially blocked a driveway that she knew for a fact was defunct. The building it led to had been boarded up for five years and only the meter maid from hell would even think of giving her a ticket. She locked up and carried her new purchases home.

She heard Karen's convulsive sobs behind the closed bedroom door as she stepped into the apartment. Her sister, who was as dainty in grief as in everything else, did not go in for theatrical groans and moans and the screeching of "Why? Why?" like the professional Greek and Italian mourners of long ago. Her sadness rumbled instead, like thunder that was very far away or earth tremors that registered low on the Richter scale.

Ellen dropped her parcels and went to the door, unsure whether she should knock or merely collapse to the floor and quietly beam her sister healing energy. Finally, she tapped lightly on the door and opened it without waiting for a response. Karen sat on the futon leaning against the wall, a pillow clutched in front of her into which she cried. Olivier and Mutley, huddled together at the foot of the futon, were watching her as if she were a movie made for kids and dogs in their age range.

Ellen rushed in and threw her arms around her sister. "I was out," she said, wanting to assure Karen that she would never have left her to cry alone. "I just came in." Karen's rib cage fluttered and her shoulders shook as if centrifugal force were trying to rip them from her body in different directions.

"Mornings are the worst," Karen sobbed.

Mornings, Ellen thought, when Cocho would wake up, profess his love to his lungs, and begin to play his flute as a morning prayer.

"I wake up and for the first second I think it was all a bad dream, and then the truth hits me. It's real, it's real." She buried her face in the pillow, muffling her sounds. "I don't want Olivier to have to go through this, but . . ." This time she threw her arms around Ellen's neck and pressed her face into her shirt.

"You can't help it. It's okay, it's okay."

"How can I live?" Karen asked. It sounded like a genuine, not a rhetorical, question, and Ellen was tempted to say "One day at a time." But even in the mental flash in which she imagined herself saying it, Ellen knew it was too trite. Karen wanted real words, real wisdom, not a cliché from a bumper sticker in the parking lot of the AA meeting. "How can I live?" Karen asked again.

"You can't live the same life," Ellen said into Karen's ear. "That one is over, but—" How could she finish her sentence? She had no comfort to impart. "But you'll make a new life after a while. It'll be hard and awful at first, but after a while, it'll be okay. It will." Ellen glanced up and noticed Tommy's yoga mat and his open yoga instruction manual. He was on to a new life himself. And so was she. And so was Karen, except her old life had been violently yanked away while Ellen and Tommy had simply opened their fingers and let theirs go. Ellen, ashamed of thinking of herself at such a moment, turned her full attention back to Karen, who had untangled herself and was sitting up and wiping her eyes on her T-shirt. "The storm is passing, I think," Karen said. She said something in French to Olivier. Ellen recognized the word *douche* and assumed they were headed for a shower, as, in fact, they were. She quickly made up Tommy's bed and then sat at the kitchen table to write him a note. Images of Rodney, Sr., skated through her mind as she lifted the pen.

Dear Tommy,
   Sorry to have missed you on this whirlwind trip.

Ellen stopped. It sounded like a note she would leave for any Tom, Dick, or Harry, someone in the category of casual acquaintance or next door neighbor. She tore it off the telephone pad and crumpled it up.

Yo Tom!
   Good to see the old block but bad not to see your face.

She stopped again. This one was certainly more cheery but it felt put on, like a performance instead of a heartfelt communication to her husband of seventeen years. She wadded it up, pitched it into the trash can, and put the pen down. Maybe, she thought, she should try Karen's "let me think and feel" system, which seemed to have netted a definitive course of action quite efficiently in the airport parking lot. Ellen closed her eyes. Impulsively, she wrote "Kilroy was here" and stuck it onto the fridge with a magnet in the shape of chili peppers.

It wasn't until after breakfast had been eaten, the car had been loaded, and they were crossing the George Washington Bridge, with the city prevailing in a cloud of humidity behind them, that Ellen's thoughts returned to her odd-ball note to Tommy. "Kilroy was here" was a pop culture moment that took place in her parents' time, not hers. The truth was, she had never even known the whole story—only that someone named Kilroy had painted those words in various places sometime in the past. Was he a prototype performance artist? A graffitist? A murderer flaunting his evil presence to the police? Would Tommy get it? Or would he think that she had gone demented in the North Country? Ellen had read that isolated people in the extreme northern latitudes often developed an irresistible desire to howl like wolves. Was "Kilroy was here" her first official bay?

She shook her head and reminded herself that she was neither isolated nor in the northernmost latitudes. In fact, she was about to exit the bridge onto the Palisades Parkway, with traffic coming and going in all directions, not to mention below her on the lower deck and above her on the overpasses and cloverleafs that curved down to the Jersey side of the bridge.

Karen was turned in her seat to catch a last glimpse of the New York skyline. "I wish I could've gotten to see Tommy," she said.

"I was just thinking the same thing." Suddenly Ellen realized that, in her general confusion, she had forgotten to leave her husband his new Chinese robe. It was still tucked in among the others in the bag she had grabbed just as they were leaving the apartment.

"Are things okay between you two?"

"Why do you ask?"

"Well, really, the last clear moment I remember was when you came up to see us in May, and you bought the house on the way. Tommy wasn't talking to you then."

"We talked after that."

"I should hope so. That was two months ago."

Nobody said a word for a few slow seconds.

"I think we're both reevaluating."

"Oh."

Ellen peeked at her sister, who was regarding her intently from behind her sunglasses.

"There's nothing technically wrong."

"But?"

"But we're sort of alienated. We didn't have a major fight or anything. It's just . . ."

"Is he mad at you for leaving?"

"Jeez, I didn't leave. I just went away for a while. But then I got shipwrecked and I don't know how to get back." She paused, thoughtfully. "This is normal in long-term relationships. Shit happens."

"I know," Karen said.

For a few moments, Ellen had forgotten about Cocho and now she felt repentant. If anyone was acutely aware that shit happens, it was surely Karen.

"I don't think it's time to freak-out yet. But when it is, you'll be among the first to know. Now, on a totally different subject . . ."

They had just passed the Kingston exit, ninety miles from the city, before Ellen had completely recounted the whole saga of the father and son Rodneys and the ups and downs of Rayfield's hard-on. She had told it breathlessly, as if she had been waiting for an audience for a long time, and Karen asked for the details and clarifications that proved she was truly listening.

"It sounds like you're deep into the intrigue of Eagle Beak," she said. "You arrive and everything's on simmer, as it has been for years, and before they know what hit them, the heat's up and all the secrets are boiling to the surface."

"Is that how it sounds? Because if it does, I'm telling it wrong. I'm not a key player there. I'm a spear carrier. All I'm doing is noticing."

"You don't get it, Ellen, which is part of your charm, but you're like a walking chemical catalyst. You come along and—"

"Shit happens?" Ellen interjected, going with the flow on the surface but feeling resistant inside.

"Shit happens," Karen repeated.

At the New Baltimore rest stop, they pulled off to allow Mutley the opportunity to pee. Ellen threw the Frisbee a few times in the grassy field at the extreme edge of the parking lot while Karen and Olivier went inside the busy junk food and souvenirs complex to use the bathroom. Her whole life, people had called her a shit disturber, normally when they were mad.

"If it ain't broke, don't fix it!" Tommy frequently roared when she began, in his opinion, nit-picking their relationship.

"It's called maintenance!" Ellen always shot back. "You don't have to wait 'til there's a crisis to pay a little attention!"

"Shit disturber!" Tommy accused.

And Reginald Eubanks had called her a shit disturber when she had questioned the small size of the coproducer's name in the credits of his last film. "Just leave it alone. It's not your business."

"You're the almighty boss," she had snipped as she left his office in a huff.

Karen had called her a human catalyst. But for what? Nothing ever changed, really. The surface might reconfigure for a while, but in the end the dust usually settled over the same old forms. Leopards didn't change their spots, old dogs didn't learn new tricks, and all the changes she or anyone else brought about added up, in the long run, to much ado about nothing.

Ellen sighed as Mutley bounded back to her with the Frisbee in his teeth and dropped it at her feet. "One more time, Mutley," she said as she sent the Frisbee sailing toward the pine trees. What would become of Mutley after all the change reverted to normal? He would probably end up in Rayfield's yard with nothing to show for his interlude with Ellen except a pink Frisbee and a grown-in fur coat.

Sometimes Ellen wished she had been born in Asia instead of America. In Asia, the average person didn't fall for the myth of the happy ending. They didn't believe that progress was the most important product and measure everything by a standard of happiness that was absolute rather than relative. Even their writing system cooperated. Instead of the phonetic system of the West, which exercised the logical left half of the brain, they got ideograms, which exercised the art-and-music-oriented right side. Westerners got arbitrary sounds strung together like links in a chain to make meaning, and Easterners got whole concepts at once in the form of a picture.

She turned and saw Karen and Olivier coming across the parking lot, like a mirage in the searing summer heat. Olivier was setting the pace, and Karen trotted along beside him, wearing a pair of seersucker overalls, a sleeveless T-shirt, and a baseball cap. She looked like an unwed, inner-city teenage mother from the Midwest, so much less murky than Ellen, so much cleaner, so fresh.

She had always seemed that way. Even as a child, Karen had been happy-go-lucky, carefree, and extremely confident. Ellen, thirteen years older, had loved her with the passion of an adolescent girl first experiencing the thrill of maternal hormones. Strangers who saw the way Karen fit onto Ellen's hip often asked if they were mother and daughter, and Ellen was just as involved as her mother was in events such as Karen's first rollover, first tooth, first word, and first step.

When Ellen had gone away to college, Karen had sobbed hysterically and clung to her leg. Her mother reported that Ellen's high school graduation picture, which sat on the piano, was constantly smeared with kiss marks. And for a long time, more than a year, Ellen had come home every weekend, not to see her parents, whom she had lost all interest in, but to be with her baby sister. She had walked across parking lots in exactly the same way Karen and Olivier did now—hand in hand, engrossed in each other, totally attuned. Often, she had looked at her own aging parents and wondered how they could possibly have produced such a magical child, and more than once she had asked them to let her take Karen back to Boston to raise, a suggestion that Joyce and Norman only laughed at.

"You raise her?" her mother said. "In a hippie commune? Over my dead body."

"You're living in a dreamworld," her father had piped up. "You don't have the first idea about responsibility. Raising a child is a full-time job. Besides, she's not yours."

"She's not yours either," Ellen had answered hotly. "Children are the sons and daughters of life's longing for itself," she added, quoting, she hoped correctly, from Kahlil Gibran's *The Prophet,* which was all the rage in Somerville.

"Yeah, well life's longing for itself doesn't put the bacon on the breakfast table," said Norman.

"You shouldn't be feeding her the meat of the pig anyway!"

Inevitably, every weekend, Ellen left in a huff, and during her sophomore year at Tufts, she began to skip weekends home and spend them with various boyfriends instead. She called, of course, and she attended every important event in Karen's life, including her birthday parties, her kindergarten graduation, and a talent show in which Karen played a glowworm. She happily hung Karen's drawings on the fridge and routinely liberated, as an act of political anti-consumerism outrage, little outfits for her from Filene's Basement.

She had maintained weekly contact with her little sister for her whole life, until Karen had joined the Peace Corps and disappeared into the green hills of Honduras for six years. And even then, she and Tommy had visited her not once but four times. So it was safe to say that she was a constant in her sister's life, and vice versa. They followed each other's plots with extreme attention, and needed to.

"Ready to rock and roll?" Ellen said as Karen and Olivier approached.

"Yep."

They settled back into the Honda and were soon merging into the flow of northbound traffic. Olivier and Mutley conked out in the backseat and Karen stared moodily out the passenger window as if she were mesmerized by the mileage markers posted every mile. Occasionally, Ellen saw her sister raise her fingers to her cheeks and brush away unruly tears.

"Do you want to talk about it?"

Karen shook her head. "I'm just leaking," she said. Five miles later, she added, "It's so final. I keep saying to myself, 'Cocho's life is over.' But in my heart I can't believe it."

"It was too short. Too short."

"You know, I didn't understand one word they said when they buried him. They were speaking Quechua."

"I bet in some deep way you understood every word," Ellen said, but then she remembered her mother's funeral and then her father's. They had had

Catholic services, as they wished, and during both the phrase "the communion of the saints" was thrown around like verbal confetti. Ellen had survived eight years of Catholic school, not to mention kindergarten and weekly religious education classes during high school, and she had never once heard an explanation, or even a mention, of the communion of the saints. She sat at the funerals mulling it over, feeling gypped, duped, and outraged instead of comforted. The words were like a roadblock that kept her off the natural path of grief and recovery.

"But maybe not," she felt compelled to say.

"Maybe not what?"

"Maybe you didn't understand the words at all. I don't want to dismiss your feelings or cover them over with some empty, rote response." She reached across the front seat and touched Karen's shoulder. Karen undid her seat belt, dove into Ellen's lap, and sobbed her heart out. Ellen pulled off the road. "Poor Karen," she said as she patted her. "There, there. Poor Karen. There, there."

Tractor trailers barrelled by within a few feet as she repeated the same words over and over again.

forty-one

The day was scorching and, four and a half hours into the ride, the engine light came on in the dashboard of the Honda. Ellen had faced this mechanical problem before, many times, and she knew that the immediate solution was to cool it off by turning on the heater, full blast. Karen, unable to take it, climbed into the backseat. Mutley moaned in protest as she crowded him but he finally resettled, his long nose resting on Karen's leg. The windows were wide-open but sweat began to pop out in little bubbles on the bridge of each person's nose, and by the time they got to Saranac Lake, Ellen was actively nauseous. Fortunately, there was a public beach at the lake, and Ellen careened into the parking lot, opened her door, and tumbled onto the pavement moments before she would have thrown up. Karen peeled Olivier's clothes off him and sent him into the cool water in nothing but a clean diaper while Ellen ran across the street to a sporting goods shop and purchased bathing suits for herself and Karen. Soon they were splashing among the ripples cast ashore by a passing powerboat. Even Mutley got into the act. He stood with water swishing around his ankles as if his feet were stuck in fresh cement. Observing him, Ellen remembered a dog fact from Reginald's calendar: dogs have no sweat glands except in their feet.

No one wanted to leave, so Ellen bought vegetarian subs and they had a picnic, complete with fresh watermelon slices and carbonated apple juice. They were just one hour from home, if Eagle Beak was Ellen's home, and Ellen was happy about returning. She had only been gone overnight, but it seemed much longer. Time in the city was somehow condensed. She had been in three restaurants, an airport, and a Chinese department store. She had walked Mutley three times and repaired a broken car window. Here in the North Country she wasn't busy, but it was borrowed idleness, wantonly charged to her credit card at 19.7 percent interest—a rate that guaranteed that she would be paying it off for years to come. Her timing was terrible, too, because she was right at the age at which women's chances of landing a new job plummeted. The younger generation wanted to put her out to pasture, but how could she retire when she didn't have a pension plan? She always got fired before she could become vested. Of course, Tommy was careful about future planning, but what would happen to her, individually, if she and Tommy were destined to go their separate ways?

"Karen," she suddenly asked, "do you save money for retirement?"

Karen laughed out loud. "Where did that come from?"

"I was just wondering."

"I do the standard things. Save ten percent of my income and contribute to IRAs, and Regine-Marie and I are trying to buy a small apartment building."

Ellen was shocked. "That's standard? Sheesh." She had missed the boat.

"Oh . . . I also have a college fund for Olivier," Karen added.

"Wow." Ellen sighed. "Sounds like the café business is booming."

"It's okay. But I'm neurotic about living below my means."

"You? Neurotic?"

Karen swung her legs off the wooden dock. "Cocho called me the family CEO. He saw no point in planning. He said life was too unpredictable."

I guess he proved that, Ellen thought.

"He lived more in the moment," Karen said wistfully.

"Did he seem irresponsible?" Ellen was thinking of herself.

"Yes and no."

Ellen waited for more, and when Karen didn't continue, she prodded. "Yes and no?"

"Yes in my value system, but no when I looked at things from his." She turned to look directly into Ellen's eyes. "Sometimes I wish I was somebody else, somebody more like Cocho. Or you."

"Me?" Ellen replied. "Don't wish for that."

"You're such a free spirit." Karen's eyes filled with tears and she shifted her sunglasses down off her head to cover them. "Let's bug out of this creep joint," she said.

As they sped north, the last forty-five miles, Ellen felt not free but shackled to a personality that was out to get her. She didn't pursue it, though, because Karen seemed exhausted. She fell into a light sleep and didn't wake up until Ellen turned off Route 30 onto the bumpy back road to Eagle Beak. Then Karen sat up straighter and glanced to her left and right. "God, you really are in the boonies."

"Yep."

The road ahead looked like the winding path that Hansel and Gretel had followed into the forest. When it disappeared around a curve up ahead, the trees seemed to simply close over it.

"What a crazy twist of fate that you would end up buying a place here."

"Yep."

When Ellen had arrived in Montreal just after purchasing Viola's old home, she had told Karen the whole story, minus one important detail. Now she wanted to share it. "You know the real reason I bought the house?"

"I remember you said you'd surrendered, with glee, to a moment of spontaneity, which you said were becoming few and far between in your middle years and—"

"Sheesh, you're just like Tommy. You remember every word." Now Ellen felt less inclined to talk, but she didn't want to cut herself off from Karen so she pushed verbally on. "The real reason," she said, "was, I had seen that house in my dreams for years. And when I saw it in real life, even though it was just a shack, I just had to have it." Suddenly, Ellen felt upset.

"Really?" Karen said.

The woods along this stretch of road were dense and it seemed noticeably darker and cooler than it had just seconds before. "Yep," Ellen replied as she steered around a sharp curve. Karen stared at her, waiting for more. "It's . . ." Ellen wanted to deliver the perfect one-sentence summary of the whole experience, but she felt constrained by her own requirement for clarity. "It's not over yet," she finally mumbled.

"Remember when I was a kid, I used to ask you over and over again if we were just characters in a giant's dream?" Karen asked.

"I haven't thought of that in years. You were obsessed."

"I had long, involved discussions with the other kids about it. This was in kindergarten and first grade. Everything I did, I'd wonder, Is this me doing this?"

Ellen chuckled. "Ah, the carefree days of childhood."

"You know something?" Karen said softly. "Lately I've been wondering the same thing. Like when I was sitting by Cocho's bed, I kept having this feeling that I was some kind of a hallucination—that I could fade away if I or maybe somebody or something else got distracted and lost concentration for a few seconds."

Ellen wanted to be careful. At tender moments like this, she often stormed ahead with the zeal of a missionary whose task was to provide comfort though she just as often destroyed it. Rayfield had not called her Florence the Ripper for nothing. "I wonder why you felt like that," she said neutrally, a direct contradiction of her basic impulse, which was to announce to her sister that she had been disassociating. "That's perfectly normal in a period of stress," she would have begun, and then launched into a list of coping strategies from barbiturates to Zen meditation.

"I think being with somebody who's stuck between life and death really makes you question what's real."

"Did you think you were losing your mind?" Ellen asked. Just recently she had been shocked when Rodney suggested this same possibility in relation to Rayfield.

"I didn't think about it."

This whole conversation felt murky and dark, the way Viola's house had when Ellen first slept there and didn't know where the light switches were. She would take baby steps, flailing her arms in three-hundred-sixty degree circles in search of some object that would orient her before she tumbled down the kamikaze stairs to land on the living-room floor with her neck broken.

"Well," she said tentatively, "the Buddhists say that this life is just a chance to prepare for being somewhere else for all eternity."

After a few seconds, Karen said, "Really? Well, I think I got a glimpse of it."

"Was it comforting?"

"No. It was neutral."

Ellen was startled. Had her sister received a little peek into the Big Nothing? She gripped the wheel a little tighter, floored it around the bend, and burst out laughing when the hand-painted WELCOME TO PORKERVILLE sign appeared on her right.

"What's funny?"

"We're in Porkerville." Ellen giggled. "The name kills me."

Within a minute, they passed the orange tires that marked Rayfield's driveway. Mutley scrambled to the sitting position and put his nose out the window, perhaps catching a familiar scent. Maybe traces of Debbie still swirled in the air on the microscopic level, or perhaps Rayfield had neglected his weekly bath for too long, and Mutley could smell him from a distance of three hundred feet. Reginald Eubanks's dog calendar said that dogs had six million scent-detecting cells in their noses and smelling what had long since disappeared from the visual field was business as usual for them. Did Mutley miss his former life as the canine child of Rayfield and Wide Load Geebo? Ellen would never know, though she did notice a sharp tug of longing for a glimpse of Rayfield in her own heart as she hit the accelerator and proceeded homeward.

The late afternoon was immensely still, as if the entire landscape were sealed in a jelly jar, when Ellen finally shut off the motor in the driveway. "This is it," she said as she opened the back door to let Mutley out.

"Silence about the dream house," Karen said. "What a gorgeous setting." She stretched, placing one foot on the hood of the car and then bending over it like a dancer. Then she unbuckled Olivier and stood him on his feet in the grass. He waddled off toward his dump truck, which he had previously parked in a pile of dirt near the house.

Suddenly Ellen felt apologetic. Other people probably dreamed of mansions with marble halls, crystal chandeliers, and paintings by Rubens, Rembrandt, or Titian on the walls, but her unconscious produced only shacks and dives, while in her waking life, she dove into debt to purchase them. This broken-down house was a screaming statement about her own inner disrepair, and now she felt silly. Beside her, a mushroom-shaped cloud of vapor rose from the Honda.

"Ellen, what's wrong? You look like you're going to be sick." Karen said.

"I am sick. I'm looking at this house through your eyes, and I'm realizing I'm very mentally ill."

Karen laughed.

"Look at this dump," Ellen cried.

They both turned to stare at the house. The new green roof that she had forced Rodney to put on was definitely the best feature, along with the lacy curtains visible through the wavy pane windows.

"All it needs is a paint job, and you'll have the perfect cottage in the dell," Karen said.

"You think so? Because I'm suddenly overwhelmed with horror."

"I want to see the garden before we even go in," Karen said. "*Olivier, mon petit chou-chou, ou est le jardin?*" Olivier climbed to his feet and started across the lawn. Karen followed, and Ellen trailed along behind, much more slowly, as if the lawn were made of glue. Each step forward required her to overcome the force of suction that wanted to hold her feet in place.

She had bought her house because she thought it was an entrance portal into a parallel personal universe. Now she felt like the blades of grass in the lawn had a grip on her ankles and no matter how much she wanted to, she couldn't catch up with her sister and her nephew. They would enter the garden without her, and she would remain mired just outside the gates of paradise. She stopped trying and just sat down.

"Tomatoes, cucumbers, and beans!" Karen hollered. "Arugula, corn, and broccoli rabe! Peppers, lettuce, and yellow squash! This is a gorgeous garden. It's a cornucopia." Ellen watched as Karen picked a Roma tomato and bit into it. "Oh, my God! This is the best tomato I've ever had," she said, offering it to Olivier. "Let's make a huge salad. Go get me a bowl, Ellen. I want to start picking."

"I'll be right back," Ellen called as she got up and went, without further drama, into the house. It looked neat but smelled stuffy, as if old odors had begun to reaccumulate in a single day. On the table was a note, propped up against the sugar bowl.

Dear Ellen,
> *Please give me a call the second you get back. VERY IMPORTANT!!*
> Rodney

This cheered Ellen, who worried that she had alienated one of her only friends in the North Country. Besides, at this point, she knew more about Rodney's past than he did. It was, in a way, a burden, and she hoped he would relieve her of it, though she would not selfishly thrust it upon him. She decided to call him as soon as she delivered the salad bowl to Karen.

When she got to the garden, Karen's arms were full of nature's bounty. "I look at a lot of organic produce," she said in a matter-of-fact voice, "and yours is really exceptional."

"Really?"

"Definitely. You must have great topsoil here."

Karen had studied agricultural techniques during her six years in the refugee camp. The number of residents there grew exponentially as the months went by, the war displacing everyone on its violent path. Karen had personally researched not only the methods but the long-term consequences of ground water pumps and irrigation. As a community, the refugees had mulled over and ultimately balanced their need for food and fresh water with their concern for the depletion of the aquifer, the potential salinization of the fields, and the possibility of toxic runoff from their makeshift outhouses. When Ellen and Tommy had visited, they had been astonished that Karen, so musical and language oriented, had suddenly burst forth with a science side.

"That's what survival mode does to you," Karen quipped at the time. "The problem is the whole planet's in a crisis and only the powerless people are hurt enough on a daily basis to realize it. And they're too desperate to think calmly."

Ellen had known in her heart that it was true but saving the planet was totally beyond her. Still, every time she returned from Honduras to New York, where the water consumption was more than two hundred and fifty gallons a day for each of its millions and millions of people, she was dismayed at the level of reckless oblivion. For days, she would police the faucets in the kitchen and bathroom for drips, take just one bath, and not flush the toilet unless it was absolutely necessary. But inevitably, she and her raised consciousness would tumble into the black hole of forgetfulness, and the supply of available fresh water would once again become something she took for granted.

Now, five years later, Karen was praising her organic efforts, and Ellen was about to purchase the very same water purification system, one approved by the Red Cross for use in disaster areas that Karen had set up in Honduras, so the yellow water in her own well would be 100 percent safe and potable. It was a miracle. She handed the salad bowl to Karen and stood back to watch the harvest. She herself had consumed at least two dozen tomatoes and numerous other vegetables but seeing her sister, a food pro, delighting in her vegetable patch made it so much more real.

Not that she knew what was real anymore.

"I'm going to go in and call Rodney," she said. "He left me a weird note." Ellen had not seen Rodney in more than seventy-two hours, but time measured against the events of those three days, which included Cocho's death, trips to both Montreal and New York, and the reading of Rodney, Sr.,'s love letters to Viola, was truly inaccurate. Ellen chuckled as she pulled open the screen door, knowing she had come full circle, from railing against the concept of inaccurate time to embracing it.

Rodney answered on the third ring.

"Hey, Rodney, it's Ellen."

"Can you come over? Right now?"

Ellen had visions of Rodney as the victim of some disaster that befalls old people who live alone. "Are you okay?"

"I'm fine, for heaven's sake. Just come over. I'm in my shop."

Ellen could not and would not say no, but she didn't especially want to leave Karen alone before she had even crossed the threshold of the house.

"My sister's here and—"

"Good. Bring her," Rodney said, and he hung up. Ellen was mystified. Maybe Rodney, when he was working, always barked out orders like a four-star general, but she had never heard nor imagined such verbal abruptness from Rodney de Beer. It took three seconds for her to recover enough to replace the receiver on its hook. Then she picked up her car keys and headed out the door.

Karen was just coming around the corner of the house. "Going somewhere?" she asked.

"To Rodney's. Let's all go."

"Really? We just got here. I haven't even been in the house."

"I know, but Rodney basically ordered me to come over right now. Something's definitely up."

"I think I'll wait here."

"No, come. Think of it as some crazy tangent you would take in a dream."

"Where should I put the veggies?"

"Let's take them. Come on, Olivier, back in the car." She put him in his car seat and off they putted. Though Ellen had told Karen all about Rodney, she had intentionally left out the part about his sculpture-covered hillsides. That was a visual that no one should be prepared for in advance of the experience. She felt a buzz of anticipation as they drove up Rodney's long driveway, knowing that once they hit the clearing at the top, Karen was in for a wonderful shock.

"Stop!" Karen cried just as Ellen had when she and Rodney had emerged from the forest into the clearing where his imagination ruled. "Oh, my God!"

Ellen put the car in park but left it running.

"Where are we? Is this a holy place?" Karen asked.

"It's the cathedral of St. Rodney de Beer."

"Can we get out and walk around?" Karen was clearly under the same spell that had captured Ellen when, weeks ago, she had wandered over these hillsides for hours.

"Of course, but first let's go up and check up on Rodney. He's acting very weird."

"Mutley?" Olivier asked, pointing out the window at a statue of a wolf howling at the moon. Ellen stepped on the gas and proceeded up the hill.

On her one-day retreat to this place, Ellen had not entered Rodney's wood shop. She had thought it would be a violation of his privacy, or more correctly, one too many violations, for she had already entered his house to snoop and dozed in a rocking chair with wooden arms that had notches where his fingers fit.

She drove to the barn and parked, and they all climbed out of the car. After a second, Rodney appeared in the double barn door. His overalls were thick with sawdust. It was also in his hair and eyebrows. His shirttail had somehow begun to work its way out the armhole of his overalls, and the long lock of hair that was usually draped over his bald spot was hanging down to his shoulder on one side. He looked wired, a mix of exhaustion and nervous energy that Ellen knew all too well. She had it herself on occasion and so did Tommy, but Reginald Eubanks lived in that space all the time.

"Rodney, are you okay?"

"Come inside."

"Rodney, this is my sister, Karen," Ellen said, gently reminding him of basic social protocol.

"I figured," Rodney said, not unkindly. Then he stopped and stepped toward her to shake her hand. "I usually have better manners, but you've caught me in one of my frenzies."

Both Ellen and Karen laughed. Rodney certainly looked like he was in a frenzy, but it seemed odd that a man his age would still have what it took to get into one. He turned and moved quickly back into the barn as if he were a ball bearing at the mercy of centrifugal force. Karen lifted Olivier to her hip and all three entered a half beat behind Rodney. "I came home from your place the other night after all that commotion about them letters and my father, and I was all shook up," Rodney said over his shoulder. "I tried to sleep but all I did was toss and turn, and in the middle of the night I couldn't take it no more and I got up and come down here and started to work on a new statue. I dug out some cherry wood I got years ago off'n my own back woodlot, and I started in. I ain't had one of these frenzies in a long time, but before I knew it, it was morning and I was still at it. I been at it for a couple days now." He stopped. "It's in there," he said, pointing through a door at the very back of the barn.

Ellen felt a tingle along her spine. "Jeez Rodney, I feel like I'm about to see Rosemary's baby." After she said it, she realized he had probably not seen that movie, but he had ignored her anyway.

"I thought it was me," he said, "like I got all riled up and something deep inside me about me and my father was coming out, but . . . Ellen, it ain't me. It's . . . well, see for yourselves." He opened the door to a smaller room whose walls were covered with gleaming antique hand tools. The statue, which was life-size, faced the other way.

They moved in a group around to the front with Ellen in the lead. Her eyes fell upon the most finished part, the part that had already been sanded and polished. "It's Olivier!" she whispered in awe, but right behind her she heard Karen catch her breath and moan as if she'd just been severely wounded. Then Ellen felt a rush of air and she shifted her attention, though it was hard to pry it off the wooden likeness of Olivier, with his wild ringlets and his beautiful inquiring face, and she saw her sister crumple to the floor.

"Karen!" she cried as she dropped to her knees to support her sister's back. Karen stared up at the statue from the floor. Ellen had never seen such a look of pain on anyone's face.

Rodney squatted down and took Olivier. "Is it your husband, dear?" he asked.

"It's Cocho."

"I thought so," Rodney said, and then he lost his balance and landed on his ass in the sawdust. "Did he pass on?" Rodney asked and Karen rolled over, threw her arms around his waist, and cried into his chest.

Ellen, baffled, turned back to the statue and saw that, because her eyes had snagged on little Olivier, she had simply not looked up. Because there, with one hand holding the boy's little fingers in his own and the other holding a wind instrument that Rodney had probably never seen, was Cocho. Life-size.

"How? How?" Ellen shrieked.

"I don't know. I don't even know the guy," Rodney said. He wiped his brow nervously.

"But you . . . how . . . ?"

"I just don't know." Rodney's blue eyes were both weary and wild. Olivier was now standing up, transfixed, as his wooden twin stared back at him. Meanwhile, Rodney held Karen in his arms like a cross-gendered Pieta.

Ellen turned back to the sculpture. On closer examination, she realized that Cocho's likeness was strongly suggested but not yet totally refined. His body shape and proportion, height, hair, and posture were so correct that Ellen hadn't noticed that his face was perhaps three-quarters of the way into shape. "Oh, my God," she whispered. In Florence, she had seen incomplete sculptures by Michelangelo in which figures seemed to be unwilling to step forth from the cover provided by the stone. They stayed back where it was safe. Cocho, though, seemed impatient to be seen. He seemed to want to shuck off all the excess wood chips and simply be.

"Rodney, this is unbelievable. It's gorgeous. It's . . ." Ellen sputtered.

"It ain't finished yet."

"But how did—" Ellen could not even finish her sentence. It was as if her vocabulary had deserted her.

"I'm getting wore out but I don't dare to stop," Rodney cut in. "Karen, you're gonna have to help me, so pull yourself together." He said this in a tone that was neither bullying nor touchy-feely, and the words worked like magic on Karen. She stopped crying and sat up.

"What do you want me to do?"

"Talk to me about his face."

Karen stood up, extended a hand to Rodney, and hauled him up. "I have a picture in my wallet," she said.

"I'd rather just go along talking and see what happens." They moved toward the sculpture in a trance. Ellen heard their conversation far in the background, as if they were on the radio with the volume turned too low. "He had a fairly long face, am I right?" Rodney was saying. "And somewhat of a pointy chin?" He picked up a chisel.

"Rodney," Ellen said again, "how did you do this?" She wanted a simple explanation, but he was not listening to her. She turned to observe Karen and him more closely. It was clear they were in an altered state together, and she was on the outside, looking in. Ellen collected Olivier in her arms.

"It was more pointy when he smiled," Karen said.

It was such a private moment, so intensely personal, that Ellen felt like a movie extra who had been sent to the wrong stage set by the casting office. "I'm gonna take Olivier home," she said. "Give you two time to work." It seemed like the right thing to do.

"Okay," Karen said, totally distracted. She forgot to kiss Olivier and only called "Thanks" after Ellen was halfway through the door.

Ellen felt lonely and a tiny bit resentful as she carried Olivier out of Rodney's workshop. What had happened was a miracle—a phenomenon that could never be explained no matter how many scientists or theologians tried. But it wasn't her miracle. She looked back toward the barn with a sense of longing. But then, deep in her heart, she actually felt something let loose, as if a part of her had finally been lifted off some inner meat hook, and a wave of relief, gratitude, and amazement rushed over her. It made her dizzy, and she reached for the car roof for balance. She was hot, as if each of her cells was a sun, bursting with healing energy, and her eyes seemed to open wider and see more than ever before. Spontaneous combustion, she thought, and she glanced down to see if she was still encased in her skin. She was. Her fingers, gripping onto the car roof to steady herself, looked like pale tree roots that had suddenly been exposed to light.

Ellen pivoted to take in the panoramic view from Rodney's mountaintop. The first shards of darkness were extending across his lawn, and the frogs were revving up. Something smelled good, and the warm air lay across her shoulders like a handmade shawl. "Hey, Olivier, you want to drive?" she asked as she took a deep breath and opened the car door. He climbed into her lap and she turned on the ignition. The lights in Rodney's shop windows looked friendly and kind as they eased away, with Olivier at the wheel, toward home.

forty-two

By nine o'clock both Ellen and Olivier were exhausted, and they went to bed. Ellen left a light on in the dining room with a flashlight and a note directing Karen up the darkened staircase. She lay on the new luxury bed and thought about Rodney's statue. Seeing Cocho unexplainably there had left her breathless and sent her consciousness spinning like a top. She was thrilled but disoriented, and she badly wanted to hear what Karen had to say on the subject. No one else would do.

But when morning came, Karen still had not appeared, and Ellen was torn between surrendering to her earthly curiosity by heading immediately to Rodney's or savoring the mystery in the place it had flung her. She was certain that the finer details of Cocho's face would emerge from the wood as surely as his body had, and forever more, whenever she felt trapped by the iron predictability of life, she could conjure up this strangest of all the moments to prove to herself that it truly was a magic kingdom in which she lived. She hummed as she powdered Olivier's bottom. The Dalai Lama was reported to have, at just Olivier's age, understood a language he had never heard and recognized the members of the Buddhist search committee charged with finding him. That was amazing; look how he turned out. And what had happened to Olivier was almost as good.

As she waited for her open-the-heart tea to brew, Ellen considered where the statue would ultimately reside. Surely Rodney would not just add it to his backyard gallery. Or would he? Her thoughts meandered on, arriving in due course at her documentary. What a twist it would be if it made it to Cannes, Sundance, or Toronto. Rodney would become a made guy, and people from all over the world would arrive at his door asking him to channel their loved ones into cherrywood logs. Would he want to? Ellen, while researching for Reginald, had once met a renowned charismatic. This man had bona fide healing hands, but had not known it until he was over forty. He had taken on the healer's mantle after a religious experience at Lourdes and had subsequently restored hundreds of people to health, but he meticulously avoided publicity. He no doubt knew that the maimed masses would suck him dry.

"Let's go out and water," she suggested to Olivier, and he charged toward the door. Ellen retrieved Mutley's Frisbee from her bag, and Mutley, seeing his love object, rose to his feet, his ears erect and one front paw lifted in readiness. Ellen let it fly, and the combination of the prevailing wind against the trajectory of the Frisbee allowed Mutley to arrive at its landing place precisely at the right moment to snag it from the air. "Bravo!" Ellen cheered. "Bravo!" Mutley soon returned it to her feet, and so her day began: water, weed, throw the Frisbee. Repeat, repeat, repeat. The sun beat down, and soon she was planning a dip in the lake.

Ellen had removed the topic of her marriage to the back burner of her mind in the wake of Cocho's death, but her trip to New York, to the apartment in which she felt like a visitor, hadn't really helped. A sick feeling came over her, but she willed it away. Let that wave of nausea crash on some other shore today, she thought. It was strange that she and Tommy had essentially stopped communicating, though, except on a need-to-know basis. This was by far the oddest phase they had ever gone through as a couple. But for now, for today, Ellen was in Wonderland in the wake of Rodney's miracle, and she flat-out refused to be a sad sack.

With Karen occupied elsewhere, she decided to call Rayfield. He picked up on the first ring. "Look, you dumb cluck," he said instead of hello, "I already told you I ain't gonna take the goddamn newspaper. You call me one more time and I'll come down there and ram the whole printing press straight up your ass."

" 'Morning, Rayfield," Ellen said sweetly.

"Oh hey, Ellen," he said. "What's shakin' with the bakin'?"

"Feel like going for a swim with me and Olivier?"

"Where? Peak Pond?"

"Yeah, unless you know a better place."

"I know a million better places, but you better hope the people that own them don't come home while you're there."

"Let's go to one of those," Ellen said devilishly.

"I'll meet you at the post office."

Ellen collected her beach paraphernalia with a sense of adolescent rebelliousness. It made sense that Rayfield, who had lived here his whole life would know the best swimming places from the days before the lake was sold off in lots to private parties whose first act of ownership was to slap up a large NO TRESPASSING sign.

Once, in the sixties, she and a whole VW busload of hippies had set out to spend the night in New Hampshire at the home of their housemate, Valerie, whose parents had gone south to a high school reunion for the weekend. They followed the directions precisely and arrived at a white farmhouse, as they expected. Valerie was nowhere to be found but the door was unlocked, so they went in and made themselves at home. They raided both the fridge and the liquor cabinet and were about to settle in for the night when Ellen happened to notice that the number indicated on the phone did not match the one they had for Valerie. This motivated a search for identifying documents, and, sure enough, they soon discovered that the name on the assortment of bills on the table was not familiar. Quickly, they cleared out, not even doing the dishes or removing the half-smoked joints from the ashtrays. Continuing down the road another half mile, they found Valerie waiting, alone and rejected, on the front porch of another white farmhouse.

"So where we going?" she asked Rayfield as he settled into the passenger seat.

"Onward toward Peak Pond!" He pointed stiff-armed out the windshield like a member of the U.S. cavalry of yesteryear, directing her past Baldy's store onto a road that she had never suspected led around the lake from this direction.

"Heard from your sister?" Rayfield asked.

"Yep. She's here. I have a story to tell you, but let's wait until we get to . . . where we going?"

"Just tell me now."

"Come on, Rayfield, I'll tell you when we settle down. I want to ham it up."

"If it's a good story, it don't need them extra frills of yours."

"So humor me."

"Okay, okay." He turned around in the seat. "Ready for a swimming lesson, my man?" Olivier raised his little hand to slap Rayfield five. "Today the dog paddle, tomorrow the world," Rayfield cheered.

"Why didn't you and Debbie ever have any kids?"

"Oh . . . Wide Load had her pipes tied off long before I met her. She said she had better things to do than wipe asses."

"Like what? Make fork bracelets?" Ellen was instantly ashamed of both her words and her tone.

"Hey, don't disrespect fork bracelets. She sold a lot of 'em."

"I know. I own one myself. I don't know why I said that. It just came out."

"Mean as a snake," Rayfield said, though he didn't throw much oomph behind it.

Ellen let it settle, then she said, "So are you still feeling blissfully free of all your self-defeating ties to Debbie?"

Rayfield looked at her. "Damn, Ellen, speak English."

Ellen giggled.

"Take that left," he said.

She turned down a narrow lane with tufts of long grass growing up between the tire tracks. After a half mile, the road widened slightly and a second later a beautiful rustic retreat on the lake came into view. "Whose house is this?" Ellen asked, alarmed now that reality was upon her.

"Some doctor's. Park over there in the trees."

"What if he's here?"

"*She* never comes here," Rayfield said, emphasizing the feminine pronoun with glee. "She's had this place for five years and she really only showed up once for a week. Probably needed a tax write-off."

"If you say so," Ellen said, but sudden fears were kicking up left and right. What if she ended up in the hoosegow? It would be thoroughly humiliating to have to call Tommy at work to bail her out, or, worse yet, represent her in criminal court. But she wanted to end her life as a stiff, so she collected Olivier and his toys, which now included a blow-up turtle five times his size, and followed Rayfield toward the dock.

"Who keeps up the grounds?" she asked. The grass was cut, and flowers bloomed all around the porch.

"Guy I know."

"Did he give you permission to be here?"

"Look Ellen, I'm from here, okay? I go where I always went. Besides, look around. Do you see anybody? Who's gonna report us?"

"I suppose you're right," she said halfheartedly.

"Damn right I'm right," Rayfield said, peeling off his T-shirt and barrelling toward the dock. At the end he took a flying leap, formed himself into a human cannonball, and disappeared into an explosion of spray. Obviously, they were not going to keep a low profile.

Ellen slipped off her shorts and shirt without self-consciousness and edged slowly into the water with Olivier. He shrieked with delight when she placed him on the inflatable turtle's back and paddled him around her in circles. It was truly a glorious summer day, and kids were splashing all along the lake's shores while teens water-skied by. Canoes, pontoon boats for two with foot pedals, and powerboats crisscrossed the lake, and dragonflies that looked like miniature helicopters darted hither and thither, looking for a human landing pad. Rayfield, like a soaked rat, swam up until he beached in about a foot of water.

"Feels good, don't it?"

"Sure does."

"Take a good swim. Me and Ollie'll stay here and play with the turtle."

"Great." Ellen walked out a few feet, did a surface dive, and frog-kicked her way toward the center of the lake. In her grade school years, she took to water naturally. Her mother had called her a fish. There was even talk of her making it to the Vermont swimming championships in the under twelve category, but when her tiny breasts had begun to form, Ellen abruptly stopped swimming. She refused to display her budding, betraying body in public. In private, at home, she developed the odd habit of holding a pillow in front of her chest whenever she sat down, for example, in the living room for *Alfred Hitchcock Presents* or *The Ed Sullivan Show*. What a shame, she thought now, as her breath became labored. She could've been a swimmer with long, lean muscles and low body fat. She probably would've progressed to scuba diving and she could have taken exotic diving vacations in the Galapagos Islands or Cozumel, Mexico. She was so involved in lamenting what might have been that she forgot, for a moment, that many of the events she longed for had actually happened. She *had* been to Cozumel, where she snorkeled the reef in complete contentment. And by her hippie years, she had so scorned the concept of bathing suits that she essentially refused to go to any beach that forbade nudity.

Ellen flipped onto her back and stared at the passing clouds. She waved to Olivier and Rayfield, who had situated himself on top of the turtle and placed Olivier on his tummy. They bounced gently in the lake ripples. He's a good guy, Ellen thought as she headed back in, doing a fast butterfly stroke like in the olden days. She climbed onto the dock, lying on her back and enjoying the heat of the wood beneath her bottom.

"So tell me this great story," Rayfield said as soon as she had stretched out. Suddenly Ellen didn't want to. She wanted to keep it to herself but she had painted herself into a corner, so she simply said, "The night Cocho died, Rodney started a new statue. He didn't know Cocho died, and he's never seen a picture of him. He worked on it like a madman, day and night. Guess what? It's Cocho." She stopped. "And Olivier," she added.

"You're shitting me," Rayfield exclaimed, his eyes wide. "You mean like, it looks just like him?"

"Yep. Rodney even included his zampoñas, the kind of flute that Cocho plays. They make them in his village in Peru. In South America," she added, just so he wouldn't again confuse it with Peru, New York.

"Damn," said Rayfield.

"My sister's over there now. They're working on the face. Know what happened when she saw it? She fainted."

"So would I," Rayfield said. He took a moment to digest it. "Da da da da, da da da da," he chanted—the theme song to *The Twilight Zone*. "Damn," he said again, "it makes you wonder, don't it?"

"Yep." Both were silent for several minutes.

"What happens to people when they die?" Rayfield finally asked.

"I can't imagine."

"Like, do you think your sister's husband possessed Rodney?"

Ellen sat up and tried to think clearly. "Well, Cocho couldn't sculpt. If his spirit possessed Rodney, wouldn't Rodney suddenly start playing the flute or speaking Spanish or something?"

"Shit if I know." Rayfield went back to bobbing quietly in the water on the blow-up turtle.

"Edgar Cayce said that when he went into trances, he tapped the collected knowledge of all beings, living and dead," Ellen offered after a few minutes.

"Who?"

"Edgar Cayce. A real guy who would fall asleep and then diagnose sick people. Most of the time he could tell them what to do to get cured."

"He talked in his sleep?"

"Yeah. But the point is, he said when he slept he had access to all the knowledge there was. Maybe Rodney's spirit and Cocho's crossed paths out there in the great beyond."

"Maybe," Rayfield said, uncharacteristically pensive.

"There's so much we don't know and never will know," Ellen said. "That's why science pisses me off so much. I think science is the greatest myth of the last three centuries."

"Oh, no, don't start to Ellen me. Okay? Because I might as well tell you that you generally lose me after about the fourth word."

Ellen felt giddy. She had been the object and the subject of many sentences, but she had never been a verb before. "What do you mean 'Ellen' you?"

"You know, start in with all that book shit. I been watching you for almost two months now, and it wasn't until right now that I figured it out. You're just like that Edgar guy you was just telling me about, except you go into a trance when you're wide-awake and all the shit you read starts pouring out of your mouth like it was you who thought it all up."

Ellen's elation disintegrated.

"Yeah, that's it," Rayfield remarked to himself, obviously satisfied.

"Well, that makes me feel like shit," Ellen said.

"What the hell for?"

"Because you're diminishing a part of me that I take very seriously, that I think has value, and that I've really worked hard to—"

"Don't Ellen me," Rayfield said. "I'm floating around the lake on a turtle. Don't fuck it up."

Humph, Ellen thought, but she just lay back. The wide boards of the dock were hot, and it felt good. A chuckle began to form in her stomach, and a nanosecond later, she was howling. She rolled over onto her side, barely able to push herself to the sitting position, and gasped for breath. Soon, her sides ached from exercise, and she had to cross her arms and hold her ribs in place. Rayfield and Olivier watched for a few seconds and then joined in. When it was all over, when the tears had dried on her face and Ellen had simmered down with only occasional chuckles instead of tidal waves of laughter, she felt just as good as she had countless times in the past after exceptionally wild sex. This reminded her that she had not so much as mentioned Rayfield's area of prime concern.

"So what's happening in the hard-on department?" she asked. "Any more morning surprises?"

"I'm running about fifty-fifty, which ain't bad."

"A positive trend," Ellen said.

"I ain't making no official statements."

"Smart."

"I mean, I was living like an old man long enough to get used to it. Why should I get nervous now?"

"High hopes, low expectations," Ellen contributed in her wise woman voice.

"I ain't hoping and I ain't expecting."

It entered Ellen's mind that perhaps she had attached more significance to the unraveling of Rayfield's penis than he had. To her, the return of the functioning masculine member was the red carpet to the door of enhanced living for males of a certain age. But right from the beginning, from their initial meeting during which he blurted out his whole story, Rayfield had seemed amazingly unself-conscious about his problem.

"Are you back in the market for a girlfriend?" Ellen asked.

"Why? You want to put in an application?" He raised his eyebrows twice like a cartoon lecher.

In their morning coffee klatch, Rodney had told her about a Boston woman who had owned a second home on the lake. She'd come up one summer with her two sons while her husband, a wheeler-dealer in sports equipment, stayed behind to make even more money than they could possibly ever need. After a lightning storm knocked out her power, this woman had called a local electrician. The second he walked in the door, according to Rodney, sparks flew, and before anyone could count to ten, he had moved in with her and she had filed for divorce. Her big-shot husband took her to court and got not only the house on the lake but the two kids, too, which nearly broke her heart, but she moved into the electrician's small cabin in the woods and took a job as a rural mail carrier. Ellen had seen her, sitting almost in the passenger seat of her Toyota Tercel, steering with her arm stretched out full length, as she drove from mailbox to mailbox. She was always intent on her work, whipping correspondence into the open mouths of the mailboxes like a mother bird feeding her young. What if a crazy twist of fate wrenched her out of Tommy's arms and deposited her in Rayfield's? Ellen felt herself go pale.

"No offense, Rayfield, but I'm not the girl for the job."

"Why not?"

"Because I'm married," she said simply.

"Oh, right," Rayfield said as if he had totally forgotten about Tommy. "Seriously," he added, "I'm taking some time off from women. I gotta rest up before I get back in the ring."

So many people thought of relationships and marriage as a fight, Ellen thought. Even the language, or at least the concepts behind it in the West, linked love and aggression. All's fair in love and war. Win somebody's heart. Lower your defenses. Fight for your man. There were probably a dozen other metaphors like this.

"Rayfield, why do you think people stay together? I mean, it's so much trouble, but we keep at it. Why doesn't the institution of marriage just crumble away once and for all?"

"You're asking the wrong man."

"Why?"

"Because my marriage did just crumble away, Ellen."

"Oh, jeez, of course it did. I'm sorry. I just—"

"You were just Ellening," he said, and then added, "Don't you ever get sick of it?"

"Yes but . . . what else can I do?"

"You can shut up. No offense."

"None taken," Ellen said as she slipped off the dock into the water. "Just one more question," she said. "What do you think of men having extramarital affairs?" She was thinking of Tommy, of course.

Rayfield thought for a few seconds. "I think it don't matter where you get your appetite just so long as you eat at home."

Once again, Ellen thought, that all depended on the complex definition of home.

forty-three

When she pulled into the driveway two hours later, Ellen left Olivier in his car seat and ran in to see if Karen was there. She tiptoed up the stairs to peek into the bedrooms, but both were vacant and she went back outside. "Let's go see Mommy and Uncle Rodney," she said. She felt amazingly clean, as if the acid rain in the waters of Peak Pond Lake had eaten away any tendency to worry that she might be intruding where she didn't belong. The inflatable turtle, stuffed into the backseat with Olivier, obscured her rearview mirror in a delightful way, and pulling onto Rodney's road, she saw the familiar vehicle of the love-struck mail carrier in the distance and made the blessing sign of the cross in her direction with her right hand.

Rodney and Karen, seated next to each other in matching rockers on the front porch, were eating salad from bowls in their laps. "Hey!" Ellen called.

"Hey!" they answered.

Ellen moved toward the porch. Black half-circles had formed under both Karen and Rodney's eyes, and Rodney's hair was greasy while Karen's face looked red and somewhat chapped. Still, there was a sense of quiet about them.

"So, are we finished here or what?" Ellen asked.

"It's done," Rodney said.

Ellen was baffled. He might as well have announced that a load of laundry had just made it through the spin cycle.

"We just finished a half hour ago," Karen said as she reached over and touched Rodney's hand.

"Can I run down and take a look?" Ellen had already taken a step in the direction of the woodshop.

"Ellen, wait. Rodney wants to finish polishing before anyone sees it."

A small part of Ellen wanted to protest, but instead she smiled. "Rodney's the boss," she said, and she sat down on the steps. Olivier had climbed into his mother's lap and was dipping his fingers in the remains of her salad dressing and licking them.

"I ain't been this pooped in years," said Rodney as he forked a fresh green pepper slice into his mouth. "I'm gonna get in the shower and then crawl into bed."

Karen rose and kissed him on the cheek. "Call us as soon as you get up," she said.

"Okay. See everybody later." He shuffled inside and the door gently closed behind him.

Karen stared after him. A moment later, they got into the car. Karen held her son on her lap for the short hop to Ellen's. "All night long, I watched Rodney work. I know it's a miracle, and I've had my own hands on the proof. But my mind keeps wanting a logical explanation. It wants me to doubt. I keep wondering why."

"It beats me, but I have the same feeling," Ellen said.

"It's like I'm afraid I'm going to lose something if I just give in and believe."

Ellen knew exactly what Karen meant. She had bought the house, had Viola dreams, found the letters, and built (against many odds) a relationship with Rodney, who had delivered the statue as a cosmic knockout punch. Each step of the way, she had doubted, yet she had crossed the cosmic finish line. So had Karen, who had come into the race late.

"Believing is not easy."

"You get a miracle, and you don't . . . you don't . . ."

"You don't know it's going to deconstruct your whole personal universe? And blow your mind," Ellen supplied, and they both laughed nervously for a little while. Ellen turned into her driveway, turned off the ignition, and reached for her door handle.

"Ellen, wait," Karen said, "I want to say something. To me you have always been a miracle worker. But this one? This one is saving my life. Thank you."

"I didn't do anything," Ellen stammered.

"Yes, you did."

There was nothing to do but move toward each other and hug, as if the circle of their arms around each other would somehow seal the experience into their cellular memory. Ellen had hugged a few people that she knew she would never see again in her life, like her friend Harold before he died, with this same intensity. She didn't want to let go, and didn't until the strange electrical current that had engulfed them subsided and allowed them to get out of the car.

Karen inspected the house for the first time with great interest and enthusiasm. She admired the craftspersonship in Viola's doilies and said she could just imagine the pantry full of jars of whole grains and dried fruit. She threw herself down on the porch swing, declaring it perfect, and laughed with delight at the kamikaze staircase.

"So you think you'd ever come down here for a weekend—sometime when you need a break from the city?" Ellen asked shyly.

"Absolutely. I want a key."

Ellen had already made one for her and scampered off to get it. "*Mi casa es su casa,*" she said as she handed it over.

Karen managed to stay awake for just over an hour before she climbed into Ellen's new bed and plummeted into a deep sleep. Ellen had sacrificed her room quite happily. Olivier's port-a-crib was already there and the bed was excellent, which Karen needed in her exhausted state. Being in the old iron bed in the other room was like sleeping in a ditch, but Ellen looked oddly forward to it.

That night, it was very dark and strangely quiet, as if the frogs were on strike, or perhaps avoiding some predator. As Ellen stretched out, she replayed the conversation she had had with Karen just before her sister collapsed.

"Rodney gave me the statue," Karen had said.

"I thought he might. You should have it—you and Olivier."

"But it's so generous." Karen was silent for a minute but fluffed the heavy bed pillow with nervous intensity. "I'm going to have an unveiling. A memorial service for Cocho and an unveiling."

Ellen decided at that moment that she would not look at the statue again before the unveiling. Waiting would allow her to become a contributor to the group response of Cocho's friends to Rodney's statue, which would be an honor.

"I want you to tell the story of the statue," Karen had said as Ellen tucked her in.

"In detail? Because Rodney is a very private person and . . ."

"Let's ask him," Karen said as she drifted off.

Ellen went outside to stare at the passing stars. She couldn't imagine telling the story without including the letters from Rodney, Sr., but maybe Rodney, Jr., would not want that part of his life broadcast to the good people of Old Montreal. If he said yes, though, she would work hard on the job Karen had given her. Short and sweet would be her goal.

In bed, listening to the silence, Ellen wondered where to start. She wanted to tell the tale of the statue with as little personal intrusion as possible. But where should she begin? With the day she bought the house? With her dream vision of Viola, sprinting across the field toward the cover of the cave? With the letters sewn into the chair? With the night Cocho died?

It was a huge responsibility, which she would take on gladly, but it would be a lie to say it was not intimidating. She pulled the covers up to her chest and gripped onto them like a child in a dark room. She could hear snoring from the other room. Suddenly, it occurred to her that she was probably sleeping in Rodney's old room. He had perhaps hidden under the covers, maybe these same quilts, waiting for sleep to carry him forward to a new day. He must have listened to his mother's snores, probably with relief that she was, however temporarily, not running amok.

What a life Rodney had had! He had been deposited by fate in a whirlwind of insanity, rage, and hatred. Somehow he had survived, harboring his dream of joining the Ice Capades. He had probably fallen asleep in this very bed imagining himself in a sequined tux doing triple lutzes in rinks all around North America, maybe reaching speeds of up to thirty-five miles per hour before launching into an in-air split. Then, he had found Leland, a hermit and a lover of beauty, who had taken him under his wing. Rodney had remained loyal to his savior, staying by his side as Leland had slowly died. Rodney had given everything while somehow, cruelly, being miscast by the local real-estate agents as a no-goodnik and a layabout. He had taken up the chain saw to keep from murdering Viola. He had worked obsessively, been driven to create, until the precise moment when all his sensitivity and training combined to permit him, or perhaps force him, to transcend the known boundaries between this world and the next.

That statue was a freaking miracle.

But miracles, thought Ellen, were like fireworks. They dazzled when they ignited, but, like gunpowder waiting to explode, they were also dangerous when they didn't. Maybe every moment in life was like that: ready to detonate with just the right jostling into a miracle or a tragedy. And no matter which way it went, the recipients asked the same questions: Why me? What did I do to deserve this? What do I do now?

Like a meteor that had crashed through the atmospheric force field and splashed into the psychic sea, Rodney's miracle had sent out ripples large enough to swamp many little life rafts, including her own. And even though she was joyous and filled with amazement and wonder, the fact that it had come in exchange for losing Cocho was unbearable. Ellen had spent years spouting off her beliefs in the collective unconscious, the Self, and the order of synchronicity beneath the surface chaos. But face-to-face with the proof, she felt, ironically, not more but less able to believe because believing, like Karen had said, was the passport into no-man's-land. Behind your back, people called you a Born Again, and you yourself lived in fear and dread of the moment when your bubble might burst.

It was frightening.

Ellen began to doze off. When I wake up, Dear God, she prayed, please let me be a new person. Whatever I have to leave behind, I let it go. "Thank you, old attitudes, for serving me so loyally in the past, but I ask you now to set me free," she said in a whisper. And then she slipped over into the night and had no dreams at all. And somehow, she slept through the noise of Karen and Olivier waking up and maneuvering themselves down the creaky staircase. When she finally made it into the dining room, Karen was already on the phone, babbling away in French and sounding both efficient and sexy. She covered the receiver with her fingers and whispered, "I'm giving directions to some people I know—art movers."

Ellen nodded, kissed Olivier's head, and padded into the kitchen to heat up her special tea. It was eight thirty—practically the middle of the day for Ellen, who had been a witness to dawn almost every morning for the past month. She glanced at the table, saw no donuts, and assumed that Rodney had not come over. In fact, Olivier was munching on a bowl of cut-up fruit in yogurt and a slice of twelve-grain bread, which Karen had thoughtfully purchased after their swim in Saranac Lake.

Ellen had totally dropped the reins of healthy eating during her guardianship of her nephew. Karen would go pale if she ever found out how many empty calories Ellen had fed Olivier in the form of jelly donuts and chocolate eclairs. She herself was shocked to think of it.

Karen hung up. "All set. They're coming tomorrow afternoon. That gives Rodney the day and a half he said he needed to finish the sanding. And I'm setting the memorial service for Cocho for Friday at sunset." Her voice faltered, and the bottom rim of her eyes suddenly filled with salty water.

"Are you sure you're up to this? Wouldn't you rather just stay here for a few weeks and rest?"

"I would but . . ."

"Regine-Marie would want you to rest a little," Ellen said. "I know she would."

"I've been gone six weeks. Almost seven. She's done enough. And you need your privacy."

"No, I don't," Ellen said quickly. In fact, she was a little afraid of the inevitable return to the normalcy of isolation. "I'd love for you to stay here."

"I have to get back to my life."

Ellen poured her tea and said nothing. She had been away from her own life for longer than Karen had, but she felt no compelling need to get back to

New York. More often, she felt she couldn't fit in there if she tried, or, worse, that there simply was no former life to return to at all. Then she remembered her bedtime prayer. How could she become the new person she felt was possible if she held on to the old? "Whatever I can do to help, I want to do," she said.

"I have to stay busy," Karen said.

Ellen sat down at the table. "That's a good idea." She knew that whenever she herself knocked off work, she suffered a period of intense despair as all the feelings she avoided by overdoing it rushed at her like kung fu experts. "Are you going over to Rodney's this morning?" she asked.

"Not until he calls. The poor guy is completely beat."

"I'd like to be a fly on the wall of his mind," Ellen said as she sipped her tea.

"I did ask him how he was handling it all, the weirdness, and he mumbled, 'I'm just doing my assignment.'"

Ellen mused on this as she sipped her tea. "At least he knows what his assignment is," she said.

"Maybe we're all doing our assignments."

"You think so? Because if life is homework, the dog ate mine," Ellen said. "If it's a test, I think I'm failing."

"You think too much." Karen laughed. "Let's do something." She looked around. "Let's go buy some paint scrapers and scrape the house. It needs a facelift. Let's give it a coat of paint."

Could that possibly be their assignment, Ellen wondered as they sped down the mountain with the windows down and the heat blasting so the engine wouldn't seize up before they even made it to the hardware store on Main Street, Lamone.

forty-four

Ellen scraped back and forth, forth and back, on the north side of her little farmhouse. Filthy paint chips, probably composed entirely of lead, fell, or in some cases seemed to leap with joy, into the grass, and the squawk of the scraper over the hundred-year-old clapboards became peace-inducing white noise as soothing as the song of the nightingales of Taipei. Even though her shoulders ached and her neck felt as if a steel rod had been permanently wedged between her vertebrae, she scraped on. When blisters rose, she donned leather gloves. She became totally at ease perched fifteen feet above the ground on the rung of a rickety wooden ladder.

"You're a maniac!" Karen laughed when Ellen declined to knock off for lunch on the first day.

"I'm deep in meditation," Ellen answered.

Ellen had once written an article for a pop psychology magazine about a rabbit ranch run by the developmentally disabled. All day long, the residents combed Angora rabbits, collecting the soft fur into clear plastic garbage bags and selling it off in large lots to a manufacturer of expensive sweaters for the rich and trendy. The counselor had told Ellen that the repeated motion of combing was comforting to the men and women who did it. He thought it also developed hand-eye coordination, exercised their concentration skills, and provided a sense of accomplishment as the mound of Angora fur grew larger. At the time, Ellen had assumed that the comfort actually came from cuddling the bunny rabbits, but now, she thought, as she had glanced down at the accumulation of paint chips along the edge of the house, she wasn't sure which part of her chosen chore was really driving her. Maybe it *was* the size of the pile. People fell into behavior patterns and had a compulsion to mindlessly repeat them, no matter how many psychic aches and physical pains developed along the way. And still she scraped.

On the first day, Karen went at it with almost equal gusto, but midway through the second, the art movers from Montreal arrived, two starving actors with chiseled cheekbones and washboard bellies, and off they went to Rodney's to pack up the statue. Four hours later, they were back. As planned, Karen and Rodney would follow them back to Montreal in Rodney's truck. The memorial service for Cocho was scheduled for the next day, at sunset, and Karen had many preparations to make. She had told Ellen that she wanted to spend one night alone in the loft with Rodney and the statue. Ellen had simply nodded and promised to drive up the next day with Olivier. She had held Olivier in her arms and watched as the tiny caravan disappeared down her personal dirt road. She even felt a twinge of concern for Rodney, the country bumpkin off in the big city, though she knew Karen would take good care of him. Ellen's heightened attachment to Rodney was taking all sorts of bizarre forms, but primarily fear that all this excitement and hard work would kill him. She didn't want him to keel over as a direct result of her having turned up in the North Country. She didn't want to lose him before she found a way to show him how much she cared.

This awareness of caring soon delivered her to thoughts of her husband, her estranged husband she would have to say at this point, and she went inside to call him. He would want to come to Cocho's service and he belonged there. She saw by the clock that it was almost seven, which was a good time to catch him at home. It was the cocktail hour, though now that he had cut down on his drinking, she had no idea what had replaced it. Maybe a frosty glass of noni juice.

He answered on the second ring.

"Hi, Tommy. It's me, Ellen."

"A.k.a. Kilroy?" Ellen could tell there was no smile in his voice. "Nice of you to leave a note."

"Yeah, well, it was the best I could drum up at the time," she said defensively.

"Christ, Ellen, I would think you would've tried a little harder on your note when, one, I didn't even know you were coming, and two, you're not even talking to me anymore."

Ellen's face went hot. "Hey! I've only been on the phone with you for five seconds and you've already filed two criminal charges against me."

"I'm not filing criminal charges, I'm saying it would've been nice to get a real note instead of a joke note for once, especially at a time like this. You've cut me totally out of the loop. What's going on? How's Karen? Where's Karen? I left four messages on her machine."

Ellen felt her heart go steely. It happened whenever she felt under attack, even if she deserved it. "Well, actually, the reason I called was to put you in the loop—though, I should point out, my phone also rings."

"I tried to call you at least ten times. You're never home."

Ellen ignored that. "I picked Karen up at JFK, which is what I was doing in *your* apartment. There's a memorial service for Cocho tomorrow night, at sunset, in their loft in Montreal." Each sentence felt like a bullet aimed at Tommy.

"Tomorrow?" he said. "You couldn't give me a little more notice? So I could at least have had a shot at changing a court date so maybe, possibly, I could come?"

"Let me just make sure I'm getting this. You can't come to Cocho's memorial service because you have to be in court."

"I can't come *tomorrow* because I need more than a few hours' notice to change an important trial date that's been set for two frigging months."

"Well, that's fine, Tommy. I hope you win in court."

"That's incredibly unfair. You don't call me to tell me anything, and then when I react you play the victim. You're fucking impossible, Ellen."

"Correction. I'm upset and disappointed. In you." Some part of her felt satisfied, as if she'd just scored a point against him.

"Well, let me tell you something," Tommy said, very softly. "The feeling is mutual. I'm gonna go now. Goodbye, Ellen."

She barely had time to mumble "Goodbye" before the line went dead in her hand.

Whenever Tommy went quiet in a fight, it brought Ellen to her senses. Quiet words resonated longer than yelled words. He had said he was disappointed in her. She had left him out of the loop, come and gone from their apartment with nothing more than a three word note, and not been at home to receive his phone calls. Now she felt repentant and quickly dialed his number. There was no answer, and the phone machine did not pick up. Every interaction with Tommy went haywire.

She tried his number again, and this time it was busy. Maybe he's trying to call me, she thought as she quickly replaced the receiver. But her phone didn't ring. She slumped into a chair. The Dalai Lama advised the people of the world to rectify their mistakes as soon as they became aware they had made them. Ellen had made several. She *had* left Tommy out of the loop. And why? Because she was afraid he was gone anyway, or she was, and she desperately wanted to avoid facing it. She dialed again. Still busy.

Probably Tommy was talking it all over with the yoga teacher, she thought, but then she took it back and just sat there with her own fear hijacking her heart cells, one by one. If you didn't run from such feelings and there was no one to lash out at, what could you do? The fight or flight instinct was a gyp, Ellen thought, and being taught about it so glibly in science class was a disservice that only made life worse. Nobody ever mentioned the flip side of those options: if you ran away, your fear and sense of terminal wimphood increased over time; if you fought and lost, you could end up a bloody mess with your front teeth missing and multiple bruises about the jawline. If you froze in your tracks, hoping the danger would pass you by, you were probably scheduled for nightmares for years to come, and if you simply gave up, you got plowed under, buried alive and suffocated by your own powerlessness.

"There has to be more to it than this," Ellen said to Olivier. "There have to be more options. This just can't be it. It can't." How could seventeen years of fairly good rapport suddenly blow up in a couple's face? Her marriage was burning down around her and she was trapped in the flames.

The phone rang. Ellen practically yanked it off the wall. "Hello? Hello?" she repeated as if the phone was not in working order.

"Ellen," Tommy said, "you seem to be doing everything you possibly can to sabotage our marriage, and before you succeed completely, I want to ask you one question. Do you really think, realistically now, that there's something better out there for you than our life together? And someone better out there for you than me?"

Ellen felt moisture squeeze out her pores onto her forehead and fingers. "Tommy," she said softly, "it would be hard if not impossible to imagine a better life for me or a better person for me than you. But if it all falls down, that's what I'll have to believe. And so should you."

"Okay," said Tommy in his lawyer voice, "I just wanted to clarify that." He hung up.

Ellen felt a rumble of laughter building in her intestines. This retreat into helpless hilarity was happening all too frequently of late. It would be unnerving if it wasn't so fucking funny. "Here I go again," she said to Olivier as an avalanche of laughter dislodged her from her emotional space and carried her off. "That's what I'd have to believe!" she crowed in awe as her eyes filled with tears. "That's what I'd have to believe!" she repeated, louder this time. She lifted Olivier off the floor and performed a St. Vitus dance in the kitchen. He giggled and placed his little brown hand on Ellen's cheek.

"Happy?" he asked.

"Yes, yes, happy!" Ellen said, though she didn't have a clue in the world if that was accurate or not. "Let's go out and scrape the house!"

forty-five

Ellen had promised Karen that she would arrive in Montreal by three in the afternoon to help her prepare for Cocho's memorial gathering and the unveiling of Rodney's wonder statue. In the morning, she collected vegetables from her garden to take along for the food table and spent two hours on the porch swing with a notebook in her hand, composing a speech about Rodney. It seemed odd. Memorials were supposed to be about the deceased, not the living. But in this case, the lines were blurred, so Ellen plodded on, though she ripped up everything she wrote. When she didn't have a working draft by eleven, she finally went upstairs and climbed into the bathtub with Olivier. His favorite water toy was a plastic submarine, and, as she sunk it for his amusement, it hit her that once this bath was complete, she should pack it up along with his other things because today was the day Olivier returned home.

No more submarine in the bathtub.

No more pots and pans clanging on the kitchen floor.

No more little boy in the pile of dirt with his dump truck.

It was too sad. She climbed out of the tub, dried them both off, and got dressed. She put Olivier in a white T-shirt and a pair of dungarees like a tiny Marlon Brando. "Say, *Stella!*" she prodded, doing her very best Stanley Kowalski. Olivier complied, and they played *Streetcar* until it was time to hit the road.

But when she turned the key in the ignition, expecting the Honda to roar to life as usual, there was nothing but dense silence interrupted by a feeble click. "Don't even *think* about it, you motherfucker!" she screamed, jamming the gas pedal to the floor until her knee locked and rattling the ignition switch in hopes of catching that one small spark that would get things underway. When it didn't work, she released the brake, put the car in neutral, opened her door, stepped out, braced herself against the car frame, and rocked the whole car forward until it passed a small bump and began to roll through the yard toward the garden. If she couldn't jump-start it before it hit the first row of tomatoes, she was a goner.

With long experience in the sixties at the art of pop-starting recalcitrant cars, Ellen waited until the perfect moment to release the clutch. The Honda sputtered slightly, a small cough, but didn't catch. "You shitbox!" Ellen roared. "You piece of living shit!" Olivier started to cry.

"I'm not yelling at you, Sweetie," she said in the syrupy sweet voice of a woman with multiple personality disorder. "Auntie Ellen's just mad at her fucking car." Defeated, she yanked up the emergency brake so the Honda wouldn't plow into her garden, freed Olivier from his seat, and tore into the house.

There were no car rental businesses listed in Lamone and only one 800 number for bus information. Quickly, she dialed it, only to find that the one daily bus that offered a connection to Montreal went east toward Plattsburgh, where a change was necessary, and took four and a half hours to get to the city. Plus, she had missed it.

Tugging at the neckline of her travel dress, she called both local taxis, but neither had a free cab to drive her into Canada. "Look, do you know anybody who's out of work who has a car? I'll pay two hundred bucks."

"I know one guy," the dispatcher said. "Gimme your number." She did, and then nervously paced the kitchen. This is a disaster, she thought. Stranded in a one-horse town without car rental companies or decent taxi service! In New York, she could snap her fingers and anything the mind could imagine would be delivered to her door within an hour. Here, she could snap, crackle, and pop until she was blue in the face, and absolutely nothing would happen.

Suddenly she thought of Rayfield and she quickly dialed his number.

"You rang?" he said on the fifth ring.

"Rayfield, thank God you're there!" she screamed into the receiver. "I'm fucked, Rayfield. I'm hysterical. Can you lend me your truck right now? This minute? Can you bring it over here right now?"

"My truck?"

"Yes, yes. My car crapped out and I'm here with Olivier and we have to go to Montreal for Cocho's memorial service in"—she glanced at her watch. It was now almost four—"in three hours. I was supposed to get there early to help Karen. And I can't get my frigging car to start."

"Where's it at?"

"Who cares? Who gives a shit? It's in the garden!" She was yelling. "Please, Rayfield, help me out here."

"I'm on my way," he said.

"Thank you, thank you," Ellen said. Saved by Rayfield! She ran outside to remove Olivier's car seat from the Honda. Twenty minutes later, when Rayfield roared into the driveway, Ellen had the seat, Olivier's suitcase and toys, her vegetables, and her change of clothes piled up neatly next to the driveway.

"I thought about it on the way over," he said as he opened the door, "and I'm gonna drive you. My truck ain't really seaworthy, you know. You wouldn't make it on your own to Montreal. Hell, you probably wouldn't even make it to Lamone."

"Fine, fine," Ellen said, "whatever. I'll pay you, Rayfield. I'll pay you and I'll owe you, too." She knew she was babbling, but he wasn't really listening anyway. He began to fasten Olivier's seat into the truck cab while Ellen pitched the bags into the back. She put her vegetables on the floor in the front seat, though, because she didn't want them to absorb the toxins from Rayfield's useless exhaust system. Then she ran into the house to call Karen.

She got the answering machine. "Karen! I had a car disaster, but it's solved and we're on our way. We're leaving now. It's four thirty. Don't worry. We'll be there." She hung up and ran out, slamming the door behind her. Olivier was already secured in his seat, and she had to climb in the driver's door and sit with her legs crossed to the right so Rayfield could shift. Each time he did, his hairy paw moved along her thigh line within an inch of her private parts, though he seemed oblivious to that, and her body was actually pressed against his as closely as it would be in a crowded subway car. She tried to move away but Olivier's chair had her completely wedged in. She simply surrendered, and when her half spinal twist became unbearable, she shifted her legs so the gearshift was between her legs and just hoped Rayfield wouldn't take advantage during downshifting. At the border, he had the presence of mind to turn the engine off and coast to a stop in front of the custom's agent just in case they wouldn't welcome a redneck with a problem muffler into the quiet country lanes of Quebec.

"*Bonjour,* hello," said the customs agent, whom Ellen recognized after so many border crossings.

"*Bonjour,*" she said around Rayfield, playing the French game.

"*Où allez-vous?*"

"*Nous allons à Montréal,*" Rayfield said. "*Nous prenons le neveu de mon ami chez sa mère.*"

"*Elle habite à Montréal?*"

"*Oui.*"

"*Est-elle canadienne?*"

Rayfield turned to Ellen who was slack-jawed listening to him. "Karen a Canadian citizen?" he asked.

"She's a landed immigrant," Ellen said in English to the border guard. "She's lived in Montreal for five years."

"*Et vous n'avez pas quelquechose à déclarer?*

"*Non, rien,*" said Rayfield.

"*Bon. Passez-vous et bienvenue au Québec.*"

"*Merci.*" Rayfield waited until the officer went back inside before he fired up the noisy truck and took off.

"Rayfield," Ellen said, "you speak French!"

"Only when I have to."

"I'm impressed. I'm amazed."

"For chrissakes, Ellen, what kind of a name do you think Geebo is? Serbo-Croatian?"

"French Canadian?" Ellen asked rhetorically.

"My grandmother and grandfather never talked English at all. I grew up talking French."

Ellen was silent for a few seconds. "It's such an accomplishment to be bilingual." She paused. "Why didn't you speak French to Olivier?"

"This is America," Rayfield said, even though they were now in Canada.

"Oh." Ellen let it drop. It was hard to hold a conversation over the roar of the muffler anyway. Finally she yelled, "Do you know the way?"

"To Old Montreal? *Bien sûr. Mais oui. Naturellement,*" replied Rayfield.

Onward they sped. Children in the tiny river towns stopped what they were doing to stare and point at the noisy truck. It was six before they arrived at the Mercier Bridge and rush-hour traffic was in full swing. Rayfield slid between lanes with the precision and grace of a New York cabbie, and in due time, Ellen directed him to a parking space a half block from Ng's fruit and vegetable stand.

She piled out the driver's side after Rayfield and staggered a few steps around the car to get her circulation revved up again. Meanwhile, Rayfield freed Olivier and began to collect the bags that needed to be schlepped inside. Ellen turned toward him in the building doorway. "Rayfield, I can never thank you enough for this. You saved my life this time."

His face looked blank, as if he didn't really grasp the fact that he was being dismissed. And until Ellen saw that look of incomprehension, she hadn't realized that she *meant* to send him on his way—to use him for the ride and then bar the door. "Jeez, Rayfield, did you want to come up?" she said apologetically.

"Well, I thought . . . I . . . ." He seemed quite flustered. "I guess I thought I could go to the memorial service," he said. "As Ollie's friend and your friend. But if it ain't public, I understand and—"

"Of course, you're welcome," Ellen said. "It just didn't occur to me that you'd want to come." She felt ashamed of herself for treating Rayfield like a nonentity. Hadn't he broken down and sobbed when he learned of Cocho's death? Hadn't he been the only one—the only one—to whom Ellen had told the story of Rodney's miracle statue? Hadn't he just rushed her to Montreal on his trusty, or at least rusty, steed? "Please, please come to the service," she said. "Let's hurry."

She turned around again and was just about ready to enter the building when an old van pulled up and double-parked. "Hey," called a man in the passenger seat wearing a do-rag, "you going up to Karen and Cocho's?"

"Yeah," Ellen said, experiencing a sharp stab of sadness. It really wasn't Cocho's place anymore.

"Carry some of these chairs up, will you?" He hopped out and began to unload a huge stack of metal folding chairs.

"I got 'em," Rayfield said as he hung Olivier's bag over Ellen's shoulder and draped her dress there, too.

"Fourth floor," Ellen said as she hooked the front door open. Olivier was already scrambling up the stairs. Without a free hand, she could only position herself behind him in case he lost his balance, but on the second-floor landing, she dropped her various bags and picked him up. She could hear Rayfield and the do-rag guy clanking up the stairs, and when she peeked over the railing, she saw them ascending with chairs hanging from both arms.

The door to the loft was wide-open and a photo of Cocho had been enlarged and hung on it as if he himself were there to greet you. In it, Cocho sat on the wide windowsill of the loft with nothing but rooftops, river traffic, and sky behind him. With a start, Ellen recognized it as a photo she had taken the previous year when she and Tommy had come up for Olivier's first birthday party. At the time, she had thought that Cocho, seated on the sill with his feet pulled up, looked as if he had just flown in to perch there—a new species of urban bird. Now, oddly, it looked more like he was about to take off into the wild blue yonder. It was actually a stunning photo, Ellen thought, taken in the context of today. She lowered Olivier to the floor and he ran in calling, "Mama, Mama!"

Ellen stepped across the threshold. Cocho's whimsical melodies filled the room, and exotic floral arrangements, in which birds-of-paradise seemed to have paused midflight to appreciate the intense colors of the flowers around them, rose from every surface. Rodney's statue was covered with a canvas tarp that permitted just the barest suggestion of what was inside. It was like a church—perhaps Holy Week in the Catholic chapel of her youth, when, for some forgotten reason, all the statues were hidden under mysterious purple drapes. Once, decades before, she had visited the Acoma pueblo in New

Mexico, a Native American village atop a four-hundred-foot rock, which had been continuously inhabited for a thousand years. The guide had described it as "very peace and quiet," and now the phrase emerged from her memory like a sealed cask rising to the surface of the open sea. The serenity seemed to wash through her like a warm river of light, and she felt herself breathe deeper.

"Ellen! Oh, my God, thank God you made it. I was freaking out!" Karen said as she ran to embrace her sister. Karen wore a skintight, sleeveless white dress with a boat neck and a hemline that stopped a good five inches above her knees. She had silver bracelets on both wrists and a pair of delicate pink ballet slippers on her feet. She looked iridescent and somehow luminous, like a moon goddess or a vestal virgin, forever pure and undefiled.

Behind her, Ellen saw Regine-Marie and Rodney involved in a project that included scissors, paper, and a tabletop laminating machine, while two other women whom Ellen recognized from the café were cutting and speed-chopping in the kitchen area. Ellen wanted to tell Karen that the loft felt like sacred space, but now the frenzy of activity had captured her. "The chairs are right behind me," she said instead of hello, "and I brought vegetables from my garden. They're on the landing downstairs. I'll go get them. I'm sorry to be so late. Oh, Rayfield brought me and he's on his way up."

Suddenly, Ellen realized that Rodney might not want his personal enemy here for the unveiling of his mystery statue. She glanced at him and saw that he was totally focused on what he was doing. Paranoid, she felt he was purposely avoiding eye contact, and she made a mental note to explain and apologize as soon as it was logistically possible. In that second, Rayfield stepped into the doorway. Perhaps it was the show of strength, what with a dozen folding chairs hanging from each arm, or the atmosphere of quiet appreciation in the loft, or the fact that now Ellen knew he spoke French, but Rayfield seemed somewhat more rakish. A manly man, as her mother would have said.

"I prefer my men to be sensitive," Ellen had shot back in the sixties. "Attila the Hun as the model of masculinity has been officially evicted from the mass female psyche, Mom. And good riddance! Let him rot!"

"I like a manly man," Joyce had repeated, rather mildly.

"Oh, brother," Ellen replied in disgust, "give me brains over brawn any day."

And now, twenty-five years later, she was noticing that the muscle definition of Rayfield's arms, which she had never noticed before, was actually very attractive. And there was something to be said for being able to hump eighty-five pounds of folding chairs up four flights without flinching.

"Chair biped," Rayfield called as if to announce himself to the group. "Have chairs, will travel." Karen moved toward him and Ellen saw Rayfield straighten up to better appreciate her. There was no doubt that Karen was a beauty. Ellen, at her peak, had just been pretty. She had just had a taste of the adoration Karen evoked and even that had kept her fucking full time in the sixties. If she had had Karen's looks, she probably would've gone into orbit, perhaps reached the moon before the Apollo spacecraft did.

But why was she even comparing herself to Karen? With shock, she traced it to the look of interest that had caused Rayfield's eyeballs to bug-out of his head for a split second before Karen said, "Hi, you must be Rayfield. I guess between my sister and me, we've really got you working today."

"Where do you want 'em?" Rayfield asked.

"There," Karen said, pointing toward the covered statue. "Could you set them up in a shallow arc with a center aisle?"

"One shallow arc, coming up," Rayfield said. The do-rag guy, carrying half as many chairs, arrived, and they went to work. Ellen scampered down the stairs to bring up her bag of veggies. It was just a half hour until the memorial service would begin.

"Can I jump in the shower?" Ellen asked. She felt gritty, as if exhaust fumes from Rayfield's truck had hardened on her skin.

"Sure. I think we're covered here."

Ellen looked around. Platters of healthy food were assembled on the kitchen counters, chairs were being arranged as requested, and Rodney and Regine-Marie were cranking out cards with miniature versions of Ellen's photo of Cocho for each mourner to tuck into a wallet or place on the fridge with a magnet. Cocho's flute gently filled the space with curves and spirals of music, and the river out the window was a silver stripe in the afternoon sun.

"It's so beautiful here." Ellen sighed.

"Tommy sent the flowers," Karen said. "All of them."

Ellen surveyed the room. Flowers stretched skyward from every tabletop and windowsill. In addition to the large flock of birds-of-paradise, there were sunflowers enough to provide numerous jars of seeds for future snacks. Tommy must have spent five-hundred dollars, Ellen thought.

"I talked to him for a long time last night," Karen said, her voice neutral but her eye contact intense.

"Yeah?" Ellen said uncertainly. "How'd he sound?"

"Heartbroken," Karen said.

Ellen, feeling as if she'd just received a hard sock in the solar plexus, rushed into the bathroom and jumped into the shower, where her tears became just so many additional droplets of water destined for the cosmic drain.

forty-six

Ellen emerged from the bathroom fifteen minutes later. She had pulled herself together because no matter what might happen or had happened between her and Tommy, it was minor in comparison to what Karen had been facing for weeks and would continue to face for years to come, if not for her whole life. The first of the mourners had already arrived and collected around the food table in what could have been a poster celebrating the wonderful world of racial diversity in Montreal. The music had been turned up very slightly, as if Cocho were breathing life into the party from beyond the pale. Ellen noticed that Rayfield was seated on the couch with Olivier in his lap reading a picture book, while Rodney was on the far side of the loft listening to a woman a third his age who wore a large "Jews for Jesus" pin on her eyelet sundress.

It suddenly occurred to Ellen that no one who would climb the stairs to this little paradise knew about Rodney's statue. Karen had decided to keep it a secret until the whole story could be told. Cocho and Karen's friends were simply here to offer their sympathy and support. Perhaps they had experienced a kind of dread as they entered the loft or been uncomfortable about how to approach the grieving widow. But each and every one of them was going to leave with their mind blown. In a few hours, they would spill into the streets of Old Montreal in a kind of daze, as if they had been catapulted into someone else's crazy dream. The statue stood, covered and mysterious, as the focal point of Rayfield's arc of chairs. From where Ellen stood, if she squinted her eyes just a little, the shape of the arc was like a canoe and the statue, in the middle and covered with white canvas, was the mast. Where were all the passengers going? Destination: unknown. And the identity of the captain? Up for grabs.

Ellen wandered toward the food table where her beautiful organic veggies waited in pretty, color-coded rows. She grabbed a tomato wedge and stuffed it into her face, which made it somewhat difficult to talk when she was introduced to the first of Karen and Cocho's friends. Ellen shook hands and smiled crookedly, like a chipmunk whose cheeks were full. She noticed that Karen had a fistful of Kleenex and kept dabbing at the corners of her eyes, as if she didn't want her tears to get away from her, perhaps to splash down on the floor where someone might slip in them and fall. Watching her, Ellen wondered if Karen felt hostess pressure or if she was past that now that she had to cope with the raw emotions of the well-wishers. Maybe having her secret to tell was a source of strength. Karen was a person who established a goal and worked tirelessly toward it. When she reached it, she set another and carried on. Now, she wanted to both honor Cocho and share with his friends the magic of Rodney's sculpture. After that? Perhaps her long-range plan was to stay in touch with the mystery. Not only to endure, but to triumph over the world of doubt and live in the realm of belief.

When Carl Jung was asked if he believed in God, he had said something like, "I don't have to believe. I know." Ellen had been simultaneously charmed and appalled by his smug response. At what point did zealous belief so imprint itself on the cells that it felt like sure knowledge? Was something lost or gained in that process? It was hard to overlook the mayhem that religious belief created, but perhaps knowledge was a different thing. Her attention drifted again toward the statue. Given it as proof, was there any point in doubting anymore? Yet she still resisted surrendering. Somehow, "I don't know" was preferable to "I know." It seemed more honest. It seemed easier, too, because it required less personal commitment.

The loft was crowded now and people were beginning to sit down on the folding chairs. They talked softly among themselves, smiled warmly when they caught Karen's eye, and reached out to touch one another, perhaps more than was usual. It struck Ellen that she would soon be expected to say her piece, the speech about Rodney that she had not prepared. She moved toward the arc of chairs and sat down in the front row, hoping to clear her mind for the talk ahead. No sooner did she land, though, than Olivier toddled over. He raised his arms like a sun worshipper, and Ellen lifted him to her lap. Rayfield came over and sat down next to them. Ellen noticed that the children's book he had in his lap was in French.

"Good book?" she asked with a smile.

"It's about a lonely cucumber that gets lost in a pea patch."

"Happy ending?"

"I don't know. The kid lost interest halfway through." She saw then that his finger was stuck in the middle of the book, holding the page.

"Why don't you finish it? I'd love to hear you read in French."

"Really?" Rayfield looked skeptical.

"Yes, really."

"You won't be able to understand it, will you?"

"I'll look at the pictures," Ellen said with a slight edge. "Besides, I know how it feels to be a big, fat cucumber in a pea patch." Rayfield opened the book and Ellen shifted Olivier onto her other knee so he could see better. In the picture, a green cuke with white oval eyes and slash eyebrows—not unlike the ones she had received in the trendy salon three blocks away—towered over all the little peas like a tyrannosaurus rex on an ant farm. The cucumber, which was dressed in overalls like a farmer, looked ready to cry.

"Ellen?" Rayfield said before he started to read, "sometimes misfits are just people who are larger than life." He looked directly at Ellen and, to her surprise, his eyes began to sparkle with tears.

My God, Ellen thought as he immediately turned his attention to the book and started to read, he's talking about me. Even if it was just a momentary feeling, brought on by the intense emotions all around them, this was stupefying. People had accused her of being a pain in the ass and a shit disturber; they had fired her for insubordination and stormed out of her presence in a rage. But nobody had ever hinted that she was larger than life. It was a great shock, especially coming from Rayfield Geebo, who called it like he saw it. She felt humble. It was a clean feeling in which she experienced awe and insignificance in equal proportions and felt free.

All around her, the lovely sounds of French rose like smoke signals, and one by one the chairs filled, and after a while, a kind of hush filled the room. Even the music stopped. Karen walked to the front of the group. Behind her, the sun was a flaming orange ball and, from certain angles, Karen seemed like a modified human lightning rod, designed to channel the last of the day's solar power into the room.

"I want to start with a moment of silence," Karen said. She stood with her arms at her sides, palms slightly open and facing front, and closed her eyes. It was a familiar position that Ellen recognized from the bathtub Marys of Eagle Beak. Of course, those Marys were not clad in skimpy mini-dresses, but then, Mary had lived in the desert where sun protection was an absolute must. The quiet in the room seemed to pulsate and Ellen felt heat engulf her. It made her dizzy, and she reached for Rayfield's hand to keep from swooning, falling into a heap at Karen's feet. Rayfield's hand was cool compared to hers, and he exerted just enough pressure to ground her. With her free hand, she held Olivier around his waist. She could feel the expansion and contraction of his body and breath beneath her fingers, and when she opened her own eyes to peek at him, he was quizzically turning his head from his mother to his auntie, from Rayfield to Rodney, and then the Ngs, Regine-Marie, and all the others. He didn't make a peep. In the silence, Ellen could hear soft whimpers, like puppies dreaming, and she thought, though it was probably her imagination, that she could identify the splash of individual teardrops on the floor.

Softly, the sound of Cocho's flute began to rise again, and when Ellen opened her eyes, Karen had shifted, as if she had to place her feet in a different location in order to speak. She looked so small and vulnerable in her white dress. In Ellen's youth, the image of Jackie Kennedy, black veiled and mysterious, had established the archetype of the young widow. Darkness had seemed the only way to express such monumental grief and loss. Karen was the complete reverse. Her face was scrubbed clean, her hair was pulled straight back into a simple ponytail, and she had never looked more open. Grief had many faces, Ellen knew, and suddenly she felt afraid, and without meaning to, she buried her face in Rayfield's shoulder and tried to smother the sobs that she felt would weaken, not strengthen, her sister in her hour of need. When he put his arms around her, she sank even deeper into his chest. Karen began to speak.

"When Cocho died, I was sitting by his bedside in a tiny hospital in Peru. I spent six weeks there, just staring into his beautiful face. I learned that when you spend a great deal of time with a dying person, you become completely tuned into the subtleties that we rarely notice in each other at other times. A slight change of skin color, a fleeting look of anxiety or peace, a change in the rhythm of breathing—these become significant and important. They become everything. So I am sure that I know the exact second when the spark of life disappeared from Cocho. Life was there and he was there, and then life went away and Cocho was gone, at least from that body that I loved so dearly.

"I knew I couldn't die and go with him, though in a way I wanted to. I couldn't bear to be separated so soon. Our little boy is not even two. His parents and I took his body to the village where he was born, and I saw my great love put in the ground and covered with dirt and rocks, and I thought, I can't go on. I really can't. But somehow I got back to Lima and I called my sister, Ellen, and she told me to get on the first plane out, which was going to New York, and she picked me up there. I was in a black hole, a deep lonely black hole for three days. My sister was my lifeline and my strength."

The whole congregation was riveted. Ellen could feel the heightened attention pulsating in the air. It was the power of the story. For her whole life, while listening to or sometimes telling stories, her insides would begin to shake and knock against her ribs as if there were impersonal secrets there that were desperate to be released. Stories transformed people. They changed lives and had the power to heal.

Karen took a breath. "The three days are important," she said, "because somewhere else, far away from Peru and New York, something very strange was happening." Even Ellen leaned forward in her seat to listen, and was therefore somewhat shocked when Karen said, "My sister will tell you this part."

As she rose to her feet, Ellen felt unprepared in every possible way. Her eyes were so flooded with tears that she saw the assembled group as patches of watercolors bleeding into one other. She moved toward Karen and took her hand. She had probably not held her sister's hand since Karen was a child who had had to reach up, up, up to grasp Ellen's fingers. Now they were the same size, two grown women cut from the same genetic material. Ellen squeezed, perhaps too hard.

"Three months ago, on an insane whim, I bought a tumble-down farm-house. The owner, Viola de Beer, had died years before and left it to her son, Rodney. Rodney and I got off to a rocky start." She glanced quickly at Rodney, whose face looked pink with expectancy. And suddenly, she was telling the story of the leaky roof and the rain barrel, and though her tears kept coming, she began to hear people laughing out loud. Karen giggled too, and Ellen realized that she had never told her this story. All the laughter came dangerously close to triggering a fit, but Ellen jumped the tracks in time. "Over time, I learned about Rodney's life. I pried it out of him, really, and"—her voice broke, but she continued—"and I began to love him."

The giggling stopped abruptly, and Ellen had to swallow hard to continue. She glanced helplessly around the room, and in her blurred vision, she thought for a second that she saw Tommy at the very back of the crowded room. Her heart jumped before she realized it simply wasn't him. Tommy wasn't there.

"Anyway, I hope I'm not saying too much about his personal life when I say that it was hard. Very hard. He never knew his father. But the day before Co-cho died, I decided to yank the slipcover off an old chair in Viola's living room, and I found three letters hidden there, hidden for decades, from Rod-ney's father to his mother. And the night that Cocho died, before I even knew Cocho had passed on, I told Rodney about the letters and he got very upset and mad at me for butting into his life and telling him about the father he never knew, and he stormed out of my house and went home."

She wiped a layer of tears away and looked at Rodney. His chin was quivering and his fleshy old face was blotchy and red. "Your turn, Rodney," she said.

He seemed shocked, but he got to his feet and came forward. Karen and Ellen dropped hands and drew him in between them, holding his fingers tight. They stood there like paper dolls cut out of an old brown sack. "I couldn't sleep that night. I went down to my wood shop and I started to work." He stopped. "I guess that's it," he added after thinking for a few seconds.

"That's it?" Ellen asked, and a few people laughed.

"Jeezum, I didn't know what was happening to me," he said. "I thought it was something about my father, but it wasn't. The plain truth is, I don't know."

Olivier had climbed off Rayfield's lap and toddled over to his mother. Karen picked him up. "Nobody knows how it happened," Karen said, "but we do know *what* happened. Remember that Rodney never met Cocho and he didn't know that he died. And, really, Rodney didn't have the chance to know much about the father-son bond." She stepped to the side of the sculpture and cut the rope that held the drape. The canvas fell away, and there it was.

A collective gasp erupted in the loft, followed by complete silence. Then Olivier said, "Papa?" and pandemonium broke loose. People shot to their feet. Someone cranked up the music. Rodney was spontaneously placed in a sturdy chair, lifted above the group, and paraded around the loft like the groom at a Jewish wedding. And of all the people cheering, raising Rodney higher and higher, Rayfield, who had a hold of the front left leg of the chair, was hollering the loudest. And then, like a kaleidoscope, the image shifted and everyone formed circles around the statue, two circles, and then they began to dance, one circle to the right and the other to the left, and they chanted the name, "Cocho! Cocho!" And Cocho smiled down on them all from within the wooden statue. And then the kaleidoscope shifted again, and everyone turned to the next person and hugged for dear life. Ellen threw her arms around Grandmother Ng and saw, over Grandmother's narrow shoulders, Karen and Regine-Marie holding each other, and just to their left, Rayfield and Rodney were locked in a bear hug. And then boxes of votive candles were produced from a paper bag, and Karen asked each person to think of a memory of Cocho, a beautiful and good memory, and when they had one, to light the candle and hold it high. When the whole loft was ablaze with candlelight and sunset, Karen said, "We will never forget you, Cocho. We are with you as you are with us, now and forever." A few people said, "Amen," and then they all put the candles in a circle around the statue, which seemed to absorb the light and positively glow from within.

forty-seven

Adrenaline, thought Ellen as she lay, exhausted, on the couch at four in the morning with her eyes wide-open, is a violent thing. It releases from the adrenal glands like rocket fuel, giving the human body oomph enough to do the impossible, but then it evaporates and leaves you wasted. So it was definitely not an adrenaline burst that had exploded like an A-bomb over the memorial service group. True, the collective energy level had shot off the charts in the minutes after the unveiling, and all hell—or more correctly, all heaven—had broken loose, but instead of passing, it had built up into some metaphoric cube of space that made any other memorial service, or any other wild party for that matter, merely two-dimensional by comparison. Instead of idle party chatter or morbid or sentimental remembrances, strangers were asking one other if they believed in God, if the soul existed and if so, was it individualized in the afterlife, if disembodied spirits lingered on earth to protect their loved ones. People clasped Rodney's hands in wonder and stood in front of his glorious statue in reverie. Karen floated from person to person, sometimes smiling beatifically and sometimes crying, as if her system were intent on gently flushing out some of the grief. At one point, Ellen saw Rayfield and Rodney standing together in the corner, and she maneuvered herself into earshot and shamelessly eavesdropped.

"I think I *was* scared shitless," Rayfield was saying, "and I *did* want to get the hell out of there, and that's why I ran. You were right, but I couldn't see it."

"I probably would've did the same thing," Rodney said, and Ellen drifted away, quietly amazed that they had each reversed position and were thus able, finally, to meet in the middle. Later, Ellen saw one of the chubbier women pass Rayfield a folded note, which he carefully placed in his T-shirt pocket, and when Karen's antique grandfather clock struck midnight, Rayfield and Rodney left together for the drive home in Rayfield's truck. Rodney left his for Ellen, who planned to follow the next day, after cleanup.

The last guest did not depart the loft until two thirty, at which time Karen found, outside the door, a cardboard box with a hand-painted sign above it. LEAVE SOMETHING FOR OLIVIER, it read. A PERSONAL MEMENTO OF THIS GATHERING FROM YOUR POCKET. She had carried it inside and placed it on the kitchen table. "I'll look tomorrow," she said as she joined Ellen on the couch. They sat up to watch the subtle, shifting moonlight on the statue.

"Do you think you'll ever get used to it?" Ellen asked, mesmerized.

"God, I hope not," Karen said. After a half minute, she added, "Peak experiences do have a way of flattening out, though. I'm really afraid of that."

Ellen reached for her hand. "Maybe when they do, they raise your basic elevation." And it can happen to anyone, this uplifting. Anybody. Any minute, she thought.

She turned to face the contours of Cocho's cherry wood face in the dim light, and she felt that she had raised the anchor and sailed away from her former self. She had left her baggage on the cosmic dock, and she felt light, free, and unencumbered. In the sixties, her hero, Janis Joplin, had sung about freedom. It's "just another word for nothing left to lose," Janis had said. Ellen had liked the song but doubted the definition. Now, decades later, she found herself wondering. Had she lost everything already? It was an awesome thought. During the memorial service she had seen a shape she imagined for a second was Tommy. Her heart leapt and then crash-landed in disappointment. Had she really lost her husband? And if so, how long would it take for the hallucinations of him, like the one she'd experienced during the memorial service, to stop?

She stood up, feeling drawn to the statue, and placed a chair next to it so she could climb up and have eye-level contact with Cocho. For the first time, she saw that the pupils of his eyes were actually little holes, carefully dug out of the wood, perhaps by one of the tiny drills that Rodney had hanging among his antique hand tools. She leaned even closer and peered in, even though she knew there was nothing to see.

If Tommy was gone now, he had probably been gone for a long time. She reached out to touch the statue of her brother-in-law, whom she knew more now that he was dead and gone than she'd ever known him when he was alive and well. She placed her hand on his chest and for a second she thought she felt the fibrillation of a beating heart. "I love you, Cocho," she said. "Now and forever."

She climbed back down off the chair, returned to the couch, and buried her face in its overstuffed pillows. "I love you, Karen, I love you, Olivier. I love you, Ellen. I love you, Rodney. I love you, Rayfield. I love you, Tommy," she whispered.

"I love you, Tommy, even if you are gone. Even if I am," she said again into the pillow, which she held tightly against her body, as if it were her lover. Or her husband.

forty-eight

Ellen woke up gently with Olivier patting her face as if he were massaging the cells of her forehead, cheeks, nose, and chin back to life for a new day. "Hello, my honey," she said as she opened her eyes. From her perspective on the couch, there were two Oliviers—one standing in front of her and the second several feet away, holding his father's hand. She heard the muted sound of Karen in the kitchen, and soon the aroma of Central American coffee beans filled the loft. A random fact arrived in her head: in the world consumer market, coffee is second only to oil. How odd that barrels of oil and burlap bags of coffee were crisscrossing the seas of Planet Earth in record numbers, all because people, by nature, desperately wanted what they didn't have in their own backyard. She stretched and sat up. Then she went to the kitchen area to collect her coffee. Karen took one look at her and burst into laughter.

"Gee, that does wonders for the aging ego," said Ellen.

"Go look in the mirror."

When she did, Ellen saw that self-stick postage stamps were plastered all over her face. "Wow," she said loud enough for Karen to hear, "that kid has great manual dexterity for someone his age." Her nephew loved to dig in her purse and had strewn its contents over the kitchen floor numerous times in the past six weeks. She pulled the stamps off her skin, balling them up and tossing them into the trash. Soon her face was bare again, and she took the opportunity to study it in the mirror. There she saw a woman of a certain age. She had crow's-feet that were stretching toward her temples, two deep vertical lines between her eyebrows, a few wiry gray hairs amidst the brown, and a general downward trend to her facial features.

When the baby boomers first began to hit menopause, the mass consciousness suddenly expanded to include the possibility that women who had gone over the hill had possibly arrived in an interesting new place. "Sageing, not aging," read the classified ads in the back of *The Village Voice*, announcing no less than three crone circles forming each week. Ellen had blocked it all out of her mind, but now, as she stared at herself in the last days of being forty-six, she thought that maybe there was something to it. Youth had definitely vacated the facial landscape, but there was a sense of stability around her hills and vales. That had to be worth something.

She scampered back to the kitchen table, where Karen was examining the contents of Olivier's carton. "Look at the stuff!" she said. "It's a treasure chest." Ellen sat down. Shiny quarters, dangling earrings, and a St. Christopher medal were mixed in with lucky marbles, felt-tip pens, and even the do-rag directly from the head of the chair guy. Ellen recognized Rayfield's lapel pin, which read "Sounds like bullshit to me" in block letters, and she was quite certain that Rodney had tossed in a small piece of wood that looked like a pine knot.

"Olivier's going to have a weird life," Ellen said. She looked again into the cardboard box that, no doubt, would become one of Olivier's kooky personal treasures. It was a time capsule in reverse. Instead of commemorating a whole age, with carefully chosen objects, it was a tribute to a brief moment, and the objects were completely random. And the miracle of Rodney's statue, it was random, too. Maybe all over the planet, there were random recipients of amazing gifts from unknown, unexplainable donors. It was a cheerful thought.

Ellen and Karen toiled diligently all morning, and when the noon bells of Notre Dame Cathedral rang, the loft was sparkling, the folding chairs were stacked on the landing, and both sisters had showered and changed in preparation for a long walk through the sunny streets of Old Montreal. Without a word, they had agreed not to talk about last night. Having had the experience, just being in its glorious afterglow, was conversation enough for the moment. The gleam of the river was pleasantly blinding, and even the impatient honks of the car horns had an element of charm, like an urban musical score based on the twelve-tone scale. Eventually, they meandered their way to the Café L'Alibi. Flower boxes spilled over, and purple and pink flowers looked like miniature fireworks against the faded bricks.

"Guess this is when I climb back into the saddle," Karen said.

"And what a comfortable saddle it is," Ellen replied.

Karen stopped on the first step. "You know, I missed this place."

"It's a great place. A temporary rest ranch for the world-weary." Suddenly, Ellen realized that she had never seriously questioned Karen about her work life. She simply took it for granted that her sister was content in it. While she herself was getting exploited, abused, and ultimately canned by one egomaniac after another, Karen was among friends, changing the CD and spearing kiwi slices for both decorative and nutritional purposes. "Do you ever get sick of the job?" she asked.

"So far, so good. But things change."

"That they do," agreed Ellen.

"Anything can happen," Karen said.

"And often does," Ellen replied. She felt poised in the exact epicenter of an important moment.

"Hey," said Karen, "you like tropical birds?"

"Uh-huh," Ellen smiled.

"Take a wing," Karen said, and Ellen tucked her fingers beneath her sister's elbow. In the sixties, just before she had become a vegetarian for life, Ellen had had a boyfriend, a playwright she was crazy about, who had always invited her to take his arm by saying, "You like chicken? Take a wing." Then she had given up meat and couldn't in good conscience reply in the affirmative to the "You like chicken?" setup. Oddly, this had distressed her. The undaunted playwright had tried many alternatives. You like airplanes? You like angels? You like the White House? The tropical birds had been the most satisfying, or perhaps the boyfriend had become history before any dissatisfaction with the substitution set in.

Ellen thought about that sexy playwright as she sat in the café and watched Karen reenter her former life. Like a rocket ship reapproaching earth's atmosphere, Karen had to come in at exactly the right angle to avoid bursting into flames. Graceful and strong as she was, this was not a problem. For Ellen, though, slamming in, head-on, was a way of life. Even as a kid, her every dive into the White River turned out to be a belly whacker. It was her destiny to smack into life's four walls before she had the presence of mind to position herself at the correct angle for reentry, exit, or safe passage through the moment.

Though maybe all that was behind her now. She drove west over the Mercier Bridge in Rodney's truck into the setting sun. She felt essentially different, as if each summer step, from taking the credit card advance and buying Viola's house to participating in the Dionysian frenzy that followed the unveiling of Rodney's statue, had blasted her through the sound barrier or the time barrier or perhaps her own personal Great Barrier Reef. Suddenly, everything seemed more beautiful. At a stoplight in Chateaugay, she noticed that the leaves on the oak trees seemed bigger and better able to soak up sunlight than ever before. The pinks and blues forming in horizontal bands across the sky were unbearably perfect. And when she reached the crest of the Eagle Beak hill, she pulled to the side and climbed out of Rodney's truck. The sky had lost its color now, become a black disk with little star-shaped holes through which the silver light of the great beyond shone. On the horizon, she saw a glow, just a half circle of dim light rising above the edge of the earth, a reverse shadow, and she realized that on a clear night like this, she could see all the way to Montreal. Perhaps Karen and Olivier were curled up there on the couch reading about cucumbers and peas while Cocho stood gentle guard. Or maybe they were at the window, staring up into the night sky. Somewhere behind her, Rodney and Rayfield were moving through the minutes of their lives. Perhaps they, too, had paused for a second and looked up toward the star path with wonder. And Tommy. Even though the stars were barely visible in New York City, maybe he was feeling a momentary urge to climb the steps to the roof of the building, crane his neck, and peer into the pea soup above his head.

Ellen hiked herself up over the edge of Rodney's truck bed and then, as if that weren't high enough, she scrambled up onto the roof and lay down on her back with her feet dangling off, and her eyes wide-open to the night. It was absolutely quiet in Eagle Beak, as if all the noise had emptied out into the empty, spacious sky. And so had her mind. And her cares and worries, her plans, her hopes, her fears. Splayed on the roof of Rodney's truck, Ellen simply was.

forty-nine

The next morning, Ellen stretched out on the swing and watched the rain pour out of the black sky. It pelted into the screen, leaving a dark brown border of wet wood all around the edges of the porch. The mud released a specific smell, *eau du sweat socks* Ellen called it, as a reminder that a whole different world operated beneath the visible surface. Under the lush green summer carpet, beings, microscopic and larger, were hard at nature's work—breaking down, moving, building, breaking down, moving, building. Ellen took deep breaths, noting the similarity of the odor to a certain sexual stimulant of her younger years. It, too, smelled like sweat socks, but when the little yellow bottle was uncapped and the fumes inhaled near the moment of orgasm, the physical sensations of pleasure intensified to produce a frenzy state in which participants would say or do anything. Years later, she had learned that this aphrodisiac was amyl nitrate in disguise, a heart attack dared to happen.

She smiled at the memory. Death by orgasm was not a bad way to go.

Ellen had expected that she would feel lonely with her main man, Olivier, gone, but she didn't. For days, she scraped the house and then bought twenty gallons of white paint and started the hypnotic act of layering on crisp, clean color to the old boards of her dream house. Rodney, who had fallen behind his schedule during his cosmic detour into trance channeling, had to finish a statue of a grizzly bear raiding a beehive and leave town for a few days to deliver it to Buffalo, and Rayfield came by on his way to Montreal, where he was going to visit Monique, whom he had met at Cocho's memorial service. He reported that he was ready and willing to give his restored erection a test run, if Monique felt inclined to cooperate.

"Do you have condoms with you?" Ellen asked.

"Yes, Mother," Rayfield said, adding that his mission in life was to get Monique disenrolled from Overeater's Anonymous before she lost too many more inches from her rear and thighs.

"You're one of a kind, Rayfield," Ellen said, patting him on the back. "Good luck!" she called as he pulled out of the driveway. She noticed that his muffler had been fixed; the truck purred down the road. She did not call Tommy and he did not call her, either. Just do nothing, she advised herself whenever the urge to grab the reins of the relationship came upon her. It was an interesting experiment. Would the marriage roll on, like an old stagecoach, if no one was in control of it, or would it slow down and stop? She had no idea how much momentum was built up over seventeen years. Often, she pictured Tommy, going about his day, defending innocent people as well as career criminals, amidst the bustle of the Big Apple. He had nobility, she thought with pride. She hoped he was happy. She hoped, from time to time, he thought of her with affection, but who knew?

Her forty-seventh birthday circled closer, and soon it was just three days away. Staring at the calendar, she decided to throw herself a little birthday bash. Karen and Olivier, and Rayfield and Rodney were soon invited, and Ellen set to planning a vegetarian feast, contents courtesy of Mother Earth. She gave her little home the housekeeper's equivalent of a facial peel. She scrubbed and swept and ran a mop along the baseboards in every room. Upstairs, under a pile of laundry that had spilled over the side of Viola's wicker laundry basket, she uncovered a large white plastic bag. Inside it were the silk and satin robes she had bought on her morning expedition to the Chinatown department store.

I forgot all about these, she thought in wonder as she dumped them all out on the spare bed. Dragons, flying cranes, and lotus blossoms suddenly floated in a sea of bright, shimmering colors. Then it hit her: she would have an Asian feast for her birthday. They would all dress in robes, and she would prepare one dish each from China, Japan, Korea, Thailand, Indonesia, and India. It was perfect, and she immediately set up her ironing board and carefully pressed each robe and hung it on a hanger in the one and only closet in the house. Afterward, she spread out the curtain doorway so neither Karen nor Olivier, who were coming down the day before the party, would catch a glimpse of her surprise. Then she hopped into the Honda, with its brand-new radiator, and sped to the library, where she waited her turn on the computers and then downloaded several exotic recipes. She even made a secret trip to Montreal to pick up special ingredients like coconut milk, plum wine, peanut sauce, seaweed, and bamboo shoots. As she poked along the aisles of the Asian market, with ginseng roots piled like mutants into boxes and a huge selection of durian, a fruit that she knew from her researching days stunk so much when it was cracked open that it was banned from the majority of the hotels of Singapore, Ellen felt the slow return of her long lost hippie fantasy: to see the whole, wide world. She had felt certain that traveling would reveal the hidden plans and purposes of humanity, and she considered herself a seeker of such knowledge. She realized with shock that she hadn't taken a big trip in years. Her passport was no doubt expired now, and she had recently given up on the concept of figuring out the secrets of the universe. But when she whipped out her credit card to pay for the cartful of imported goods, for the briefest second, she mistook it for a boarding pass and a smile began to form at the edges of her mouth. Egypt, she thought. The Nile, hieroglyphics, the Great Pyramid, and the Sphinx. What was a little more credit card debt when there was a whole, wide world just waiting for her to arrive? She hummed as she left the store, a tune that she imagined could be plucked on a stringed instrument by a desert shepherd.

On her birthday, Ellen had so many pots and pans going that it took her full concentration not to let the basmati rice boil dry, char her homemade egg rolls, or scorch the hot and spicy sesame sauce. Karen, consulting both the recipe and Ellen for her interpretation of it, floated pear slices in sweet and sour nectar in individual bowls, and both sisters puzzled over a diagram demonstrating the ancient art of transforming a simple table napkin into a swimming swan. Rodney and Rayfield arrived within five minutes of each other. They had obviously coordinated, because Rodney carried a birthday cake and Rayfield brought the ice cream.

"Smells like a Japanese whorehouse in here," said Rayfield.

"Like you would know," Ellen replied.

"Hey, I got my secrets." He straightened up and assumed a confident, James Bond-inspired sneer. "The name is Geebo. Rayfield Geebo," he said. "Otherwise known as double-oh-nothing."

"I've got a mission for you. Put this on the table for me."

Rayfield complied. Ten minutes later, Ellen called the group to order. "Time to get in our birthday suits!" she said with a sharp pang of sorrow, remembering Tommy and Truro so many years ago.

"Yahoo!" said Rayfield.

"Wait here," Ellen ordered before he could whip off his pants. She ran up the kamikaze stairs, stripped off her clothes, and put on a robe upon which giant bumblebees flew like airborne tigers. She carried the rest downstairs, over her arm.

"My goodness," said Rodney as she handed him his.

"Atmosphere!" Ellen said. She felt warm triumph as Karen admired her selections, then went upstairs to change. Rayfield simply peeled off his T-shirt and stepped out of his jeans in the middle of the living room, while Rodney went into the kitchen to remove his overalls. By the time they assembled at the table, they could've easily passed for an emperor's court straight out of the Ming dynasty. Looking from face to face, Ellen felt a deep happiness. Not a resolution but a willingness to simply be here now, as Ram Dass had long advised. Sorrows, there were plenty to go around, but this particular moment had the power to hold them at bay. Rayfield soon let it slip that the whole town thought Ellen was in the Witness Protection Program, which thoroughly delighted her.

"Why else would you have boughten this house?" asked Rodney.

Ellen didn't answer. She was thinking of the local folks, like Baldy and the love-struck lady mail carrier. Maybe they imagined that she had given personal testimony against a Mafia don, the *capo di tutti capi* of one of the New York crime families. Perhaps they thought she had discovered a white-collar criminal, like the junk bond king Michael Milken, and taken it upon herself to send him up the river to some low-security country club to live at the taxpayers' expense.

She leaned back in her chair and indulged in a little fantasy. There she was, on the witness stand, nervous but committed to putting the bad guys away ASAP. She stared out over the packed courtroom, though she couldn't decide whether the press corps members were hanging over the balcony or if only sketch artists were permitted in that particular courtroom. The audience was hanging on to her every word, because she, and only she, had had the courage to come forward to testify, knowing that her words could result in her own death contract. She took a deep breath, in her daydream, and prepared to speak her piece. She looked up at the attorney for the defense.

And there was Tommy. This is a guy I could love, she thought. He opened his mouth and said, "Is this a private party, or can anyone get in?" Ellen was so astonished that she was completely unaware for a few heartbeats that the question had not come from her fantasy adversary but from the real-life Tommy, standing just on the other side of the screen door. She blinked and rubbed her eyes, like in a cartoon. He was still there, his old carpenter's toolbox in one hand and his Georgio Armani suit bag in the other. "I thought I'd come up and do a little work around here for my vacation," he said, as the entire group stared at him as if they had been forbidden to react until Ellen did.

She finally snapped out of it. "Tommy! I was just thinking about you," she said as she jumped to her feet. There was no need to tell him that she had been about to pole-vault over his defenses, whatever they were, and put his bad guy away—for life. She pushed the door open and threw her arms around him.

Having him there in the flesh was an instant reprieve from alienation, and it felt right to be in his arms, right to feel the scratch of the five o'clock shadow from which she had sustained many a whisker burn, right to experience the familiar circle of his arm around her waist.

Behind them, the party revelers snapped into action. Rayfield rounded up a chair and wedged it in next to Ellen's, Karen set another place at the table, and Rodney took up the duties of bartender, filling Tommy's miniature cup with warm sake and adding a little to everyone else's, too. Tommy went immediately to Karen and wrapped his arms around her. She fell against him and, for the first time that day, Ellen saw tears form in her sister's eyes. Tommy held her tighter and for a tiny second, perhaps because Karen was so slim and young, Ellen imagined her husband with the sylphlike yoga instructor. But when she saw the comfort Tommy provided to her sister, just by the way he rested his chin on the top of her head and placed his fingers, spread wide, across her back, the unruly image disintegrated. She ran up the stairs and yanked the last robe from its hanger, and when she returned Tommy was shaking hands with Rodney and then with Rayfield. Ellen had cried big alligator tears when she pressed this robe, sorry she had forgotten to leave it in New York, sorry she had ever bought it, certain it was destined to gather dust in her little closet under the eaves. But now, as she held it up for Tommy to slip into, it felt like the last piece of a complicated puzzle finally snapped into place, and she felt tingly inside, as if little stars were twinkling into the darkness of her insides.

"I have so much to tell you," she whispered into his ear.

"It's been so long," Tommy answered, and he kissed her chastely once on the lips.

In the wee small hours, after the party had ended and the guests had left, including Karen and Olivier who had gone to Rodney's to spend the night, Ellen and Tommy climbed the kamikaze stairs together and fell onto the new mattress. Perhaps it was the fact that her metabolism had been swamped with successive waves of sugars, proteins, fats, alcohol, and birthday cake, but Ellen felt genuinely giddy as she smoothed out her robe beneath her and leaned back against the pillows. "So tell me," she said, "did Karen tip you off about the party?"

"I plead the fifth," Tommy said. "Anyway, it wasn't as if she had to do that much prodding." He shifted onto his side and looked deeply into Ellen's eyes. "What did you think? That we would just fizzle out, never speak to each other again? Go immediately to divorce court without passing Go?"

"I just didn't know," Ellen said happily. Even she could hear the joy in her voice. "I still don't know," she added, smiling widely. She felt as if she were floating through deep, indigo space, maybe on the magic carpet she had always wanted to ride in her youth. It flew calmly along, heading everywhere and nowhere at once, and Ellen didn't even feel the need to hang on, let alone know the destination.

"Tommy," she said suddenly, "I thought for a second I saw you at Cocho's service. Were you there?"

He hesitated. "Yes, I was. But when I came in, I saw you holding hands with Rayfield and crying on his shoulder, and I felt afraid of what I would say or do. I just felt afraid in general, so I ran away. I left a little bit after you started to speak. I wandered around the streets for hours. Then I got a plane home."

"I thought you were there," Ellen repeated, but she felt dreamy. If Tommy needed some kind of reassurance, if he needed her to explain that there was nothing going on between her and Rayfield, he was headed for disappointment. She was too free to worry. And then the flying carpet in her mind made another turn, and she knew in her heart that she would never ask him about the yoga teacher, either. She turned to stare into his placid brown eyes. "I have no idea what's going to happen," she said.

"No doubt, the universe is unfolding as it should," Tommy replied, quoting some of Ellen's favorite words of wisdom from her hippie days. She reached for his hand. And when she felt his strong fingers intertwined with hers, she realized that, in this important moment anyway, she actually wasn't alone on the carpet ride into the heart of the mystery. She didn't know how, when, or why, but Tommy was right there with her.

And so were Cocho and Karen, Olivier and Rayfield, Rodney and Viola. She felt as if her heart might burst with love, as if every red cell and white cell in her blood supply were dripping with it. She looked out the window at the night sky and felt passion for the universe and all the beings in it, great and small.

She pulled her fingers free, climbed on top of Tommy's hips, and sat down. She didn't even try to support some of her own weight by assuming the deep knee bend position. She didn't really care if he knew how much she actually weighed anymore. If he couldn't take it, he had options, after all.

She leaned forward and placed both hands on Tommy's chest. "Tommy," she whispered, "let me tell you what I'm feeling right now. I feel like I'm standing at the very edge of the remote possibility that I might be in the neighborhood of perhaps entertaining the notion that I might be ready to think about making a commitment to you."

"Ellen," Tommy chuckled, "does this mean you want to get married?"

fifty

Long before dawn, Ellen slipped out of bed and into her homeboy outfit. She stole downstairs and quietly put on her pot of open-the-heart tea. The kitchen was a disaster zone as she had refused both to do the party clean-up and to allow anyone else to do it. Viola's old plates were crusted with exotic foods from the Far East, and the stove top looked like modern art for its random splotches of color. The chaos soothed her. Every spill seemed to shout, "Hey! It was worth it, wasn't it?"

She carried her tea to the porch swing to observe the arrival of the sun over the crest of Eagle Beak Mountain, wincing slightly as she sat down. Tommy, in his new state of physical fitness, had given her quite a workout between the sheets. In the sixties, she would have said that he gave her a ticket to Happy Twatland, but now, as a mature woman of forty-seven years, she was less prone to isolate her body parts one from the other. And while she wanted to acknowledge Tommy's contribution to her pleasant state of body and mind, she could certainly not give him total credit for it.

What had happened between them—before, during, and after this summer interlude—was a big blank to Ellen. She had not actually known they were in a deep rut until, in an act of desperation (or perhaps inspiration) she had liberated herself (and him) from it via the purchase of Viola's ramshackle house. This had catapulted them both into separate and different lives. Resentment and tension had built up, though she didn't understand why. Maybe it was just the walls of the rut collapsing. She and Tommy had been in such a state of panic induced by the emotional landslide, or loveslide, that they had blamed each other instead of attributing it to the force of nature. The falling debris ultimately wiped out everything but the one frayed thread that connected them.

It had felt so tenuous that Ellen truly believed if it had snapped, they would barely even have remembered each other.

But it hadn't snapped, at least not yet. And while they made love, Ellen had found herself making such crazy sex comments as, "I'm not promising you anything," "There are no guarantees," and "I have no idea what will happen."

"That is *so* sexy," Tommy had panted, obviously meaning it.

They had slept in each other's arms, and she had awoken calm and happy. Who could figure?

Before her eyes, a golden glow, a suggestion of light, began to infiltrate the darkness in the sky above the mountain. It made her think of Viola's gold coins, and she suddenly felt compelled to collect them out of the drawer and hold them in her hand. They had such a history: saved by Rodney's father for who knew how long, sewn into a ratty slipcover for more than sixty years, discovered by accident by a stranger, a New York nutcase who both belonged in that chair and didn't.

Ellen stepped through the screen door into the dawn. She immediately felt warm patches on her skin, a gentle gift of the distant ball of fire that supports all life. She opened her palm and studied the miniature replications of the golden sun overhead. She glanced from her hand to the mountaintop above which the whole solar disk had risen. Below it, like a photographic negative, was a black circle. The entrance to Viola's cave.

Suddenly, Ellen was running. She could feel the morning dew through her sneakers, and the brambles were snapping against her calves, scratching them. She felt solid and surefooted, as if her whole life had been a preparation for this mad dash toward the cave. She would find Rodney, Sr., and Viola's flat rock, the one they used for a bedside table during their love trysts, and she would place their gold coins beneath it as Rodney had. Perhaps Viola's spirit was waiting there in the cave, hoping to find her way to the next world where she might join her own true love. Maybe she had waited all these years for the return of the gold coins that would buy her passage across the River Styx into eternity. And if that were all a cracked fantasy and some future spelunker came upon the gold coins, that was fine, too. Let them all into heaven, Ellen thought, as her feet pounded over the earth.

Like an Olympian, she ran, sweat forming into rivulets off her brow and in circles on her palms under each coin. "I'm coming, Viola," she whispered, as her heart beat loudly in her chest. Soon, she arrived at the cave entrance. With one wild glance over her shoulder, Ellen disappeared into the darkness within, knowing for certain that she was on the right path—the one that led straight into the heart of the mystery.

FIC   6/08

MARS

  ANYBODY ANY MINUTE $25.

Dobbs Ferry Public Library
55 Main St.
Dobbs Ferry, NY 10522